Christmas Journeys

A Trilogy

Helen Brown

Reading Stones Publishing

Unless otherwise stated Scriptures quoted here are from the King James Version (Authorised version). First published in 1611. Quoted from the KJV Classic Reference Bible, copyright 1983 by the Zondervan Corporation.

Any people depicted in stock imaginary provided by Shutterstock are models and are being used for illustration purposes only.

Angel Picture Photo by Kasper Rasmussen on Unsplash

Published by: Reading Stones Publishing
Helen Brown & Wendy Wood
Woodwendy1982.wixsite.com/readingstones
Cover Design: Wendy Wood

For more copies contact the author at:

Glenburnie Homestead
212 Glenburnie Road
ROB ROY NSW 2360
Mobile: 0422 577 663
Email: hbrown19561@gmail.com

Dedication

To my daughters:

Jennifer, who pointed me to the destination and
Wendy, who came along for the ride.

Prelude

But now **faith, hope, and love** remain—these three.
The greatest of these is **love**.
1 Cor 13:13

1

Everyone was smiling! The drought had broken! The rains had finally come, and the grass was already starting to grow. Last week, at church, the minister had announced that all members of the congregation would meet in the church after the service for a fellowship luncheon to give thanks to the Lord for His mercy. The ladies were asked to bring a main meal and a dessert that would be shared amongst everyone who attended. It was going to be a great time of rejoicing.

Many of the families had not been able to attend for months, as the stock needed to be fed, even on a Sunday. There just wasn't enough time in the day to get those jobs done and drive to and from church. The minister had carried out many miles of travelling to visit those families to make sure that they were still alright. He had carried with him many packages of flour, biscuits, and sugar, things that these people were unable to afford or get to town to buy. He also carried some small gifts, donated by the town's people for the children who had birthdays and something for the wives to help them feel special. Most farmers killed their own meat, had their own fowls for eggs, made their own bacon and milked their own cows for milk but he also knew that in some cases some farmers didn't have those either as the drought took its toll on the livestock. If it was needed, he would arrange for water to be carted out to some of the farmers as their supplies dried up.

Mary noticed that the minister had looked increasingly tired as the drought had dragged on. But for now, the rains were giving everyone a much-needed break and it was time to celebrate.

The members of the congregation were starting to move back into the church, many of them had been chatting outside in order to give the ladies room to get lunch ready. She had been helping her mother in the kitchen, which had been built off the side of the church, setting the tables with plates, cutlery, glasses, cups, and saucers. Her best friend from school, Julie, who helped pack the books away when they were able to attend church had just walked back in from the vestry, which was on the opposite side to the kitchen, so Mary paused her duties to say hello. While they were talking, a young man walked in. He was tanned, with well-developed muscles that filled his shirt to capacity. He stopped just inside the door, looking around, it seemed he was in search of someone in particular.

'Who's that handsome bloke?' Mary asked Julie.

'Oh, that's John, John Cooper, silly.' Julie giggled.

'You're kidding.'

'Nope, they haven't been to church for months now because of the drought.'

'Well, he's certainly grown up while he's been away, the drought wasn't all bad by the looks of things.'

John spotted them, or Julie in particular and started walking in their direction.

'He's coming over', Julie moaned, and Mary shot her a startled look, what was wrong with her, he was handsome and had his own farm and that was something that he and Julie had in common, they were both from farming families. Many people would consider this to be a match made in Heaven, but Mary discovered that she didn't like the idea very much.

'Hello, Julie', with a quick glance, 'Mary', and turned back to Julie, 'How are things at your place. Have your dams filled up yet?' Mary felt very uncomfortable, John was pointedly ignoring her, so she made her excuses and returned to the kitchen to help the ladies.

During lunch, she had found that her eyes were constantly drawn to John. He was sitting with some of the men and engaged in talking about the latest price of stock, rain, crops, and the like. Occasionally, their eyes met across the room when he would scan the room during breaks in their conversations. Mary would blush with embarrassment, quickly drop her eyes to her plate, placing more food on her fork, even if her mouth was full.

After lunch she made sure she helped the ladies in the kitchen with the washing up and stayed well out of John's way, all the time praying that no-one else had noticed what had happened during lunch.

That night, as she had laid in bed going over the day, the picture of John standing just inside the doorway looking around seemed to be burned into her brain. She went over all the reasons why John wouldn't be interested in her. *She was a townie. He was a farmer. They had very little in common, he was an only child, she had three brothers who made her life difficult when she was little.* Mind you, it meant that she managed to get her fair share of her mother's attention as the boys were now living away from home, working with families of their own. They had moved away, she really could consider herself an only child, more or less. What she couldn't understand was why Julie hadn't seemed interested in this handsome hunk of a man.

Julie had left school before her; she was old enough to leave when her mother had fallen ill. Julie had told her the day before at lunch. Her father had insisted that she leave school to look after her mother. Julie wasn't happy. She was desperate to leave the farm and go into nursing. She had always loved looking after animals and always declared that if she had been a boy, she would have become a Vet, but that was a man's job and women were not allowed. Mary remembered how Julie would wish she had been born a boy so many times and didn't understand why God had made her a girl. On one such occasion, Mary had shot back at her, 'well, He made you a girl so I could have at least one friend at school, because if you had been a boy, I wouldn't have even liked you. Boys are silly and there is nothing silly about you.'

Now, of course, because of the distance between them, they rarely saw each other except at church on Sundays. Julie's mother had got better, but her parents still insisted that she stay at home and work on the farm with them until she managed to secure a husband. Mary knew that Julie still hoped that one day she would be able to go nursing. She told Mary that there wasn't a man in the district that she would be interested in marrying and that included John Cooper.

2

Over the next few months, Mary was very aware of John's attendance or absence at church. If he was there, it seemed to brighten her day, even though she never actually talked to him. If he wasn't, she was aware of something being missing.

When he was around, she would engage in conversations with other members of the congregation but remain fully aware of him being in her peripheral vision. Julie continued to try and keep her distance, but it was obvious that John had her clearly in his romantic sights. After all, Julie was also pretty to look at and with her farming experience she would be a great asset to any farmer.

One night at the dinner table, the conversation had briefly covered the possibility of John and Julie getting married. Her father had told her that farmers couldn't afford to marry someone who wasn't prepared to get their hands dirty, muck in, and work as hard as the men. She worked in the general store around the corner. Like Julie, her parents only saw it as a stop gap job until she got married and her father had indicated that a farmer wouldn't be a suitable match for her. She was never sure if it was because he thought she wouldn't measure up or if a farmer wasn't a suitable son-in-law for him, the town's doctor.

Just before Christmas, Mary had walked out of church, having stayed behind to help clear away the books, when she noticed that John and Julie were having a serious conversation. Julie had asked her before church if she could take her place, as she had something important to do straight after the service. Mary couldn't hear what was being said, but it was clear that John wasn't happy. In fact, he looked as if she had hit him across the face, even though her arms were tightly crossed across her chest. Julie turned and walked away, leaving John staring after her. Mary slipped around the side of the church and caught up to Julie.

'Hey, Julie, what's going on?'

'Oh, Mary, sorry I was going to come and see you, but John just made me so mad that I almost forgot to talk to you. You see, I'm off to the city, I've got a position nursing down there. I leave straight after the New Year.'

'Wow, that's wonderful. How did you get your parents to agree?'

'I sent the application in myself and told them after I'd been accepted. I have to do six weeks training, and if I pass that than I do three years with final exams at the end. I thought dad was going to have a heart attack, he was so wild, but I told them both that I needed to do this before I got married. Besides, it would be something that would be useful if I ever had to come home and care for them and I would be sending any spare money I have home for them, not that there will be very much left over. They told me the next morning that they weren't happy about me going behind their backs but had prayed about it and decided that I could go.'

'So, what happened with John?'

'Oh, I told him that I was leaving to go nursing. You'd thought I was asking for a divorce. I mean, we weren't even going out together. He just assumed that I was going to marry him and live on the farm with him. The cheek of the man. How dare he! I've been telling him for ages that I'm not interested in marrying him and living on his farm. He has always known that I wanted to get away from farming, but it seems to have gone right over his head. The man's as thick as a brick! Mary, I've got to go, mum and dad are waiting. I have a lot of packing to do before I leave and with

Christmas and New Year coming up there's not a lot of time to get everything done.'

Julie hugged Mary and said goodbye as she raced back towards her parent's horse and cart which was parked down the street. Mary walked around the corner and noticed that John hadn't moved. He was standing where Julie had left him, staring into space. Mary squared her shoulders, walked over to him, and plastered a smile on her face.

'It's great news about Julie being able to go nursing isn't it, John? She'll make a great nurse. She has always loved caring for the animals on the farm and I don't imagine that caring for people will be very different', she said.

John gave a start, as if he had come back to earth with a thud, and glared at her, 'If you say so', he said as he walked away and got onto his horse and rode away.

Hmm, maybe Julie was right. He might be good looking but today she had seen a side of him that she didn't particularly like.

He had been at the Christmas and the New Years' service but apart from those he didn't attend church for months afterwards. Had John only be going as a means of courting Julie, she wondered after he hadn't been there for at least three months.

Julie, in the meantime, had written plenty of letters to her. It seemed funny to Mary, that now Julie was living in the city, she found out more about what she was doing than when she was only several miles away. Her letters were full of details about how hard the work was but also about how much she was enjoying it. There were stories about what the patients and staff did. Some stories tugged at Mary's heart strings and some made her laugh out loud.

It had been September, before John had returned to church. Mary had almost bumped into him on the way out after the service.

'Oh, hello John, it's been a while since you have been, have you been away?' her heart was beating faster than it had for a long time.

'No, just working hard on the farm. I've been fixing up the house and built a new hay shed. The work never stops on a farm.'

The minister, who had been standing nearby, remarked, 'Just be careful that you don't become like the rich fool, who stores up earthly goods and neglects to store up Heavenly goods'. He extended his hand, shaking John's enthusiastically 'It's nice to see you back John, please don't make it too long before we see you again'.

'Thank you, Reverend, I won't. I enjoyed the service this morning. I hadn't realized how much I missed being part of the church until this morning. I'll see you around'. John nodded at Mary and walked away to his horse.

Although John had been as good as his word, attending every Sunday after his encounter with the Reverend on that September morning, he usually was last in and the first to leave, without engaging with anyone except the minister at the door. Mary had overheard someone speaking to the minister, nodding in John's direction as he drove off in his new ute, 'he doesn't hang around for long'.

'No, I have a feeling that there is a lot going on under the surface there. I've tried to talk to him on a few occasions when I've been out to visit but he's keeping things pretty close to his chest, as yet'. The minister looked as if he was about to say something else but changed his mind and turned the conversation to the man's family and his children's achievements.

Mary realized that maybe John had really been hurt by Julie's inattention. He might have really loved her, after all they had all gone to school together, John leaving as soon as he could to work on the farm alongside his father. His father and mother had purchased a house on the coast and left the farm for John to work as soon as he turned eighteen. Most people thought they were crazy, John being so young and all, but John's father's health was starting to be an issue and they wanted to spend some time away from the farm before he became too sick to enjoy it, or his wife had to spend all her time caring for him. She had heard that John's mother's family used to live on a farm on the coast, she grew up there. She met Roger while his family were on a rare holiday enjoying the beach. They had written to each other for years, and when he asked her to marry him, she had moved inland but had missed the beach and coastal weather for all those years. John's father had promised her that, if it was at all possible, he would return the favour and retire to the coast, and he had kept that promise to his wife, when John turned eighteen.

In November, the church decided to hold a thanksgiving service and luncheon. This time Mary was seated next to John. While he didn't really engage in serious conversation with her, apart from the normal polite hellos and simple yes or no responses to her questions, he became quite animated with the couple seated across from them at the table. Mr and Mrs Brown were farmers on the other side of town from where John was situated. Mr Brown asked John about what he was doing, and John launched into a whole excited dialog about all the changes that he was making to the house.

'I've built a new bathroom with a fancy bath and chip-heater. A storeroom separate from the kitchen and put in a brand-new Kerosene Ice Box. I've heard that they can start fires so hopefully, out there, it will protect the house more. Beside that I've put in a new laundry with a great new copper, cement tubs and a new tackle room so that Julie won't have to work around that stuff. I've even ordered a brand-new wood stove.'

'Julie?' Mr Brown asked

'Yes, I'm still hopeful that she will return home after she has finished her nursing training and marry me. I know that she will have tasted the comforts of city living so I wanted to make sure that things are as up to date as they can be at the farm, even though we don't have electricity. Next year, I anticipate being able to purchase one of those 32-volt generators for the house.'

Mr and Mrs Brown looked at each other and Mr Brown turned his enquires to the outside runnings of the farm, crops, sheep, cattle, pigs, and the like, including the weather.

Mary sat in silence. Several of Julie's recent letters had not only been filled with details about how great it was living in the city but there was also the occasional mention of someone named Steven.

3

The new year arrived with heat and bushfires again keeping everyone busy. Julie continued to write to Mary each week. Mary noticed that the name Steven appeared more and more in her letters. It seems that Julie had met him at the church she attended when her work allowed. He apparently worked at a bank as a teller. It didn't take too much imagination on Mary's part to get the idea that this relationship could be serious for Julie. She prayed that Julie wouldn't get hurt in the way she had hurt John.

After one particular letter, Mary thought about how she still looked forward to seeing John at church. Yet, he still seemed to be fixated on Julie as his life partner. Would he ever notice her? She wondered. Was she destined to watch him continue to be hurt from the side-lines? What would he do if Julie did stay in the city? Was he so in love with Julie that he would rather stay a bachelor and live on the farm as a recluse than marry someone else? She knelt down beside her bed, and prayed: 'Lord, if John is not the man for me, please take away any feelings I have for him. Help me to find someone else to love and help me to love them with all my heart without any pining for John. Amen.'

Climbing into bed, she watched the stars through her window until she fell asleep.

She was startled awake, by someone banging on their front door. She checked the sky outside; it was just breaking dawn. She could hear her father, moving quickly, closing the door to their bedroom, making his way through the house to his surgery which was at the front of the house.

This wasn't unusual, Mary's father was the local doctor. It didn't matter what time of the day or night it was, people would call asking him to attend to some sick loved one or help when someone had been hurt in an accident. It often meant many miles of travelling to farms or out-lying droving camps.

She heard the door to her parent's bedroom, open and close quietly, and knew that her mother would be making her way to the kitchen. She always made a thermos of tea and a couple of sandwiches for her husband when he was called away in an emergency. As soon as the new electric kettles were available, her father had purchased one in order to make his wife's generous actions at all hours of the night a little easier. There was no way of knowing when he would get to eat, and even though many of the farmer's wives would offer him a cuppa after attending to their children, there was no way of knowing who or why this person was knocking on their door, so food and tea was being made. Mary stayed where she was. It wasn't that she didn't want to help her mother, but she knew that her parents treasured the last few minutes that they would have together before her father raced off to do his duty. She would join her mother a little while after her father had left. She knew that her mother would sit at the table, committing both her husband and the distressed family to the Lord, and would not appreciate Mary interrupting her. It's the way that it had always been as far back as Mary could remember. Somewhere back in her early childhood, her mother had managed to teach her that this is the way it was to be, even though she didn't remember learning the lesson.

Mary also felt led to pray this time as well. Would the family in distress be someone who were close friends or someone passing through their small town? Either way, she prayed.

The prayers just poured out of her, something that only seemed to happen when these callouts were for people close, even though she didn't know who they were. This morning, her soul was crying out to God, and it was quite a while before she got up, dressed, and joined her mother in the kitchen.

Her mother's distressed face made Mary run to her and wrap her arms around her.

'Who is it?' Mary asked, knowing that it had to be a family they knew well.

'Julie's parents, there was a fire.'

'Oh, no. Are they badly hurt?'

'I don't know.'

'Poor Julie. I prayed for such a long time this morning. It's as if God was preparing me for bad news.'

'Yes, I fear that there is going to be bad news for Julie either way today. You'd better put some clean sheets on the spare bed in your room, Julie can stay here when she gets home. It will take a couple of days for her to get here but from what we have been told, the house is gone.'

Mary got up, stirred up the fire in the stove, and started making their breakfast of bacon and eggs, leaving her mother sitting at the table in quiet contemplation.

4

They had just finished making up the spare bed, after having eaten breakfast, washed up, and swept the kitchen floor when they heard their car pull up and stop outside the house. They both walked out into the kitchen, making a pot of tea while they waited for her father to come through to join them.

The tired look on his face, when he entered, told them both that bad news was coming. He just shook his head, as he sat down at the table. He took the cup from his wife and drank deeply. He seemed to relax a little then. I've sent a telegram to Julie. Peterson said that he would make sure that arrangements are made for her to get home for the funeral.

'What about John, who is going to tell him?'

The Reverend is on his way out to tell him. I have a feeling that this is going to affect him in a big way. I'm not sure that Julie will come home now. The last time I saw her parents at church they were saying that Julie seemed to be very settled in the city.

A telegram arrived later in the day to tell them which train to meet, and they returned one that said. "Yes stay us". Mary knew that telegrams were charged per letter, so it had to be as short as possible even if it didn't make sense.

Mary travelled with her father in the car to the train station. They could've walked but they felt that it would be easier for Julie not to have to engage with the town's people on the way back from the station. Julie was travelling on the overnight train; Mary wasn't sure why she hadn't taken the train that arrived later in the evening but accepted that Julie had her reasons.

It was just breaking dawn when the train pulled into the station. As summer was giving way to Autumn weather it was necessary to wear a jacket, even so, the day would be reasonably hot later.

Julie embarked from the train, her face puffy and eyes red. She placed her bag on the platform as Mary reached out and hugged her friend very tightly.

'Do you have any other bags, Julie' the doctor asked. Julie shook her head as Mary linked her arm into Julie's and led her away towards the car, leaving her father to collect the bag and follow the girls.

As they reached the house, Mary's mother hugged Julie and made her sit down for a small breakfast. She seemed to know that Julie wouldn't be up to eating too much at this hour of the morning. Mary's father took her bag to the bedroom before returning to the kitchen. Once Julie had eaten, Mable, Mary's mother insisted that Julie go and lie down in Mary's room for a couple of hours. Reassuring her that they would wake her in time to get ready for the funeral. Julie thanked them all and left the room. She had often spent time with them while the girls had been at school, so she knew exactly where to go. Mary, her father, and mother remained at the table finishing their breakfast and lingered a little longer with an extra cup of tea each. No-one felt the need to make conversation, so the silence was a bit eerie.

Once the meal was over, the women quietly started putting food together that would be taken to the church so that family and friends could gather together after the funeral and offer their sympathies to Julie. Mary's father went into the surgery to finish up some paperwork and see anyone that needed attention, but there was a feeling that no-one would dare be sick on such a day. They were aware that the doctor and his wife were also grieving the loss of close friends.

5

At nine o'clock, Mary quietly walked into her room to wake Julie and change her clothes for the funeral. While they were getting dressed, the girls had time to talk for a little while.

'How long are you staying?' Mary asked Julie.

'I have to be back on the overnight train tonight.'

'Gosh, Julie, can't you stay for a couple of days. You look as if you could use a jolly good holiday.'

'No, the hospital has been kind enough to call it sick leave to allow me to come, but I can't graduate until I've worked the extra time, so the less time I'm away the better. Mary, there is nothing here for me anymore. I'll see Mum and Dad's solicitor this afternoon, as he will be making the arrangements for the farm to be sold. As I understand things at present, if I'd been married it would have been left to my husband but since I'm not it has to be sold and the money will be held in trust until I get married.'

'What about John?'

'What about him?'

'Julie, he is still hoping that you will come back and marry him. He's done a lot of work to the house, made it all modern just for you! I sat through the last church dinner listening to him tell Mr and Mrs Brown about all the things he has done to the house, just for you.'

'Look, Mary, I'm not interested in marrying John, I never was. I told him before I left that I wasn't interested in him that way, so he has just got to accept that I won't be coming back.'

'He's going to be so hurt.'

'That's not my problem, Mary. If you feel that badly for him, marry him yourself. I'm not going to, and no-one is going to change my mind. Besides, I have a feeling that Steven will have a place in my future. We get along well, and we are both interested in doing missionary work overseas.'

'Missionary work! When did this happen?'

'I've been thinking about it ever since I left school. I just didn't want to say anything to anyone. Mum and dad wouldn't have approved and by your reaction just now, I'm guessing you might have tried to talk me out of it too.'

'Well, that depends on why you are doing it. Are you doing it because you feel it's part of God's plan or to follow Steven around the world?'

'It's definitely the first one, Steven would just be an extra blessing if it's part of God's plan. I am most certainly ready to go out alone if I have to.'

'Wow, you are full of surprises.'

'I'm hoping that the solicitor can see a way for me to use my inheritance to cover some travelling and training costs.'

'Well, John isn't going to be happy, all that work for nothing.'

'As I said before, not my problem. And besides, why would that work be all for nothing? Any wife of his deserves to live in as comfortable circumstances as he can make it, not just me. Some lucky woman, if you can call being a farmer's wife lucky, will reap the benefits that he was planning for me. Come on, we need to get going. I don't want to be late for the funeral.'

Mary followed Julie out of the room, and out the front door, pulling it closed behind her but not locking it, walking down the path to the street where her parents were waiting beside the car.

As funerals go, this one was uneventful. The locals were keen to speak to Julie afterwards, many asking what her plans were now. Most expressed surprise when she indicated that she would be on the overnight train, that evening, heading back to work.

Mary noticed that John hovered pretty close to Julie until she had spoken to about half-a-dozen people, then he quietly walked away. She didn't see him again. Around three o'clock she noticed Julie speaking to her father, he nodded, and she walked out of the hall. Mary had been gathering plates to be taken back to the kitchen at the time. Her father looked at her and gave her a sad sort of smile and then turned to answer someone who was trying to get his attention.

The family returned home without Julie around four and about an hour later Julie walked in.

'Do you mind if I lie down for an hour, it's so hard to sleep on the train?'

Not at all dear, go right ahead, Mary will get you in time for the train.

Julie walked up the hall and Mary followed, she wanted to spend as much time with Julie as she could because she had a feeling that their paths were going to take very different directions from here on.

Once in the room, Julie laid down, Mary sat on the side of her bed watching Julie for a moment.

'Do you mind if I ask how things went with the solicitor?'

'Yeah, things were as I thought but he insists that the money will not be released until after I'm married. Oh, Mary, what if God doesn't want me to get married, that money just sits there gaining interest forever. Gee sometimes I still hate being a girl.'

'I wouldn't worry, God knows about it all and I'm sure that He will work things out for you. If you marry Steven and then you will be able to use the money in the way you want.'

'Well, in the way my husband wants anyway. I'm pretty sure Steven would use it properly but what if Steven isn't the one for me…..' Mary could see Julie's eyes glisten with tears that she was trying very hard to not let fall.

Mary moved and hugged her friend, 'Julie, it's alright to cry. Life isn't fair. Not for you, me, or John for that matter.' Julie clung to her friend as if her life depended on her and cried a flood of tears.

When she had stopped crying, Mary gently laid her down again, left the room and allowed her to sleep. It wouldn't be long, but it would be better than nothing, as Julie has said, it was hard to sleep on the train.

The journey back to the train a while later was a quiet affair. On the platform, Julie and Mary hugged for what would most likely be the last time ever. Julie shook the doctor's hand, thanking him for all his help and got on the train, the doctor placing her bag in the overhead rack for her.

'Bye Julie, stay safe and God go with you.' With that remark he stepped back onto the platform closing the door securely. As the train pulled out of the station, Julie raised her hand in farewell, and leaned back into the seat. Mary felt as if Julie's departure closed a chapter in her life forever.

6

That night as she looked at the ceiling, Mary wondered what John was thinking and feeling. *Why had he left without actually speaking to Julie? Where had he gone?* She assumed that he had gone straight home, but what was happening out there now? She knew that he would be hurting, but she wasn't in a position to even help him, he didn't know that she was alive. He had been so focused on winning Julie, that he hadn't even been aware that there were other girls out there who were looking in his direction. Mary knew that she wasn't the only one who thought John was a good catch. There were a lot of farmer's wives who would have been very happy to welcome John Cooper into their family as a son-in-law.

It was still another few weeks before John returned to church. In the mean-time Mary continued to pray about her feelings for John. After all, she realized that she didn't really know the adult John, and while he had been a quiet studious boy at school, she hadn't had a lot to do with the boys in her classes.

Julie continued to write interesting letters about her work, both at the hospital and with the church. Not that she seemed to have a great deal of time to do anything other than nursing. Julie commented in one letter, that being a farmer's daughter had been good preparation for nursing because it seemed to require the same level of commitment or more.

Time rolled on and things didn't change much, there were rains and dry spells, winter came and went and suddenly, or so it seemed, Julie was writing to say she had finished her three years training and was about to sit her final exams.

Then one day the family received two letters from Julie. One was addressed to the doctor and the other to Mary. Both letters were to inform them that Julie and Steven were getting married in six months. Julie was asking if the doctor would be willing to give her away at the ceremony and would Mary be her bridesmaid. The logistics of making this happen were discussed around the meal table that night. Mary's father would need to find someone to come and cover his practice while they were away, and that would need to be at least a week, taking in travelling time and necessary preparations. Julie reassured Mary that because of the distance, Steven's sister, Grace would be the major maid of honour as it was her duty to organize the kitchen tea amongst other things. They requested that gifts be in line with their desire to go into missionary service in the next few years. The doctor said that he knew of a couple of doctors who would be able to fill in for him, and since they have been given plenty of notice, he didn't think that it would be a problem. Julie had included a pattern of the dress that she wanted Julie to wear, and a sample of the colour that Steven's sister would be wearing. Mary's mother looked at the pattern and decided that it would be easy enough to make.

So, the next few months were filled with lots of letters back and forth and steady industry as plans were made and implemented. Things moved forward smoothly, and it seemed like in no time at all the whole family were packed and embarking on their train journey to the city. As it was Wednesday evening when they arrived, Julie and Steven met the train. Hugs, handshakes, and introductions were made on the platform. Steven had borrowed his father's car to transport them and their cases to the motel. Julie, having resigned from the hospital, had moved in with Steven's family, he had taken a room at the same hotel that Mary and her family would be staying. These unusual arrangements being made due to Julie now being an orphan.

The next couple of days were filled with a lot of activity and in no time at all, the day of Julie's wedding had arrived. Mary looked at her friend, dressed in white, smiling with excitement and nerves. She had never seen her look so beautiful. Mary and Grace descended the stairs to the foyer of Steven's parent's home first, where Mary's father was waiting to escort the bridal party to the church. Mary heard her father's intake of a deep breath when he saw her at the top of the stairs.

'Oh, Mary, how grown up you look, and you are not even the bride. I can't imagine how beautiful you are going to look when it's your turn to be wed.'

They reached the bottom of the stairs and turned to watch Julie descend. A photographer had set up his camera in the foyer in order to capture her about half-way down. This had been requested by Steven's parents and they were paying for his services. There would be a few more photos taken at his studio after the wedding.

The weather was beautiful, the day went according to plan. It seems that Steven's mother was a great organizer and was very willing to take on the role of mother-of-the-bride for Julie. She had joked that it would be a rehearsal for Grace's wedding.

Everyone retired late that night, exhausted but happy. The married couple were staying at another hotel. Sunday started with brunch with Steven's parents. They wanted to thank the family for coming and were also keen to find out more about Julie's early childhood. Monday saw the family doing a little bit of sightseeing. Mary's father insisted that they do this since it was unlikely that they would be back in the city again. His country practice kept him tied to the small town and he couldn't ask his friend to fill in for him too often. The family returned home on the Tuesday with very little conversation between them because it was hard to hear each other over the noise of the train but also because each of them were busy with their own memories of the trip.

Two weeks later, Mary was walking along the street, after doing some shopping for her mother. She bumped into someone, when she stepped back to apologize, she realized it was John, sporting a bandaged hand.

'What happened?' Mary asked looking pointedly at the hand.

'I had a run in with some wire while fencing a couple of weeks ago and it needed stitches. The doctor filling in for your father said you were visiting Julie in the city. How is she?'

Mary paused, suddenly she realised that she hadn't seen John at all during the six months they had been planning to attend Julie's wedding. How was she going to break the news to John that Julie was married without causing him more pain? However, there was nothing for it. It was time for him to let go and get on with his life and the only way for that to happen was for him to realize that Julie was no longer on the marriage market.

'She's married, John. She asked my father to give her away since her father was no longer able to do so. You know what? I've never seen her look so happy or beautiful.'

John sat down with a thud on a bench that was on the street. Mary sat down beside him.

'John, it's time you realized that Julie was never interested in staying around here. They are planning on going into missionary work overseas.' John gave her a startled look. 'Yes, I was surprised by that news too when she told me about it while she was home for the funeral. I knew you still had hopes of marrying her and I when I told her about it, she was adamant that she didn't love you in the same way that you loved her...... Just because you weren't loved back in the way that you wanted, doesn't mean that you cannot be loved by someone else. There are any number of single girls in this town who would gladly line up behind Julie to be your wife and if they weren't willing, there are plenty of mother's who would push their girls into the line.'

'But I did all the work on the house for her'.

'As Julie said when I told her, any wife deserves the same respect that you wanted to bestow on her. It's time for you to let her go, John, she will never be yours. God must have someone else, or maybe he wants you to live life as a single man, either way, put Julie into your past because that is where she should be, needs to be.'

With that, she stood up and walked away, thinking that John would probably not speak to her ever again but strangely, she found that she didn't care. If he was so hung up on Julie then how would he be able to love any other woman, let alone her, since she had been Julie's best friend.

7

Life fell into a comfortable routine for Mary after her street encounter with John. However, there were still rare nights when she dreamed about him. They always unsettled her, but she was careful to commit the next day to the Lord. She also had to endure overhearing some of the older ladies in the community making snide remarks about her becoming an old spinster or being left on the shelf. Her parents, if they were privy to such comments were quick to declare that they were sure that the good Lord had someone for their Mary, he just hadn't turned up yet, or needed to learn something in order to be the best husband for her. On such occasions, Mary took a quiet delight in the stunned looks on the faces of her accusers.

The church's time of the Harvest Festival and thanksgiving came around again. The church again scheduled a luncheon after church. John had still been coming but not really engaging with members. So, Mary was a little surprised to find that he helped some of the men set up the tables in the church, while the women were working in the kitchen getting the meal ready.

It surprised her more, to find that John actually sat down beside her when it was time for people to take their places. Inwardly, she groaned, remembering the last time that he sat beside her, was she going to have to sit through another meal listening to him go on and on about Julie. The meal progressed with the majority of the conversations being between the other farmers around the table and concentrated on the price of stock and the weather. As Mary, didn't have any idea of what they were talking about she tuned out, just letting the noise flow over her. On this particular occasion the ladies had decided that dessert would be a variety of cakes and slices placed on the table for people to help themselves to whatever took their fancy. Mary had made her own contribution along with her mother. As John was about to leave to collect some cake, he paused and asked Mary if he could fetch her something. She asked for some of her mother's cake and returned to her meal. John returned placing the plate with her selection in front of her and sitting down to tuck into the three selections that he had made. Glancing at his plate, Mary noticed that he had a piece of her contribution on it. He continued to eat and talk, until he started eating Mary's cake.

'Oh, wow, this is good!'

Mary smiled, 'You know I cooked that don't you?' there was a note of accusation in her tone.

'No, did you really?'

'Oh, come on John. It's not that good, you're just making fun of me'.

'No. I'm not. I had no idea that you cooked that cake, but I do really like it.' He defended himself looking a little hurt.'

'Well, if you're sure, thank you.' She returned also feeling a little guilty about not accepting his complement at face value.

'They say the way to a man's heart is through his stomach', Mrs Jones, who was sitting next to Mary, said pointedly.

'I doubt if it is a way to heal it though', Mary responded quietly standing up and gathering dirty dishes.

'You might be right there, but God certainly can, if He is allowed', Mrs Jones said before Mary was able to move away, and Mary escaped to the kitchen.

Many hands made quick work of the dishes and the men worked at putting the tables and benches away. It wasn't long before everyone was outside, starting to make their way home. Mary and her family had walked to church that morning, something they did regularly if the weather was clear. Her father considered it good for his constitution. As she stepped down from the porch, John came up behind her.

'Can I walk you home please, Mary?' Mary looked at her father who was standing on the path waiting for her mother.

'It's alright, Mary, John has asked my permission. We'll see you later.'

Mary's mother stepped past John and her parents walked off down the road leaving her and John to walk behind. John was walking very slowly, and Mary wondered why, usually he moved as if a pack of dogs were after him. They had nearly reached her gate before he spoke.

'Mary?'

'Yes, John'

'I just wanted to thank you for what you said to me the last time we met'.

'What? In the street? That was a long time ago now.'

'Yes, you were right though. I've spent a lot of time since then talking to the Lord about letting go and trusting Him to lead me in the future. He has shown me that I have been self-centred, and I'm trying, with His help, to think about others more. In my defence I spend a lot of time on my own, so it's easier to think about myself than others.' They reached her gate.

'Well, I just wanted to thank you for being honest with me and helping to get my head on straight.'

He opened the gate to let her through, she turned to him, 'You're welcome', and walked up to the door, letting herself in. As she was closing the door, she noticed that John was now headed back to his ute at his normal pace. She headed for the kitchen, shaking her head, and feeling the need for a cup of tea.

8

'Mary?'

'Yes, John, what can I do for you?' They were standing outside the church on a bright spring day.

'I have a problem and I'm hoping you can help me.'

'Well fire away, I don't know if I can help you or not until after you tell me what the problem is.'

'Well, you see, I had some travellers turn up at my place the other day looking for help.'

'Yes, so?'

'There was a man, his wife, a boy, and a girl. I had no problem helping them fix their car but when I went to offer them some afternoon tea, I didn't have anything other than damper and honey to offer them.'

'What's wrong with that?'

'Well, nothing I guess, it's all I had. But….. you see I kept thinking that it would have been much better if I had been able to offer them some of that cake that you made for the harvest festival luncheon.'

'Oh, so you want me to teach you how to make it, is that it?'

'Well, no, I'm sure that if I made it, it wouldn't turn out to be as good as yours anyway and besides, I don't have the time to do fancy cooking. What I was wondering….'

'Oh John, spit it out. I can only say no.'

'True! If I got you the things that you needed, would you please cook me some cake and biscuits. I can do a good stew and even meat and potatoes without any trouble but there are more and more people travelling these days and because I'm so far away from town, I'm getting more and more people looking for help. Besides, it would be nice to have some of your cooking to offer my neighbours when they come to visit. I would be happy to collect what you have on Sundays after church and I can even pay you a little for your time, if you like.'

'So, this would be a regular thing?'

'Yes, please, could you do that for me?'

'Sure, why not.'

Look, how about you go to the store and buy what you need during the week, put it on my account and I'll collect them after church next Sunday.'

'You're being very trusting.'

'Mary, I know you well enough to know that there's not a dishonest bone in you. Please, this would be a big help to me.'

'Alright, I don't like to see a man beg too much, just a little.'

'Thank you, I'll see you next week then.'

❦❦❦

John quickly turned his back on her and walked to his ute, grinning from ear to ear with great satisfaction. He breathed a prayer of thanks to the Lord. 'That was a good idea you had there, thank you,

Lord.'

As he drove home, his thoughts went back over the last month. He had realised that it was now Mary that he thought of, more than Julie. Once he had gone to the Lord and asked him to help him put Julie in his past, as Mary had rightly said he should, he had buried himself in the work on the farm. It had taken about three weeks to realise that he hadn't thought about Julie at all since then. He was a reasonable cook, and cleaner, after all, you don't survive stock camps and living on your own, without some skills in that quarter. So, he had decided that being a bachelor farmer was probably the way life was going to be, and he felt contented with the thought.

However, a week later, a visit from his neighbours and the family with the broken-down car, had made him very aware that his house and life could really do with a female influence. That night as he had said his prayers, he had mentioned to the Lord that he might be better off with a woman around after all. He fell asleep quickly. That wasn't unusual, he worked hard and slept deep. What made this night, in particular, different was that he dreamed about Mary's cake, not once but three times. His dream so vivid that he woke with the taste of the wonderful concoction in his mouth.

'Well, Lord, what was that all about?' he asked as he dressed and readied for work. The day passed as normal without him giving the cake another thought. However, that night he again dreamed about the cake but this time it was ginormous. Mary was carrying it down the street, it looked heavy so he rushed forward to take it from her for fear that she would drop it. She gave it to him with a smile and he discovered that it weighed next to nothing and he almost dropped it himself. Again, upon waking he asked the Lord, what his dream meant.

That day, however, he found it hard to get the dream out of his mind. It wasn't the cake he thought about so much but Mary herself. Sure, they had gone to school together, she had been one of the better-behaved children in the class and honest, oh so honest. Once he started to think about her, he discovered that while he hadn't taken very much notice of her at school, there were a lot of memories there, simply because she had been Julie's best friend. However, those memories now seemed to be surfacing without Julie being in the forefront of his mind. Then the memory of Mary being so straight with him over Julie, made him realise that she had matured into a very straight talker, a no-nonsense person. He also realised that if he were to try and walk out with her now, she would still be worried about him being hung up on Julie. How was he going to be able to start a relationship with her in a way that avoided Julie still being the wall between them. Cake! The word hung in the air, as if someone had spoken it. John then asked the Lord if He thought she would be a willing cook for him. There was only one way to find out, he had to ask.

And so, the weekly ritual began. Mary would cook one cake and two batches of biscuits every Saturday and John would collect them after church on Sunday. It wasn't long before Mary's mother extended an invitation for John to stay for lunch, which he accepted and debated many issues with Mary's father.

On the second visit, John and her father were discussing something about which Mary had incidentally read about during the week and she voiced her own opinion on the matter. Both men had looked at her as if she had grown two heads and returned to the topic in question, ignoring her. Feeling her anger boiling up inside herself, she bowed her head and prayed, God help me with my anger and show me how to deal with this. John had, as he had become accustomed to, given her his requirement for the following weeks cooking. Mary decided that there was a way for her to teach John a lesson for ignoring her. His requests had included his most favourite of her offerings, however, he had also mentioned in passing who he was expecting to visit that week and she also knew that they had expressed their delight in something completely different to John's list. Saturday arrived; Mary cooked but instead of John's preferred list, she made up the things that his visitors liked instead. This week, John wasn't staying for lunch, so Mary's cooking was handed over in tins at the gate. Mary hoping that John wouldn't open them to check that she had made what he wanted. John was in a hurry, so he handed her his list for the following week, gave her a quick peck on the cheek, something she wasn't expecting, saying, 'Thanks, Mary' as he rushed to the ute, putting the tins on the seat, and driving off.

Mary was a nervous wreck all week. What would John have to say on the following Sunday. Would he even realise what she had done and try to work out why? John was due to have lunch with them again this weekend.

It was Mary's turn to put out the hymnals, so she walked to church earlier than her parents. Her father had been called out during the night and her mother would wait for him. If he didn't make it back in time for church then they would stay home, spending the time with the Lord and each other in the kitchen.

Having finished placing the books on the seats faster than expected, Mary found herself sitting alone in an empty church. Hearing footsteps, she turned to see John walking in, feeling her stomach do a flip, flop, she watched his face to try and work out how mad he was with her, but she couldn't tell. He came and sat down beside her.

'I'm sorry, Mary.'

'What for?'

'I've spent all week wondering what you were trying to tell me by switching my cooking. It took a lot of prayer but finally God reminded me that I had ignored your opinion at the table the Sunday before last and therefore you had ignored my choices.'

'You worked it out?'

"Well, yes, sort of. When Tom and his wife came to visit yesterday, we were discussing the same subject that your father and I had talked about the last time I had lunch at your home. His wife expressed exactly the same opinion as you did, but instead of Tom ignoring her, he looked at her, smiled and said that she was probably right as well. He hadn't thought about the subject from a female's point of view. When we went out together to check the cows, I asked him if he really thought his wife was right. He turned to me and said, maybe or maybe not, who knows what the outcome of this particular situation will be but it's always good to take notice of a different point of view. It keeps the lines of communication open, something that is very important for a good marriage and he had found that she was right more times than she was wrong anyway.'

'That was when I remembered the way you ducked your head and closed your eyes. I'm sorry, I didn't mean to hurt you.'

'I was praying, asking God to help me with my anger. I'm glad that He has helped us both with a tricky situation.'

After that, John made a concerted effort to include Mary in all their conversations at lunch. It made the conversations far more interesting.

A year later, John asked to speak to Mary's father after lunch, instead of rushing off home. Eventually, her father found her in the lounge room with her mother and told her that John wanted to speak to her, she found him at the front gate, and he asked if she would visit the farm with him the following weekend while his parents were visiting.

9

Mary rode her bike out to the farm, enjoying the fresh early morning air. She had never visited the farm before, there had been no reason to. She hadn't even visited Julie's farm as a child, Julie had come to her place.

As she rode up to the house, she noticed that it was freshly painted. The yard was neatly trimmed, and it was evident that John really had been working hard to tidy things up. Did he still hold out hope for Julie's return, even after all this time? The thought presented itself unbidden.

She walked up to the nearest door, it was open, as she knocked, she was surprised to discover that it was evidently the back door of the house not the front. Mrs Cooper, who was in the kitchen, looked up, smiled, and told Mary to come in. She pointed to the nearest chair and placed a cup and saucer in front of her.

It's so nice to see you, Mary. The men are out in the paddock and will be in shortly for smoko. I'll give you the tour of the house after you have finished. Mary looked around and noticed that there was a kerosene lamp sitting on the table. Suddenly, she realised that there would be no electricity out here on the farm.

Over the next hour, she asked Mrs Cooper all sorts of questions about how things were done without electricity and the answers were a bit daunting. She knew that she loved John and had a strong feeling that meeting his parents this weekend was his way of trying to find out if she loved him enough to be able to live out here with him. Her father's words about farmers needing wives that were not afraid to get dirty and being willing to muck in, came back to haunt her. She put the thoughts to the back of her mind. She enjoyed the day, talking with his mother and helping her around the house only seeing the men during the meals.

It was later that evening when John was walking her to the main road, pushing her bike, that the words again came back.

'Mary, I know that things are very different here to what you are used to in town, but I love you and I wanted you to see for yourself what you would be up against. Now that you have seen it for yourself do you think that you would be able to live here as my wife.'

'John, dad says that farmers need wives that are willing to get dirty and muck in, I'm not sure that I would be a suitable farmer's wife.'

'Mary, Julie was my first choice for all the reasons that your father said would make a good wife, but what I've realised since, is that what is more important is love, being able to talk, share, listen. I never had that with Julie. Yes, it took me awhile to work that out and things were a bit rocky there for a while, but I like the way you tell me when I'm wrong. You also tell me when I've done something right, most of all, we share our faith in the Lord, those things are very important. Oh, and your cooking beats anything Julie was able to cook. I'll look after the outside, if you are willing to keep the home fires burning and meals on the table.'

They had reached the front gate.

'John, this is a big change for me. I love you and yes, if you are asking me to marry you, I will, but please be patient with me. I think it's going to take me awhile to learn how to do things your way.'

'Mary, the house will be yours, you need to figure out how to do things your way. I know that it will be harder with no electricity, but you will work it out. I hope I will be able to afford a generator soon, that will give you electric lights and run some things that you are used to in town.'

'Oh, John, I love you.'

'I love you too, Mary Dawson.' With that John kissed her. A long slow kiss. After a minute he pulled away and handed her the bike. 'I'll see you tomorrow at church. I love you. Goodnight, ride safe.'

Mary mounted her bike and rode home, looking back to see John watching her until she turned the corner.

Lord, will I be able to manage to do this, it was a prayer that she repeated, over, and over again, all the way home.

A verse in the bible came to mind: I can do all things through Him who strengthens me.

A Rose of Faith

'Now faith is the substance of things hoped for, the evidence of things not seen.'

Hebrews 11:1

1

Mary felt the sigh that she had let out ripple down through her body as she relaxed back into the comfortable armchair. It had been a long day and the house felt empty. It was late and the room was dark, except for the flashing lights on the Christmas tree. Her face, hidden by the night, exhibited lines and wrinkles that come with old age and life. Yes, her life had been tough but not brutal.

She quietly watched the lights flashing. Her mind drifted back to the Christmas' of her childhood. They were looked forward to with much greater anticipation than they are today, she concluded. Life back then was routine, not so busy that things can spin out of control at a moment's notice. Christmas was special because it broke the routine of life. You only had a few special occasions to look forward to. Your birthday, cracker night, which sadly we don't do in Australia anymore, and Christmas Day; being the one that was probably the most anticipated. It was full of surprises, simply because there were so many secrets to be kept, and so many questions to be answered. Some questions you had been asking all year, others just weeks, and you looked forward to the answers. The beginnings of a smile appeared as she continued to reminisce.

Of course, there was also the school concert, with its songs, Nativity play, and other items that had to be practised over and over to get it right. This also broke the routine of school life, something that was very much appreciated by even the most dedicated student.

What surprises await? What will Santa bring me? Did he get my letter? Will I get what I want or something I need? Even as you got older, and you knew the truth about Santa and Christmas you had other questions that you looked forward to getting answered. I guess the main one was, *did mum and dad get the hints I've been dropping for weeks?*

You see, back then, you didn't get to know what you were getting before Christmas morning. These days, Mary mused, a lot of children just demand what they want. Often, they know what they are getting long before Christmas morning arrives.

Christmas paraphernalia wasn't even flashy like today's Christmas trappings. The Christmas tree was usually a bush tree cut down. The decorations were hand-made paper chains from glossy pictures from magazines that were no-longer needed. There was no main line electricity, even in town, so coloured lights were unthinkable.

Mary wondered if this was one of the reasons why, the older you got, the more you looked forward to Heaven. According to the Bible, there will be beauty beyond our imaginations. Those streets of gold and the sea as clear as blue crystal. There are so many questions that we will get the answers to. Life gets routine too, as you get older, she ventured. Heaven is anticipated like Christmas because it will certainly break the routine of life here on earth. There would certainly be a multitude of surprises that, unlike the Christmas ones, will last forever.

Her mind drifted through other memories, such as the time she had an argument with her mother about Christmas being the end of the year. What her mother hadn't realised was that to her childish mind, Christmas and the New Year were so closely intertwined that she was unable to separate the two events. Christmas did herald the end of the year! Just as the first Christmas spoke of the end of the old covenant or system of salvation that God had for His people and signalled a new arrangement, one of grace not law.

Of course, not all Christmas memories were good ones. She thought about the year she had read a story about a little boy who had snuck out of the house and bought his mother a Christmas tree to show how much he loved her. Mary loved that story and the message of love that it carried, so much that she wanted to copy it. However, she wasn't able to sneak out of her house and she had no pocket money anyway. The only way she could think of making this happen was to ask her parents to get her a Christmas tree. The plan was that they would buy it for her before Christmas. Then she could give it to her mother on Christmas Day, just like the boy in the story. However, her parents hadn't read the story or understood what she wanted to do, how could they, it was supposed to be a surprise? Oh yes, the Christmas Tree had arrived, it was sitting on her bedside table on Christmas morning. How could she surprise her mother, it was too late? Mary realised that there would be many people who thought they knew what Heaven was going to be like or how the end of the world would come about. Just as her parents had no idea of what she was thinking back then, they really have no idea of what God has in mind for our future either. How can they, no one can understand the mind of God? Mary was pretty sure that there would be many surprises in store for everyone when the time comes.

The Christmas lights continued to flash rhythmically. She let out another sigh, shifted her head back a little more trying to find some cool air. The night was hot and humid, a common thing in Australia at Christmas time. Summer was in full swing. The windows and doors were opened in order to let what breeze was available flow through the house. She was grateful that out here, in the country, far away from civilisation, she was able to let the air flow naturally through her home. If she lived closer to the main road or in town, she would need to keep her doors and windows locked against the danger of thieves and invasion. These things were becoming more common in the world that existed now. Again, it was so different from the days of her childhood. 'It felt safer back then'.

She had not always appreciated it of course. As a child she had been lonely, her brothers had left home as they were older and her best friend lived out of town, but back then it was part of normal life. People didn't move around like they did these days. They visited occasionally, but generally, people were just getting on with the routine of life and travelling wasn't easy. However, if you did visit you stayed for several hours, a whole day, or even two, not just an hour or less. You had more time to talk and to get to know those guests, it was a much bigger deal than just 'dropping in' which people now call a visit.

There was the mandatory Christmas Church Service each year which she quite enjoyed as a child but as she had got older, she found that many church goers really didn't practice what they preached. They ignored her, particularly when the children had been very small, tried to tell her what they needed and made very little effort to actually get to know her circumstances. After John had died, she hadn't been visited by anyone, there hadn't even been a phone call. In the end, she had given up going to church all together and this most likely contributed to her bitter attitude towards people in general.

Mind you, loneliness really wasn't an issue for most children she mused. You had your imagination to keep you company. It became your best friend. It took you to all sorts of places and allowed you to reach the greatest heights of achievement. Your dreams were realised to great acclaim through this friend, and you felt good about yourself, if only for a moment in time. It was good for your self-esteem she concluded. Yet, even with your imagination in full flight, you were still able to tell the difference between fact and fiction.

A frown formed on her face as she contemplated how poor today's children were, when there were so many facts and reality checks thrown at them every day. Children, even babies, needed to be taught right from wrong and given boundaries, that was true, but the fact was, there was so much incorrect information being presented as true. How adults could expect children to sort out fact from fiction anymore was unknown.

She sat up, it was getting late, time for another cup of tea before going to bed. She walked to the kitchen and switched on the electric jug. Placing the teabag in her favourite mug, she automatically massaged her shoulders to relieve the pain that was constantly there. She was wearing out just like her mug was, she thought, noting that the gold edging around the top had almost worn off from constant use but the roses painted on the side were still distinguishable even after all these years. How it had survived this long was a mystery, the chips in the ceramic around the base being testament of the number of times that it had been dropped or knocked off the various surfaces around her home.

Still waiting for the jug to boil, her mind drifted back to her first tea set. It was made out of empty tins; she couldn't remember what might have been in them. The lids became the plates and the cans her cups. A larger tin had been bent out of shape to make a spout on one side. Unlike the toy ones she had seen in the shops, this tea set would change its style according to where she pretended to be on the day. It could be made out of pure gold, fine china or even crystal. It didn't matter to her back then, that these were not suitable materials for a teapot or a cup. Ceramic mugs were not in common use in those days either, only the big clunky ones that the men took up the paddock. They were made of enamelled tin and were very large to suit the huge thirst that the men developed working on the farm, even her father had one that her mother used to pack with the food for him when he attended his patients.

The jug boiled and, with her tea made, she moved back to the armchair that she had vacated. It was still warm, which made her briefly question the wisdom of a hot cup of tea instead of a glass of water but as she sipped it slowly and allowed the flavour to seep through her, she dismissed the thought and allowed her mind to drift again to the toys of her childhood.

There was not the abundance of toys back then that are available now. Your toys were bottles, rocks, sticks, even the slats on the fence of your home. Rocks were probably her favourite, they were students in a game of schools but an hour later they easily transformed into packages on a shop shelf, a loaf of bread or even a wonderfully decorated birthday cake when she decided that she was tired of being a teacher and wanted to be a shopkeeper. You could even make the most wonderful wedding cake out of those rocks using your imagination. Boys did the same things with sticks, turning them into guns, rifles, or bow and arrows. There was no limit to what you could do back then.

As you played with these improvised toys, yes, there were accidents, cuts, and bruises. Most of them weren't serious; some were, of course, but life back then was considered a gift, not a right, and not taken for granted like nowadays. The cuts and bruises also served to help toughen you up for life as an adult in an adult world. You learnt that, while it was painful, it didn't last forever and unless you kept irritating it, it would, in time, heal. Yes, it might leave a scar, maybe, but the skin and you were stronger because of it. You had learnt to be careful next time and what to avoid, or maybe that life just had to go on, pain and all. Her mind flashed back to the hands of the men that worked around her then. Their hands were scarred, and rough from physical work but that didn't stop them being gentle and kind when the need arose.

She remembered playing house under the big apricot tree while staying with her grandparents. Again, the toys were empty cans, rocks, and sticks. However, at grandma's there was the special addition of her old clothes that had been put away. She was also allowed to use some blankets and rugs to put on the ground. Sometimes, you even got to use some of her chipped china instead of the tins and rocks. Good old grandma, she didn't seem to mind all the extra work that having grandchildren stay created. Mary was a little guilt-ridden about how she just didn't seem to cope with her grandchildren as well as her own grandmother had. As a child, she had sometimes wondered about what life was really like when her grandmother was a little girl.

Finishing her tea, she moved to the kitchen, the floor creaking as she walked across it, she placed the mug on the sink, picked up a bottle of water and headed to bed. She was known to be very set in her ways, almost to the point of being obsessive. Tomorrow would be the same routine as it had been ever since her husband had died. She had everything planned right down to the last minute. It was just the way she was these days, and it didn't matter to her that her family didn't like it very much. Somewhere in the back of her mind she knew she could change but she kept pushing away that thought. She was too old to change, and she had a right to be the way she wanted to be, that was her argument anyway. She made her way back into the hall, resting her hand on the railing just for assurance as she climbed the curved staircase to her upstairs bedroom, which she had started using again after the death of her husband. She was thankful to still be able to climb the stairs reasonably easily, knowing that the day would come when it would be necessary to return to the downstairs bedroom. It had been easier to use it while he was sick, but the view from upstairs was less cluttered by the trees in the garden. Through the window she could see the great expanse of the sky all the way across the valley. The stars at night and the sunrise in the morning was something that she had always enjoyed. Even lightning flashing during storms seemed more spectacular from a higher perspective. Walking into her bedroom, she automatically checked the view through her window as she crossed to the bathroom on the opposite side to carry out her personal care routine. The night sky was one of those special black velvet ones with diamond stars all over it. *Another real Christmas sky,* she thought. When she returned to the room, she moved to the window and stood there marvelling at the wonder of such a beautiful sight. *The night Jesus had been born would surely have had such a sky.* It made sense to her, even if no one else even considered it, that this would be how the sky would have been on the first Christmas night. *What a stunning backdrop to the angel choir when they sang to the Shepherds. No wonder they were afraid when the first angel appeared, it would have been the last thing that they would have expected to happen, particularly on such a calm and gorgeous night.* She imagined they loved the nights that were like this as much as she did. Stormy nights would have been very frightening and, had the angels appeared on such a night, they would have put it down to a trick of the storm. *On such a night as this, there would have been no doubt about what they saw.*

She moved to the side of the bed, placed the glasses on the table, and, as she undressed, she found herself wondering what it really would have been like for Mary as she rode the donkey from

Nazareth to Bethlehem. If time travel was possible, she would travel to many of her favourite times to find out for herself about how life really was. She knew that many of the stories she read were not always the most accurate accounts. She carefully placed her shoes under the bed where they could be found in the morning; bare feet were one of her many pet hates. Slipping her nightdress over her head, she separated the sheet and blanket making sure that the later was in easy reach near her feet just in case it cooled down enough during the night for her to need its warmth. Climbing into bed she pulled the sheet up; it gave some protection from the mosquitos that decided to come out once the light had been turned off.

She checked the clock, it said 2 am, that was a bit later than usual, she really had lost track of time. She surprised herself by thinking, *oh well, it doesn't matter!* Turning out the light, she relaxed, rolled onto her side, and watched the stars through the window. It was one of her favourite things to do, particularly when she was feeling flat. As she drifted off to sleep, listening to the birds singing outside, her final thought was that she didn't really enjoy Christmas these days because societies expectations had changed so much.

2

Mary stirred! *Did she hear someone calling her name?* There was something very strange about this particular morning. Half-awake she looked towards the window; it was missing! The light coming into the room came through French doors which had replaced the solid door that led to the balcony and indicated that it was just breaking dawn. *That's funny* she thought, but it was Christmas morning, there was no need to hurry. The children wouldn't arrive until nearly lunchtime. She rolled onto her back and looked at the ceiling. *What has happened to my ceiling? Why does it look like that? That's odd, where am I?*

The birds were giving their usual magnificent rendition of tweets, twits, and squawks; however, they did seem to be in extra fine voice this morning. Was it her imagination or were there a lot more than usual? Oh, how she enjoyed the birds singing each morning but this morning she could hear other noises under the beautiful bird songs. A couple of dogs were barking, somewhere nearby. She didn't have any dogs now that her husband had died. They were too much work to look after. A rooster crowed several times, she didn't have chooks anymore either. Her husband had not been able to look after them during the time he was sick, so they had given them to their son who lived on a few acres on the other side of town. She was trying to work out what these noises meant when she heard her name again.

'Mary!'

The voice sounded annoyed. Mary sat up! Her bones didn't creak like she was used to. She swung her feet over the side of the bed, looking for her shoes that she had left there the night before, but they were missing. She frowned wondering where they were. A search under the bed failed to find them. All that she found was a chamber pot, empty, thank goodness, but it was there none the less. *That's very odd* she thought, *everything feels very odd this morning.*

There was that voice again!

'Mary, will you hurry up!' Someone was definitely yelling at her.

Right, well, I had better go and find out what the problem is. As she walked towards the French doors, she heard the familiar creaking of the floor. *Well, at least that's normal!* She peeked at the mirror that was hanging on the wall above a table with a large bowl and jug sitting on top that also seemed to have materialised overnight. *That hadn't been there last night!* What she saw in the mirror though, made her stop in her tracks. Who was that looking back at her? That girl was only 15 or 16 not 86. Where were her wrinkles, frown and laugh lines? They were gone. She took another look around, fully awake now, where was she, this really wasn't her house! Who was the girl looking back at her in the mirror? She glanced down; you'd swear she was only sixteen. Still trying to work out what was happening she opened the door and stepped out. This should have been the landing at the top of the stairs, but instead, she found herself standing on a verandah staring across a valley. Even now, this early in the morning, the orange misty haze on the horizon gave an indication that the day was going to be hot. At least that was familiar. She could hear Kookaburras singing, Galahs squawking, pigs grunting and horses neighing in the distance, which was not so familiar. Mary became conscious that she only had night clothes on and was about to turn back into the room when she heard another voice.

'Mary, will you hurry up and stop daydreaming child.' Mary looked up and down the verandah. Who owned that voice and where were they calling her from? Hearing footsteps, she turned to see a boy about ten years old, coming towards her.

'Mary, you'd better hurry up,' he said 'and get dressed! Ma is getting upset with you for taking so long.' Again, Mary looked down at her new body. 'Ok, Ok, just wait here a second while I get dressed.' She saw the boy roll his eyes as if to say, you're kidding, aren't you? as she ducked back through the door and looked around. Where were the clothes, she'd taken off last night? There were some clothes in the corner! She moved quickly to investigate. 'Oh dear, these are going to take more than a second to throw on,' she gasped. There was a corset, two petticoats, a pair of something that looked like a short version of loose-fitting trousers, a dress, and a pinafore. Something deep inside her knew that all of this had to be worn. She wouldn't get away with just putting on the dress. She wasn't even sure how she knew that. The clothes were all pretty plain and reasonably clean but how did one get all this gear on in a hurry.

'Oh, will you hurry up Mary!' even the boy sounded cranky. 'We are all going to get into trouble if you don't get a move on'.

Dressed as best as one could be in such a hurry, in clothes that were so unfamiliar and not all that comfortable, Mary emerged from the room. 'Right, lead on my man' she instructed waving her arm around in some sort of dramatic gesture. He rolled his eyes again and retraced his steps down the verandah. Mary followed, shaking her head, and wondering what on earth was going on.

Is this some sort of out of body experience? It couldn't be! From what she had been told, if you had an out of body experience you seem to float above the activity. The other thing that she assumed, was that no one could see you, and she was definitely seen and had a solid body.

They turned the corner and stepped down off the boards, across a small dirt gap and into another building that was separate to where they had come from. The first thing Mary noticed was the heat, quickly looking around she saw that the windows and doors were all opened but the heat was incredible even this early in the morning. No wonder, at the other end of the room was a fire burning in an open fireplace. *Oh, my goodness,* thought Mary, *no wonder its hot in here, they aren't using electricity!* Her bare feet felt funny and looking down she noticed there were no floorboards. It was a dirt floor! Packed down hard, feeling firm and cool it still made her feet feel dusty.

'YUK, I hate dirt floors,'. Her memory flashed back to her early days on the farm. She was used to dust and mud when she lived in town, after all there were very few sealed roads at the time, but once she had moved to the farm after marrying John, she found that dirt, dust, and mud moved to a completely new level. It had been a battle which she'd constantly lost, however, she still hated the feel of dusty feet.

'For goodness' sake, Mary, stop being a fusspot. You know dirt is safer than floorboards for the kitchen. Will you please get your head out of the clouds and get a move on! Your father needs you in the dairy. We have given Daniel the morning off so he can spend some of his Christmas day with his family and the aboriginal workers have gone 'walkabout'.'

This tirade came from a woman standing near the fire. *Oh, had she said that out loud?* Well at least she knew what 'walkabout' meant. The Australian aboriginal people were famous for going 'walkabout'. These people had always been a nomadic race. They moved from place to place, living in small open sided dwellings made from tree bark. These provided shade from the harsh summer sun but how they provided protection in the snowy winters further south, Mary had never been able to work out. However, when bushfires raced through the country, they were able to get out of danger without having to pack up, unlike the Europeans with all the trappings they had brought with them. The aboriginal people just didn't understand why these strange new people wanted to stay in one place all the time. They were so used to picking up spears and boomerangs and moving to new territory. This meant that they often just disappeared over night even though they were working for farmers. They would be back, but the farmers never knew when they would turn up again. It could be a couple of weeks or months. This could explain why the woman in front of her seemed to be in such a bad mood. It would be hard to get up and find that suddenly you have to do all the work by yourself because all your help had left.

'It's Christmas morning, isn't it?' she asked, waving her hand in front of her face to disperse the flies that swarmed around her.

'Yes, it is, but the animals don't know that and even if they did, they wouldn't care. The cows need to be milked and the other animals still have to be fed no matter what day it is'.

'Here, I've made you some cocoa instead of tea just because it is Christmas morning but please hurry up, your father is waiting'. The woman regarded her quizzically 'My goodness you look like something the cat dragged in. You should take more care in how you dress, Mary. If you didn't spend so much time daydreaming, you would have time to dress properly, you know'. This last remark was made as the woman crossed the room and handed her an enamelled mug. 'Now, get a move on! She finished. *What's wrong with daydreaming,* Mary wondered. *After all she had been doing a lot of reminiscing last night, wasn't daydreaming the forward version of reminiscing.*

While drinking the warm chocolatey liquid she looked around the hot and stuffy room. Where was the electric stove, the fridge? There were no signs of either. Three out of the four walls had a doorway. She also noticed that there was a firearm of some sort hanging beside each door. The fourth, the one she was facing, was taken up with a very large fireplace. There were either benches or shelves on every available space along the walls, and a large table and chairs graced the middle of the room.

The young boy was sitting at the table, munching on a piece of toast and there was a little girl sitting in front of the fire. On the table there was a mixture of cooking pans, plates, cups, food, and a loaf of bread sitting on a cloth. It seemed that it had been wrapped around the bread. Something Mary did remember doing when she was first married. Every food container had a fancy cover over it. She assumed that was to protect the food from being attacked by the flies.

'Look, Mary, I'm cooking the toast this morning and it won't fall into the fire,' the little girls' eyes were shining, matching the smile on her face. 'Pa made me my own toasting cage for Christmas,' her voice rose in excitement, 'Isn't daddy clever, Mary?'

Mary looked at the implement in the child's hand. It was obviously handmade. There were two layers of wires crisscrossed and hinged at the top with a very long handle attached to each layer. Wide enough to hold two pieces of bread, it was being held just over the hot coals in the fire. Mary had made toast on the fire but had used a two-pronged fork made out of fencing wire. The little girl flipped the cage over to reveal one side of the bread toasted, if a little darkly.

Mary felt the blood drain from her face as she saw a vision of the child's hand reaching towards the fire to grab a piece of bread that had fallen off a fork. Suddenly, with an echo of NOOOO which seemed to go on forever, two arms clamped around the child's torso at the armpit level. She was swiftly lifted off her feet, swung around and deposited into one of the chairs at the table just as the piece of bread burst into flames, quickly burning into a pile of ash.

'Mary are you alright, you look like you've seen a ghost' the women's voice held a note of concern.

Mary shook her head, 'Yeah,' she said slowly, 'I was just seeing her trying to get a piece of bread out of the fire'.

'Oh Mary,' Ma's voice softened and was full of sympathy, 'we are so thankful that you saw what Emma was going to do and pulled her out of harm's way'. A smile lit up the woman's face as she continued. 'I don't think I've ever seen anyone move so fast in all my life. That is why your father made her that toasting cage, as she calls it. That way she can make the toast, as long as I put the bread in and take the toast out. Isn't that right Emma!' The woman looked at the little girl who nodded enthusiastically. Returning to look at Mary, Ma continued, 'You know how much she wants to feel grown up by helping. Besides, even the small things make a day like today a little easier. Talking of which, you'd both had better get a move on and get to the dairy. Go on Joey, you can finish your toast on the way'.

Well at least I know the children names now, that's something but Mary still was trying to work out what was happening. *Is this some sort of 'time warp'* or *'time tunnel' experience?* She didn't have time to think about it anymore as Joey spoke.

'Ok, come on Mary, we'd better get going'. He remarked, pushing back his chair.

Mary placed her mug on the table. 'Alright, you lead the way then, let's go' Mary replied trying to make her voice sound more jovial than lost, which was how she felt as she followed Joey through the side door.

3

She found herself out in a yard. The sun was now sitting just above the horizon and the air was heating up quickly. The bird and animal noises that she had heard earlier became clearer and louder. Mary was glad Joey had been sent to help because she had no idea where to go. It wasn't that she didn't know what a dairy would look like but there were so many buildings here and she'd no clue which one the dairy would be. This whole situation was completely foreign to her and she had no inkling of where to go or what to do next. At least with Joey, who seemed to know where to go, all she would have to do is follow his lead, that way she might be able to muddle through whatever this was, even if it was only a dream but gee it felt very real.

As they walked across the yard the grass crackled and prickled under her feet. It wasn't hard to see that it probably hadn't rained a lot recently. The grass wasn't dead yet, but it was obvious that it would be if rain didn't come soon.

Joey was leading her in the direction of some sheds at the bottom of a slope. As they ran down the narrow track, the occasional rabbit jumped out of the grass and scuttled off. Each time it happened; it made her flinch with surprise. Halfway down the hill, Mary heard what might have been thunder. The noise made her look around at the sky. Yes, there they were, dark clouds in the distance indicating that a storm was brewing! It was a long way off yet. Of course, there was no way of knowing which path it would take or how much rain it would bring, if any. Storms were very unpredictable.

Joey had heard the noise as well it seemed as he started running faster while looking back at her and yelled. 'Come on, Mary, we'd better hurry up.'

They reached the shed set in the middle of a few others very quickly. Joey burst through the door, calling out, 'Pa, we're here'.

'Ha, slow down, young man, you'll spook the cows if you're not careful'. The man who spoke was dressed in loose fitting trousers held up by straps that went over his shoulders, a shirt and jacket. He was tall, broad-shouldered and muscular, evidence of the hard physical work that it took to run a farm successfully. She also noticed that he had a pistol strapped to his side. *Wow*, she thought, *I wonder why he needs to wear that while he's milking the cows.*

'Morning, Mary,' the man was looking straight at her. 'You look a little dishevelled this morning,' he smiled at her, 'Were you daydreaming again?'

Mary decided to nod but not say anything, how could she explain that she had no idea where she was or what was required of her. After all, everyone seemed to have expected that she should have been up for hours and yet it wasn't even five o'clock. She had never been a morning person, preferring to work late into the night when things were quiet. The other thing that was making Mary nervous was that she had never really felt comfortable around animals. If she was honest, they scared her. Would she be required to help milk the cows; Mary felt the butterflies go berserk in her stomach.

'Right', the man's voice took on a commanding tone, 'Joey, you let the cows back in the paddock please, Mary, you can wash the separator while I feed the pigs, then we will take the house milk back to the kitchen so we can have breakfast.

69

The relief that Mary felt was enormous, she wouldn't have to get too close to the animals. Cleaning the separator should be achievable. Cleaning wasn't that dissimilar no matter what age and time you lived in; it was just the equipment you used that was different, and that thing was very different to the one that they had used when they were first married.

She looked around again. There were several buckets filled with milk.

In the corner of the shed, was a copper filled with hot water. There was a fire burning in the grate. Through a window she could see Joey letting out the cows, all twenty of them, he hunted them down through a gate in the next paddock. On her way back to the copper, to fill another bucket of water she watched the man lift a bucket in each hand and head out the door.

I wonder what time he started work. Mary thought, *it must have been early, you wouldn't be able to milk twenty cows by hand without having to get up long before everyone else in the house.*

It seemed like no time at all, Joey was back.

'What do I have to do now, pa?' Joey asked as his father came back into the shed.

'Grab one of those buckets of milk and help me take it down to the pig pens. Put the milk from your bucket in the trough of the first pen please, that's a good boy.' The man replied. As he picked up a bucket in each hand himself, he turned to Mary and said, 'We won't be long now.'

Mary's tummy was starting to rumble from a lack of food, and she was beginning to think longingly of breakfast but first, she figured that she should wash the buckets that had been sat down near the copper.

While she worked, on some sort of instinct, she could still hear the thunder rumbling in the distance. *Somewhere, someone is getting rain. Well, maybe!* Some storms were called 'Dry storms'. These consisted of mostly lightning, thunder and very little rain. They often were the cause of bushfires. The lightning would strike trees and other high structures, sending sparks into the dry grass on the ground. The strong winds that came with the storms would fan the sparks into flames. The flames, driven by the winds and fuelled by the dry plant material lying around, would become a raging bushfire very quickly. Those fires burnt everything in their path and even jumped great distances as the embers were blown miles ahead of the original fire.

As she finished washing the buckets, she turned them upside down on the bench, not really sure if she was doing the right thing but decided that leaving them there to dry would just have to do. If she got into strife then she would cross that bridge when she came to it. She looked around to check that everything had been washed when she noticed a cloth on the edge of the bench. Picking it up, she noticed that there were a lot of cows' hair and dirt on one side. This was the strainer, she guessed, it made sure that the milk was clean before it was separated. She finished washing it and hung it over a rail to dry. She was enjoying the silence, but she really was starting to feel very hungry.

'Right then', Mary jumped, she hadn't heard Joey and his father return from feeding the pigs. 'Time for breakfast, hey Mary'. Joey's father asked as he helped her to wash the buckets that they had returned with. Then he picked a bag of what could be feed, threw it over his shoulder and headed for the door. Mary was quick to pick

71

up the bucket of milk that was sitting on the floor and followed behind.

'Oh, boy', Joey happily asked, 'I wonder if Ma has made us anything special because it's Christmas Day?' He was almost dancing with anticipation.

'Oh, yes please', Mary exclaimed.

Mary again tried to figure out what all this was about as she followed the two men back to the house. Joey did seem to be very grown up for his age. You could hardly call him a boy, except of course when he had been jumping around wondering what would be on the menu for breakfast. When he did things like that you realised just how young he was but otherwise he was a child doing a man's work and therefore deserved the respect that was due to him for what he managed to do. Turning her thoughts back to breakfast she wondered, *what did these people consider to be special?*

There were also a million other questions going around in her head. This was turning out to be the strangest Christmas Day she had ever had.

Halfway back to the house, they all looked to the sky as raindrops fell. 'We'd better move faster!' the father said picking up the pace. Joey just took off at a gallop reaching the house long before the two he had left behind. Mary wasn't sure how she was going to manage to run. She had long skirts on. These were gathered up in one hand and the bucket was in the other one. It was only half-full, but it was starting to feel heavy in the way that dead-weights do after a time. The flies were also making a nuisance of themselves in the humid air, bussing around her face and sticking to her hands. She tried to blow them off her face with her breath, by extending her lower lip and directing air upwards. It was after all the only weapon she had available as both her hands were occupied, they just stayed there annoying her. The sticky heat was the sort of weather that they loved. The perspiration on her skin attracted the flies like bees to a honeypot. If it hadn't been for the milk, instinct told her that she would have gathered up her skirts and covered that ground nearly as fast as Joey had.

By the time she had reached the house, her dress was wet, but the rain hadn't soaked through to the skin. It had only been a light shower and had pretty much stopped as she had stepped under the awning around the kitchen.

'Oh, there you are Mary, put the milk on the bench and go and wash up'. Joey's mother had only glanced in her direction and continued to serve up food as she talked. Mary, looked around, where on earth, does one wash-up? What did she mean exactly? The smell of food assaulted her nostrils, she was so hungry. She felt as if she could eat all day and not stop the rumblings in her stomach.

Joey appeared in the doorway on the other side of the room. He looked at her quizzingly, leaving Mary to wonder if he also knew that there was something strange going on.

'Go on Mary, Pa's out there washing up and you'd better do the same.' Mary threw him a grateful smile and moved to the door that Joey had come through and found Joey's father stepping back from a basin on another washstand, similar to the one that had been in the room that she had woken up in.

'All yours, my dear,' he smiled as he grabbed a towel and wiped his hands and face. Mary stepped up to the basin. and looked at the dirty water. You could see the flakes of soap floating around left behind by Joey and his father. Oh, well, there was nothing for it, she would just have to get on with it. Gingerly she placed her hands in the water, cupping her hands, it was surprisingly cold, she lifted the water to her face, making sure that she kept her mouth firmly closed. She didn't want to taste any of that water even by accident.

'Come on child' the man was getting impatient, mind you Mary herself wasn't in any mind to dawdle either, she was hungry, 'I'll make you water the plants if you don't hurry up'.

Mary quickly rubbed her hands together and moved away. There was no way she wanted another job to do that she had no idea how to carry out. She took the towel that the man was holding out to her and while she dried her face and hands, she watched him pick up the dish and walk out into the yard and throw the water around the base of a rose planted near the gate. Well, that would have been simple enough she thought but the strangeness of the situation was making her so unsure of herself.

There was a rail on the side of the washstand, Mary folded the towel and hung it over the rail. Joey's father placed the empty basin back on the stand and walked into the kitchen and Mary followed. Hoping that it really was time to eat.

4

Joey's mother was moving towards the table, both hands held plates piled with food. There was bacon, eggs, potatoes, sausages, tomatoes, fried onions, and toast. Mary looked at the table, in the middle there was a large platter of pancakes as well as jam, honey, cream and butter. Joey and Emma were already seated and fiddling with their cutlery. It was evident that they were as impatient as she was to eat.

'How is my Rose this morning?', the man walked up to Joey's mother and kissed her on the cheek. 'Merry Christmas, my dear', he remarked as he sat down on the chair at the end of the table facing the door that she had first entered the kitchen through, which to Mary, seemed to be a long time ago even now.

Sitting down in the chair on the right side of her husband, she replied, 'Your Rose is fine, thank you, Joe, you'd better say grace before the children disgrace themselves please.' Mary moved quickly and sat down in the empty chair on Joey's left side. Closing her eyes, she waited edgily for grace to be said.

Mary placed her hands in her lap, noting that her dress was already dry. The heat dragged water out of everything it seemed, she guessed the same would be happening outside. The heat would be dragging the water out of the ground.

Joe finished saying grace and everyone tucked into their meal. Mary looked around for the salt. A grinder was sitting in the middle of the table directly in front of Joey. Without thinking, Mary reached out to pick it up, saying 'Excuse me' as she did so.

'MARY!', Rose's voice was sharp with rebuke. 'Where are your manners? The salt is directly in front of Joey. You should have asked Joey to pass it to you and not only that, why didn't you wait until the adults had used it?'

Mary quickly pulled her arm back to the edge of the table. Looking down at the table she muttered 'Sorry Mam'. Mary hoped that she sounded respectful. The salt and pepper grinders were then passed around the table starting with Joe and finishing with Mary.

As she continued to eat with some enjoyment, she also had time to think in the silence. At least now she knew the names of all the people involved in this completely bizarre story, dream, or whatever it was. She just could not bring herself to call the parents Ma and Pa, she just didn't feel as if she belonged here amongst them. However, this also created a bigger dilemma for her. At some point, she was going to have to actually address these people and she knew that calling them by their Christian names was not going to be acceptable. How long would she be able to get away with not speaking to them directly?

The family had been eating silently for about ten minutes, hungry stomachs must have started to feel a little better because the food was beginning to move slower from plate to mouths.

'So, how well did the girls behave this morning?', Rose directed the question to Joe.

Mary frowned, she had been the only girl with Joe, why was Rose asking him about how the girls had behaved. She opened her mouth to say something but stopped herself just in time. Instead, she put the food on her fork into her mouth as Joe answered Rose and she realised that Rose had asked about the cows, they called them 'girls'!

'Oh, they were pretty good. Bessy should deliver her calf in the next couple of days. Molly is starting to dry off, but the others managed to give plenty of milk.' Joe responded.

'Has the sow delivered those piglets yet?' Rose continued the conversation between finishing mouthfuls of food.

'No, not yet, but that could still happen later today, I will have to go and check on her on and off, particularly since Jacky has gone 'walkabout'.' Joe had waited until he had finished eating his mouthful of food before replying.

Mary looked around the table, did these people really celebrate Christmas Day or was it just another workday to them?

'There wasn't very much rain in that storm,' Rose sounded a little despondent,

'There was plenty of thunder, I could hear it while we were in the dairy', this remark was made by Joey.

'Where there is thunder, there is always lightning,' Joe said, 'Let's hope it doesn't start a bushfire. One Christmas Day without fighting a fire would be a rare Christmas indeed'.

'That's true,' Rose noted.

Joe looked at his wife. 'You look tired, my dear, you didn't sleep very well last night.'

Rose swallowed the mouthful she was chewing. 'It was so hot, and as it's our turn to host Christmas lunch this year, I kept going over everything that needed to be done today.'

'You have been working very hard for weeks now, Rose, I'm sure that everything will go according to plan, it usually does, you are very good at making people feel comfortable and at ease, it's a talent that the Lord has blessed you with and next year you will be able to relax and enjoy being a guest.' Joe's voice was full of concern mixed with pride. 'Who are we expecting for lunch today anyway?'

'I've been over the RSVP's several times, there's Mrs Jones; Mr Bradshaw; and the Goldsmiths from down the road. Even though they have been part of the community for nearly six months, it will be their first Christmas away from their family, so I've asked them to come today. Chloe has walked home from school with Joey nearly every day and I'm sure their little boy will enjoy playing with Emma. Oh, and old Mr Smith as well, this will be his first Christmas without his wife and since it's only a couple of months since her passing I feel sure that some company would be welcomed.' Rose returned, 'that makes seven extras. They all sent very nice acceptance cards. I think that Mrs Goldsmith's little girl might have handmade the one that came from them. It was a very good effort for someone who was only seven years old.'

The food gradually disappeared from the plates and the cups of tea were being finished when Emma asked. 'When are we going to open our Christmas presents?' this plea from Emma seemed like a signal, it was time to move on, the meal should be finished.

'Not until its morning smoko, darling,' Joe spoke and looked around the table, 'Right then,' he continued, 'It's time to get the chores done. Mary, you can help with the cleaning up of the kitchen and water the vegetable garden. Just use the medium dipper and make sure you only put the water around each plant. We can't afford to waste the water at the moment because we don't know how long this dry spell is going to last. Do you understand me?' Joe's voice held a stern note. 'There was no ring around the moon last night and I haven't heard a Kookaburra singing in the morning for a long time. Even the Black Cockatoos seemed to have disappeared.'

'I heard a Kookaburra singing this morning' Mary interrupted.

'Oh, well we had still better be careful with the water and please pick anything that is ready to eat. Your mother will need whatever is available to help feed our visitors today. I want you to give her all the help she needs, she has worked very hard to make today special and she doesn't need you going off into your own dream world, please, not today'. Joe's tone held a dismissive note as if he didn't quite believe her and wasn't impressed with being interrupted.

'Yes, sir,' Mary replied, wondering if she would even be able to find the garden and being amazed that there were still more chores that had to be done. In her other life, today would have been a holiday, most chores were left undone but not here, it seemed there were extra chores, she discovered this as she listened to Joe's instructions to Joey.

'Joey, you can let the chooks out, so they can get a feed and collect the eggs for your mother. Take Emma with you and she can bring the eggs back to the house. Then I want you to come down to the stable to help with the horses. The stalls need to be cleaned and horses fed. You can give them an extra brushing as a special treat for Christmas. While you are doing that, I will check on the pigs and go out around the sheep. We might even have some piglets by then.'

Joe turned his attention to Emma, his voice softened, there was an extra sparkle in his eyes and a smile played around his mouth. 'And you, young lady', there was a smile in his voice as he spoke, 'your jobs will be to go with Joey, he will give you the eggs, so take the egg basket with you and be very careful not to trip over on your way back to the house. We don't want scrambled eggs again today. Then you feed the cat and her kittens, don't play with them too long because you can also help Mary water the garden. You use the small dipper, Mary will carry the bucket, all right?', Joe asked, as eyes briefly flicked to look at Mary and then back at Emma. 'Now, I want you to remind me of what you do if you find a snake in the Washhouse?' Joe asked as his face took on a serious look.

'I don't move, I yell SNAKE and ma will come running with the shovel', Emma replied with a look on her face that indicated that she thought she was very clever to know what to do.

'Very good, alright, time to move', the smile returning to Joe's face. It was obvious that this little girl had a special place in her father's heart.

Some things hadn't changed, even in her other world, Mary knew that the youngest daughter often seemed to be able to wrap their father around their little finger in a way that no other child could.

Joe turned to Rose, 'I'm so glad that our wheat crop ripened early, it's all harvested and stored away. The men at Blacks on the other side of town are still trying to bring his crop in today, if the storm didn't stop them working, that is.'

Mary was about to stand up thinking that it was time to go to work when Joe returned his attention to the rest of the family, 'Right, we will say our return thanks to the Lord for his good provision and then we will get going. 'Lord, we thank you for the food that you have delivered for us to enjoy, we thank you for the provision of a good night's sleep and for the gracious way that you have provided for and protected this family in so many ways. Make us truly grateful, until you come again. Amen.' *That would be a good prayer to use for grace in our time,* Mary thought.

Chairs scraped against the floor as everyone moved at the same time. It was as if a button had been switched on, automating action.

Mary gathered up the dishes and looked around for the sink. Eventually, she spotted a large square tin that had been cut in half, with boards fitted over the sharp edges, sitting in the bench under the small window between one of the doors and the fireplace. The heat in the kitchen was climbing. What made it worse was that Rose was now stoking the fire to make it burn better. Putting the dishes on the bench, Mary decided that the only way to get some hot water to wash the dishes with would be to use some of the water in the kettle near the fire. Looking down she noticed a bucket sitting on the shelf under the bench, it was filled with cold water, she assumed that it would be used to refill the kettle. *Man, there is a lot of lifting in this house,* she was thinking as she poured some hot water into the tin. She let out a moan while refilling the kettle and adding some to the basin to cool the water down to a temperature that she was able to put her hands in, before replacing it back where she had got it from.

'Oh, Mary, will you please just get on with the dishes without moaning for once,' Rose reprimanded.

Mary knew how hard it was to raise a teenage girl, after all, in her other life she had raised two girls of her own. She should behave with a lot more energy and cheerfulness, after all, as she got older, she had promised herself that if she could go back in time, she would do things differently. However, she found the confusion of the situation was really making her just as moody as she had been when she had been a teenager the first time. Picking up the bucket to fetch some cold water, Mary walked out the nearest door. The rain had stopped, and the skies had cleared to a hazy blue. She walked towards the tank that was situated at the end of the awning and near the verandah of the other part of the house. She needed to walk around it a bit to find the tap, as it was on the other side, out of sight.

5

She watched Emma, who was scampering across the yard. She disappeared inside a shed just inside the fence that was around the house. Well, that had to be the washhouse, she would have to find an excuse to find out exactly what was in there later, other than a mother cat and her offspring, if she got the chance. The small building beside it had to be the out-house, she knew from her history that that would be where the toilet was. It would be one of the original, of what her other world called the "eco-friendly" variety. A great big hole in the ground with a wooden seat over it. She had heard horror stories, during her other childhood, of snakes and Redback spiders. Most likely there would also be a variety of other creepy crawlies such as lizards and the like but hopefully no snakes. Given the heat outside, she knew that she would have to be careful when the time came, as it inevitably would, for her to visit there. Even as she contemplated this, she knew that the time was drawing near. She would have to venture out into a scenario that, thankfully, no longer existed in her other world but was very real here and now.

She carried the bucket, now full of water back into the kitchen and placed it on the shelf where she had taken it from.

'I have to go to the outhouse,' Mary turned and spoke to Rose.

'Ok, you know the drill. Open the door slowly. Check carefully and if there is a snake, wave your arm. I will bring the shovel. As for the spiders, just roll up some of the newspaper, wack them and brush their flattened bodies down the hole' Rose said calmly. However, Mary was feeling anything but calm.

Mary walked towards the outhouse, aware that Rose was watching her from the kitchen, for once she was glad that she had a long dress on, even if it was hot to wear. The dress was covering her legs which were shaking so badly with fear that she had a job to even walk. *Goodness me*, she thought, *it's only an outhouse. She wasn't going to die!* She thought about Jesus and how he had faced the cross, and He was going to die. *It would've been much harder than this.* These thoughts made her lift her shoulders and straighten her back. *I can do this,* she told herself, but it didn't stop her legs from feeling a bit like jelly.

Reaching the building, which was all of five-foot square and eight-foot-high, she carefully opened the door. It swung out silently, on well-greased hinges. *Joe must be very diligent with the maintenance of his property,* Mary thought as she looked carefully inside. There was a bench across the back wall with a lid in the middle, a pile of newspapers was stacked to one side. No modern toilet paper here either, Mary noted. Oh well, the newspaper will have to do the job. Mary checked the floor, nothing there but before she stepped inside, she took the time to look all around the building, the walls, and the roof in place. There was no ceiling leaving a space. A sparrow flew out through the gap between the wall and the roof startling Mary and making her jump. Then, there curled around the rafters was a snake! It was about three feet or a metre long with a brown and white pattern on its skin. She waved her arm at Rose who was still watching from the kitchen window. Rose came running with shovel in hand which she must have collected from just outside the kitchen door.

'Move back,' she said as she approached. Mary stepped back pulling the door open wider so Rose could have easy access. Rose was ready to deal with the snake but stopped when she noticed nothing on the floor or bench at the back.

'Where did it go?' She asked incredulously looking at Mary.

'It's up there, in the roof,' Mary said her voice quivering with fear. Rose looked up.

'Oh, Mary that's only a Children's Python! You know we don't kill those because they eat mice and rats. They are very helpful and not poisonous; he won't hurt you'. Rose turned and walked back to the house, shaking her head. Mary stepped inside, closing the door behind her. She couldn't help it, but she kept her eye on the snake the whole time while trying to manage the clothes, praying all the while that the thing would not move. She made sure that she didn't stay any longer than was necessary. How did people live with this much stress, she wondered? There was no way she would be reading any of the newspapers that were stacked beside her.

Having finished, she went to the wash-house to wash her hands and while she was there, she had a good look around. A bench was against the wall, with a very large tub sitting on it, various buckets and dippers were stacked underneath. There were hooks on both the side walls on which hung various bits, bridles, leather straps and saddle bags. The laundry was also the tack room, Mary mused.

'Look Mary, the kittens are so beautiful' Emma was sitting in the corner watching a black cat, curled up on some rags nursing four black and white kittens. They weren't that old it seemed. They were staying very close to mum. Mary wasn't an animal person really, but she could understand why Emma might be taken with these particular kittens.

'Yes, they are, but I have to get back to the kitchen and do the washing up' Mary replied.

There was a tap low down on the back wall. Mary washed her hands and returned to the kitchen feeling very relieved that the exercise had been uneventful.

She finished washing the dishes, placing them on a cloth on the bench. She could see a towel, made of Linen hanging on the wall. Pulling it down, she wiped the dishes and thanks to the fact that most of the china was sitting on open shelves rather than in cupboards with doors, she was able to see where they needed to go.

This done, she turned to the table, lifting the cloth carefully, folding it roughly to the centre so the toast crumbs were held in it and wouldn't fall on the floor, she carried out the cloth to shake the crumbs outside, hoping the birds appreciated the tidbits being flung in their direction.

6

Before going back indoors, she gave Emma a call. She didn't know exactly where the garden was and like Emma, she was anxious to get to morning tea and see how this family celebrated Christmas and what presents would be exchanged.

Emma's head appeared in the doorway of the shed. 'Come on, it's time to water the garden. Bring the buckets and dippers with you, please.' Mary hoped that her voice sounded far more confident than she felt. Emma disappeared again, no doubt to say goodbye to the cat and kittens. Mary returned to the kitchen and by the time she had replaced the cloth back on the table Emma was standing in the kitchen doorway, hopping on one foot.

Mary turned to Rose asking, 'Is there anything in particular you need from the garden and what do I use to carry them in?'

The puzzled look on Rose' face made Mary wonder if she had overstepped again, she just didn't know how things worked in this strange world. Yes, she had read about it but living here, if that's what she was doing, was way more complicated.

'Please, I need whatever is available. A lettuce for tea but leave the rest for the moment.' Rose responded, 'and you'd better take the big cane basket there.' Mary's eyes turned to where Rose was pointing. It sure wasn't what she expected to be using, that big basket looked heavy. *Oh well,* she thought *whatever is available. So much for our world's new thing of recycling. It wasn't new, it was just a forgotten way of life.*

Picking up the basket, she walked towards the door, still very aware of just how hot it was and how she felt in the clothes that were still unfamiliar and uncomfortable. Mary checked to make sure that Emma was walking in front of her. She still didn't want to let on that she needed Emma to show her where the garden was. Emma walked in front of her, dancing around in circles, her excitement was hard to miss.

'Make sure you come straight back to the house if you see anyone about and don't forget to shut the gate even if you have to come back in a hurry,' Rose said as they went through the door. *I wonder what that was all about,* Mary thought as they walked towards the garden.

'Ma is always worried about us being attacked by the aboriginals' Emma said as they stepped out from under the awning into the hot sunshine. Her tone suggested that she thought Ma worried unnecessarily but thinking about how many guns she had seen already this morning, she wasn't so sure that Emma wasn't being a little naïve, but then, she was only a child. Mary guessed that her parents wanted to let her have a childhood as well as keep her safe. This always meant that you were constantly trying to work out how and when you tell your children certain things about the dangers of life. Such are the difficulties of being a parent.

'What am I going to get for Christmas?' Emma asked bringing Mary back to the present.

'I have no idea', Mary said truthfully.

'Oh, Mary, please tell me, I want to know what you are going to give me,' Emma pleaded.

'No, way,' Mary responded, realising that Emma had no idea that she didn't know. Emma was trying to get her to share a secret that she thought she was keeping.

They walked past the tank behind the washhouse and filled the bucket with water. Mary followed Emma to the garden. As she looked around her, Mary saw a large mob of Kangaroos in the distance. They were grazing on the stubble of what Mary assumed would have been the wheat crop that Joe had spoken about at breakfast. She was startled as a rabbit jumped out of a tuff of grass just in front of her and raced away. By the time they had reached their destination there must have been a dozen or so of these creatures breaking their cover and running off to hide somewhere else. As they approached the gateway, Emma gave a squeal, Mary looked up to see three kangaroos jumping over the fence on the other side in one single bound. It always amazed Mary how high these animals could jump. A fence had to be well over six feet or around two metres in height in order to keep these creatures out of any paddock. It seemed that they had quickly developed a taste for the new feed that was now available since these strange people had arrived in their country.

The garden was a reasonably large area surrounded by a high wire fence with a slab fence dug into the ground about 4-foot-high around the base. The gate was about the size of a door, made with planks crossed in the centre to keep it square and covered in wire. The whole thing reminded Mary of an abandoned tennis court from her time. She knew from her history that rabbits had been a big problem in Australia but hadn't seen as many as the pictures had indicated there would be. Obviously, she was back in time before the plague hit its peak. They very quickly reached plague proportions causing a lot of damage to the country. The amount of feed they had consumed meant that the animals were left without forage. In a lot of places, they had turned the country into a barren land. Many a horse had to be 'put down' because the ground underneath its hoof had collapsed into a burrow, even on the dirt roads, no animal was safe because of the pestilence. The fence had been buried down into the ground, Mary could see where the men had dug up the earth and replaced it, all the way around the yard. Joe had also made raised beds by placing some large beams together in rectangles inside the yard, giving the lettuce, carrots and beans a little better protection from the rabbits. However, Emma noticed her looking at the fence and, in the innocent way of young children, offered up the information that the fence was there to stop the bandicoots from eating their vegetables. She also noticed that the vegetables were easier to reach and wondered if Joe had organised things this way so that Rose would be able to tend the gardens when she was pregnant with the children, as it was obvious that they had been this way for a very long time. It also occurred to Mary, that Joe had organised things this way in order to protect the gardens from the various native animals looking for an easy meal, after all, without food, survival was unlikely. Mary thought about the people in her world. Many assumed that food just appeared in supermarket shops by magic. They had no idea of what it took to grow food or how tenuous your survival was without it. The girls worked together filling the dippers and placing the water around the roots of the plants. Mary registered that there were beans, peas, tomato plants, lettuce, and carrots. Some of the plants had been covered by hessian strips strung between tall stakes in order to protect them from the heat of the day while still letting in plenty of sunshine. Looking around it occurred to Mary that Joe may have been far more innovative than most of his peers.

Mary listened as Emma chatted on about all sorts of things as little children were prone to do. She tried not to appear too interested in what the child had to say just in case it gave away just how much of the information was important for Mary to hear. Emma chattered about her toys, in particular, a doll named Sue. She went on about how Joey was glad that school was finished for the year. He hated school mostly because he had to walk seven miles each day and that's why he wanted a horse of his own. She also talked about her trip to the pig sales last week with pa, excitedly telling Mary how their pigs had been the biggest and fattest there. The pigs would then be turned into ham and nice thick fatty bacon, Emma declared.

'Did you know that some of the fat is used to make soap?' Emma asked Mary.

'Yes, I do' Mary replied trying to keep her answers brief so not to interrupt the child and not letting on that she had forgotten that she had actually read that somewhere in her other life. Other information gleaned related to how the family made money by selling the cream to the butter factory. They took the cream in the cans that Mary had seen being filled up that morning, each week to be made into butter for townspeople to buy, her plans to be a mother one day and keep her house just like her mummy did. How the potatoes they grew were sold, along with the wool off the sheep that were in the back paddock. Rose, according to Emma, also sold any vegetables from the garden, if there were any left after the preserving had been finished. She couldn't wait to be big enough to help Mary and Rose with that job it appeared. If there were families who were poor or sick, they were always the first ones to get vegetables and they were for free. Emma's voice was full of pride as she went on about which families she had visited with her mother. She went on to tell Mary about how the horse had played up when

Rose was trying to put it into the sulky and how Joe had come along at just the right time to help.

'Mummy said that it was an answer to prayer', Emma said. She then turned the chatter to what she might do when she grew up, she was going to be just like her mother. She was never going to leave, and her husband would come and live on this farm. Suddenly, she stopped, straightened up, looked at Mary and asked: 'Why do you want to go away, Mary?'

What! she thought, *wow, here is a question that I have no idea how to answer.* Why the real Mary wanted to leave, she couldn't even guess, but she had to assume that there was a real Mary in this family, she had somehow taken her place in some weird time shift. In the end, she decided that she could be honest but still be very general in her answer. Emma was waiting for her reply.

'Well, you see Emma, I know that the world is much bigger than the farm. There are lots of new things happening out there, the world is changing, and I want to be part of those changes.'

'Oh,' Emma said thoughtfully, 'I don't want anything to change, I want things to stay the way they are' Emma looked so serious, she looked like she might even cry.

'Oh, darling it's ok.' Mary put down the bucket and the dipper and hugged the girl tight. 'I know that is what you think right now, you want things the way they are but one day when you get older, you too will want to try new things, spread your wings and see how far you can go'. Little did Mary realise what affect her words were having on the little girl.

'No, no' cried Emma, 'I don't want to get my wings, I don't want to die' Mary could see that she was very distressed.

'I didn't say you would die,' Mary was struggling to work out why what she had said was distressing Emma so much.

'But, if I get my wings that means I am going to be an angel, and to be an angel you have to die, like Grandma and Grandpa and then you go away forever. Is that what you are going to do Mary, are you going to die, so you get your wings and go away forever.' Emma stuttered tearfully.

'Oh, Emma, I didn't mean those sorts of wings', Mary held her a little tighter, the wings I was talking about will take you to different places around the world and you can always come home for a visit.

'What' Emma struggled out of Mary's arms, 'what do you mean! Do you mean wings like the birds have then?' The little girl was frantically trying to look over her shoulders, first the right and then the left. 'When will I grow wings, you don't have any', she cried as she quickly moved to look at Mary's back.

Mary laughed, 'Not real wings, honey, just thinking wings, ones where you will want to learn how to do new things and go to new places, it's just part of growing up. Learning helps to make you a stronger and better person. Anyway, we had better finish this and get back to the house'. Mary decided that this conversation was getting the child all tangled up and she could end up in trouble if she wasn't careful. She had forgotten that aeroplanes must still be a concept in the making that Emma would have very little knowledge of.

They went back to work, only now Emma was silent as she went from plant to plant. She seemed to be thinking pretty hard about what Mary had said and Mary was hoping that it wasn't going to cause more drama back at the house later. She knew that little ones could be depended upon to repeat conversations, often at the most inappropriate times. She had a bad feeling in the pit of her stomach that this wasn't the end of the story.

They finished watering the plants and just to make sure that it was all done properly, Mary turned to Emma and asked: 'Well, what do you think, have we got them all now'.

'Yes, I think so' Emma replied distractedly.

'Right, then, let's put these away and see what we are having for morning tea.' Mary was already heading back to the washhouse as she spoke. She couldn't believe that she was already feeling hungry again and the hot humid air after the storm was beginning to make the perspiration run not only down her face but soak into her underclothes.

'Oops, we forgot to pick the vegetables' Emma called after Mary.

'Oh, dear I did forget, well we'd better get on with it then, can you pick the ripe tomatoes while I pick the beans and carrots.'

'Don't forget that Mumma wants a lettuce, Mary, I heard her tell you that she wanted one,' Emma said, and Mary noted that she seemed to be getting back to her chatty self.

'Well, thank you for reminding me,' Mary said, glad that the shift in the conversation seemed to be distracting Emma from the previous one. 'Then you and I can pick the peas together, ok?' Mary said, lowering her voice enough to make it seemed like they were sharing a secret.

The vegetables loaded, Mary handed Emma the bucket with the dippers in it, picked up the basket and they headed carefully back to the house. Again, Mary wondered how this day would continue to unfold.

7

They entered the kitchen with Emma chatting about the cat and her kittens.

'Oh, there you are, I was beginning to think you didn't want any morning tea, you were taking so long. Just put them on the table for now, Mary, we will deal with them after smoko. Come on, your father is in the parlour waiting for us, please bring that plate of biscuits and Emma you can carry the other plate, don't eat any on the way' Rose spoke as she headed for the door that led back to the rest of the house.

Emma followed Rose and Mary moved behind them both, making sure that she kept them in sight. The last thing she wanted was to get lost and have the family accuse her of daydreaming again. Besides, she was still waiting to see how the rest of this Christmas Day would unfold. It was like turning the pages in a storybook, only she was walking, talking, and living each word written in it.

When they left the kitchen, they crossed the verandah and entered the main part of the house through a set of French doors that were open. The room had a large fireplace on the outside wall to her left. There was a sofa against the opposite wall facing the fireplace beside a door into a hallway. A chair and side table were situated in the corner on the left side of the fireplace in front of the only window in the room. A small round dining table took pride of place in the centre and a tall grandfather clock stood in the other corner filling the space on the other side of the doorway. Tones of green dominated the room, giving it a cool feeling even though it wasn't a particularly airy room. Other than a photo of Rose and Joe, on what

Mary assumed was their Wedding Day, and a couple of pictures hanging on the wall, there were no other furnishings in the room. In modern terms, it would be called minimalist but here it just seemed normal.

Mary crossed to the table to place the plate of biscuits in amongst the various plates of food which consisted of sandwiches, other home cooked biscuits, and Christmas cake. In the centre, Rose had gone to the trouble of placing a very pretty Christmas centrepiece. It was a very simple arrangement of apples, roses, and candles, but it was very effective and beautiful. There were a nice set of teacups, saucers, cake plates and a tea set of nice china. This was undeniably a special set that only came out on special occasions. After putting down the plate, Mary turned around, pausing briefly as she noticed a large branch of gum tree standing in a bucket of water behind the French doors. It was decorated with paper chains, folded paper decorations and a few coloured balls made of fabric with beautiful hand sewn motifs on them. There was a handmade angel in the top of the tree as well as a scattering of coloured crocheted stars. Lots of Gifts wrapped in mostly brown paper adorned with hand-drawn pictures were piled around the base, almost hiding the bucket. The sight of it brought back memories of the Christmas trees that had graced her own childhood.

'Come on, everyone, it's time for us to read the Christmas Story before we eat.' Joe, who was sitting in the armchair, said as he picked up a Bible that she could see on the side table. He opened it and started reading. Mary recognised the story from the book of Luke.

After he had finished reading, Rose moved to the table and poured cups of tea for everyone, making sure that there was plenty of milk in Emma's so that it wouldn't be too hot. Mary held her breath as she watched Rose hand Emma the teacup and plate. She thought how brave Rose was to allow such a small child to use the good china. After all, what were the choices, if the tea set was too precious for Emma to use then the other alternatives were to give her the ordinary kitchen china or a tin mug, both of which would have made Emma feel left out. She remembered all the times she had given her own grandchildren plastic cups so as to not endanger the good china. There was no plastic here, it was china or metal, nothing else. Suddenly, Mary realised that even her good china would not have cost as much in money terms as Rose's did. Yet, she was still willing to put Emma's self-esteem above her china.

'Can I have two biscuits, please,' asked Emma.

'Only after you eat a sandwich,' Rose replied.

'Which present are you going to open, Mary?', Emma asked between mouthfuls of food, 'Mumma told me that we only get to open one now, the rest have to wait until all our guests arrive.' Mary breathed a sigh of relief; Emma had no idea how much her chatter was helping her keep up.

'Well,' Mary paused for effect, Emma was watching her carefully, 'I think .....' (again, Mary paused), 'Um, Oh, I know, I'll open ...... yours', Mary exclaimed as a look of pleasure came over Emma's face.

'Alright Emma, when you have finished, you can put the plate and cup back on the table, then you can find the gift for Mary and she can open it,' Joe said as he accepted a refill of his teacup from Rose. 'Careful child! Don't get into too much of a hurry, you will choke on your food', Joe reprimanded her as it was easy to see that Emma was having trouble containing her excitement. Mary continued to drink her tea while observing everything carefully.

Emma finished her tea, sandwich, and biscuits, stood up, and placed the china on the table, which Rose subtly shifted further towards the centre, then headed to the Christmas tree and dug in to find the particular parcel she wanted. Mary had just finished eating a really nice scone topped with jam and cream by the time Emma stood in front of her holding out the parcel, wrapped in brown paper covered in hand-drawn stars in every colour imaginable and tied up with string, no sticky tape in sight Mary noted. The string went through a tag that had Mary's name on it. She could see that the drawings would have kept the girl occupied for some considerable amount of time, probably allowing Rose to get some work done undisturbed.

Mary took the parcel in her free hand, the other was still holding a cup and saucer, which Rose took from her, having moved to her side unnoticed.

'Well, let's see what is in here' Mary smiled at Emma as she carefully untied the knots, rolling the string up as she went. Something told her that this is what would have been expected of her and also, she was trying to draw the process out as long as she could. It was fun watching Emma's excitement. She parted the paper and there laid a square of hessian. Mary picked it up. It unfolded to reveal a square bag, with a strap. As Mary turned it around front to back and back again. She could see stitching in wool on one side. Emma had sewn her name on it in cross-stitches and some flowers. Rose must have spent a great deal of time, not only supervising Emma's handiwork but putting the bag together after she was finished. What a patient woman Rose must be. Mary ran her fingers over the stitches that spelt out her name.

'It's for your books', Emma said, 'did I do good?'

'It's beautiful Emma, I love it, thank you very much and I'll keep the paper as well. You did a very good job with this; you are so clever.' Mary said hugging Emma as she flung herself at Mary.

'Alright, Joey, it's your turn to pick one,' Joe said.

Joey hunted amongst the parcels until he found one that he was looking for. This time it had his name on it. 'I wonder what's in this one, it says it's from you, Pa'.

'Well, you'll never find out if you don't open it boy' Joe chuckled.

Joey carefully opened the parcel with the same care that Mary had instinctively taken to find a small box. Opening the box revealed a penknife, with a bottle-opener, a blade, and a screwdriver. His smile was a mile wide as he thanked his father for the gift. It appeared to Mary that Joey grew two inches taller in that moment as he stood up. This was a grown-up's knife, he was a man now and to prove it, he walked across to his father and shook his hand.

'Thanks, Pa', Joey said

'You're welcome lad, but don't let me see you do anything silly with it or I'll take it off you, understood' Joe admonished Joey.

'Yes, sir', Joey's chest expanded a little more as he responded.

'Emma, you'd better find a gift under there for you now', Joe said.

Emma went hunting again and like the others opened her gift carefully, finding some very nice dolls clothes made by Rose. To Emma's delight, the dresses were made out of the same material as her own dress, and one was even the same style. She stood up and headed for the door.

'Excuse me, young lady' Joe's tone was firm, and Emma stopped in her tracks, 'Where do you think you are going?'

'To get my doll' she replied.

'Not until you thank your mother for those dresses, you don't,' Joe said.

'Oops, sorry,' Emma hung her head and ran to her mother, flung her arms around her neck 'I'm sorry, thank you, I love them.' As she stood back, she looked at her father and said: 'Can I go now please?'

He nodded 'yes, you can, but walk please, don't run.' Emma was already in the doorway by the time Joe had finished speaking which made Joe shake his head, but Mary noticed that he was also smiling.

'So, are you going to open a gift each?' Mary asked.

'Joey, would you like to find a gift each for your ma and me please', Joe directed his son.

Joey didn't need to be asked again and quickly found two gifts. One he handed to his mother and the other to his father. They opened both and smiled. Rose thanked her son for the large packet of seeds that she found inside. Joe thanked him for the new hankies that he received. 'Well done, son.' Joe said, 'just what I needed.'

'The vegetables will be really nice once they grow, thank you, Joey, you will be able to help me plant them when the time comes' his mother's thanks followed Joe's quickly along with an indulgent smile at her son.

The clock in the corner chimed ten o'clock, making Mary jump, as Emma walked back into the room carrying her doll.

'Right then, Emma, you can come out to the kitchen and play, while Mary and I start getting the meal ready for our visitors. Rose said as she stood up and moved towards the doorway.

'I'll go out and check on the pigs, Joey, you can come for a walk with me', Joe said as he too stood and crossed the room towards the door. 'I'll see you in about half an hour Rose, then I'll get the tables together on the verandah for you'.

Mary also stood up, gathering up some of the china off the table and being careful not to drop the precious items, followed Rose back to the kitchen.

She wasn't looking forward to working in the kitchen again as the day was getting hotter, even here in the parlour it was hot now, at ten in the morning.

They entered the kitchen and as expected it was hot even though the fire had died down. The first thing Rose did was to add some more wood and stir the coals in order to bring it back to life. Mary crossed to the tin on the bench and Emma installed herself under the kitchen table with her doll and dresses. They worked together, Mary was very careful to listen to what Rose asked her to do and carefully watched everything that she did, so she didn't feel too much out of her depth and tried to make as few mistakes as possible. At some point, while they were working, Emma emerged from under the table and pleaded with Rose to let her help.

'Ok, here is a butter knife, you can scrape the carrots for me', Rose instructed.

When being asked to peel the potatoes, Rose handed her a knife instead of a vegetable peeler like she was used to, Mary knew that knives were used before the peelers were invented and so she set to work as carefully as possible, but no matter how hard she tried a lot more potato was attached to the skin than she was used to in her other world. She was surprised when Rose complemented her work by saying, 'That's much better than you usually manage, Mary, well done'.

The one thing that did cause some concern was when Rose asked Mary to get the chicken and roast out of the Meat Safe. Mary knew vaguely what she was looking for, she had seen photos in that other world, but precisely where the one for this home was actually located and exactly what it looked like was an unknown.

'Can, Emma come and help?', Mary asked, realising that she was very dependent on the small girl.

'Oh, if you wish, but really Mary, one day you are going to have to do everything for yourself you know', Rose retorted.

'Thank you, …. Emma, you want to help me get the meat', Mary appealed very sweetly.

'Ok,' Emma climbed down off the chair where she had been sitting scraping carrots for Rose and headed towards a door. This was exactly what Mary had hoped for because that way she could follow her and not let on that she was uncertain of what to do. It was nice to walk out on to the verandah; it was much cooler out there. The grapevine climbing along the bearers and hanging down provided natural shade and had a cooling effect on the slight breeze that was drifting in from the yard. Mary took a deep breath, filling her lungs with the cooler air. As they walked to the corner where there was another tank, also helping to shade the verandah. She noticed that Joe and Joey had returned and were pulling a table out through a set of French doors. There was another table which was standing against the wall of the home which the men pulled out and placed against the end of the table which they just dragged out of the house.

Joey was sent to get a bucket of water and a rag to clean down the second table. Low benches and a variety of chairs materialised allowing enough seating for all the people expected for lunch. Emma had reached the meat safe and was opening it, Mary, looked at what resembled a metal cupboard sitting in a metal tray with a tray on top. Water in the top tray was soaking hessian cloth which hung down on the three other sides of the cupboard. As she reached in to collect the roast, she noticed just how cold it was inside. Shade, wet hessian, and a breeze made it an effective cold storage unit. Mary took another lung full of cool air before returning to the kitchen with Emma in toe carrying the chicken. She had also noticed that there was a large leg of ham in the Meat Safe. Lunch, it seemed was going to be pretty much the same as to what she was used to. What she was to learn later is that this was the only time of the year when the family ate chicken. Roast mutton was reserved for Sunday lunch and ham, pork and bacon were the basis of their general meals.

The meal preparations went on for what seemed like ages, although in reality, it didn't take as long as Mary thought it might.

The food preparations finished, Mary and Rose started setting the cutlery and things out onto the tables set up on the shady verandah by Joe and Joey earlier. Once these arrangements were finished, the whole table was covered in a cheesecloth cover to protect it all from the flies and bugs. It had some beautiful hand worked embroidery around the edges with a nice trimming sewn all the way around it. Again, Mary marvelled at the time and energy that went into the everyday items used by these people.

No sooner had they finished when there was a noise in the front yard.

'That will be our guests arriving,' Rose said, 'Mary, go and tidy yourself up while I greet our guests. You really do look like something the cat has dragged in and find your shoes. If you put them away properly, they should be under your dresser. It's a special occasion, so you are allowed to wear them. Please make sure that you put on a clean pinafore as well'. Mary moved around the table that they had just finished setting up for dinner and disappeared around the corner into the room that she had woken up in that morning. It was the first time that she had been back in there since she had walked out. She wriggled around, pulling her clothes into some sort of smoother arrangement. She looked under the dresser and there was a pair of very solid leather shoes and a pair of socks. They were thick, hand knitted in wool by the looks of them. *Wow, these are going to be hot to wear* she thought, but she put them on, aware of just how dirty her feet felt after running around in bare feet all morning. While she was doing this, she heard Rose lead the visitors past her door along the hallway to the parlour.

8

This time when she left the room, she exited through a door that led into the hallway. Walking down the hall she went back to the parlour. She entered the room to see an elderly gentleman sitting in the chair that Joe had occupied earlier in the day. He had a bushy grey, almost white beard, portly stature, and sparkling eyes, if he had been wearing a bright red suit, he would have been a perfect portrayal of Santa Claus.

'Santa', she said, not realising that she was speaking loud enough for the others to hear her.

'Excuse me? What did you say?' The gentleman asked with a puzzled look on his face.

'I'm sorry', responded Mary, 'You look just like Santa'.

'Who is Santa?' Emma, who had been playing with her doll under the table, crawled out and was looking at Mary with great interest.

Mary realised that this was another thing that her world made a bigger deal about than this world. She also realised suddenly that she needed to be very careful about how she answered the little girl. She decided the best course of action was to tell her about the origins of the Santa story.

'He is a magical jolly happy man, who wears a bright red suit and is supposed to live at the North Pole. He brings children, who are not going to get anything at all for Christmas, a small gift. He leaves it in a sock that they hang on the fire mantle. If they have been bad, they only get a piece of coal but if they have been very good, they get something that they really wished for.'

'How does he know who isn't going to get something for Christmas?' The gentleman asked, making Mary wonder if he was playing along or wanted to know.

'Well, that's where the magic comes in' Mary responded, looking from Emma to him. 'he can see what every child is doing, and he knows if they are being naughty or nice'.

'But I thought God was the only person who could see what everyone was doing all the time'. Emma said thoughtfully.

'You are so right Emma,' Rose said. 'You know that we don't follow that tradition in this family. Please stop filling your sister's head with silly notions that will destroy her faith in God.' Rose was clearly not happy with what Mary had said so far.

'I'm sorry, but I think it could be a great way for people to secretly help those who aren't going to get something for Christmas. You give a gift, put Santa's name on it and then they don't know who it was that is trying to help them. It would work well for those who are too proud to ask for help'. Mary's voice was deliberately thoughtful. 'The Bible tells us to give in secret, but it's hard to do that if you have to put your name on a gift,' Mary said.

'But isn't that lying?' Emma asked. 'Why can't we say God sent the gift'.

'Would people believe that?' Mary asked Emma, trying to keep her voice light.

Emma thought for a moment having put her finger in her mouth. She looked so cute; Mary had to smile.

'I guess not,' she said at last.

'Alright, that's enough of this talk'. Rose said firmly, putting an end to the conversation just as more noises came from the front of the house. Rose walked out of the room leaving no more room for the conversation to continue anyway. Emma disappeared back under the table to play with her dolls.

A few minutes later, Rose returned with a lady who she introduced as Mrs Goldsmith. She had her arms full of gifts, and a little girl and boy were right behind her. The little boy clinging to her skirt.

'Emma,' Rose said as she entered the room, 'Chloe and Paul are here. You can take them outside to see the kittens if you like. Be careful to watch out for snakes, won't you'. Emma approached the children and held out her hand to the little boy. Mary watched to see if he would leave with Emma or if he would refuse to go and need some encouragement from his mother. However, it seemed that Paul wasn't as shy as he first appeared and ran outside with Emma. Maybe it was the mention of kittens that had done the trick.

Turning to Mr Smith, Rose continued 'Mr Smith, do you know Mrs Goldsmith, our new neighbours? They have only been there for a few months. Her husband, Henry is just seeing that the horse is fed and watered and will be along in a few moments.' Turning to look at Mrs Goldsmith, Rose went on, 'That's a very smart Sulky you have there.'

'Yes,' Mrs Goldsmith replied, 'My father gave it to us as a Wedding present many years ago and Henry makes sure that it's kept in good order. Do you think you might be able to call me Jane, please? I know it's not considered proper, but I would like it if you would. Mrs Goldsmith makes me feel very old because it's the name that everyone calls Henry's Grandmother.'

'Only if, you are sure?' Rose replied with a frown on her face that clearly indicated that she really wasn't sure that this was a good idea.

'I'm absolutely certain' Jane responded as there was a polite knock on the parlour door.

'May we come in?' Everyone turned around to see a gentleman standing in the doorway with a lady hovering behind him.

'Henry,' Jane stated. He smiled at Jane with love lighting up his eyes.

'I believe this is Mrs Jones,' he said, 'She walked up the drive as I was finishing with the horse.'

'Yes, Yes, come in, both of you. How nice to see you again Mrs Jones? I hope that you have been keeping in good health. This heat is so draining on a person. Mary would you please go and get a jug of water out of the meat safe I put it in there earlier so our guests can have a cool drink.' Rose said, leading Mrs Jones gently to the sofa. 'Take a seat, Mrs Jones, you look as if you need to rest.'

As Mary stepped out on to the verandah towards the safe, she heard Mrs Jones say to Rose 'Thank you, Rose, yes, it's certainly hot outside, oh, this gift is for you.' Mary realised that she hadn't seen Joe for some time. It was then that she heard more noises in the front yard. After a brief silence, she saw Joe heading to the stables with a horse and sulky. He appeared to be taking care of one of the guest's horses.

Returning to the parlour, she discovered that there was now another man in the room. She decided this must be Mr Bradshaw as he was the only guest that had not yet arrived. He was dressed in a smart suit and a top hat. He looked every bit the gentleman. Mr Smith seemed to have left the room.

On his return he was carrying some baking dishes. He walked towards Rose saying: 'Mrs Renshaw tells me that these might belong to you. They were left on my kitchen table some weeks ago.' Rose looked at Mary as she entered the room. 'Put that jug on the table please dear and take these dishes to the kitchen'. As Mary left for the kitchen, she heard Mr Smith thank Rose for the meals she had provided. Moving slightly to engage with Mr Smith, Rose continued to speak. 'I do hope that they have been some help to you. I understand that it must be very difficult without your wife, particularly at night. Strangely, silence can sometimes be very deafening. If we can be of any help to you, please let us know.'

Mr Smith, nodded, 'Thank you for your kind invitation. You are a very kind woman. We were not blessed with children so yes, I find the house very quiet, particularly at night, like you said. It's good to still have to go to work, that helps fill in the time during the day.'

It's the least I can do. We have been blessed with three beautiful children and a good year on the farm, it's my pleasure to have you here. Sharing some meals is such a small thing compared to the blessings that God has showered on us', Rose said as Joe entered the room. Rose handed him a glass of water silently, 'Well, as we are all here, we should call the children, and Mary and I will dish up our meal. Where is Joey?' Rose looked at Joe.

'He's outside with the children, they are making a fuss of the cat and her kittens' he replied.

'Well, that's good. Joe, can you call the children and help them to wash up please, and show our guests to the table, we are eating outside in the shade as its cooler out there. Mary, the kitchen awaits.' Rose smiled as she spoke and almost curtsied as she moved to the French doors.

It wasn't long before the food had been loaded onto platters and placed on the table. Rose and Mary joined the others and Joe again said grace. Plates were passed to Joe who carved the meats, serving portions to each person. The plates were then passed to Rose who added vegetables to each plate before they were returned to the owner.

There was mostly silence as people ate their meals. Mrs Goldsmith attended to the children from time to time if they were struggling to cut their meat or vegetables. There was some polite conversation between the adults, but the children were quiet. On the rare occasions that they tried to speak, looks from the adults quickly suppressed any conversation.

9

They were about half-way through their meal when a horse and its rider could be heard arriving. 'Please excuse me, I'll go and see who that is,' Joe said as he pushed back his chair, walked along the verandah and around the corner. Those left at the table could hear muffled voices and soon Joe returned.

'I'm sorry everyone, there's a fire at the Jackson's place I have to go. It's getting very close to the house so they need all the help they can get' Rose stood as he continued, 'Terry Burns has gone to get more help. Joey, please go and get my horse out of the stables.'

Oh, of course, this is the only way people managed to communicate before there was such a thing as a telephone. I wonder what these people would think if I was able to show them a modern mobile phone, thought Mary.

'I'll get you some food together to take with you while you get changed.' Rose had almost reached the kitchen door before she finished speaking.

'Is there anything we can do to help?' the other two ladies in the group said in unison as they also pushed back chairs and followed Rose.

'Children stay right there, please', Jane Goldsmith instructed gently 'we will be back soon.' Mary noticed just how gentle this young woman was.

'Joe, would I be of some help if I came with you,' Henry asked Joe's retreating back. Joe stopped and turned around.

'Yes, of course, I'll get you some old work clothes to wear, come with me' Joe responded as Henry caught up with him.

'Mr Bradshaw, do you think you could give me a lift home. I will leave my horse here, it's in the stable, thanks to Joe, that way if the ladies need an extra horse, they can use mine. I need to get changed and then I will head out there as well,' Mr Smith was looking intently at Mr Bradshaw.

'No problem, sir. I have to go past your house anyway. We will see you there, Joe', he called at Joe's retreating back. They left the table without even saying goodbye. Mary knew that it would have been considered rude in high society, but she also knew about the urgency of dealing with a bushfire in the Australian summer. Even in her world, everyone downed tools to deal with the firestorms that happened every year somewhere in Australia.

Mary also got up and followed the women to the kitchen. When she entered, Rose was already cutting a loaf of bread into slices, Mrs Jones was in the process of buttering the slices as Rose passed them to her.

'Mary, can you get the meat platters off the table and the cheese out of the Meat Safe please', Rose asked without looking up from what she was doing. 'Jane there are some cakes on the shelf over there,' Rose pointed the knife in the general direction of the opposite wall, 'Would you cut some slices please and pop them into one of the empty tins from the bottom shelf?'

Mary made her way to the Meat Safe, this time she knew what she was looking for, having been there earlier, so she moved much more quickly this time.

When she returned to the kitchen, Rose asked Mary to get the basket that they had used for the vegetables from the garden that morning. Meat and cheese were quickly sliced, and the sandwiches completed, wrapped in brown paper, placed in another tin and into the basket just as Joe and Henry came into the kitchen from the direction of the house. Joe moved to Rose, kissed her on the cheek, taking the basket as Rose handed it to him and gave him a quick return peck. At the same time, Henry had moved to Jane's side, kissing her. 'I can take the basket with me in the sulky,' said Henry as he headed toward the door.

'Excuse me, Mr Goldsmith, would you mind giving me a lift as well. I will go and help the other volunteers serve food to the men.' Mrs Jones said, turning to Rose she continued, 'I'm sorry Rose but I'll take my leave. I want to be of as much help as I can. When it's all over I will go straight home. Thank you for your kind invitation but I really feel that I must go.'

'That's alright Mrs Jones, thank you for coming and the gift, I will get yours and you can open it later when you get home. Emma had so much fun making biscuits for you, she would be very disappointed if you didn't take them.'

'How delightful, not only will I enjoy them but I'm sure that the fire-fighters will enjoy them as well. Again, thank you for making me feel so welcomed.' Mrs Jones responded.

'Mary, get your bonnet, you can go as well. You can help Mrs Jackson to bring the twins here. Be careful all of you and we will see you when you get back,' Rose said, then looking at Henry, Rose continued, 'Jane and the children can stay here until you return, even if that means staying the night.'

'Thank you, Rose, I'd appreciate that,' Henry answered. They all made a quick exit from the kitchen, walking along the verandah where they had been eating. Surprisingly, the children were still sitting at the table. Emma, it seemed, had kept them occupied with some stories about life on the farm. Joe quickly kissed Emma's head as Henry also quickly kissed his children goodbye.

'Stay close to the house please children and do exactly what the adults tell you, we don't want any of you to go missing. Rose, keep that gun handy while we are gone. The natives might be watching,' Joe said as he stepped off the verandah, taking the reins from Joey's hands and mounting his horse. Mary, Mrs Jones, and Henry climbed into the sulky. They were off.

Mary looked back to see Rose picking up the teapot. She could just hear Rose say: 'We need another cup of tea' as she returned to the kitchen. Mary learnt later, after they had returned with the twins, that the children had enjoyed Christmas Pudding and Custard. Emma told her proudly that this time Rose handed the plates to the children first, a rare treat it seemed.

'That was because we had been so good while daddy was getting ready to help with the fire,' Emma had gushed, with a smile. 'And we ate every last bit. We even got to have extra playtime'.

Mary looked around the countryside as the sulky rattled over the rough tracks. They were travelling as fast as they could, and Mary hung on tightly as she was jolted from side to side. The sun stung the exposed skin along her arms. She saw the gum trees with their ghost white trunks stretching out their branches up into the sky; the great bunches of leaves gathered like bouquets of green on each end. The trees stood like sentries along the waterways with the paddocks in between cleared to allow cropping to occur. The grasses along the road, such as it was, stood high and had turned the colour of straw. It appeared that the country was drying out and you could see the heat haze and smoke rising in the distance. Kangaroos, Rabbits, snakes, wombats, and birds were all fleeing the fire, crashing through the bush on both sides of the track.

As they got closer, they could see that there were a number of people gathered along the fire front. They were attacking the fire with wet wheat bags. The bags were made out of hessian, not plastic like the ones in Mary's other world. This meant that they didn't melt when they were near the hot flames. They were soaked in water to prevent them from burning. It was hard, hot work. There were no fire trucks and long hoses around. Mary could see the perspiration running down the faces of the men they passed as they drove up to the house. As they approached it, Mary found herself looking at a building very similar to Joe and Rose's. Henry drove around the back and left the horse in the sulky near a water trough. 'That's so it will be ready when we have packed up the family,' said Henry. Mary jumped down; Henry handed her the basket of food before helping Mrs Jones to alight. Mary headed through the gate into the house yard. As she approached the kitchen she called out: 'Mrs Jackson, its Mary here. I've been told to bring you and the children back to our house. What would you like me to do?'

A small woman met her at the door. She was of thin build, about five-foot-tall, her blond hair tied up in a bun at the back of her head. Strands of hair that had escaped the bun were sticking to her face with the heat.

Mrs Jackson seemed surprised to see her. 'Mary! I see you have brought some food. I was beginning to wonder what I was going to feed the men; they will need some respite soon. There are so many out there and there is no time to actually cook anything. Please put it on the table out there on the verandah so they can help themselves when they need to. Could you please take that bucket of water out as well and fill the empty one? Some of them are needing a drink. While you are doing that, I'll get the children ready to leave.' She said without a smile.

Mary looked around the neat kitchen. It wasn't as big as Rose's but very much the same sort of layout. An open fireplace, benches, and a table in the centre of the room. The one thing that was very different was, that in one corner there was a cot. Mary noticed two children, about three years old, sleeping in it. One stirred briefly but settled again. They must have been tired, Mary thought.

Mary filled buckets with water and placed the tins of food on the table Mrs Jackson had indicated. Mrs Jones thanked her and continued to serve drinks and food to the men who were taking a break from the back-breaking work of trying to beat out the flames. The wind had picked up and the flames were racing across the paddocks of stubble left behind after the wheat harvest. Hot embers were being lifted up, carried by the wind into paddocks, some miles away, depositing them there, spreading the fire even faster and further than Mary could have envisioned.

Mary knew that these fires took hours of hard work to get under control. Henry Goldsmith banged on the kitchen door. 'Time to go, Mrs Jackson, you need to get the twins and yourself out of the house. The wind has changed direction and if you don't leave now you may not be able to get away. Joe says to take my horse and sulky and head back to his house. He will double me on his horse back to his place when we are finished here.'

Without any comment, Mrs Jackson grabbed a couple of blankets for the children. She also picked up a suitcase. 'This is the only case we have; I'm taking the photo of our wedding and one of the children, just a few clothes and the twins' favourite toys, I don't have time to get anything else,' Mrs Jackson said. Henry helped them load the sulky. Mrs Jackson picked up the little girl, handing her to Mary, she gathered up the little boy who was a bit bigger than his sister. They headed to the sulky. As they climbed aboard, Mary sat down in the back of the sulky as Mrs Jackson handed Mary the children, she placed the little boy under her left arm and the little girl under her right. *Boy, I would feel so much safer if this contraption had seatbelts, I will never complain about them again if I ever return to my other life,* she thought in panic. Mary put her arms around each child without a word and hugged them tight as Mrs Jackson climbed into the seat, took the reins, and headed back down the track the way they had arrived. Mary, with her back to Mrs Jackson, was able to watch the workers beating furiously at the flames as they retreated from view and wondered if she would see Mrs Jones again. Fires were so unpredictable. She knew people often got caught with no way of escape and died.

The ground was now black as far as the eye could see. The smell of burnt stubble and scrub was overwhelming. Burnt Eucalyptus leaves and oil had a strong odour that assailed her nostrils. Even the horse was skittish and didn't settle down until they were well away from the area. With the growing distance she saw the rest of the fire burning in the scrub away from the farms. What surprised Mary was that, while it was still a large and dangerous thing, it didn't seem to be as furious as the wildfires she had witnessed on the Television at home. It was in fact almost benign in comparison. *Why is this fire different to ours?* Then it hit her! *I must be far enough back in time for the bush to still be mostly under the care of the aboriginal people. They looked after the bush in a way that prevented the wildfires that were common to the country in her other life. Oh, will aboriginal common-sense ever prevail again in this country?* She doubted it and the realisation made her incredibly sad.

The children, having been disturbed from their sleep, started to cry and fidget, bringing her sharply back to their current situation. It took a lot of cajoling to get them to settle down. The sky had that weird orange tinge to it, that gave it that eerie feel, as the smoke spread out above them, blown around by the wind.

It didn't take long to get back to Joe and Rose's place. Mrs Jackson drove the horse and sulky just as fast as Mr Goldsmith had. Mary was again glad that she hadn't been required to drive, something that she had never done before. Of course, those around her had no idea that was the case.

Once they arrived back at the house, Rose appeared on the verandah. Mary was easily able to hand the children down to her as they seemed to know her. Jane Goldsmith appeared just behind Rose and took one of the children as Rose reached up to receive the other child. Mary climbed down while Mrs Jackson had disembarked on the other side. Joey appeared from somewhere and started to attend to the horse. 'Thank you, Joey', Mrs Goldsmith said. Mary glanced at Mrs Jackson and could see just how tired she looked. It seemed that now they had reached safety, tiredness was taking over, she actually looked like she was about to collapse. It was still very hot and, like every other woman around, Mrs Jackson had multiple layers of clothing on.

Mary moved to her side: 'Mrs Jackson, I think we had better get you inside. A nice cup of tea seems like a good idea,' she said. Mary wasn't sure she would, but she didn't want Mrs Jackson falling down outside in the dust and heat. Mrs Jackson pulled herself up and shook off Mary's helping hand. Mary let her arm fall to her side and walked towards the door through which Rose had taken the children.

Mrs Jackson followed Mary into the house, down the hall and into the parlour. Once inside the room, Rose encouraged Mrs Jackson to make herself comfortable on the sofa. The children immediately scrambled up onto their mother's lap. Mary guessed that they were looking for reassurance after the disruptions, thinking back to her other life and when her own children were so small. Mary turned around to find that there wasn't another child in sight.

'Just sit there for a moment', Mary said to Mrs Jackson. She then walked out onto the verandah and spotted Emma playing with Chloe.

'Emma and Chloe, do you think you could do something for Mrs Jackson, she needs to have a little rest and the children need someone to play with them.'

'Yes, we can do that, do you think they would like to see the kittens,' Emma and Chloe said in unison. They both raced into the parlour and enticed the twins outside to see the kittens. Rose appeared with a tray, containing a plate of sandwiches, cake, a pot of tea, milk jug and sugar bowl.

'Here you are, Mrs Jackson, some tea with sugar, and food will help to revive you'. Rose said. 'Now, don't you worry, Emma will take good care of the twins. You just sit there and rest for a while'.

'Okay' Mrs Jackson said, her voice indicating that she was very close to crying, 'I have no idea what we will do if they are unable to save the house. Timber houses burn so fast in a bushfire.'

'It will be alright, the community will help you out, you will be able to rebuild. At least you and the children are safe and that's what is really important.' Rose's voice was strong with confidence.

In the background, the clock in the corner stuck three o'clock. At the same time, there was a knock at the French doors.

10

Rose directed her attention to the young man standing in the doorway, he too was wearing a pistol on his belt. He was tall and skinny. He still had that gangly look that boys have when they are between boyhood and manhood. Mary noticed that he had very blue eyes and a smile that seemed vaguely familiar. 'Oh, hello Daniel, Mr Campbell is helping at the Jackson place with the fire. You will have to enlist Joey's help for the milking this afternoon. The two of you will have to manage on your own as Jacky has gone walkabout. Please check on the pigs before you start today as there is a sow who is supposed to deliver, and she hasn't been checked all afternoon. Did you have a grand time with your family this morning?'.

'Very good Mam,' Daniel replied, 'Where might I find Joey then?'

'I'm right here,' Joey called, as he stepped up onto the verandah, 'I spotted you walking across the paddock. I'll change my clothes and meet you down at the dairy.' Daniel nodded and they went their separate ways.

Two things made Mary smile, here was a ten-year-old boy acting so much older than many of the twenty-year old's that she knew in her other world and she had finally found out what surname belonged to this family. It had taken more than half a day to get that piece of information.

'Mary,' Rose directed, 'can you get Emma and the children to help you with the afternoon jobs, please. It's a little earlier than normal but if we get them out of the way we can sit down and enjoy our guests properly. You can even lock the chooks up early tonight; it won't hurt them for one day. Thank you, dear.'

Mary nodded, walking out of the room, she was very aware that she now had to find out from Emma what really was involved in the doing the afternoon jobs. This was another time when she really didn't want to mess up, but she really wasn't sure what was expected of her as a sixteen-year-old in their time. The adults were busy trying to deal with the dramas in their own lives and those of their neighbours. She felt that it would have been imperative for her to help in any way she could.

Walking to the edge of the verandah she could see the children playing a game of cricket in the backyard. It was still very hot, but the children didn't seem to feel the heat. They were using homemade bats made from sticks, they weren't even straight, and balls made from fabric filled with scrunched up newspaper that were far more suitable for the smaller children to play with than traditional cricket balls.

'Children,' she called, 'can you come and help me do the jobs please.' She was thinking hard and fast about just how she was going to get this to work. 'Right,' she continued, 'Emma, if you were grown up and in charge which job would you get us to do first?' Mary was hoping that she sounded convincing in trying to making Emma feel grown up.

Emma put her finger to her lips and thought for a minute. 'I think we should water and feed the dogs first. There are lots of meat scraps left over from lunch today because the men had to leave before they ate it all. Next, we need to fill up all the buckets, so mamma has enough water in the kitchen and before we feed the chooks and lock them up, we should fill the wood box for the fire.

Emma did her best to look all grown up but just ended up looking cuter than normal.

'Okay, you are in charge, so let's get going. Do we have to have a treasure hunt for the meat?' Mary said.

Emma giggled, 'Noo, it's in a bucket on the bench in the washhouse'.

'Right then, let's go, everyone to the washhouse. Keep your eyes open for snakes ok.' Emma led the way, all the other children following her, and Mary brought up the rear. Mary had to smile at Paul who was carrying the stick that they had been using for a cricket bat, he had placed it over his shoulder like a gun and was marching like a soldier. 'I'm going to shoot any snakes we see' he declared. When they got to the washhouse, Emma pulled out a covered bucket. Chloe stepped up beside Emma to grab the handle on the other side of the bucket, the little troupe then turned around. Mary picked up an empty bucket for the water, following the others as they headed out the yard gate towards where the dogs were tied up under the trees. There were only two dogs. The meat was divided between them while Mary topped up the water containers, having filled the bucket as she passed the tank behind the washhouse. Emma, still acting as head of the troupe marched everyone back through the gate, she turned to Mary, we have to wash the bucket, so the flies stay away, I think you should do that job,' Emma said.

Mary smiled and said 'Aye, Aye Mam', you go and get the buckets from the kitchen for the water while I do this then.' She had only just finished washing out the bucket when Emma and the others returned. 'So, who is going to carry the full buckets of water?' she was looking down at the children. Seven hands went up into the air. Again, Mary smiled because the twins had both put both arms up.

'They will be heavy,' she cautioned.

'We are all very strong', they chorused together.

'We only have two buckets', Mary said, hoping that the twins wouldn't get upset at being left out.

'The twins can take the empty scrap bucket back to the kitchen,' Emma said. Mary then suggested that maybe Paul might help her find the cart for the wood while everyone else was taking the water and buckets to the kitchen.

As they walked away, she took the little boy's hand and led him back out the gate towards the wood heap, which was also under a tree away from the house. As they got closer, Mary could see a small wooden cart with wheels and handles sticking out the front, a little like the shafts on sulkies. The children could load it with wood and pull it to the wood box that was situated just outside the kitchen door.

The children were soon back, and they made a game out of loading the wood onto the cart. The boys relishing in who could lift the biggest piece. The girls were not so keen but still worked alongside the boys. It was loaded very quickly, and Mary ended up having to organise the children to take turns at pulling it in order to prevent an all-out revolt.

The only job left was the chooks. Emma collected the wheat and the rest of the children started to round them up and hunt them into the henhouse. Mary was a bit worried that the children might excite the chooks too much, but the exercise went pretty smoothly, and it was soon time to return to the house.

Walking back to the yard, Mary spotted a man riding away from the house. The children didn't seem to notice and returned happily to their game of cricket. Paul's toy gun again becoming a cricket bat. Mary headed back to the parlour. As she entered the room, she could tell that something was wrong.

Mrs Jackson was crying, 'I can't believe that it's all gone, I knew it was possible, but you always hope that it doesn't happen'. It didn't take much to realise that the worst had happened. The Jackson's house had been burnt in the fire. The fire had beaten the men. She wasn't sure if it was out yet but knew that now wasn't the time to ask.

The children must have heard Mrs Jackson crying for they stopped playing and raced towards the house. The Goldsmith children and Emma hovered around the doorway, but the twins ran into the room and climbed on to their mother's lap. Distressed at seeing their mother crying, they started crying themselves. Mrs Jackson wrapped her arms around them and looked like she might never let them go. It was quite an odd scene, these people huddled together, tears running down their faces. *So much for this generation not showing their emotions,* Mary thought. Rose came over and steered Mary out of the room. 'We will leave them alone for a little while,' Rose said quietly. As they reached the door, Rose put her hand on Emma's head, also steering her away from the distraught group. Jane Goldsmith was right behind Rose and also moved her children towards the kitchen where Rose had taken Mary and Emma. The kettle was put on the fire. Rose and Jane set about putting some food together for the next meal.

'How bad is it?' Mary asked Rose.

'They lost everything, except what she brought with her in that suitcase,' Rose replied as the children started to get restless.

'I wonder?' Mary asked guardedly, still unsure of the boundaries of being a teenager in this world, 'would it be possible for us to put some things together for them.'

'Mrs Jackson is a very proud woman, I don't want to offend her', Rose replied thoughtfully.

'How about,' Mary paused, and Rose looked up at her, 'how about,' she repeated, 'we get some of the toys that we don't need, and clothes and wrap them, and just quietly put it under the tree with a tag that says from Santa.'

'She may not understand who he is and I'm sure that she will know exactly where the stuff has come from, but if you want to, go ahead, it will give the children something to do while Jane and I prepare some food. The men are going to be very hungry when they finally get back.' Her tone indicating that she wasn't convinced that what Mary had in mind would work but was glad that the children would be occupied with something that would leave the ladies in the kitchen free to work and talk and the children wouldn't be disturbing the family in the parlour.

Mary whispered to the children who had by this stage managed to crawl under the table, a favourite spot for Emma it appeared. 'Do you kids want to come with me and help me make a surprise for the twins? It's a secret and we have to be very quiet,' she placed her finger across her lips to indicate that they really should be silent. She led them out of the kitchen and around the side of the house to what she had worked out would be Emma's room. Once in the room, Mary asked Emma to find any toys that she didn't need anymore.

'Why?' Emma asked Mary, fear showing in her eyes.

'Well, you know the fire that your pa went to fight at lunchtime.'

'Yes, it was on Mr Jackson's place,' she replied.

'That's right, the thing is, it burnt their house down and they hardly have any toys or clothes left so I thought we might pretend to be Santa. You remember the story, don't you?' Emma nodded, 'If we wrap up some toys you are willing to give them, then that might make them feel a little better.'

'Okay, I can do that. Did the fire burn all their clothes as well?' Emma's face showed concern.

'Yes, they only have the things they are wearing, and their night clothes', Mary replied.

'I know where mummy put my old Sunday dress that is too small for me, do you think it might fit their little girl,' she asked hopefully.

'It might, would you like to go and get it and I'll have a look. I will go and get some brown paper from the kitchen while you do that and then we can all wrap these things up together, what do you think?'

'It's a wonderful idea,' Emma said running out of the room.

'Don't forget to be quiet' Mary cautioned, 'remember it's a secret.'

Emma slowed down to a walk and after Mary had made sure that Paul and Chloe were sitting on the floor, she went back to the kitchen to get the brown paper and string, so the wrapping could begin.

As Mary walked into the kitchen, Rose looked at her, the unspoken question on her face.

'I've come to get some brown paper and string to wrap up some toys for the twins and a dress Emma won't fit into anymore for Mrs Jackson's little girl,' Mary said quietly, in response to Rose.

'I have a better idea,' Rose said, 'there is some fabric in that blanket box over there that I was going to use for Joey's new shirt, but he has had such a growth spurt lately that it's no longer sufficient. You will also find some ribbons left over from the last dress that I made you. How about you wrap the gifts in that instead of brown paper, tie it with the ribbon as a substitute for the string. It will be a more festive presentation since Santa wears a red suit and then she can use the material to make some clothes for the children.

Mary opened the box and found a length of fabric. She lifted it out and turned to Rose, 'Is this the piece that you were referring to,' she asked.

'Yes, that's it, and there should be some red ribbon you can use.'

'That will make it very special,' Mary said as she picked up the materials and headed back to the room.

By the time she had got back to the room, Emma was already back with a couple of dresses. One showed signs of having been worn a lot, but the other was still in quite good condition. *This must be the Sunday dress,* Mary thought and wondered whether it would be suitable for the little girl, it looked a little too big. Truth was, they had nothing, and they would probably be glad to have anything to wear, at least until someone had time to sew something new.

'Look what I have here, we are going to wrap the things in this cloth and, instead of string, how about we tie it up with ribbon to make it look really special,' Mary said as they all nodded enthusiastically.

Mary knew that children in her other world would often be offended if they were given something that wasn't new, and she still wasn't sure that the same thing wouldn't happen here. After all, Rose had said that Mrs Jackson was a proud woman. It's sad how so many things happen to us in this life, that make us deal with those personality traits that need a little bit of adjustment from time to time. She had realised during the day that some of her own traits needed to be adjusted, if only she could be sure that she would be returning to her own world sometime.

The children had a great time, wrapping up some toys and the dress. It wasn't much, but Mary was hoping that at least it would show the family that someone cared and was willing to help where they could. It was plain that no one had a great excess of goods around here.

When they were finished, Emma jumped up, all set to take the parcel out and put it under the Christmas tree.

'Sorry Emma, you need to wait. Remember this is a secret. If Mrs Jackson sees you put that package under the tree she is going to know who it's from. We have to wait until there is no one in the room. Then someone needs to sneak in and place it under the tree without anyone seeing it happen.' Mary looked sympathetically at Emma because she knew just how keen she was to get that gift under the tree.

'Oh, yeah, that's right' Emma sat down with a thud.

'Ok, I think its time for you all to go back outside to play,' Mary figured that the distraught family would probably have had enough time together. Besides these children were starting to get restless again, it was time for them to burn off some energy. 'How about you go and play a game of rounders.'

Wow, where did that come from? Mary wondered. She wasn't even sure if they knew how to play rounders.

There was a chorus of subdued okays and the children got up and returned outside, leaving Mary alone in the room. She heard the clock in the parlour strick the fourth hour. This was such a strange day and it seemed that it was a long way from being over yet.

Returning to the kitchen in search of Rose, Mary discovered Mrs Goldsmith, Daniel, and Joey sitting at the kitchen table enjoying tea and cake.

'Would you like a cup of tea,' Rose asked.

'Yes, please' Mary replied sitting down, she was starting to feel a little weary despite the fact that she still had the body of a sixteen-year-old.

'How are the children?' Mrs Goldsmith asked

'I've sent them outside to play again. I figured they had spent enough time inside for the time being and it is a little cooler now.'

Rose placed a cup of tea on the table in front of Mary.

'Here you go, drink up, you have been a great help and there is still a lot that needs to happen before we get to bed tonight.'

Mary sipped her tea and let the warmth and flavour seep through her body.

'What do you want me to do now?' Mary asked looking at Rose.

'I think we can rest for a little while, then we'll put the evening meal together. We have no idea when the men will be home, so we will feed the children in a couple of hours and then the gifts can be opened when the men return.' Rose paused as Mrs Jackson appeared in the doorway.

Daniel stood up, 'I'll be off home now, Mrs Campbell.'

'Yes, alright Daniel, Mr Campbell will see you in the morning. Thank you.'

I'm sorry Mrs Campbell, I didn't mean to be rude.' Mrs Jackson sat down at the table having crossed the room while Rose was dismissing Daniel.

'Not at all, it's a distressing time for all of you. Would you like a cup of tea?

'Yes, thank you, that would be nice. I've sent the children outside to play just for a while', she said.

11

'Mary and I will set up a couple of camp beds in Emma and Joey's rooms so the children can get to bed at a reasonable hour. You and Mr Jackson can use the double bed in Mary's room. She will be fine on a camp bed on the verandah tonight.' Rose turned to Joey. 'When you have finished that cuppa, please go and get the camp beds from the dairy.' Joey only nodded in response as he had a mouth full of food. 'Emma can sleep in our bed and Mrs Goldsmith can sleep in her bed. The men will have to use the 'swags' I'm afraid, but I imagine they will be so tired they won't care where they sleep.'

Mary marvelled that this situation must not have been that uncommon, as Rose seemed to have everyone's sleeping arrangements worked out with little fuss. It was going to be rough, but these people were tough and prepared to put up with a little more discomfort in order to help their neighbours.

'You are such a great neighbour, Mrs Campbell' Mrs Jackson said. 'I don't deserve such kindness, I haven't treated you very kindly in the past, I'm sorry. Can you please forgive me?' Mrs Jackson was looking down into the cup that she had her hands around, they were starting to shake.

Rose gently reached across the table, placing her hand on Mrs Jackson's wrist. 'It's alright, my dear. We are called by God to be kind to everyone regardless of how we are treated. It doesn't impress Him if we are only kind to those who treat us nicely. God sees your heart and the troubles that lie there. He understands you and He loves you regardless. As His servant, the very least I can do is behave in the manner that He instructs me to in the Bible.'

Mrs Jackson looked up at Rose's kind face, tears filling her eyes. 'But... Mrs Campbell, I was so mean to you. I told lies about you and your family. I deliberately tried to spoil your reputation. I knew it wasn't Joey who let out the pigs at Renshaw's farm. I left it unlatched by mistake that day after having tea with Mrs Renshaw. I had been telling her how irresponsible you were, letting your children roam around by themselves. I hate letting my children out of my sight. You see my little brother drowned in the river when he was little. I was supposed to watch him, but I got distracted and when I looked back he was floating face down. I guess I never forgave myself. My mother wasn't quite the same after he died. I never understood how much a child gets into a mother's heart until I had the twins.' Tears started to run down her face.

Maintaining eye contact, Rose squeezed Mrs Jackson's wrist a little firmer. 'It's good of you to tell me this. We trusted Joey when he told us that he hadn't left the gate unlatched. He is not perfect, he makes mistakes like all of us, but we'd guessed that it had been an accident, although we didn't know who was responsible. Joe and Joey went over and helped Mr Renshaw round them up when they noticed them out on the road. You see, Mrs Jackson, that's the good thing about knowing God sees everything we do. He knows the truth. In the end, it doesn't matter what others say about us. Yes, it makes our lives more difficult when people hurt us. Life was hard for Jesus too when He was here on earth. He was kind to me, you see. I hurt Him before I understood why He came to earth as a baby. That's what we celebrate at Christmas time. He came, grew up, lived here for thirty years or so, and then died so my sins could be forgiven. So, I trust Him to give me the strength to be kind to everyone. He loves you, Mrs Jackson, He cares for you and He wants to be your friend as well. All you have to do is say that you are sorry for the things that you have done wrong. He will forgive you as well. He will help you to be the kind of person that He wants you to be.'

'Is that all I have to do?' Mrs Jackson asked in surprise.

'Yes, it is that simple.'

'But how do I find out what sort of person God wants me to be?'

'You find that in the Bible.' Rose cocked her head to one side, 'Can you read, Mrs Jackson?'

'No, my parents decided that it would not be necessary for me to be able to read to look after my husband, besides, there was no school close by and mamma was too sad and too busy to teach me. Actually, I'm not even sure that she could read.'

'Well then, we will have to get together at least once a month and I will read it to you. I can even help you to learn to read if you would like? My mother wanted all of her children to be able to read God's word for themselves, that way if people tried to lead us astray, we could make sure of what God really said. My mother was a very unusual woman.'

There was a noise on the verandah that indicated that Joey had returned with the camp beds.

Mrs Goldsmith and Mary stood up and left the room to give Joey a hand to put them together leaving the two women to talk further.

'You have an amazing mother; do you know that, Mary?' The awe that she felt could be heard in the way she spoke.

About fifteen minutes later, Rose walked out onto the verandah with another pot of tea, Mrs Jackson was behind her carrying a tray laden with china, cakes, sandwiches, and biscuits. They all sat around the table talking.

Mrs Jackson was looking at Rose, 'Rose, are you alright? you look very tired, maybe you should go and lie down for a little bit. I know that a farmer's wife's day is very long and hard, and today has been exceptionally difficult.'

'I'm fine, Martha.' Rose smiled tiredly and Mary noticed that Rose and Mrs Jackson were now on first name terms, which she was sure was due to the forgiving nature of Rose, 'I think that I might be with child again. I haven't told Joe yet, because I wasn't certain. However, with each passing day I become more convinced that my fears are real. You are right Martha; the farmer's wife's lot is hard. I don't even remember what it was like to have half the energy that I had when I was Mary's age. Being with child just drains the life out of one. It must have been very difficult for you when you were with the twins. Childbirth is such a dangerous thing for us. Men face great dangers in the paddocks, but we deal with greater dangers inside the walls of our homes of which our husbands are oblivious.'

'Yes, it was difficult,' Martha Jackson looked out into the distance as if remembering, 'Mr Jackson employed a girl to assist me, particularly towards the end. It was so hot, since they were born in January, I really struggled to get out of bed most days. There is something that I must do soon,' she said changing tack, 'in view of now trying to live the way God wants me to live.'

'What's that?' Jane Goldsmith asked.

'I must go and apologise to that poor girl who worked for us. I must admit that I wasn't the easiest of employers and was unnecessarily hard on her.' Mrs Jackson said hanging her head in shame.

'I'm certain that God will give you the opportunity and the strength to do exactly that' Rose said with a watery smile. She really did look tired.

'Rose,' Jane Goldsmith said, 'I think you should at least come into the parlour and rest on the sofa. I think you need to put your feet up for a while. We have no idea what time the men will return so please do so now, while you can.'

This time Rose didn't protest, she allowed Jane to assist her into the room and sat down rather heavily on the sofa, lifting her feet up. She rested her head back and sighed deeply. Mary, watching through the doorway, noticed that her actions were very similar to her own when she reclined in her favourite chair in her other world. Jane left the room, quietly returning to the table, leaving Rose to rest for as long as would be possible.

The clock had struck the sixth hour before Joe and Henry returned. Mr Bradshaw and Mr Smith also returned to the house with them.

'We won't stay long, Mrs Campbell. It's been a long day and my ageing body feels the need for some sleep very soon.' Mr Bradshaw said.

'Please stay for a cup of tea, the gifts haven't been opened yet?' Rose beseeched politely.

Joe stepped to his wife's side. 'Rose, we still have plenty of food, don't we?' Rose nodded 'May I make a suggestion then. Let's have a cup of tea and then if you ladies wouldn't mind giving Rose a hand to put a meal together, I suggest that you all stay for a meal. We will give the children their gifts before we eat, then the adults can open theirs after dinner. I know that these gentlemen want to discuss something with Mr and Mrs Jackson that relates to their future. I think that if they know what suggestions are going to be made now, it will allow them to sleep a little easier tonight. Don't you agree Mr Bradshaw?' Joe placed his arm around her shoulder, 'Mary, can you please make the tea, I want your mother to sit down for a while? I'm a little worried about how tired she is looking.'

'I've had a rest this afternoon', Rose returned.

'Well, it doesn't look like it was long enough' Joe said, 'Come and sit down.'

You are right Mr Campbell,' Martha Jackson said. 'Rose, go and sit down, Jane, Mary and I are taking over your kitchen.'

'Thank you, ladies' Joe said taking hold of Rose' arm and steering his wife out on to the verandah with enough force to ensure that she didn't have any means of escape.

Mary delivered the tea to the men and Rose. They were deep in conversation. Mr Jackson appeared dumbfounded as he looked at the people around the table. 'Are you sure! This is incredible, I've never had such a generous offer'. Mary returned to the kitchen and mentioned that Mr Jackson seemed to be surprised.

'I really don't know what we are going to do until the house is rebuilt' Mrs Jackson said, 'but do you know, I have a real peace about it now.'

Five minutes later, Joe came to the door. 'Ladies, are you right to come into the parlour and watch the children open their gifts now?'

'Yes, we can, this can cook while we do that,' Jane answered,

Mrs Jackson, looking a bit odd said: 'I'll stay here and finish if you like. After all, we didn't bring anything, and we are imposing on your kindness.'

'Oh please, Mrs Jackson, please come in and at least enjoy the company', Mary said. She hoped that she didn't make the woman suspicious but also didn't want her to feel embarrassed either.

'Oh yes, alright, it would be nice to have a sit down again,' she said as she followed Jane and Mary back to the house. Just as they entered the room, Mary saw Emma whispering to her father. She seemed very animated.

Mary sat on the end of the sofa nearest the door. Emma came up and stood beside her. She linked her small arm around Mary's elbow and clung to her. Mary could see that she was having trouble containing her excitement.

Jane and Martha joined Mary on the sofa, Rose having been installed in Joe's chair in the corner. The children sat on the floor. The gentlemen, having brought in chairs from the verandah, sat in various vacant spots around the room.

'Alright then,' Joe announced, sitting on a chair close to the gifts and decorated Gum Tree. 'Let's see what we have under here.' Mary could see that he was trying to build the anticipation. 'This looks as if it's something special', he said picking up a parcel wrapped in cloth. 'The tag says, To the Jackson twins from Santa!'

'Who is Santa?' the twins both asked, looking very puzzled and turning to look at their parents. Both parents just smiled. 'You had better open it and find out'.

They untied the ribbon, Joey lending a hand as he had been sitting on the floor not far from them. Every eye in the room watching with anticipation.

They opened the gift to find the dress of Emma's, some soft toys and a couple of small wooden cars. Mary looked at Emma, those cars weren't there when they had wrapped it that afternoon. Emma smiled. 'I told Joey about what we did when no one was around and he said that he had some toys that he had made but didn't know who to give them to, so he helped me add them to the parcel.' She said very quietly, particularly given that she was only five and was having real trouble, still, containing her excitement.

'These are very nice' Mrs Jackson said, 'how very nice of Santa.'

'He is a magical man who lives at the North Pole and finds ways to give things to children who are sad,' Emma blurted out.

'Oh really,' Mrs Jackson smiled. 'Well as it seems you know all about this man, I guess you had better thank him for us, please Emma.'

Emma looked at the floor, she didn't mean to give the secret away, but she somehow knew that she had. 'It's alright dear,' Mrs Jackson said smiling 'This is really lovely.'

Joe, who had been watching his daughter's discomfort, decided to rescue her by giving out another gift. They were handed out and each child opened their gift carefully, folding the paper and rolling up the string. Joey had made Emma a pin cushion, stuffed with wool on a wooden base, covered in some colourful fabric. There were a variety of wooden and soft toys and the occasional book. What Mary noticed though was that each gift represented a lot of time, effort and thoughtfulness by the giver and that effort was very much appreciated by the recipient. *Her other world didn't seem to put that much effort in anymore. Things were too easily come by and were not valued to the same extent as the gifts being handed out around her. She was as guilty as anyone she mused. She never knew what they wanted and often resorted to asking them for suggestions. She even bought gift cards sometimes so they could buy something themselves rather than face disappointing them with something they didn't like.*

Once all the gifts for the children were handed out, Joe decided that now they had started that they might as well hand out all the gifts as it was getting late, and the children needed to get to bed once their meal was over. There were only a few left, Mary received a pair of handmade knitting needles from Joey and a rolling pin from Joe, for her bottom drawer. She decided that she needed to investigate that when she could. Joe gave Rose a new wooden sewing box, with lots of compartments for various threads, needles, fasteners, and the like. Mary could see that it had taken a lot of time, a lot of love and care had been poured into its creation. Like God's love and care into us, his creation, she concluded. Rose gave Mary some linen tea towels, also for her bottom drawer and for their guests there were homemade biscuits and cakes, all presented and wrapped with ribbon in festive homemade boxes. *Was there no end to Rose's talents?* Mary wondered.

With the gift giving concluded, the women returned to the kitchen and the children ran outside to play, making the most of the slightly cooler evening air. Joe insisted that Rose return to the table on the verandah and join the men as he wanted her to rest as much as possible. Joe hung some lanterns on some hooks and lit them. The sun had just about gone down but the twilight lingered on during these summer nights. It was still hot though Mary noted. Just like her other life, the nights were hot long after dark, and the multitude of garments did not make it easy, she was suddenly very thankful for the changes in fashion standards through the years.

When the meal was ready, the ladies returned to the verandah bringing the food with them and sitting next to their respective husbands. Mary collected the children, supervised the washing of hands, and directed them to the table. However, the twins were not with the other children. Mary felt her stomach lurch, remembering the conversation that Mrs Jackson had with Rose earlier. *Where are they!* A quick search around the yard failed to find them and Mary decided that she had to tell Mrs Jackson that they were missing. She stepped up to the verandah and as she did so, just happened to look through the French doors. There they were curled up on the sofa fast asleep. Mary let out a very long, relieved sigh as her heartbeat returned to normal.

She approached the table, Mrs Jackson looked worriedly at her and Mary could tell that she was about to ask where her children were.

'The twins have gone to sleep on the sofa, Mrs Jackson, do you want me to wake them?'

Mrs Jackson looked at Rose who shook her head gently, 'I'd let them sleep if I were you. Go and check on them, if you like, but I'm sure they will be ok there. It has been a long day and they probably could use sleep more than food right now.' Rose said.

12

Once everyone was seated, Joe said grace and the meals were distributed in much the same way as they had been at the mid-day meal.

A few minutes into the meal, Mr Jackson looked at Mr Bradshaw and Mr Smith, 'Would you mind if I tell my wife about what we were discussing now? I would like to put her mind at ease as soon as possible, if you don't mind.'

'Not at all,' the men spoke in unison.

Mr Jackson turned to his wife, 'Martha, Mr Smith is allowing us the use of his home until we can rebuild our own.'

'That is really very generous Mr Smith, but the twins will be noisy and will get under your feet. Are you sure that you want that much inconvenience?' Martha asked.

'It's alright, Mrs Jackson, Mr Bradshaw has offered me the spare room at his place so you can have the house to yourselves. Tomorrow I will pack up the few things that I will need to take with me and that way you will be able to make use of the furniture, utensils, and linen while you re-establish yourselves. Honestly, Mrs Jackson the house is not large, but it is silly for me to be living there all by myself when you have nowhere to go. Mr Bradshaw assures me that there is more than enough room for me at his home.'

'Well, I don't know how I can thank you, Mr Smith. You must join us for Sunday lunch as often as you can. It's the least we can do.' Martha looked at Rose, 'I was saying to the ladies while we were in the kitchen that I had a real peace about our immediate circumstances. This amazes me. Is this what happens when you ask God to look after you?'

Rose smiled, 'God shows His love to us through so many different ways, so yes, I believe that this is His way of proving to you just how much He loves you and your family.'

'What are you saying Martha? I didn't think you believed in God?' Mr Jackson said giving her a puzzled look.

'Oh, I believed in a God, John, but not a God of love and kindness. The God I knew was one of judgement and rules that had to be obeyed. I had to work hard and be good to be acceptable. I guess that's why I was so critical of others. Judging them, just like I thought God was judging me. Rose showed me today that God isn't like that. Yes, He wants us to be perfect but the only way that we can achieve that is through God's grace and the blood of Jesus, not our works. Today, I made a promise to myself, and to God that I would accept His grace and that I would allow Him to work in me and make me a much better person.'

John smiled, leaned over, and hugged his wife. 'Do you know how many years I have prayed to God, asking Him to do this for you?'

'No?'

'Well, it doesn't matter', he said still smiling, 'it happened today, my prayers have been answered and that makes this the most wonderful Christmas Day I have ever had'.

When they had finished the meal, Joe suggested that they have a time of thankful prayer before putting the rest of the children to bed. The twins were still sleeping soundly on the sofa. Each member around the table said thank you for something. Notably Mr and Mrs Jackson thanked God for showing them how much He loved them and for keeping them safe through the fire.

When they were all finished, Rose and Jane put the children to bed, Mary and Martha did the dishes, while the men sat around the table talking. They discussed arrangements for rounding up Mr Jackson's horses, which had been let out before the stable had been burnt down. It appeared, from what Mary could hear, that the dairy wasn't too badly damaged, and the men discussed what repairs and help would be needed. Once they found the horses, they could be stabled in the shed attached to the dairy. Mr Jackson would have to ride out to work on the farm each morning and back in at night.

Their duties carried out, the women returned to the table to hear Mr Bradshaw say: 'There is enough room in my stable for your horse, Mr Smith, which will free up your stable for Mr Jackson to use. I'm sorry,' he added with a sigh, 'it's been an unusually long day'. *He has no idea how unusual,* Mary thought as he continued, 'I need to return home. Like those twins in there, sleep is what I need more than anything. Thank you, Mrs Campbell, you have been most kind. I'll see you all tomorrow, there is still a lot of work to be done before this family is put to rights again.' He stood up, and Mr Smith did the same. 'Yes, thank you ladies, that meal was excellent. I'll look forward to some wonderful Sunday lunches in the future, if that is an example of your expertise in the kitchen, Mrs Jackson.' He smiled, shook Joe's hand, turned to Rose and said 'Thank you, Mrs Campbell, it has been a day with some very special memories to keep. May God bless you for your generosity'.

'You are most welcome, Mr Smith, thank you for gracing our home today even if it was interrupted. I trust that you will have a safe journey home.' Joe showed the men out.

It wasn't long before he returned, saying to Rose, 'well, I'd better not forget the nightly ritual of winding the clock and then we can all retire for what is left of the night. He moved quietly into the parlour and with a lantern in one hand, took out a key, opened the glass of the clock, inserted the key into a hole and turned it a few times. He then reversed the procedure, closing the glass very gently as to not disturb the children.

'It's nearly midnight now, there will not be much sleep before the animals require my attention.' Turning to Mr and Mrs Jackson who had also been quietly laying out the swags, he said, 'I hope you will be comfortable enough here, are you sure you don't want to use Mary's room?'

'No, we will be fine, thank you for allowing us to sleep here tonight.' Mr Jackson replied. 'I am just so grateful that I have my family alive and well tonight. God has been very gracious to me.'

'Well, we will see you in a few hours then, since it's already a new day' Joe said and leaving the room, 'Come on Mary it's time you were in bed as well. We have trouble getting you up at the best of times, but I want you to help your mother without complaining. Now that you have another little brother or sister on the way, I expect you to help look after your mother in every way possible.'

'Yes sir,' she said and followed him out of the room. So, Rose must have told Joe about her fears sometime during the afternoon. He seemed pleased, but Mary wondered how the real Mary would receive that news.

It had been a very long day so the adults called it a night and settled down to get the small amount of sleep that time would allow. After all, there were a lot of animals on the farm and their needs still had to be met. It didn't matter to them that their human carers were exhausted. They settled down and rose at the same time each day, like clockwork.

13

In the end, the plans that Rose had for the sleeping arrangements had worked out quite differently. Rose suggested that it was not worth disturbing the twins as they looked comfortable on the sofa and their day had been stressful enough. There was no need for a blanket as the air was still stuffy with the summer heat, even at midnight. Mr and Mrs Jackson requested, in light of their children's new sleeping arrangements, that they use the swags and sleep on the parlour floor. They felt that it would create the least amount of disturbance for the rest of the house should the children stir during what was left of the night.

Mr and Mrs Goldsmith decided that since their house was only a few miles away, that they would return home to sleep in their own bed. Their horse was a gentle animal and was familiar with the journey, so even if they happened to fall asleep, it was capable of finding its own way home. The animals at their farm would also require attention early in the morning. Rose suggested that since Paul and Chloe were comfortably sleeping in Joey's and Emma's rooms on camp beds, that she would send them home before breakfast. After all, Chloe walked more than seven miles to school each day and had walked home from here many times. The children were early risers and therefore would be able to make the journey home, which was much quicker across the paddocks, before the heat became too oppressive.

This meant that Mary had her room to herself. As she had promised herself earlier, she investigated the bottom drawer. Opening it, she found all sorts of items stored in there. There were cheesecloth covers like the one Rose had placed over the table to protect it from the flies and bugs. There was a couple of wooden spoons, doilies, placemats, tablecloths, and the like. All sitting there waiting for the time when the real Mary, whoever she was, would set up her own home. One tea towel caught her eye. She picked it up and spread it out. In the middle was a handstitched picture of a house. Mary gasped in surprise. The picture looked just like her own home in that other world. She fell in love with it instantly. *Is this just a coincidence or something else?* How she would like to keep it but also realised that if and when she returned to her own time, she would be unable to take it with her. She had arrived in this time with only her memories from her previous life, so she assumed that was all that she was going to have to take back with her. Just like we cannot take any material thing from this world into eternity with us, Mary thought. She couldn't believe how much the house looked like her own. Was this a dream of Mary's, to own a home just like this. There was a sadness in her, knowing that she would never see these things again. They would become lost in the tunnel of time.

Mary thought back to the conversation that she had with Emma while they were watering the vegetables in the garden. Would the other Mary be happy being a housewife, or did she have other aspirations? What dreams did she have that were considered to be unrealistic? What would her future hold? Would she follow her dreams or remain bound by the expectations of the society in which she lived? Mary suspected that the latter was more likely. Mary thought about the big wide world that apparently the real Mary wanted to be part of. She thought about planes, cars, boats, trains, and how they had become bigger and greater over the years. Even the humble clock had changed beyond comprehension, she could imagine what these people would say if she suggested that there could exist a clock that didn't require winding, or one that could be worn on the arm, much less the newer technologies like computers and mobile phones. She thought about the wars that would take place and how hard it would be for families during the 'Depressions'. She placed Emma's bag, the rolling pin, linen tea towel and other gifts she had received in amongst the things already there. Silently she prayed for this other Mary, she asked that whatever life held for her, God would bless it in some special way.

Mary climbed into the bed, lying between the sheets with her thoughts going over and over the day's events. In the next room she heard Joe and Rose quietly going over the events as well. They discussed the new baby and what it meant for them. Joe was pleased but Rose was fearful, childbirth and childhood was wrought with danger. Mary heard him say that it would be nice for Joey to have a brother this time but, as long as Rose and the baby were healthy, he would accept whatever God blessed them with. Rose talked about her hopes for the future of her children, and the country. Mary heard her say that, while the country is now a dangerous and hard place to live, the future was under God's blessing and that one day it would be a great place to live.

Mary knew how much she had appreciated being able to share her thoughts and feelings with her husband John in her other world. He had been dead for over fifteen years now and she still missed him dearly. She had never met another person who could relate to her in the way John had, and sadly she realised, that even though she had served God all her life, she had let bitterness over John's death colour her world since his passing. After all, these people faced tragedy on a daily basis and yet they didn't allow them to make them miserable the way she had. She continued to lay there thinking about the day. Christmas was a time when people focused on Jesus as a small baby. Joe and Rose's baby hadn't been born today but they knew that he or she had become a reality to them and was being nurtured by Rose. From this day on they would always know that the baby was a real person. She thought about how Rose had been able to treat Mrs Jackson with loving kindness, even in the face of her wrong doings. While her world wasn't perfect, it had a lot more comforts than Rose and Joe had. She had found the lack of comforts challenging, maybe Jesus had found the differences between Heaven and Earth challenging as well. She thought about her own daughter. Had she turned up at her house with her family and found her missing? Mary knew that Jennifer would be devastated, because in spite of her being a bitter old woman, Jennifer still loved her and managed to show that love to her every time she visited. Jennifer had many of the same qualities that Rose had, she was always kind to her, very much like Rose had been with Mrs Jackson.

This was the miracle of Christmas. Jesus, leaving all the glory and comforts of Heaven and joining the human race on earth not as a king but as a baby. You could say that He had also gone back in time. He had stayed here though and showered the whole world with the greatest love gift there was. He made sure that we could be forgiven of our sins by dying on the cross, even though we didn't deserve it. As she laid there, she asked God to forgive her for what she had become.

She knew that He would hear her, after all, time was God's creation and He was all around it, therefore he could reach across all the time-zones that existed. She still didn't know if she would remain trapped here forever or if she would return to her own world like Scrooge in Charles Dickens', 'A Christmas Carol'. Maybe she had died through the night and this was part of her journey to her final destination. As she turned all this over in her mind, she heard the clock in the parlour strike two. *Funny,* she thought, as she finally drifted off to sleep, *that's what time it was when I went to sleep on Christmas Eve.*

14

Mary stirred, this time she was very reluctant to open her eyes. She lay in bed listening to the birds singing, wondering what today would bring. It didn't matter which world she was in; the birds still sang in the mornings. Foremost in her mind, however, was the question of where she would be when she did finally open them.

Just as she heard a door bang, she realised that the pain in her shoulders was back. Someone was calling.

'Mum!' it was her daughter's voice. Her eyes flew open, she looked at the ceiling. It was her very own familiar ceiling. She was home! She smiled.

'Mum, are you there? Are you ok?' She heard the sound of footsteps running up the stairs. She had managed to sit up just as her daughter, Jennifer, reached the doorway of the bedroom. She was definitely home! The home that she knew and felt comfortable in.

'Hello dear. What day is it?'

'Christmas Day! Mum, are you alright? It's not like you to be in bed this late' her daughter looked shocked.

'I'm ok, what time is it? I wasn't expecting you until nearly lunchtime.'

'Mum, it's ten thirty!'

'Oh dear, I really did oversleep, didn't I? Go and put the kettle on please dear and I'll be down in a minute.'

Jennifer looked at her, a frown creasing her forehead. 'Mum? Are you sure you are alright? I've never heard you call the jug a kettle before.'

'Darling, I'm fine! Put the jug on, and I will see you downstairs. I just need to get dressed.' She struggled out of bed, finding that old age was again making its presence felt. She laughed a happy laugh. She was truly home.

She looked down and found her shoes, the ones she had put there when she had climbed into bed on Christmas Eve. It was only yesterday, she supposed, and yet, it seemed like a lifetime ago. She still didn't understand whether it had been a dream, or if she had actually travelled back into history, but right now she didn't have time to think about it. She needed to get downstairs and spend the day with her daughter, son-in-law, and their families. If she had learnt nothing else through that strange experience, it was that family and people are very important. The rest of her family were planning on visiting her on Boxing Day, as they also had commitments with their in-laws.

She slipped her feet into her shoes and dressed as quickly as she could manage. Her clothes were loose and comfortable, a far cry from the garments the other Mary had been required to wear, she was thankful, as the day was already hot. She could feel it in the breeze that was coming in through the window.

She descended the stairs to find her family crowded around the bottom of the staircase, all looking at her with concern on their faces. The only ones who seemed unconcerned were the twin babies in her granddaughter's arms. There was a chorus of 'Good morning Gran'. Mary looked at her family and smiled.

'Good morning everyone, I'm sorry to be late, I don't often sleep in like that.' Jennifer was coming in from the kitchen carrying tea in her favourite mug.

Mary gratefully accepted the mug, sipping the tea as she walked to her armchair.

'Mum, sit down and drink that, what do you want to eat.'

'Well, it's a bit late for breakfast, so let's see,' she paused and looked at the children who were now sitting on the floor in front of her, 'what do you think we should have for morning tea? How about some ham sandwiches and Christmas Cake?' she asked. 'Then I think we will open our gifts,' There was a lot of nodding and smiles from her audience.

'Mum, you usually insist on leaving them until after lunch, are you sure there is nothing wrong?' Jennifer's voice was still full of concern.

'Darling, I'm alright', Mary added with emphasis, 'But I've decided that sometimes it's good to do things differently, to mix it up a bit, so today we will open the gifts before lunch. The children can put them up while we are eating. Besides, you all have other people to visit, and they are entitled to have a bigger share of your time today.'

'Okay, if you are sure', but Jennifer didn't seem convinced.

'Yes, I am. Now let's have some food, I'm feeling quite hungry all of a sudden. Another tea would also go down a treat, please.' Mary gave Jennifer a pleading look. She smiled back; the mention of another tea seemed to reassure her that her mother was, in fact, fine. Jennifer and her husband, Tom headed back to the kitchen. Mary knew that they would get all the meals ready for the day, together. Of course, they were only going to have ham, chicken, and salad for lunch. No one was interested in cooking a hot meal on a day like this, no matter what tradition said.

They soon reappeared with sandwiches, cold drinks, and Mary's tea. She relaxed back in her chair with her cup.

'Now, before we eat,' Mary said, 'I want us to say a new grace. Lord, we thank you for the food that we have enjoyed, we thank you for the provision of a good night's sleep and for the gracious way that you have provided for and protected this family in so many ways. Make us truly grateful, until you come again. Amen.'

Half an hour later, Mary watched the children as they sat on the floor chatting away, reminding her of little Emma. Her granddaughter, Susan, had four children, a boy nearly seven, a girl five-years-old and the twins who were only a few months old. Jeff, Jennifer's son, wasn't married yet. He just sat quietly in a chair and watched. The children told her all about their school concert, the parties that they had attended in the weeks leading up to Christmas, the places they had been with their friends. The scene gave her a strong sense of déjà vu. Rather than just let the voices wash over her like she usually did, Mary listened intently, just as she had to Emma. She was determined to glean as much information from the chatter as she could. That was another thing that she had been reminded of by Emma, a lot of things can be learnt just by listening carefully. Something she and her current world wasn't very good at anymore.

'Alright, it's time to see what is hiding under that Christmas Tree,' Mary announced. 'Paul, you're nearly seven now, how about you pick up the gifts and hand them to the people they belong to.' The gifts were handed out. Mary's gifts were a variety of perfumes and ornaments. The others received things from the latest computer games to elaborate toys designed to teach the children various skills, all very expensive, massed produced items. They seemed to lack the personal touch. She looked around the room, noting the untidy piles of wrapping paper that had been discarded in the rush to see what was inside. She thought about the stark contrast it was to Rose's parlour where everyone had taken such care, not only with the wrappings, but with the gifts themselves.

All the gifts had been handed out save for one, a large, flat, two-foot square, pale green box, a few inches thick. Susan reached for it, 'This is yours Grandma, we hope you like it.'

Mary took the parcel, there was something in the way Susan had handled the gift that told her it was something special.

When Mary lifted the lid, she found herself looking at a beautiful scrapbooking album. She looked up at Susan.

'We've been researching our family history, grandma. It's not finished yet, so there are some blank spaces, but I wanted you to have as much as we've been able to put together. I would like to come and visit sometimes and help you fill in the spaces as we find out more. It's also expandable, so future generations can keep adding to it, that way, someday, long after you and I are gone there will still be a complete history of our family. That's why the box is so much thicker than the album. Everyone has helped' Susan's serious look made Mary smile, she reached out her hand and touched her cheek for reassurance.

'It's beautiful, thank you'.

Mary opened the cover, revealing a folded sheet of paper glued to the front page. Unfolding it, she found herself looking at an amazingly designed family tree. At the bottom, there were the names of her great-grandchildren. Her eyes followed the branches up to where she found her own name, alongside that of her husband's. It was the only one in that section that had two dates with it. The one he was born and the other, the day he died. Through tear filled eyes she continued to scan the page. Her husband's linage on the left-hand side of the paper and hers spreading out on the right. There was still room at the top of the page to fill in more names. Hopefully, more research would enable them all to go back further than the four generations that were currently displayed. Mary skimmed over the page, looking with interest at the names of previous family members. Many of the names were repeated over and over again, Mary, Jeff, and Jennifer among them. *Funny how names seem to repeat themselves in families,* Mary was thinking when suddenly one name came into focus, Mary Campbell. Mary Campbell was the name of her great-great-grandmother. The lines above it were blank. Could this be the person whose life she had lived the day before? Without the names of her parents, Mary could not be sure. Mary gave her head a little bit of shake, folding the sheet back into the book, she glanced at Susan and smiled. She started to turn the pages to see what the other pages held. Each page was covered with photos of each person on the family tree. Susan had written up lots of information about each member, where they had lived, what they had done for a living, their birthdays, and the day they died. *She really is a talented writer and artist,* Mary thought. Trying not to appear in a hurry, Mary turned each page until she reached the one that had Mary Campbell's name on it. There was a photo! While it showed a little more maturity, the image in that photo was definitely the face that had looked back at her from the mirror and had stopped her in her tracks in the early stages of, what she was starting to believe had not been a dream, but an actual trip to the past.

Mary looked up at her family, they seemed to be holding their breath, waiting to see if she liked it or not.

'It's beautiful, I will treasure it.' Looking down at it again she thought, here is a gift that spoke of the volumes of love, personal effort, and thoughtfulness of the giver. Maybe her world hadn't completely forgotten the really important things after all.

'Now, it's lunchtime.' She said as she stood up, closed the book, and placed it on the table beside her chair. Giving Susan a hug, she whispered. 'Thank you darling, that is really special, I'll have a closer look at it later after everyone has gone.'

It was about two o'clock before they had finished lunch and the family moved on to their other commitments. Mary stood at the front door until all the cars had disappeared up the driveway. She closed the screened door and headed straight to the kitchen. Making a cuppa, she moved quickly back to the armchair in the loungeroom. She put the mug on the table and almost reverently picked up the book. First, she studied the family tree. Mary Campbell had married a Daniel Renshaw. Was it the same Daniel who had knocked on the French doors and milked the cows while Joe was still at the fire? She hadn't heard his surname; it had never been mentioned. She moved on to the Mary Campbell page, turning to the next page she was not surprised to see a photo of Mary's husband Daniel. This image too, showed more maturity, but yes, it was clearly the same young man who worked for Joe Campbell.

Mary turned back to the family tree and with a pencil, carefully wrote in the names of Mary's parents, Rose, and Joe. She realised that her family would have no idea how she knew their names. She wasn't sure that she would ever be able to explain how she knew either, but she was certain that when the research was completed, the records would show that she was correct. There wasn't a lot of information on Mary, she was a mother of two children, a girl and a boy, and Daniel was listed as being a farmer.

She sat, reading, and looking at all the photos for hours. She thought about Rose, a woman of faith. She proved by the way she lived that God loves us. What was that saying again? 'The only Bible some people read is the life that you live'. If you took the time to read Rose's life, then you are very sure to understand that God loves us and wants to have a relationship with each of us. Sure, Rose wasn't perfect. She had been sharp with Mary in the morning, and she expressed fear at being with child again. She was human, but her willingness to serve others first, her generosity, and forgiving spirit went a long way to show others about the love of God.

Feeling weary, she checked the time. It was eight o'clock, her tea had gone cold, and she hadn't even touched it. Taking the mug to the kitchen she made a fresh cup and, still feeling the fullness that comes with a large meal, decided that she would go to bed early, even though it wasn't really dark yet.

She showered, put her shoes beside her bed just like she did every night and climbed in. She pulled up the sheet, settled her head into the pillow. Her last thought as she closed her eyes was: *so, Mary married Daniel, I wonder what her journey to love was like.*

Mary's Journey to Love

1

'Hear this, you elders; listen, all you inhabitants of the land. Has anything like this ever happened in your days or in the days of your ancestors? Tell ye your children of it, and *let* your children *tell* their children, and their children another generation.'

Joel 1:2-3

1

Mary was sitting in her favourite armchair. Her hands wrapped around a hot mug of tea, listening to the birds singing outside. The wood heater was starting to give out some warmth. The hot weather had given way to an unusual series of colder days as a cold snap made it feel like winter when it should have been hot like a normal Christmas. Strangely it was cold enough for her to have the fire burning as she felt the cold more these days.

Christmas was still a few weeks off; Mary had finished all her shopping and preparations already. She would be spending Christmas day with Susan and Greg. They were hosting the family lunch this year. Until a couple of years ago, when she had seemingly travelled back in time, she would have insisted that the family came home to her place, but the memory of how the people she had visited shared the celebrations by taking turns to go to a neighbour's home each year, made her realise that sharing the responsibilities was a good thing.

Days like today reminded her of winter, with its cold starts then warm days that would sometimes be hot enough to take a layer of clothing off and then things would cool off again once the sun went down. Mary often found this frustrating particularly if she had to spend the day in town. You had to pick your clothes carefully. She called it the layer weather. You'd had to put on things that would keep you warm in the morning but could be shed as the day warmed up and put back on by the time you were ready to come home in the evening.

When the children were little, it was during this sort of weather that many articles of clothing seemed to get lost, particularly jackets and coats. They would start out on their backs but would be removed once they got warm. The trouble was that they would be put down in a hurry and then forgotten. She had to admit though, they usually found them within a day or two, but it was always necessary to have a couple of coats in their wardrobes to make sure these lapses were covered.

Mary looked out the window, today it seemed, was going to be wet. Rain was always welcomed by farmers, not so much by busy housewives, between getting the washing dry and keeping the mud off the floors, it just added to the workload. She found that once the children had left home and her days were slower, rainy days could actually be enjoyed.

So, today looked like being a good day to just sit in front of the fire and stay warm. She would be able to read, knit, or do some hand sewing. A bad night meant that she wasn't in an energic mood. As it was wet, it was unlikely that it would warm up that much. One of her favourite things was to watch the flames dance around in the wood burner and she welcomed the opportunities that arose on days like today.

She still missed John every day but more on days like this. These were the days when he wasn't able to do a lot outside. He would spend the day catching up on the paperwork. As he didn't enjoy that task much, he always welcomed the distraction of having a cuppa with her as often as he could. They would talk about the children and put the world to rights for about fifteen minutes and then he would return to the paperwork. With the paperwork finished, he would then catch up on those little house repair jobs that needed to be done. Farming was more of an office domain these days with all the new technology and paperwork that authorities required. There was very little time left to do actual farm work outside after you filled in all the forms that were required. You just couldn't make a go of it now without being able to understand how computers worked let alone not being able to read. That was the saddest thing about farming now. Once, farming gave those with very little education a very reasonable standard of living. As much as the authorities would like to deny it there were still plenty of people out there who had fallen through the educational cracks.

She looked down at the family tree album laying on the coffee table beside her. It had been given to her for Christmas a couple years earlier by her family. That was the Christmas when it seemed she had travelled back in time to a Christmas Day in the late 1800's. She still often wondered about that experience, was it real or just some silly dream? It had felt very real at the time, that much she was sure of, even though the memories were starting to fade. She continued to be intrigued by the lives of those she had met on that strange day. Had Rose been able to teach her neighbour Mrs Jackson to read? Did Mrs Jackson continue to become the new person that she declared she was going to be? What of the lives of Mr Smith who seemed to be such a generous, happy man? Had Mary found her wings or were they clipped by convention? Did Rose, who had realised she was pregnant, have a healthy boy or girl? What become of Emma and what path did Joey's life take? These questions and more continued to dance through her mind from time to time. The search for more details had so far proved to be difficult and unfruitful and there were times when she wished that she could travel back in time again to see how things turned out.

As she looked back at the fire burning, she relaxed into her chair, sipped her tea, and let the flavour soak through her. She sighed with pleasure, there was nothing more enjoyable than that first sip of tea in the morning.

She was enjoying a second mug of tea when the phone rang. She picked up the portable handset lying on the coffee table beside her, pressing the 'talk' button in the one movement.

'Hello'

'Grandma, it's Susan' the voice on the other end sounded excited.

'Hello, dear, how are you? You sound pleased about something. What can I do for you?'

'I've had an email from one of the ladies I contacted about our family history. She said that they were cleaning out their parents' house after her mother died and guess what!?'

'Darling, I have no idea, what?' she giggled. Susan was good at creating drama. It was part of her artistic nature.

'She said they have a desk that they are fairly sure belonged to the family. She sent me some photos and were wondering if I would like to have it. I said yes, Greg and I have been looking for another desk for my studio. It's exactly what we have been looking for!'

'Well, goodness me, that's amazing. What happens now?'

'Greg is driving over sometime in the next few days to pick it up.'

'That's wonderful, darling. I'm so pleased that you have been able to find something you like and possibly belongs to our family. Families are always connected throughout time. I'll come into town and have a look at it sometime after it arrives, if that's ok.'

'It sure is, I'll ring you when we get it,' Susan said and hung up.

Mary put the handset down, Susan was always in a hurry. Mind you she was very busy as well, along with four children, a boy, a girl, and a set of very active twin girls to attend to, she ran a very successful commercial art business from her home. Susan had decided, even before she got married to Greg, that she would build a business and work from home. She wanted to be able to be around her children and be available for people to visit. Mind you, Mary knew there were times when Susan had struggled with that decision, as the theory never exactly works out in practice, but Greg had been her greatest backer. He had made sure that he was a hands-on dad particularly when the children were babies. He would often look after them for hours at night, so Susan had time to work. He didn't have a real father growing up. Susan's dad had been the nearest thing to a father because his own dad had died during his mother's pregnancy. His experiences had made him determined to do what his father hadn't been able to.

Mary watched the flames as she took another mouthful of tea. Wow, a desk that might have belonged to the family, what about that! she marvelled. She couldn't remember seeing a desk that Christmas Day. Of course, it could have been purchased or made by another member of the family belonging to the many generations since Mary Campbell. It might have even been made by Joe or Joey in the years following her visit. She had seen the sewing box that Joe had made for Rose that Christmas and even the small toys that Joey had given the twins told of great craftsmanship.

Mary thought about the conversations she and Susan had had over the last couple of years. She hadn't told the rest of the family about that strange Christmas, but she had told Susan. Mind you, she hadn't been really honest with her to start with, she had just told her that she had experienced a very realistic dream. Susan, bless her, had got right into the drama of the situation.

Her face had lit up 'Oh Grandma, it sounds like a 'Time Travel' experience, how cool is that!' she had hugged her, but somehow Mary still had the feeling that Susan wasn't convinced that it was real. Susan might have a dramatic streak in her, but she was also a realist.

'Well, it felt real enough,' Mary had replied.

Mary and Susan had made a pact not the tell the rest of the family about it. After all, she was getting old and the last thing she wanted was for them to think that she was going crazy and needed to go into full-time care. She wasn't ready for that yet, that was for sure. She always prayed that she would never have to but that was for the future.

2

'Grandma, it's here!' It was late in the evening. 'Greg picked it up yesterday and we started pulling it apart so we could do it up. You wouldn't believe what we found!'

'Oh, Susan, don't tell me that it's full of wood worm and you can't use it!'

'No, no, nothing like that. We found a secret compartment and there was a bag with the name Mary on it. We didn't open it. I told Greg that I wanted you here and we'll open it together. He doesn't understand why I'm so excited but is putting it down to just a family history thing. He just shakes his head about me and his mother when we start talking family history.'

'How about I come in for lunch tomorrow then, if you're not too busy.'

'Tomorrow would be a good day, it's the twins' day to go to day care, so it's the one day a week I have to catch up on the housework and shopping without them. It's just nice to have one shopping trip without getting to the check-out and finding half the stuff has to be put back because they have grabbed it. So, I'll do my shopping on the way home from dropping them off and we can have lunch together. I'll see you around noon then?'

'Yes ok, I have a couple of bills to pay and a few groceries to get. I'll do all that before lunch. It really will be interesting to see what's in that package.'

'It will be, won't it? I am really looking forward to us opening it together. Grandma, I've got to go,' Mary could hear the children fighting in the background. She hung up. Children were much the same throughout time, even though there hadn't been any fights among the children on that strange Christmas, Mary was sure that would have been the exception.

Mary's thoughts turned to the package that Susan had mentioned. It would certainly be interesting to see what was in it.

The next morning, she woke and listened to the birds singing outside her window. There wasn't a morning when she didn't enjoy listening to them. She turned her head and looked at the sky through the window. It was bright blue; the rain was gone, for today at least.

She wondered what she would discover today, her stomach buzzed with excitement. She was having lunch with Susan and they would get to see what was in the package, would there be any clues that would help them in their quest to find out more about her family history and if there are any connections to the Mary Campbell she had impersonated two years ago? There were plenty of Campbell's who had travelled from Scotland to Australia to start a new life in the early stages of European settlement, so it seemed unlikely that there would be a connection. She was still looking forward to seeing what was in that package though, no matter what it held. History of any sort was intriguing. The morning was clear, even though it was cool, so instead of lighting the fire, Mary rugged herself up in her dressing gown, wrapped her hands around her mug and sat in the morning sun until it was time to get ready for town. Such was her life of leisure these days.

Susan was ready for her when she arrived. She quickly took Mary around to the shed where the desk had been pulled apart. 'This is where the secret compartment was', Susan exclaimed. It's in very good condition for its age and it won't take long for us to fix it up. Greg and Paul are going to work on it in the evenings together. Mary ran her hand over the surface of the top. It wore the marks of many years of use, probably from many generations of the family, if indeed it had belonged to our family, she thought. Regardless of who had owned it in the past, it was now part of Susan's family history and she knew that it would be treasured. 'It's beautiful, you have a real treasure there', Mary said as they walked back to the house.

Susan had set the table and a prepared a meal consisting of chicken and salad. It was still warm enough, particularly today, for a salad lunch. They ate their lunch in the sunny nook off the kitchen, almost in silence. Mary asked a few questions about how Paul, Mandy, and the twins were doing at school and day care. She asked how Greg was going at work and about his mother and her husband who lived in a town a few miles away. Greg's mother had moved there after her recent marriage. She had been a single mother while Greg was growing up and had finally found happiness with a wonderful man and Mary was really pleased for her. Susan's latest art project was also discussed briefly. They certainly didn't talk about the package. It was as if they would destroy the mystery of it by doing so.

With lunch now over, Susan gathered up the plates and sat them on the sink. It wasn't like her to leave dirty dishes there, but today she did. She made them both a mug of tea and brought it back to the table. 'Let's go into the lounge room, I want to open that parcel and see what we've got', She implored.

They walked up the hall into the lounge room. It was an older house that Susan and Greg had renovated. During the renovations,

173

they had installed larger windows giving it a much lighter and larger feel. There was very little furniture in the room, a lounge, two armchairs, two lamp tables and a coffee table in the middle. The walls were adorned with a couple of large paintings and the television was attached to the wall above the mantle of the old-fashioned fireplace, which housed a modern wood-burning heater.

Susan picked up the parcel that had been sitting on the mantel. Mary sat in one of the armchairs, Susan sat on the floor, moved the coffee table closer and she started to unwrap the parcel.

'Whoever put it in the compartment, made sure that it was well wrapped', Susan said, as she turned over the hessian bag, which was worn with age. The name Mary and some flowers sewn in faded wool, could still be made out on one side. Some of the threads had broken but it was clearly the work of a young person. Mary felt the hairs on the back of her neck rise. Her hand started to shake as she picked up the bag that Susan had put on the table. Susan stopped what she was doing and looked at her grandmother with awe, as if she too felt a sense of the mystical.

Mary's stomach was starting to churn with a peculiar feeling that she hadn't ever felt before. Susan continued to watch her grandmother. She held the bag up and turned it front to back and over again. It was the same bag that Emma had presented her with on that Christmas Day. Mary closed her eyes and ran her fingers over the name, just like she had done the last time.

'Oh, my,' Mary exclaimed as tears filled her eyes and started to run down her cheeks 'This is the bag, Susan! The one that Emma gave me as a gift on that Christmas Day two years ago. It's real, it's very real! It feels just the same as it did then, only older'.

'But it can't be, it's hundreds of years old by the look of it', Susan said as she returned her attention to the package, giving Mary the feeling that Susan wasn't sure what else to say. In the bag was another package wrapped in what looked like linen cloth. As Susan unfolded it, three notebooks were revealed. Susan lifted the books off the cloth and spread it out on the table and gasped! It looked like a tea towel, yellow with age, but what got Susan's attention was the embroidered picture of a house that could still be clearly seen in the centre.

'Grandma!' she cried, 'That picture is just like your house!'

'That's the tea towel that I fell in love with', Mary said as she reached down and picked it up. Mary laid it out on her lap to look at it. This hasn't been used for drying dishes, she thought, more likely it had been thrown over scones and wrapped around bread all its working life. It was still in good order even though it was showing its age.

Mary took the tissue that Susan was holding out for her, wiped her eyes, and looked at her granddaughter. She noticed a guilty look on her face. 'You didn't really believe me, did you?' she asked.

'Grandma, I'm so sorry, I just wanted to make you feel as if someone was on your side. Most people don't really believe in Time Travel, do they? It's only the stuff of fiction and movies, isn't it?'.

'It's alright, I still have trouble working out what happened that day myself, I wouldn't have believed me either. Time Travel is only something that writers use, not God. Come on let's have a look at those books and see what's written in them.' Mary tried to lighten the mood.

They both turned and looked at the books still sitting on the table. They were hand bound with handmade decoupage covers.

Susan handed them one by one to Mary, who turned them over in her hand, opening some of the pages to look at the writing in them briefly before putting them back on the coffee table. There was something almost spiritual about holding them. Mary was amazed at the amount of work that had been poured into just making the covers. Each book was different. Each one was covered with various pictures and a number worked into the design. Susan opened the volume that had "one" on the cover. The pages were covered in a neat medium sized handwriting. She started to read out loud to Mary.

Boxing Day

Today I decided that I need to start writing down everything that happens because I have had the strangest day ever. I woke this morning feeling as if I had slept for a week. I know that I had a dream, but I cannot remember it. Just as I was waking, Pa knocked on my door. After I told him to enter, he came in and told me that he just wanted to make sure that I would get up early to help Ma as she was with child again. He also thanked me for being so helpful yesterday. He said that it had made Ma's Christmas Day so much easier because of my kindness to the children. I couldn't believe that he said that yesterday was Christmas Day. When I went to sleep it was only Christmas Eve.

Susan looked at Mary with a puzzled look. 'Wow, how about that Grandma! Maybe you really did time travel that Christmas two years ago.' She chuckled, turned back to the book, and continued to read.

I got dressed, walked down the hall and, as I passed the parlour, I noticed two people sleeping in swags on the floor. I couldn't see who they were, but I didn't understand why they were sleeping on our floor. Why Ma had let them sleep there instead of in my bed, I had no idea. Ma usually makes sure that visitors, even if they arrive in the middle of the night, long after we have gone to bed, are made comfortable in my bedroom. I've lost count of the times she has woken me and asked me to go and sleep in the smaller bed with Emma so unexpected guests could have mine. The day continued to get stranger. In the kitchen there were two children sitting at the table talking to Ma who was making more bread. This was odd because we had cooked extra loaves on Christmas Eve. Where had four loaves of bread gone overnight?

It turns out that the two children were the Jackson twins. I just hadn't recognised them straight away. I guess that was because they were in our kitchen, not theirs. Ma looked at me as if I had lost my mind when I asked why they were staying with us. One of the children said something about their house burning down in the bushfire yesterday.

Emma turned up at this point rubbing the sleep out of her eyes and asked Ma if she could make toast again. Ma said yes! I couldn't believe that. Ma was letting her near the fire again! After the time I had stopped her from trying to pick up the bread that had fallen into the flames, Ma had declared that she was never to go near the fire until she was as old as Joey. I was beginning to think Ma had lost her mind. Emma picked up some funny looking wire thing and asked Ma to put the bread in it. I had to ask what it was, as I had never seen anything like it and even Emma looked up at me as if there was something wrong with me. She called it a toasting cage and said that Pa had given it to her for Christmas.

Breakfast was different as well. The adults had breakfast out on the verandah, and I had to stay in the kitchen with the children. Ma gave me a really strange look when I asked where Jackie was, informing me that she had told me yesterday that he had gone 'walkabout'. Daniel, the farmhand, also got to eat with the adults, even though he is the same age as I am. I think he is a nasty boy. I still hate him for laughing at me in school.

The rest of the day was taken up helping the Jackson family find their livestock, repair their dairy, and help them get settled in at Mr Smith's house. It seems that he is letting them use his home until their new house is built. Mrs Jackson never seemed to be a very nice woman. My friend Janice said she was nasty to her when she worked for her. Today though, she seemed to be happy, lovely, and kind. She thanked me for helping with the twins yesterday and I was beginning to think that Janice must have been making up stories about her being a nasty witch. However, while we were at Mr Smith's house, Janice came over to help pack up some of his very special things that had belonged to his wife. Mrs Jackson actually said sorry to Janice for treating her so badly when she had been working for her. What I still don't understand is why I cannot remember anything about Christmas Day. It seems so much happened and I don't remember a thing.

Susan stopped reading and they looked at each other.

'I can't believe this, this is incredible', Mary said.

'Take them home, Grandma, I think you are going to enjoy reading these if that is anything to go by', Susan placed the books back into the bag. She left the room and quickly returned with a box.

'This might make it easier to carry them', she said, placing the books and bag in it. She then folded up the tea-towel, placing it on top of the books.

Handing it to Mary she said, 'It's time for me to get the twins before the other two get home from school. It's been fun looking at these.'

Mary stood up and hugged her. 'Thank you, darling, these do look interesting. I think I'm going to be drinking lots of tea over the next few days', she laughed. 'I'll give them back to you when I've finished with them. You can keep them for one of your kids when they are ready.'

Driving home, Mary's mind was in a turmoil. Had she really time-travelled on that Christmas Day. It seemed like she might have, given that the real Mary didn't seem to be able to remember anything from that day. Maybe she should have left her a letter telling her at least some of the things that had happened, but she hadn't been sure what was happening herself, so how could she have known to do so?

3

Arriving home, Mary quickly put the groceries away. She knew that once she started to read those diaries, she would have a hard time putting them down. It looked like she was going to find the answers to her questions after all.

Her time was her own and looking after herself was her only occupation. The older Mary got, the less she liked town. Even though it was now seventeen years since John's death, an effort to get back into community life had not really been made. Most people would be glad not to have to deal with her critical attitude anyway, she thought. True, she had tried to be less critical of her family over the last two years but was finding that habits of a lifetime were hard to break.

A mug of tea in her hand, she headed to her favourite chair with the box of books under her arm. She looked at her chair, no, this called for a more relaxed situation. If she sat in the chair, even at eighty-eight, she would want to curl her feet up under her and, given the length of time she would be sitting, that might create too many aches and pains that she wouldn't like dealing with later. She decided that it would be better to stretch out on the lounge. Moving the coffee table within easy reach she sat down and put her legs up on the lounge, just as Rose had done on Christmas day. So many memories were triggered by the smallest things.

She opened the book to where Susan had stopped reading. The next entry seemed to be a few days later. Flipping through the diaries, Mary noticed that there were no dates, just a fancy line drawn between each entry.

Today is Sunday and we are resting today. Despite the extra workload, Pa still insists that we make Sunday as a day of rest as much as farmers can, although, the cows still have to be milked and the animals fed like any other day. Our meals will be taken together properly, and we don't rush like we do on normal workdays. We also gather in the parlour to listen to Pa read from the Bible. The last three days have been really busy. So busy that I've been too tired to write anything. So much for me writing everything down like I wanted to on Boxing Day.

The Jackson family are now living in Mr Smith's house. I went out with them to the farm the other day to help Mrs Jackson find anything that might be usable. Someone had to help look after the twins. The last thing they needed was for one of them to get hurt in the hot ashes. Mrs Jackson didn't even cry when she saw that there really wasn't anything left. The water tank was sitting on the ground next to what was left of the fireplace which had graced the entire kitchen wall just a couple of days ago. She just said that God had been so good to them since the fire that there was no reason to cry, but it really was a mess. They didn't have anything left, even the garden was completely burnt. Mr Jackson has suggested that they might build the new house somewhere else. The ground where the old house was could eventually be ploughed and used for cropping.

Ma and I spent Friday going around to the neighbours' homes collecting some donations of food and clothes for the family. We still had to do all the jobs at home as well, even Pa is working very long hours. Yesterday we spent most of the day cooking and cleaning, getting ready for Sunday like we normally do.

It occurred to Mary that these people had gathered together, probably over an extended period of time, to form a community that enabled them to support each other in what she knew was a very difficult time in Australian history as Europeans tried to establish a new way of life in a strange new land. A land that seemed to be upside down to what they were familiar with. It was summer when they were used to having winter and both seasons were hotter than anything that they had experienced back in what was referred to as the Mother Country. Making Christmas and New Year celebrations very different and uncomfortable. Parts of Australia did get snow in the winter, but there never was as much as what Great Britain got and it certainly didn't last as long. The native animals were nothing like what they had seen before. Some, like the Kangaroo, hopped on hind legs and could jump up to six feet high in one single bound from a standing start, travelling at around thirty-five miles per hour as they bounded along the ground covering over twenty-five feet with each leap. These kangaroos could kill a large strong man simply by slicing his torso wide open with one blow of his hind legs. Then there was the platypus, bandicoot, and koala to name just a few. The culture shock must have been overwhelming for most of these new inhabitants.

Pa and Daniel have started milking the cows a little bit earlier, so they have more time to help with the Jackson's repairs. They were lucky because they only lost two fences, but they still have to be replaced. Felling trees and cutting posts and rails is very hard work. I remember watching Pa do it when I was little. They still have to cut all the timber for the house. Pa said that the nearest mill is too far away so it's all going to have to be cut by hand with axes and crosscut saws. It is nice seeing everyone working together and I like listening to the laughter when I visit with food. Pa is allowing me to drive the horse and sulky now that Ma is so tired. She told me that the new baby will arrive sometime early in June.

Mr and Mrs Jackson joined us after lunch today. Pa and Mr Jackson sat out on the verandah and talked while Emma played quietly with the twins. She is allowed to read to them and play with the toys but there is to be no running around outside. Ma and Mrs Jackson are in the parlour. Ma is helping Mrs Jackson to read the Bible. It seems that this is going to happen most Sundays. She is also coming over two days during the week to learn how to write. This cannot be done on Sunday as it's considered to be work but Pa has decided that helping her read the Bible on Sunday is alright. It looks like I will have time to write most Sundays even if the weekdays are too busy. I will be doing it in my room. It's not the writing that is work but the teaching it seems.

Mary noted that it seemed nearly a week before there was another entry.

Each day last week was the same. I cannot see the point of writing the same thing over and over again. At least I do not seem to have 'lost' any other days… yet. All this week I helped Ma with the gardening, cooking, and cleaning. I'm still taking meals over to the Jackson place each day to feed the men as they continue to help build the new house. Mrs Jackson comes on Tuesdays and Thursdays for writing and reading lessons from Ma. The days seem so normal and routine now.

When Mary turned the page, Mary had continued.

It has been so long since I've written anything. I'd nearly forgotten about this diary. I'm starting again to try and do something at least once a week. The Jacksons have moved back to their farm. The new house took a few weeks to build. It's not a large home, and it's very unusual. At the moment it only has three rooms and a kitchen. A room for the twins, a parlour, and a bedroom for Mr and Mrs Jackson. The kitchen is facing the south, Mr Jackson said that would be cooler for Mrs Jackson in the Summer. It has a dirt floor with the fireplace on the eastern wall. The parlour is as wide as the rest of the house and the two bedrooms are on the east side. The parlour is on the western side which will make it very hot in the afternoon, but Mr Jackson said that they will be using it mostly in the wintertime. There is a wide-open area in front of the kitchen covered by the same roof. Mr Jackson told Pa that when the time is right, they would be able to add more bedrooms on the north end of the house.

Mary could see a hand-drawn outline of the house plan on the side of the page. She realised just how unusual this type of plan was for Australian people at that time. They hadn't changed their orientation from being in the northern hemisphere where kitchens were placed on the southern side of the home so they would be warmer in the winter. It took some people a long time to switch their thinking around because the sunlight came in from the north in Australia. She read on.

It is April and it's already getting colder in the mornings. It's a good thing that the Jacksons are back in their home before

Winter arrives. Mr Jackson would have found it very cold riding his horse back and forth if they hadn't moved. It will be interesting to see if their house is as good as Mr Jackson hopes it will be. It will be Easter soon and Pa always says to expect the first frost around then.

❧❧❧

Mr Smith is to marry Mrs Burns next Saturday. He is finding that not only is it lonely, but he is unable to look after himself properly now that he is living back in his own home. I overheard him tell Ma that Mrs Jackson's Sunday lunches were the highlight of his week. Mr Bradshaw has a housekeeper come in every day to clean and cook for him and Mr Smith says that he just cannot afford to pay for such a service. Mrs Burns lost her husband many years ago and her son Terry has the responsibility of looking after her. He started walking out with his fiancé two years ago, but it appears that his mother doesn't like her and, until now, they would all have to live in the same house. I heard Terry tell Pa on one of his visits that he could get married now as he knew the two women wouldn't have to live together in the same house. I wonder if people will always be restricted by such things.

❧❧❧

We attended the wedding of Mrs and Mrs Smith yesterday. It was a small affair. The service was held just before lunch with a small meal afterwards in Mr Smith's home. This meant that we could go and get home in time to do the afternoon milking and chores. Mrs Jackson had cleaned the house and found some nice wildflowers to decorate his parlour with. Mrs Burns looked very nice in a new, plain pale-green dress which she had made. She didn't look or behave the way I expected a bride would. After they had said their vows, the preacher told Mr Smith that he could kiss his bride. He leaned over to kiss her and she turned her head so that his kiss landed on her cheek. I thought brides were supposed to be happy but there was a stiffness about her that made me feel a bit sorry for Mr Smith. He is always such a happy person. I've heard that Mrs Burns is grumpy, a bit like Mrs Jackson was before she asked Jesus into her heart. Maybe now that she is married to Mr Smith, Mrs Burns might become a happy person too.

❧❧❧❧

I had a dream last night which I think was part of the dream that I had on Christmas Eve. I was flying around and there was a couple getting married in a park. The bride was wearing a long white dress. There were four other women standing beside her all dressed in bright red dresses and they were all carrying bunches of white flowers. The park they were in had flowers everywhere even over an archway that the minister stood under, well I think she was the minister. The groom was dressed in a white suit and beside him stood four men in dark suits with ties that matched the colour of the ladies' dresses. Lots of *people were seated watching them as they promised to love and care for each other. These people were dressed in all sorts of different clothes, some of the women wore dresses that didn't cover their knees and even trousers. It seemed very big and very happy compared to the one we went to yesterday. What was really strange was that afterwards, no one went home, the meal, which I heard was called a 'reception' went on long into the night. I wonder if this means that women will get to be ministers one day?*

Mary stopped reading. Mary Campbell could have been describing Susan and Greg's wedding, twelve years ago, right down to the white suit that Greg wore. The bridesmaids had worn red dresses and carried white flowers. The ceremony had been carried out by a female Marriage Celebrant in the middle of spring. The garden was often used for weddings. There was an archway, a large lawn area for the congregation to sit in which was bordered by flower gardens. There was even a dining room and kitchen at the venue which meant that the Wedding Reception could also be held on the grounds. The owners had put in a lot of effort to make sure that there were plenty of flowers for Susan's big day. Rain had been plentiful that year as well, so it meant that everything was green, something that was very unusual these days.

The thing that had Mary puzzled was how had Mary Campbell been able to describe the wedding in such detail. Had she seen it for herself? They obviously hadn't exchanged places because Mary had only been gone for the one night. It seemed that Mary Campbell had also time travelled but sadly, it seemed to Mary, she would never know.

Greg and Susan had met as toddlers. Mary smiled as she remembered Greg going to Susan's father at the ripe old age of three and asking him if he could marry Susan. That story had been retold so many times with laughter. They had both gone off to the same University, even though they were studying different subjects. Yes, they had had their ups and downs, worked through some difficult times, and worked hard for years before they got married to enable them to buy the house that they now lived in.

Susan had always planned to work from home, even before she had the children. Mary realised that Emma might have been a bit like Susan. She was very much a home body. Something that didn't always sit well with her friends or society these days, for that matter. Young women were expected to go out and climb to the top of the business world. If you didn't, there was often an unspoken perception that you lacked ambition or worse, you were lazy. It was the way Susan had wanted it though, so that when the children arrived, she would be established and hoped that the adjustment wouldn't be so problematic. Mary had often witnessed many aminated discussions between Susan and her friends defending her choice and sometimes wondered what would have happened if Susan hadn't been able to have children. That was something that never seemed to have been contemplated but Mary figured that there would have just been more energy poured into her career as a commercial artist.

Mary shook her head. Why did she constantly entertain these silly "what if" questions. Susan had four beautiful, bright energetic children. There was no need for any of that now.

She returned to reading the diary.

Easter

It's Good Friday today, we always take time to read the Bible after the chores are done. Pa reads about the crucifixion from the book of John every year. It's becoming a habit. I'm not sure anymore about how God is going to work out my life. Everyone expects me to just get married, have children, and work as a farmer's wife just like Ma but there are so many new things happening in the world. If what I remember from my dream and read about in the newspaper is true, women should be able to do more than what is expected of me. I want to see all these wonderful things. The papers are full of the new things that are being invented. Things like a telephone, sewing machines, and dishwashers, things that we will never see out here in the bush because they need electricity. I've even read about a women's college at the University of Sydney. There has to be more to life than washing dishes, cleaning up messes, and trying to battle the elements day in and day out. If it rains, the crops drown, if it doesn't, they die. The sheep have to be fed during the droughts and when it rains the flies come and bite the sheep until they get sick and die. Every Summer the bushfires burn crops, houses, and the bush. I just don't see the point in fighting all your life for nothing. I've tried to talk to Ma about this but all she says is that the grass always looks greener on the other side of the fence, but it isn't really, it's just weeds. I feel so sure that there is another paddock out there somewhere that really does have better pastures. Ma tells me that all the dreams I have of seeing the world come from the devil, but it doesn't matter how many times I tell him to go away I still want to see the world. Surely God gives us dreams to aim for as well, otherwise all these wonderful inventions *would be the work of the devil and they can't all be evil when they do so much good.*

Mary started to feel cold. The weather really was strange for this time of year. She checked the time. *Oh dear, I didn't realise it was getting that late*, she thought. Putting the book down, she closed the curtains to keep the heat in and set about lighting the fire. While she was doing that, her thoughts turned to what she had been reading. It appeared that farming had always been a difficult occupation, especially for women. She remembered well her own internal battles over the problems that farmers faced. For her, at times the farm had felt like a prison, they could rarely go anywhere because, unlike Mary's family, they didn't have the workers to look after things when they wanted to go away. The community that Mary and her family had built just doesn't exist in Australia now. It wasn't just the weather and the hard work but the lack of respect that society showed to farmers. It seemed to Mary that people today had lost their connection with where their food comes from. Most folk appear to think that food materialises in supermarkets by magic and doesn't cost the farmers a cent to grow. She knew there were some ladies who loved farming and getting dirt under their fingernails, but there were others that were there just because they loved the man who had the earth flowing through his veins. Which one would "her Mary", as she had started to think of her, end up being? Mary wondered.

Once the fire had been lit, Mary discovered that she was also feeling quite hungry. She had been so engrossed in the diary that she had failed to notice. She made herself a snack and a cup of tea and checked that the fire had enough wood on it before returning to the book. Only this time she also made sure that the throw rug was over her feet, another one of her pet hates, cold feet. The next entry read:

Yesterday, we again spent most of the day cooking extra food. Ma invited some more people for lunch today. I don't think she is going to be able to do much from now on. This baby is taking so much of her energy. Mrs Jones and Mr Bradshaw were among our visitors today. I think Ma would like to see them married. She seems to think that men should not live alone. I heard Pa say last night, when they were talking, before they went to sleep, that Mr Bradshaw probably likes living by himself as he does a lot of reading and works very late into the night for his business. I don't even know what sort of business he is in. Pa thinks that a wife would be too demanding for him, he is just happy employing his housekeeper. With ten children to feed, I guess the family could use the extra money that he pays her.

4

It's been a month now since I wrote anything. Pa came home from the markets today with the news that the factory has dropped the price for the cream and, since there was less of it because the cows were struggling with the dry weather, there is a lot less money to work with. The price for pigs has fallen as well. Ma didn't seem to be too upset, all she said was that she was going to have to be more careful with what money she had. She said that God had seen them through bad times before and He wouldn't fail this time around either.

This is so unfair because it means that I don't get a new pair of shoes this year as Emma's feet are growing very fast now and she will need shoes for winter. I will have to do with the ones I had last year. It's just as well that my feet have stopped growing. Pa said that he will fix the soles so they will be a bit warmer and keep my feet dry. Even if I prayed for the money for those new shoes that I like, Pa would need to use the money to buy extra feed for the cows. So, I don't see the point in praying.

This is one of the things I don't like about farming. You have to take the price that you are given. If the buyers don't want to pay as much as last year there is nothing you can do about it. My parents think I'm too young to know any of this. I can hear them talking through the wall. I'm not going to tell them either because if I do, they will stop talking and I will stop learning. According to Pa, there are a lot more pigs being sold now since there has been less rain than usual, and feed is short. Farmers would rather sell their stock than have them die but with so little feed around there are very few people interested in buying.

I understand how she feels, thought Mary, *some things never change. These days the buyers are big companies, paying the farmers the lowest price they can get away with, and the public carry on about how expensive food is. They think that the farmers get all the money, but they don't! It's all the businesses that handle the food between the farm gate and the supermarket who put the cost of the food up. Providers of transport to the market, the processing plant, storage sheds, and then the supermarket all get paid, and they get to say how much they want. Then there is the storage and any processing, such as packaging that also needs to be costed in.* She always felt sorry for farmers when food in the supermarket was priced at about a dollar a kilo because she knew that in order for it to be sold that cheaply, the farmer didn't get very much at all.

Daniel stayed for breakfast at our place again today. It seems that his mother isn't well. Ma said that he could stay for breakfast to save her from having to get it when he got home. It was apparently arranged last night. Pa told Daniel to take any other work he was offered, and he would let him know if he heard of any work going. He would get Joey to help him before he went to school but he'd manage the afternoon milking on his own. That means Joey will have to get up much earlier to get to school on time. Pa told Joey that Mr Jackson offered him a spare horse that Joey could use to get to school when he helped in the dairy. He would have to put Emma in front of him though. Joey's smiling face was something to behold.

Mary smiled at the touch of the dramatic.

I have a feeling Joey is praying that Daniel will find work elsewhere but not because Daniel needs it but so he can get to use the horse. I told Ma and she said that God doesn't answer selfish prayers. I heard her talking to Joey later when she was hearing his prayers. Emma likes school, she is already very good at writing and her teacher says that she has a talent for storytelling. I wonder if she will be a famous author one day.

The next entry written at the bottom of the page it was short but shocked Mary when she read it.

Daniel's eyes were red from crying this morning when he came for breakfast. Ma told me that his mother had died yesterday. Men don't cry, so that means Daniel is still a boy.

'Wow', Mary said out loud as she looked at the words again on the page. This was the first time that she had seen a nasty side to her Mary. Her eyes locked onto the sentence. She just stared at it for ages. Were these words really written out of nastiness or did they indicate just how childish her Mary had been? Even if you didn't like someone it was hard to believe that you would have that sort of attitude about them.

Mary turned over the page.

The whole family went to Mrs Renshaw's funeral on Friday. It was held at the graveside. We drove out through town to the cemetery. The circuit preacher did the service. He rides from town to town doing services such as baptisms and funerals. He told Ma, that he would be back in about six months and he looked forward to doing the baptism of her new child.

At the funeral, the preacher talked about when Lazarus died and the shortest verse in the Bible and that it said that Jesus wept. He told everyone that if Jesus cried then it was alright to cry because we miss a loved one, even men. We live in a world where bad things happen. Jesus will give us the strength to carry on. If God is not ashamed of his tears, then how can we be ashamed of tears ourselves? He also talked about how Mrs Renshaw will be in Heaven and would not want her friends to be sad for her for too long.

We went back to the Renshaw's farm afterwards. Mrs Jones had been going there every day, while the men were in the paddocks, to clean the house and cook an evening meal for Daniel and his father. Mrs Jones is a very kind lady. Ma told me later that she thought that she had lost her husband not long after they got married. It seems her parents had lots of money in the city, so she is one of the rare women who doesn't have to have a husband to look after her. She was their only daughter, so she inherited their property. She decided to move out into the bush for some reason that no one seems to know. I wonder if she is hiding from someone. The schoolteacher, Miss Thomas, who was boarding with the Renshaw's went to stay with the Jackson's when Mrs Renshaw got sick as it's their turn to have the teacher boarding with them next year.

I noticed that Daniel slipped outside, after a while I went out to see if he was alright. After what the preacher had said I felt bad about what I wrote in my diary, even if Daniel doesn't know, God knows. He was sitting on the top rail of the fence when I found him. He didn't answer me when I asked him if he was alright. I didn't know what to do but there were so many people inside that I didn't want to go back in there either. I sat on the ground and said nothing. After a while, he just jumped down and said he'd better get the jobs done. I asked if he would like me to tag along and he said I could if I wanted to. Pa called me as he was walking away. It was time to go home and get our chores done. I called goodbye to Daniel and ran back to the house. I don't think he even heard me.

Yesterday I went to help Pa at the dairy, but he told me to go back to the kitchen and help Ma. He figured that he and Joey would be able to manage, particularly since Joey didn't have to go to school. Ma's time of confinement isn't far away now.

5

I'm never going to have a baby! I woke up in the middle of the night. I heard noises coming from my parent's bedroom. Pa knocked on the wall and told me to get dressed and get Mrs Jones. I rushed into Joey's room and woke him, told him to saddle the horse for me. I then raced back to my room and dressed. Joey had the horse ready for me just outside my room by the time I was ready. That boy can move like lightning when he needs to. As I mounted the horse, I told him to fix the fire and put the kettle on. Pa was staying with Ma until I got back. I rode that horse as if the devil were after me. By the time I got back with Mrs Jones, that poor horse was in a real lather. I found Joey in the kitchen with Emma. She looked really distressed and Joey just looked bewildered. When Emma was born, Joey and I had gone to stay with Mrs Renshaw. So, we had no idea about what goes on when a baby starts to arrive.

Ma seemed to be in a lot of pain for a very long time. I don't think I want to have a baby ever. I sent Joey to fix the horse and I made a cup a tea for Pa when he came out to the kitchen. He told me that we would let Mrs Jones deal with things now, but he would take her a cup of tea as soon as he had finished his. I had no idea that it took so long to have a baby. Pa went to milk the cows after he had taken the cup of tea to Mrs Jones. Before he left, I asked if I should take Emma over to Mrs Goldsmiths and let her stay there, I didn't think she would be able to cope with going to school today. He thought that was a good idea, Emma didn't seem so sure, but I told her that we would come and get her as soon as the baby arrived. I wanted *some fresh air anyway. The cries from Ma's room were getting to me.*

The baby arrived around lunchtime. Mrs Jones took all the sheets out to the washhouse. It was washday anyway, but she had told Pa to tell me to leave the water in the copper and let it go cold after I'd finished. She finally came into the kitchen and ate some lunch, I asked if everything was alright, and she said yes but Ma would have to rest for a long time, and I would have to do all the housework until she got her strength back. She promised to come over and help look after Ma every day. I went to get Emma about three o'clock and we were able to see Ma and the baby, it's a little boy. Emma fell in love with him straight away. I'm not sure how I feel about him, I'm not saying I hate him, but he caused my mother so much pain and because of that I have to do all the housework now. Pa said that they are going to call him Patrick. It has been a long day. We are all going to bed early. I didn't realise that having a baby was so painful and I don't want to have a baby if I get married.

It was getting late; the fire had died down and needed attention, she would continue reading tomorrow. Time to put the electric blanket on so the bed would be warm when she retired. Putting in a bookmark, she closed the diary and climbed the stairs to switch on the electric blanket. Returning downstairs, she attended to the fire, made her meal, and cleaned the kitchen. A couple of hours later Mary ascended the stairs again and scrambled into a warm bed. *Going up and down those stairs is a good way to keep fit*, she thought, as she closed her eyes.

She woke the next morning having slept well despite the fact that she dreamed about the family again. She dreamt about Mary cleaning, washing, and cooking. In her dream, Mary had smiled at Daniel when he had stayed for breakfast one morning and Rose was sitting in a rocking chair in the corner of the kitchen nursing the baby.

She spent most of the morning doing her own housework, washing, vacuuming, and the dishes. All the while she thought about the other Mary, she was just a young girl. She thought about those books in the box. She could tell, even now, that Mary had only written about the important things in her life, but how did the girl find time to write at all? If her trip back in time was anything to go by, there would be very little time for Mary to have to herself, let alone write. She, herself, had to present reports when she was working and writing them in longhand, as it's called, took a long time, she had spent hours doing them. With a start, she realised that not many people today would even know that writing things out by hand was called that or that it even *had* a name. That was because the use of computers to write, edit, and correct spelling made the job so much easier and quicker.

Here was a girl whose life had been turned upside down. She was having to do a job that her mother was able to do efficiently due to years of experience, and yet, at about sixteen, Mary would've been expected to step up and do it just as well. Thinking about the sixteen-year-olds she knew, she shook her head, no girl she knew would have been able to cope. Her Mary must have been an extraordinary young lady.

With her housework completed, Mary decided to have an early meal and then return to the diaries. Once upon a time, before television, she would have read while she ate her meal. Even now, if a book was really interesting, she would often opt for the book over the television program but not these, they were too fragile.

Making herself comfortable, she opened the diary where she had placed the bookmark the night before. There were a series of short entries that seemed to be related to the same day because the dividing fancy lines were missing.

It's only been a couple of days since Patrick arrived and I am trying to help Ma as she is still not able to get out of bed after another bad night.

It's been an awful day!

I dropped two plates and broke them.

Emma tore her dress playing with the kittens.

Pa was disappointed that I also burnt the dinner. He told me to stop daydreaming, but it got burnt because I was busy fixing Emma's dress.

The entry finished with some words written in bold letters.

I HATE MY LIFE. I FEEL SO OLD.

Mary wasn't surprised by this entry, given her own thoughts that morning while doing her housework, she could tell that there was a large amount of anger in it. One thing was for sure, Mary herself knew that lonely people do feel old. She had felt old herself when she was nursing her sick husband. Again, it struck her how little people took notice of those who do the caring.

It's often unintentional, but they focus on the patient, not the carer. She thought back over the times when the country had experienced drought. Even then the farmers, the carers of our country, were the last people to get support. They were often ignored or, worse still, punished for trying to help themselves. It did not surprise Mary that this young Mary was feeling old, even though it wasn't intended, given the busyness of the time, it seemed that she had been ignored and was lonely. She also knew that sometimes loneliness was brought on by the carers themselves. They were too busy and tired to bother asking for help or to engage with other people.

She remembered the way Rose had been willing to give and engage with others on that Christmas Day, even though she must have been so exhausted. Mary's youthfulness and self-absorption meant that this lesson still had to be learnt. I wonder how she coped? she thought as she turned the page. Maybe that's why Rose had been so hard on Mary over her daydreaming. She saw it for what it really was and knew that the consequences would be unpalatable.

Today I have time to write. Life is still hard, but I feel a bit better today. All I have been doing for days now is wash, cook, and clean the house. I just don't know how Ma managed. The garden has been given to Joey to look after but he doesn't have enough time to fit it in during the week as he has to help Pa with the dairy in the mornings before school. The aboriginals have gone on walkabout again and at this time of year there is very little daylight left by the time he gets home. So, it's been up to me to make sure that it is watered, and the vegetables picked. That just leaves the weeding to Joey on the weekends. Ma is still struggling to just feed the baby. Mrs Jones is coming over a couple of days a week to check on her and make sure that the baby is alright. I have been feeling so lonely and tired. Pa is so busy trying to keep the farm going, particularly as he is working on his own now. If the garden dies then there will not be enough food for us to eat. Prices are still not very good for the pigs or the cream. Daniel doesn't come over anymore as he has found work in the next town. He works during the week and has to help his father on Saturday afternoon and Sunday as he works Saturday morning. His father isn't doing so well either since his wife died. Mrs Jones is going to his place as well to clean and make sure that he has at least one good meal a day while Daniel is away.

I only found all this out on Friday. Mrs Jones came to visit Ma and found me in the kitchen bawling my eyes out. She asked me what was wrong, and I yelled at her, I told her that I was sick of being forgotten, everyone was cuddling Emma because she was so little and cute, they came to visit Ma and the baby because she was so sick and the baby was so small, even Joey gets attention because he is younger and is doing man's work, but no one cares about me. They just expected me to do everything that Ma did and look after her. I don't have any time to do anything I want anymore. She just wrapped me in a big hug for ages, then made me a cup of tea and made me sit down at the table. She kept saying that she was sorry about not checking that I was alright earlier. She thought I was doing such a good job that she didn't realise that I wasn't coping.

When she asked me what I wanted to do, I just looked at her and said I don't know. I just want to have some time to myself. It sounded weird even to me. I guess I just want to be able to make a choice about what I do sometimes instead of just having to go from one job to the next all day, every day. It's not that I don't love my family, I do. Patrick is cute and I love to see him smile, but I didn't expect life to be like this yet. I told her about being so tired most nights that I couldn't even write in my diary. I didn't tell her about not being able to remember Christmas Day and how that still frightens me sometimes.

She then did the most amazing thing. She promised to come over every Sunday afternoon and spend it with Ma, Emma, and Patrick so I could have time to go for a walk, write in my diary or just catch up on some sleep.

I really like this lady. I asked her not to tell Ma, I didn't want her to worry about me too, she needs to get better, and she will try and get up if she thinks that I'm not doing the work properly. I'm worried that Ma might think something is wrong if she comes over every Sunday, but Mrs Jones said that she would be careful. She told me that she did need to talk to Pa. I shook my head, and she came around the table to hug me again and said 'Honey, he loves you very much, but he is a man, he needs to be told. Men don't get this stuff any other way.'

I don't think I will ever understand men either.

Last Sunday was the first time that she came over. When she arrived, she came to the kitchen and asked me what I wanted to do, I told her I just wanted to sleep, she said that was fine and she would wake me just before she went home. I slept all afternoon. She had even made dinner for us all, so I didn't have to. She is truly a good friend.

Mary paused, tears rolling down her cheeks. She could so relate to this entry. When her husband had been sick, there were so many people who took the time to come and visit him. It had been very good for him. It helped him to stay connected with the outside world. To start with, she had appreciated having someone to keep an eye on him while she caught up with the housework and small jobs that are just left when you get busy. However, it wasn't long before she noticed that they only visited her husband; they ignored her. They would sit outside on the verandah and talk to him for ages but as soon as he needed to go back to bed, they left. Some people implied that she was at fault for not taking time to sit with them. No one seemed to realise that she also needed to talk, and it would have been much nicer if sometimes they had stayed a little longer, joined her in the kitchen, allowing her to unburden as she worked, instead of expecting her to down tools. On the few occasions that someone had spent time with her she had felt so much better about things. They didn't have to solve the problems she went on about, often she would find the solutions herself just by talking the problem through to someone who was willing to listen.

In the seventeen years since her husband had died, it had made her mindful of thinking about those who do the caring. Knowing what to do is not always easy. It shouldn't stop people from making the effort though, as long as it's done for the right reasons, that is, really caring for the person, not just trying to get attention for yourself. She had known people who made so much fuss about what they were doing for someone in need that you ended up feeling sorry for the recipients. She often thought about how Rose had cooked the meals for Mr Smith. There didn't seem to have been any fuss, just a caring act.

A lot of carers didn't even want to talk about their problems, they were just grateful to talk about anything interesting. She was always careful to ask about cooking meals for people as so many people today have bad reactions to food. There didn't seem to be those issues to the same extent when Rose was cooking for her neighbours. Mary was also aware that you cannot force people to accept help, but it is important to try.

Feeling the need for a break, Mary put the book down, stirred the fire and made herself another mug of tea. Drinking the tea just didn't seem to help her settle in the way it usually did, so she decided on a different strategy, grabbing her warm coat she left the house. She needed to walk.

It was nearly an hour before she returned to the house. The air had been cold as it was getting towards sunset. She now made another cuppa and sat in front of the heater to warm up.

She decided that more reading could now wait until tomorrow.

I don't feel so tired today, I was in the middle of making bread this morning when Janice appeared at the kitchen door. She had been sent over by her mother to give me a hand. She did the washing for me. While we were having a cup of tea before she went back home, she asked what Emma was doing to give me a hand. I said that she wasn't doing much because she just wanted to sit and talk to Ma or the baby. Janice was thoughtful for a minute and then said, 'Emma likes to feel grown up right?'

"Yes," I replied.

"I've got a plan; I'll see you tomorrow." I tried to find out what her plan was, but she wouldn't tell me. Being able to look forward to someone to talk to makes it easier to cope.

❧❧❧

Janice turned up again at morning break. She was holding a small broom in her hand. It was a clever miniature version of a grown up one. She told me that a relative in the city had sent it to her sister, Mandy, for her birthday when she was five, but she hadn't played with it much. Her father had already cut off the handle of a large one for her and she liked it better. I asked her if she was willing to tell me what her plan was yet. She told me to watch and see what happened. She called Emma, who turned up looking pretty unhappy. Emma looked at the broom and I could see that she was impressed with the way it looked like a proper grown up one, only smaller. Janice knelt down in front of Emma and asked her if she would like to have the broom. Emma nodded but still didn't smile. Janice then told Emma that if she was willing to sweep the verandah each day to help me, Mandy said that she could keep it. I watched Emma try not to smile but she couldn't help but give a small one and she nodded and asked if she could go and show Ma. It wasn't long before she was back and told Janice to thank Mandy for letting her have the broom and promised to do the verandah every day. When Janice was leaving today, I hugged her very tightly and thanked her so much for her help.

❧❧❧

The minister came to see Ma today. He talked with both my parents for ages. I heard him pray for them both, then the minister baptised Patrick. The Jacksons, Goldsmiths, and Renshaw's arrived just before Pa carried Ma out to the parlour and we all gathered to watch. Ma really smiled when Mrs Jackson read Proverbs 22:1-16 from the Bible. She has been continuing the reading lessons with the help of the new schoolteacher. She has been staying at their place since Mrs Renshaw died.

The minister talked about how, if we raise children in the love of God while they are young, then they will remember these things when they are older. But he also said that it had to be more than just telling them, we had to show them by the way we lived. He looked at Ma and Pa and said that he knew that they were fine examples of how to live the way Christ wanted us to. We had a cup of tea before he left but Ma had to go back to bed. She looked really tired.

ళఇ-ళఇ

Ma is not getting any better. The baby is doing much better, Ma and Mrs Jones decided that it would be alright to use cow's milk all the time for him now. Pa is hoping that Ma will improve now that she isn't feeding any more. However, I have a bad feeling in my middle a lot these days. I don't understand why God isn't answering our prayers for her. Ma says that God always has a better plan even if He doesn't respond to our prayers the way we want them to be answered. How can he have a better plan than Ma being with us.

Over the last few weeks, Ma has asked me to spend my Sunday afternoons with her, to talk. She didn't take long to work out what Mrs Jones was doing. It seems that Ma doesn't think that she is ever going to get better. She has been asking me to read to her the Psalms as well. Telling me to remember that King David had a lot of bad days too. She told me that, like David, I need to remember how good God is to us even in the bad times. She even told me about how hard it was for her to do that herself. I found that hard to believe, I didn't realise that she had bad days.

We have talked about what real love is. It seems that she thinks that it's doing what is right more than anything to do with how you feel about a person. This is the way we can love our enemies the way God tells us in the Bible. It seems that if Pa decides to get married again after she dies, I am to be kind to the lady no matter how much they don't understand what I am feeling. I cried so hard when she said this, that Mrs Jones came in, gave me a hug, and suggested that I go for a walk. When I came back, Mrs Jones was giving my Ma a hug, she had been crying too. I always thought that being an adult meant that you could do what you wanted but I'm beginning to see that I was wrong. It looks like that being an adult means that you have less choices than when you are a child. I don't want to grow up anymore.

I'm so sad today. Ma died during the night. I keep crying, I stop, and then I'll start again without warning. Mrs Jones and the neighbours came over. Some left food but didn't stay for long. The men came and made sure all the jobs were done for Pa. I'm trying to help but, in the end, I was told to go and lie down for a while. Emma isn't crying though; she is just sitting around being really quiet. It's a bit scary that she isn't crying.

Here was another piece of information but it was incomplete because they didn't know what year this was or how old Rose was when she died.

Today was very strange. We had the funeral for my mother. Thank goodness Mrs Goldsmith, Mrs Jones, and Mrs Jackson helped me in the kitchen. Mrs Jackson said something strange though, saying that it reminded her of the way they all took over the kitchen on Christmas Day. It was an odd reminder that I still don't remember anything from that day.

At the funeral, the Minister again talked about how we can be thankful that Ma has gone to Heaven. He said that he was sure that is where she is because she loved Jesus and had asked Him to help her to live the way He wanted.

I cried for a long-time last night. Daniel came today to help Pa and Joey milk the cows. They were a little later than usual and

the cows were not happy. They were making so much noise. I had Pa move Patrick's cot into my room yesterday so I could get up to him when he woke up. I watched him sleeping for so long and thought that he didn't seem to know that Ma isn't here anymore. Today though, he has been very unhappy and has cried a lot. Mrs Jones says that's because he can tell that everyone is so unhappy.

Daniel seems to have changed since I saw him last. I can't believe that its only about two months since he left to work in town. He seemed more confident today. His shoulders are broader now. He is starting to look a bit handsome. I don't know what he thought about me, I really looked a mess, and I was still very tired from having to get up early to Patrick. I'm still worried that Emma seems to be very quiet and so is Pa. He is doing the work on the farm, but I can tell that he is really sad Ma is not here anymore.

Mary thought back to the start of her relationship with John. They had both attended the same church for years, however, John didn't go every week, mostly because of the farm commitments. His parents were only able to attend once a month when he was small and when he took over from his father, who had retired early to the coast, he had continued to make the journey into town on a monthly basis. It seemed that he was just there until they turned twenty. They were in the church, after the service to have a rare lunch together to celebrate the breaking of the drought. When John had walked in, she hadn't even recognised him at first and even asked her girl friend who the handsome stranger was. Julie had laughed at her, 'That's John, you duffer, John Cooper' She had stared at him, as if seeing him for the first time. *Wow*, was all she could think. He had looked around the hall and, spotting Julie, had walked over to them,

'Hello, Julie, Mary. How's your father doing now that's it rained, Julie?'

'Fine, thanks John. He is very pleased that they have received a good drop of rain and the grass is already starting to grow.'

All Mary could do was stand there as if she were glued to the spot. John had turned to her, greeted her by name and turned back to Julie. She had nodded and, realising that she was invisible to him, made some silly excuse to retreat to the kitchen.

That night, she had laid awake for ages thinking about John. He had looked at Julie with interest. It made sense to Mary, that Julie would be the object of his affections. She came from a farming background and knew what farming life would entail but she couldn't get his handsome physic out of her mind. She turned back to the diary.

Emma cried today! She cried and cried for such a long time. She was starting to scare me as much as her being silent was. If I thought life was busy before, it is now even more so. How can one small child make so much more work.

It's just one month until Christmas Day. I will have to start thinking about what we will do this Christmas. Mrs Goldsmith has asked Pa to have lunch at their home. I'm glad he said yes, but I have to start making gifts for everyone. I knew there was a lot of work involved in making Christmas special but I'm just learning there is a lot more than I thought there was. Patrick rolled over by himself in the cot this morning. I asked Emma if she wanted to bake biscuits again this year and she wasn't sure. Mrs Jones came again on Friday; she knew Pa would be at the sales. She was able to talk Emma into cooking the biscuits, she even managed to convince her to do it in memory of Ma, we are going to make them in the shape of a person with coloured icing on top to look like Ma. So, we sat down and made a list of things that we will need. Pa will be able to get them when he goes to the sales again next week. At breakfast this morning, the family decided not to exchange gifts this year but to just go to the Goldsmiths and take the biscuits for them. When Mrs Goldsmith visits next, I will be certain to ask her how many guests she is inviting. I need to know how many biscuits I need to make.

❧❧❧

Yesterday, I asked Joey to look after Patrick for a little while because I wanted to talk to Pa. I feel bad for Emma and Patrick not receiving gifts this Christmas. So, I asked him if we could just get them something small and leave them wrapped at their places on the breakfast table after they go to bed, so they can find them in the morning. Emma keeps telling me some story about a magic man called Santa Claus. Apparently, it's some story that I told last Christmas, the one I can't remember. Pa thought it was a great idea. When I returned to the house, I sent Emma to the washhouse to check on the cat. The newest litter of kittens have been running around making a nuisance of themselves. I wanted to ask Joey for his help without Emma knowing anything about it. He told me that he has been making a small dolls house for her. I didn't know anything about this. He told me that it helped him when he was missing Ma. He said that it would be easy to make a cart for Patrick but didn't think he would be able to have the whole dolls house done in time. I suggest that we make it into a representation of a stable and all we had to do is make Mary, Joseph, and baby Jesus. Then each year, if he wanted to, he could make a new carving, it would help tell Emma and Patrick the story of Christmas. Next year, we could add the shepherds and then the Wise Men the year after. We could even keep going and make King Herod. Joey thought it was a great idea. I told him that I would help him by making the clothes for the people. It means that much of the sewing will have to be done before school finishes. We don't know when that will be, so I need to work quickly. I had asked Pa if he knew when school would finish and all he said was that Parliament would decide sometime soon. The teacher would most likely get a telegram when the decision was made. After school is finished, I will have to work at night after Emma goes to bed. Joey will find it easier to hide his work as he uses the old shed.

The teacher sent a message home with Joey today to say that School finishes on Friday. I'm surprised at how well the gift for Emma is coming along.

ڪوڪوۍ

It's the last Sunday before Christmas Day. Will I be able to remember this Christmas Day, I still cannot believe that I still don't remember a thing about last year. Such a lot has happened since then. It will also be the first Christmas without Ma. I'm looking forward to seeing the look on Emma's face when she gets the Nativity from us all. Even Patrick will like the cart I think, Joey has painted it a bright red. All the biscuits are packed but I still wish Ma was here. I still don't understand why God didn't answer our prayers for her to stay with us.

Mary couldn't help smiling as she started to read the next entry.

6

Christmas Day

I'm writing this down even though it's very late just in case I don't remember anything again tomorrow.

It was really hard without Ma today. I miss her so much and we really didn't feel like doing very much as it was a hot day right from the start. Pa and Joey milked the cows earlier than usual. I prayed that the children wouldn't wake up before they came in for breakfast so Pa could see their faces when they found their gifts. I wanted him to share something good this year since we are not giving each other gifts. I was really surprised when Pa and Joey came back to the house and they were still both asleep. God did answer my prayer. Pa went to check on Patrick and found him trying to sit up in his cot, so he picked him up. Emma wasn't far behind them. Emma was really pleased with the Nativity and Patrick thinks that his cart is good.

We had dinner at the Goldsmith's farm. Mrs Jones and Mr and Mrs Smith were present along with Mr Bradshaw. The Jackson's were also there. They also invited Daniel and Mr Renshaw, but they decided to spend the day with Mr Renshaw's sister who lives in the next town. Her husband was killed while riding a horse earlier this year. It appears that the horse went down, fell on its rider and was unable to get back up. By the time the family realised that something was wrong it was too late to save him.

I got to sit with the adults this year. It was Joey's turn to look after the children. They had a separate table. It seems to me that Mr Smith isn't very happy. He has got very thin; he is no longer the portly man that he used to be. The clothes he wears just hang on him, it appears his wife hasn't adjusted them to fit him. Mrs Smith, who used to be Mrs Burns, is a very buxom lady and very loud. She told us all about how she insisted on Mr Smith buying new furniture as she didn't like the furniture that her husband had in his home. Mrs Jackson turned to Mr Smith and very sweetly said: "I want to thank you so much for your generosity, Mr Smith, when we lost all our things in the fire, I had no idea how we would be able to refurnish our new home. Your furniture fits beautifully in it and is just so comfortable, it also helped the twins. We were still sleeping on the floor when you got married. The twins were so happy when the beds arrived and strangely, they stopped having nightmares as soon as they started sleeping in those beds. God has been so good to us and I thank Him every day for you." She went on to talk about how she read in the book of Luke about how if we give, God will give us back many more blessings. I'm not sure that Mr Smith is getting good things yet. Mrs Smith wasn't very happy and actually said that he should have thrown the furniture out. Mr Jackson then turned to Mrs Smith and said, "Mrs Smith, he did, he threw it out, on our front yard". He then turned to Mr Smith and said, "May I reiterate what my wife has said, your generosity is very much appreciated in our house, even if it isn't in your own home." Mrs Smith looked very angry at this but didn't say anything more. Mr Smith just gave a bit of a sad smile and told the Jacksons that he was glad that he was able to assist them. I fear that Mrs Smith will have a lot to say on their way home.

Mrs Jones then changed the subject by asking me how I was managing without Ma. I told her that things were still very busy and that often I didn't get to bed until very late because I still had to do the washing up after the children were put to bed and summer was the hardest time trying to get them to sleep because it was late when the sun went down. I often have to tell them so many stories before they will go to sleep. Mrs Jackson then told us all about how much she now appreciated that Mr Jackson did the washing up when the twins were small. "He told me that if he could wash a separator in the dairy, then he was capable of washing up some dishes. I must admit that I didn't appreciate it at the time, in fact I have had to apologise for treating him so badly a lot in the last year". She reached out and squeezed his hand. Mr Jackson's smile was so big and said that this year had been so good. He looked at Pa and said 'I cannot thank God enough for your late wife and for the way she helped Martha find Jesus last Christmas. This year has been such a blessing. Watching Martha change has made it very special. I looked at Pa and noticed that he had a funny look on his face, but he just nodded. Mrs Jackson then told us how Mr Jackson now reads to the children while she does the washing up. Mr Bradshaw was really surprised and asked about what books he reads to the children. She giggled a little and explained how Mr Jackson writes stories out and draws some pictures for the children because he wanted to make sure that they enjoyed reading. He keeps the sheets of paper in a box. I had a bright idea, but I waited until later before I asked Mrs Jackson if she would like me to put all the pages together with a nice cover and make a book for her children. She had tears in her eyes when she hugged me and told me that was a brilliant idea. She asked me if I would be able to get it ready for their birthday in January. I said I would try but I couldn't promise because I am so busy. She went and got the papers anyway.

After we got home, it wasn't long before Pa and Joey had to go and milk the cows again. Truly, farming is so demanding. I pray that one day I am able to get away from here. I want my husband to have a job where we can enjoy our Sundays together and go for a holiday at least every few years. I want to explore our country.

After we had supper, Pa declared that he and Joey would do the washing up. He told Emma to tell Patrick a story after I put him in the cot. He looked at me and told me to go and do something that I wanted to do. He told me that he was sorry it wouldn't be very long, but he promised to allow me at least some time to myself each evening. That way I would be able to put the book together for the Jackson twins. Mr Jackson must have had a talk with Pa about what I wanted to do for their birthday.

Boxing Day

Thank goodness, I still remember yesterday! I had another dream last night, I'm sure that I have had it before as well. I was floating around in a town, there were lots of houses and they all seemed to have lights in every pattern imaginable. There were animals, fat white men, men dressed in red suits, stars, boots, balls, trees covered in lights as well as houses. It seems that everyone in this dream is very rich and can afford so many luxuries. If this dream is about life in the future than it is so much better than what we have.

It is almost the end of the year. It has been very strange in so many ways. I have had to be both a mother and a sister to Emma and Patrick. My life is no longer my own and I pray that someday God will see fit to give it back to me. Pa tells me that when we serve God, our lives are not our own and we must serve Him first by doing our duty. I fear that Pa's plan for me is to stay home and look after Emma and Patrick, at least until they are grown up.

I wonder if God has a different plan for my life.

I will start a new book next year.

Mary closed the book, turning it over in her hands thoughtfully. She knew it was pointless, but she remembered praying for Mary before and it seemed that her prayers weren't really being answered, she hoped that the next year would be better for her.

7

She put the diary down and picked up the one with a number two on the cover. She was so tempted to pick up the last diary and find out what happened between Mary and Daniel. Of course, their love story might actually be in the second one anyway. Mary decided that it was time to call it a day. It seems like a good time to go to bed even though it was still early.

With one thing and another it was a couple of days before Mary was able to even think about sitting down to read again.

Looking at the cover, Mary wondered if the other Mary had found the time to make the books for the Jackson twins. Why wonder? she thought, just open the diary, and find out.

Pa has been really helpful since Christmas. I know that he is really tired and that the days are really long. But he has been taking time out around teatime to do the washing up and tell the children a story before they go to bed. He then goes back outside to keep doing the farm jobs. It has allowed me to finish the book covers. I just have to let them dry properly and then put the books together.

꧁꧂꧁꧂

I finished the books during the week and was able to give them to Mrs Jackson when she came over on Saturday. I had been reading some of the stories. One of them was about God answering our prayers. I asked her if she really believed that

God answered our prayers. She wanted to know why I was asking, and I just told her that I didn't understand why God didn't allow Ma to get better after all the times that we asked Him to. I felt that He hadn't answered because I had been bad. After all, Ma was always complaining about me being in dreamland. Maybe that's why God took Ma to Heaven. Over a cup of tea, she said that she didn't comprehend either why God hadn't answered our prayers, but because God knew everything about our futures, only He could understand what was best for us. While He wasn't happy to see any of us in pain, He knew how to help us through the troubles and also how to make us stronger. I told her that I didn't feel stronger, all I felt was weak, tired, and sad. She suggested that she bring the twins over tomorrow for the afternoon and that I should go and visit Mrs Jones. When I asked her why, she just said that Mrs Jones might be able to help me better than she could.

❧❧❧

I went to see Mrs Jones today. She gave me a hug and asked me how I was doing. I told her about asking Mrs Jackson about God not answering my prayers for Ma and that she said that I should come and see her. She got her Bible out and opened it at 1 Corinthians 2 and we read the whole chapter. I looked at her and she sat down beside me and explained that if we cannot understand what ordinary people are thinking with the little information that we have; then how can we ever hope to understand what God is planning when he knows everything that has or will happen, not only in our world, but in the whole universe. It would be silly to try and tell God what to do. She said the hardest thing, when experiencing grief, was trusting God with your future but she figured that she had trusted him before when she was married so she had to trust Him again when she wasn't. The next hardest thing was letting Him help you through it all. There is no point trying to do it all by ourselves. If He sends people to help us then we should allow them to be part of our lives. She asked me about what my dreams were for my future. I told her about wanting to explore the world so I could one day be an author not just stay on the farm like Emma wanted to. Mrs Jones looked away and just said the rest of the world wasn't always as great as it was made out to be. She decided that it was time I went home but told me that I could come and visit on another day and maybe I could bring Patrick with me next time I felt like I needed to talk.

I asked her why she hadn't been to see us for a long time. She just answered that it didn't look right and that Pa needs time to grieve by himself. I said that I didn't understand that as he wasn't on his own because he had the four of us kids there all the time. She said that I would understand when I grew older.

❧❧❧❧

Emma asked me to put her to bed tonight, instead of Pa. While I was pulling the sheet up and a light blanket, the weather has been a little cooler of late, she told me that last night she had a dream about Ma being an angel with beautiful wings. "Just like we talked about last Christmas", she said. Oh, that day still evades my memory. Then she said that all she wanted now was for Pa to be happy again. She said that she missed his smiles. Since she has always been his favourite, I'm not surprised.

❦❦❦

I cannot believe how hard life is at the moment. Daniel's father has had an accident. He broke his leg when the horse put its hoof in a burrow. It was hard to tell if it was a rabbit or native animal that was responsible. The horse fell on him and his back is hurt as well. He is very fortunate to be alive. The horse managed to get back up on its feet and limped home. Once Daniel saw the horse without his father, he knew something was very wrong and went looking for him. Fortunately, the accident had taken place not too far from the farm, so they were able to get help quickly. He is going to live with his sister until He gets better. Daniel cannot work and look after his father at the same time. I'm not sure what is going to happen to their farm. They did have to put the horse down though.

Goodness Mary, thought, farming is still a very dangerous occupation. These days farmers used two and four wheeled motor bikes to travel around the farm. The problem is that if there is an accident, the bike doesn't come home on its own like a horse used to. Not only that, but many farmer's wives work in town, earning a wage to help keep the farms going. So, there would be no one at the house to assist the injured farmer anyway. So, they could be lying out there for a very long time before anyone missed them.

I can't believe that I had part of that dream again, the one I had on Christmas Eve. I didn't remember the dream at the time, but each time I have parts of it again, I remember that it is part of the bigger one. This time I was flying along a road. The road was covered with black stuff with white lines down the middle. Instead of horses and carts, the people travelled in horseless carriages which went much faster than we can even think about travelling. They didn't look like the ones that I see in the newspapers. They are smoother, shinier, and sleeker than the ones I have seen. I was following one of these things when it suddenly crashed into another one coming the other way. The next thing, there were all sorts of horseless carriages arriving. A couple of them had Police written on the side and another one had the word ambulance written all over it. I followed the ambulance when it took the people from the scene to the hospital. As I floated along the hallways, I could see people who had a lot of cuts and bruises. Other people had a lot of bandages wrapped around their faces, arms, and legs. There was a room downstairs that was very cold, and it had a big steel cupboard along one wall. I watched as one door was opened, only to see that there was a person dead inside. Then I woke up.

❧❧❧❧

Mr Renshaw has leased the farm to Mr Jackson for a year so Daniel can keep working. I guess I won't be seeing him around for a long time. It seems funny that, if he lived in my dream, he

224

could travel to and from work every day because the horseless carriages in my dream go so fast and the roads are much smoother.

❧❧❧❧

Patrick is trying to pull himself up. He grabs hold of the chairs and tries to stand up.

❧❧❧❧

It's Patrick's birthday today. He is one-year old. We just had dinner the same as usual.

Mary flipped through the diary trying to see if there were any more entries about Daniel. Most of them seemed to cover general goings on around the farm. Mary wrote about a few visits to Mrs Jones, but on the whole, the year seemed to have been of generally routine happenings. Towards the end of the diary there were a few entries that piqued her interest.

It's my birthday today, I'm seventeen. Pa surprised me with a beautiful desk. He told me that I could use it to write my stories on or make the special covers that I do for books. He even showed me a secret drawer that he had put in it. You can hide your diaries in there and only you and I will know about this drawer. I promise I will never look in there again.'

As I get closer to the end of the first year without Ma, I find myself asking so many questions about prayer and Heaven. What is it like? Why didn't God answer our prayers. How can He have something better planned for us? Why does He answer some prayers and leave others unanswered for so long?

I went to see Mrs Jones again today; it is so nice to have someone to talk to. Patrick even let her give him a cuddle. He doesn't usually like others holding him. She put him down, so his feet were on the floor, and he actually stood up for a little while, even though Mrs Jones was holding his hands. She made such a fuss of him, making him smile so big. When we got home, we demonstrated how clever he was to Pa.

8

I'm so sick of having holes in the bottom of my shoes. My socks got wet when I accidently stepped in water going to see Mrs Goldsmith first thing this morning. I really cried out to God in my head today, you could say that I yelled, asking Him why I can't have a pair of new shoes. I know that Pa doesn't have any spare money and he probably doesn't even realise that my shoes have holes in them. I couldn't tell him because he doesn't need any more problems at the moment. The pigs' prices are still lower than what we need to pay our bills. Just after lunch, Mrs Smith knocked on the kitchen door. I was surprised and a bit worried. I remember how difficult she was at Christmas Dinner. She didn't smile but handed me a paper bag. "Here," she said, "a voice in my head told me that you need these and that I should bring them over for you. Goodbye". She walked away without even giving me time to ask if she would like a cup of tea. I called out but she kept walking. I looked in the bag and there were a beautiful pair of new shoes. I raced to my room to see if they fitted, they were perfect. Sometimes, God answers prayers really quickly.

❧❧❧❧

I went to see Mrs Jones to show her my new shoes and I told her about how I had yelled at God. I asked if God had answered so quickly because I had yelled. She said he doesn't mind us yelling at him but that wasn't why he had answered my prayer. He answered because he wanted me to understand that he loves me, and he knew that I needed that new pair of shoes. He still would have answered if I had patiently waited for him to give me the new shoes.

❧❧❧

Patrick started walking today. Mrs Jones came to lunch. I noticed that Pa was smiling again. He actually giggled when Patrick fell over as he picked him up and set him to rights again. I also noticed that he kept looking at Mrs Jones when he thought we weren't looking. It was great.

❧❧❧

Pa went out this afternoon. It's the first time that he has been out on a Sunday since Ma died. He didn't tell me where he was going, just that he was going for a ride by himself.

❧❧❧

Pa went out again today. He even smiled at breakfast this morning. He seemed more interested in what we were doing today than he has since Ma died.

Pa seems to have more energy these days. He is standing straighter. I even heard him whistling to himself when he was coming back from the dairy.

There have been so many storms this last week. Mr Jackson came over to see Pa today. They sat out on the verandah because it's too hot inside, besides Pa hasn't really used the parlour since Ma died. I could hear them talking while I was in the kitchen getting tea. Mr Jackson was telling Pa about how the wheat crop he had was saved. Pa knew that the money from that crop was the only way Mr Jackson was going to be able to pay Mr Renshaw his lease money. Mr Jackson told Pa he could see the storm coming straight for the crop. It was nasty and he was very sure there would be hail in it. "So, I went inside and prayed," he said, 'I told God that I didn't want that money for myself, I needed it for Mr Renshaw who has lots of doctor's bills to pay, I needed to honour my commitment to him, but I also told God that if the crop went, I trusted Him to help me honour my debts in some other way. I got up, went outside, leaned against the verandah post, and watched the storm," he continued, "I watched it come up to the fence, it then tracked sideways along the fence and when it got to the corner it moved forward again right around that paddock of wheat. You know what?" he asked Pa, "I went back inside to my bedroom and got down on my knees and thanked the good Lord for blessing me so graciously and answering my prayers. It really was a sight to behold."

Is this part of the thing about prayer? They should not be selfish. Mr Jackson didn't want that crop saved for himself, he wanted it so he could honour his debt to Mr Renshaw. Was I being selfish by asking God to keep Ma alive?

229

❧❧❧

Pa asked me yesterday if I would mind if Mrs Jones came to lunch again today. I said it would be alright. She came and we had a nice time. She talked to Emma about what was happening at school and played with Patrick. It's nice to see Pa really smile. He asked us all if it would be alright for Mrs Jones to come to dinner again next Sunday. Emma said it was alright with her, Joey nodded but didn't seem too happy, Patrick didn't say anything of course but smiled, and I said it was alright, but I am wondering what is going on. Pa isn't telling us very much. I talked to Joey before he went to bed and he asked me if Pa was going to marry Mrs Jones. I asked if it would be acceptable to him if Pa married her. He wasn't sure, he didn't want her to be like Mrs Smith and change everything once she married Pa.

❧❧❧

Late this evening, Mr Smith came to visit Pa after he had finished the milking. They sat outside on the verandah and talked while Pa watched Emma trying to play handball with Patrick in the yard, it was quite funny to watch as Patrick still spends more time sitting than walking. I heard the men talking while I did some mending in the parlour. Mr Smith was telling Pa that life was difficult being married to Mrs Smith. He said that he thought she was making an effort to be nicer, particularly when she gave me a pair of shoes, and he thought that was great progress, but then little Betty, her granddaughter, died and since then she has become so very sour in her attitude. He told Pa that while it was good to have his house clean, his meals cooked, and even his clothes mended sometimes, it was hard listening to Mrs Smith complain about everything. It appears that nothing makes her happy. Even the new furniture wasn't acceptable anymore. She was even making him do most of the housework some days, saying she was ill. He gave a bit of an unsteady laugh and told Pa that if the Lord chose to take her from him, he would now be able to survive on his own. Then he said something that I will never forget, "You know, I hope that in the future, boys are taught to cook, clean, and mend their own clothes so that they can make the choice to live on their own instead of needing to get married". Pa told Mr Smith that he could become a swagman and walk away. I heard him reply that as tempting as that might be, he had given his word, not only to Mrs Smith, but to God, that he would love her until death parted them. He told Pa: "I have asked God on many occasions if I could walk away and God has always answered, no. He wants me to show the sort of love to her that He has shown me. I cannot fail Him in this. Love isn't about feeling happy all the time but it's about what I do, after all, Jesus wasn't happy about going to the cross, was He? Otherwise, He wouldn't have asked God to take the cup from Him in the garden. It was Him loving us that kept Him on that cross. This is my cross, and I will bear it, just as Jesus bore His for me. I understand that God will allow some people to walk away from such a situation. He doesn't stop loving them just because they do. I know that for certain, but He doesn't want me to leave, and I am willing to stay but please Joe, pray for me because I need extra grace from God to be able to live with such a miserable wife".

It wasn't until Mr Smith had left that I realised that Joey was working quietly around the corner and probably heard the whole conversation as well.

❧❧

Mrs Jones came to dinner again. Joey wasn't very pleased and was almost rude to her. Pa asked him what was wrong, but Joey just said nothing.

Mrs Jones didn't come to lunch today and somehow the day didn't feel as good. I hadn't realised how much I looked forward to having another lady around to talk to. Joey seemed to be grumpy every day this week.

Pa told us after dinner that he was going to marry Mrs Jones. Joey left the table and walked outside. Pa snapped at him and told him to come back inside but he didn't obey him. That's the first time Joey has ever defied Pa. Pa shook his head and went into the parlour and picked up his Bible. I went in to see if he was alright. He looked at me and asked me if I knew what was upsetting Joey. I told him that I thought he might be afraid that Mrs Jones was going to change everything like Mrs Smith did and make us all unhappy. He said that he probably should have talked to us more about things.

❧❧

Joey seemed a bit happier this morning. After he left for school, I mentioned to Pa that he appeared to be happier. He told me that he was able to talk to him about why he was marrying Mrs Jones during milking. Pa said that he apologised for not talking to him about something that was so important to him. The question just came out without me even thinking about it. "So why are you marrying Mrs Jones?". He poured a cup of tea for himself and me and told me to sit down at the table. He then explained that farming was such a dangerous occupation that it was important to make sure that there was another adult around for Emma and Patrick in case something happened to him. It wouldn't be fair to expect me to look after them even though he knew I would. He also added that he had grown to love her in a different way to the way that he had loved Ma. He also told me that he has asked Mrs Jones to come to dinner on Saturday so she can explain how she feels about being part of our family as well. I'm starting to realise that there are many different types of love. After all, I have grown to love Patrick even though I still blame him for taking my mother away.

Mrs Jones arrived at morning-tea time. Pa asked me to fix morning tea in the parlour. We all gathered in there and Mrs Jones talked to us, particularly Joey, saying that she knew that it was hard to have someone else come into a family. She told us that she had been married before, but her husband had been in the army and had died overseas two months after their wedding. She didn't have children of her own. She had asked God to find her someone to love again, and she had grown to love Pa since Ma had died. It wasn't the same as she had loved her first husband either and you never forget people you have loved and lost just as Pa wouldn't be able to forget the love that he had for Ma. She also told us that Ma had asked her to look after us all when she knew that she was going to die. She told Joey that it wouldn't be the same as having his own mother around, but she wanted him to see her as someone he could talk to when he wanted to get a different perspective on a problem. She even promised not to change any of the furniture in any part of the house other than the bedroom that she would share with Pa. I asked her what she was going to do with the things that were in her house. She told us that she would sell most of them, but the special things would stay packed away until we said that it was alright for her to put them out. Suddenly, I thought about the things in my bottom drawer, they are being put aside so that when I make my home, I will have things that I like and that reflect things I love. I also remembered what Mrs Jones had said when she had found me crying while Ma was sick. She had said that Pa was a man and didn't get things unless he was told. I think I need to talk to Joey because he is now very much a man, albeit a young one and probably needs to be told these things as well.

ๆ๛ๆ๛

I found Joey in the shed doing some woodwork. I asked him what he was making. He told me that he was making some *animals to add to Emma's Nativity and some toys for Patrick. I asked him how he would feel if Emma had to go and stay with another family and wasn't allowed to put her special Nativity out at Christmas time. He looked so angry that I thought he was going to explode. I then explained that Mrs Jones was offering to hide all the things that she loved just to make us happy which was much the same thing. He looked stunned, so I walked away to let him think about it.*

Again, Mary stopped reading. How often had she put her own dreams and desires on hold or hidden them because they hadn't fitted in with the desires of her family or farming life. Some things were just not practical no matter how much you want them to be. Holidays were something that the family hadn't done very often and if they did, they were only for a few days because the animals still needed to be looked after. They were able to go away for longer periods once the children were old enough to look after the animals but that meant that the family could not all go away together. Someone had to stay home to feed the livestock. How many times had she looked forward to picking vegetables for dinner only to find that a cow had knocked down the gate and trampled all over everything? There were the times when one of the children had left the gate open and the sheep had eaten everything or, during the droughts, the kangaroos had just jumped the fences looking for something to fill their empty bellies. Even something as simple as welcoming guests at her front door was out of the question, simply because, on farms, everyone came to the back door. That was where everyone pulled up their vehicles, so they entered the house through the kitchen door. It was just too impractical to ask them to walk around to the front door. Dirt, dust, and mud accumulated in the kitchen, making her uncomfortable when people came to visit, not that it happened very often.

In the early days she had ranted and cried, making sure that John knew how disappointed she was, but he had just kept saying that it was part and parcel of farming life and we needed to keep going. So, she had buried her hurts but also learnt that plants have an incredible ability to keep growing even after all such disasters. She had eventually decided that she needed to be more like the plants and keep growing. It was about that time that she decided that routine was a good thing because it meant that everyone knew what and when things had to be done. If things were done in a constant routine, there was less chance of things going wrong. She hadn't been right of course, but it hadn't stopped her from sticking to the program. She had found comfort in the pattern and it had, on more than one occasion, given her an excuse to duck out of some social engagement or say no to some excursion or other that she wasn't interested in or didn't have the money for. The thing that had surprised her was that John had gone along with it. He was a farmer and thrived on the chaos of farming. People look at farming and think that it's a very routine occupation, but it isn't. It's more about doing what must be done as the most important job for the day. If the flies get into the sheep, then they must be dealt with regardless of what other plans the farmer might have had for that day. If you get enough rain, then sowing comes to the top of the list. If there is a drought, feeding animals is a top priority. They had talked about her need for routine, a few times, particularly after he got sick. The routine of taking medicine and regular treatments really got to him, he hated it. She had asked him why he had allowed her to tie everything down to the routine if he didn't like it? His response was that it had helped her cope with a very difficult lifestyle and, while she was coping, he could cope better with the farm work, knowing that she was more settled. She thought back to one conversation.

'You know because you were having such a hard time coping, I asked God to show me what else I could do if we sold the farm. You getting into the routine thing helped you cope, which meant that I had so many years of doing what I really loved.'

'But it seems to have got out of hand, I can't seem to quit now.'

'Honey, just do what we did with the children, we patiently waited for them to get through their stages. Remember, God is patient, very patient, and always loves us, warts and all. Somehow, He will help you to relax more and show you how to become the cheerful person you once were. I'm sorry that farming has taken that away from you, but I still love you and pray constantly for healing for you.'

'You really didn't talk about how things worked back then. Maybe if you had it might have been easier to adjust.'

'Your dad had to remind me several times that you were a town girl and that I shouldn't expect you to understand, I was still very dismissive of your opinions. It took me a long time to put into action the lesson of that Sunday lunch.'

'The one where I didn't cook what you requested?'

'Yep, and the big fight we had over Julie.'

'Yeah, that one was a doozy.'

'God showed me that night that Julie would have been the wrong partner for me because when I got home, you were still there waiting for me. God whispered to me that Julie and her family always did things differently on their farm. So, she would have found it harder to do things the way I wanted, particularly as I would never feel the need to explain things to her because she always lived on a farm, besides, she would have run away, you always knew that's how she dealt with things. He told me He had chosen well for me.'

'I don't think even Julie's parents understood how badly she wanted to leave farming.'

'What would have happened if I really hadn't been able to cope?'

'If you hadn't.... then I would have found something else to do so we could move closer to town. I don't think I could've coped with living right in town though. I know that it meant that we didn't get to spend a lot of time together as a family, however, there were some weeks when I would ask God to send me rain, not for the farm, but so I could spend time with you and the kids.'

'But you could have just taken time out and spent it with us.'

'Yes, but rain not only meant that I could take time off, it also broke your routine, which meant that we could spend time together, particularly at weekends.' Now that she looked back and thought about it, it was surprising how many wet weekends they had. God and John did seem to have a special type of relationship.

'That was one of the reasons I didn't ask you to do too much on the farm, it helped to know that the kids and you were getting things done that my chaos would not allow. It was nice to be able to come home and leave the chaos outside.'

I had a real gem of a husband, I know that, I realise that there a very few men that would be so accommodating.

Returning to the diary she continued to read.

Mrs Jones came for lunch again today. It was nice to have her
back and she arrived early enough to help me get lunch ready.
When I said that it wasn't proper, she laughed and said it was
time she got used to working in the kitchen seeing she was
marrying Pa next Saturday. We are having Christmas lunch
with the Jackson's this year which is a good thing with the
wedding happening so close. It seems that it will be our
families turn again next year, as I don't think Mrs Smith will
want to host a lunch at her home. We were talking about the
wedding when Joey came in. He asked Mrs Jones if he could
talk to her. She smiled and asked him if he wanted me to leave,
he said no, but told her that if she wanted to change some
things around after she married Pa it would be alright with
him but hoped it wouldn't look too different. He looked at her
and asked something that I hadn't thought about, he wanted to
know what we should call her after she married Pa as he would
feel uncomfortable calling her Ma or Mrs Campbell and it was
improper to call her by her first name whatever that was.
Smiling she said that it was Sarah but looking at me she said
that we could called her Mon, it was the short form of her
middle name, Monique. She suggested that it would sound
respectful enough to others, but we would know the real
meaning of the name. Joey nodded and said that he was
happy with that. Sarah looked like she was going to hug him
but shook his hand instead and thanked him. When he had
left, she told me that she wouldn't be changing things around
until there was a reason to do so. I'm not real sure what she
meant by that, but I guess I will find out later. We will be only
wearing our Sunday best clothes on Saturday. There just isn't

enough money for new clothes. I decided that I would go and ask Mrs Jackson about helping me find some nice wildflowers for the parlour since the rose on the fence isn't flowering very well at the moment, the weather is too hot.

9

Pa married Mrs Jones today. It was very similar to the wedding of Mr and Mrs Smith. It was small with only a few people there and a quick lunch afterwards. There was one thing that was very different though, Mrs Jones looked like what I thought a bride should look like. She was happy, smiling and looked radiant, even Pa looked happy. I remember him looking at Ma in much the same way. Mrs Jackson had helped me find some wildflowers during the week and this morning I went out and picked some. I made some up for Sarah to hold just like I had seen in my dream. They didn't look as good, but they still helped her look like the bride I saw in my dream only Sarah wasn't wearing a white dress it was pale blue. Pa asked Joey to hold the wedding ring for him until it was time to put it on Mon's finger and I got to hold the flowers she was holding. When the preacher told Pa that he could now kiss his new bride, I waited to see how this would go. Pa, because he is taller than Mon, bent down and kissed her full on the mouth. It was gentle, respectful, and beautiful. Mon kissed him back raising her hand to caress the side of Pa's face. My stomach flipped; it was so different to the way Mrs Smith had behaved at her wedding. I realised that I had been holding my breath as I relaxed and started breathing again. I think Pa and Mon are going to be ok.

Mary wasn't surprised that Joe had married so quickly after the death of Rose, because history told her that many men with young children remarried within a few months of being widowed in order to have someone to care for them.

Everyone left around two o'clock so they could get their cows milked and chores done. Mon went into Pa's bedroom,

241

changed her clothes, and came out to the kitchen to help get tea ready. It was work as usual with extra food needed for tomorrow as we are having some people over for lunch. It's nice that its beginning to feel like it did when Ma was alive again. I just realised that I haven't got anything to give Mon for Christmas and its only four days away. I will pray about what to do after I go to bed tonight, but I can't imagine how He is going to answer this one.

❧❧❧

This is the second Christmas since my strange one. So again, I am waiting to see if I remember everything tomorrow. There were some small gifts at our places on the kitchen table when we got up this morning. It seems like this will be our new tradition and I quite like it. God answered my prayer for something to give Mon. I felt the need to go and visit Mrs Jackson yesterday and while I was there, I told her that I had been praying about what to give Sarah for Christmas and that so far God hadn't answered, and time was running out. She told me to go with her to the washhouse and there were a number of plants in tins. She told me to pick one and give it to Mon. They were Apricot trees that she had managed to grow from the seeds out of some fruit that friends had given them. When I told her that I should be paying for it she said to take it as a thank you gift for the books that I had made the twins for their birthdays. She said that she had been praying all year for a way to say thank you in a special way. When I got home, I found some nice red material that Ma had put in the box in the kitchen, and I wrapped it around the tin. Sarah loved it and said that it would be a nice tree to mark her arrival at 'Campbelldown Farm'.

Goodness, Mary thought, she hadn't realised that the farm had a name, and this was the first time that it was mentioned. She realised with a start that she had been so engrossed in the diary that she had missed lunch and that she really was quite hungry.

After having eaten, Mary returned to the diary and finished reading about Christmas day.

I got thinking about Mrs Jackson's prayer. It took nearly a year for God to answer it. It seems that sometimes we have to wait a long time for answers, yet by waiting, we find that more than one prayer gets answered.

We had a wonderful time with the Jackson's with plenty of conversation. Mr and Mrs Smith didn't come but this year Daniel and his father did. Mr Renshaw looks frail and needs a walking stick to get around. We knew that Terry Burns' baby girl, Betty, had died from diphtheria a while back. It's one of the many diseases that claims a lot of lives. It seems that Mrs Smith blames God. Mr Jackson said that Mr Smith had asked him to pray for her as she was very bitter because God didn't answer her prayer for the child to get better. Sometimes it seems that God's answer is 'No'.

I found it hard to concentrate on the conversation during dinner as I was so aware of Daniel sitting at the other end of the table. Thank goodness Mrs Jackson didn't sit us next to each other. I would have been a complete mess. I have known this man all my life and yet, I swear it was like meeting a complete stranger for the first time. My middle just went all funny and I seemed to have lost control of my eyes, they kept looking at him. Pa, who was sitting across the table from me, gave me a stern look a couple of times which means that he must have noticed that my eyes repetitively strayed in Daniel's direction. He didn't say anything on the way home so I guess I will be spoken to later. I didn't mean to be rude I just couldn't help it. Daniel caught me looking at him once, not long after the meal started, but from then on, made a point of not looking at me. He concentrated on making conversation with everyone else at the table and ignored me for the duration. I guess he doesn't like me. It is probably a good thing because I still want to find out what else is out there in the world. It appears that once Mr Jackson's twelve-month lease is up, Daniel will be returning home to work the farm for himself. Mon told Daniel that once he returns, he should come to dinner at least twice a week. Mr Renshaw thanked her, that way he would know that he would be getting a couple of proper meals a week. Daniel said that he had learnt how to cook while he was living in town. His landlady had taught him after he had told her of his intention to one day move back to the farm to work it by himself. It seems that she had asked him if he had a wife picked out, and when he said no, she had insisted on teaching him how to cook. She had reduced his board to make up for his working in the kitchen. The other boarders had thought it was silly and had made fun of him, but Daniel didn't seem to mind. Still Mon insisted and he agreed. Now I really want to leave home. I don't want to be seeing him twice a week when he doesn't want anything to do with me.

I had that part of the dream again where I visit the hospital. I noticed that there were no warnings on any of the doors saying that the people were suffering from diphtheria. I wonder if sometime in the future this nasty cruel disease will no longer exist. I spoke to Mon today about going to town next year to get a job. She asked me what sort of work I had in mind. I realised that I had no idea what I could do other than help on the farm which means that all I would be able to do is clean houses. I told her that I wanted to write stories one day. While she told me that she understood that I had dreams, real life means that dreams often have to stay just that, dreams. As women we are given the job of being a helpmeet for men and it's up to us to find a way to work out our dreams within those boundaries. If you want to write stories, then do what Mr Jackson does, write them for Emma and Patrick but don't expect to have them published or make money out of them. I don't understand how she could say something like that when she spent so much time being a lady of independent means.

I do have other dreams as well. I see black and white pictures of the great houses my ancestors came from. They left their homes to come to New South Wales to start over, but I want to go back and see where they lived and walk the halls of the houses that they lived and worked in. I want to actually touch and see the stone walls, inside walls, tapestries, and flower gardens in real living colour. Somehow, I believe, that in order to understand myself better I need to find out about my past. It's not something that Pa talks about much and sadly, I don't think he knows very much about how or why his family came *to New South Wales. As for Ma's family, well we will never know now as she is no longer here to even ask.*

Oh, my goodness Mary thought, she had forgotten that before federation, the eastern side of the country was known as New South Wales. That area was now governed by three full states, Queensland, New South Wales and Victoria and the Capital Territory. Some of it makes up half of the state of South Australia and the Northern Territory. Mary could understand the feelings of this long-time ago Mary. She too had always wanted to go back in time herself and find out about her past, which apparently, she did and wasn't aware of it. Having finished diary number two she turned to the last one. It seemed a little thicker than the others.

10

Mary noticed that there was an address written in the front cover of the third diary and wondered what the significance of it was. It was hard to make out but appeared to be an address in Dubbo.

There have been several times since Christmas Day when I wondered what it would be like to be married to Daniel. I daydream about cosy conversations in front of the fire. Of being cuddled up together in a warm bed at night. Walking around the farm in the late evening when it's cooler in Summer.

෴෴෴෴

I'm sitting in the tearoom of a train station writing, not sure what to do next. I have enough money for a cup of tea and that's it, there is nothing left. I feel miserable, I miss Joey, Emma, and Patrick so much that it hurts but I'm too embarrassed to go home. I know Pa and Mon will be upset with me. After all, I disappeared without telling them where I was going. However, I did leave a note telling them that I was looking for work that would enable me to explore the world. I guess Pa must be worried about me, but then he has been so busy lately and when he has got spare time, he spends it with Sarah. They will sit in the parlour for hours and talk. It was nice to hear him laughing again but it was almost as if he had forgotten that I was around. The notice in the newspaper asking for someone to look after their children while they travel overseas seemed like a wonderful answer to my prayers. I didn't talk to anyone about it because I was so sick of everyone, even Joey, telling me that the idea of going away was stupid. All I did was pack some of my clothes and wrote the address down in the front of my diary, walked into town and caught the coach to Dubbo.

এওঙ্গএও

A cold wind is blowing outside, and it looks like it's going to rain soon. I know I can't stay here near the fire burning in the grate for too much longer. The conductor will be back soon, and he will tell me to move on if I'm not going to buy a ticket. He might even get a Policeman to come and take me away. How am I going to stay dry out on the streets all night? I don't have enough money to buy a ticket to the nearest station to home anyway. All I can do is pray and pray hard. God what do I do!? I remember the story of the Prodigal Son and how he had to decide to return home and ask his father to forgive him. Unlike the son in the Bible, I didn't take anything from my family when I left. I just walked away, yes, I have looked back several times and there are times when I really want to turn around and head back home, but I also want to see the world. I just couldn't see how it was going to happen if I just stayed home and waited. Daniel wasn't any help. All he talked about was how good it was to be back on the farm and the plans he had for the place. When I talked about wanting to go away, he made me feel silly. It wasn't what he said, he never had much to say to me, but he'd laugh, not loudly, just quiet giggles and he would have a look on his face that seemed to indicate that what

I was talking about was silly, stupid, or just plain madness. It's going to be dark outside soon and I have nowhere to go. Oh God please show me what to do. If I get home safely, I promise that I will stay home forever and look after Pa and Mon. God I really want to see other places, but I will try to put my selfish dreams away and just be happy where you want me to be. It's so hard to trust God to make things happen when the odds seemed to be stacked against it.

Mary noticed that the writing on this page was blotchy, it didn't take much imagination to realise that Mary would have been crying while she had written these words. She herself understood how hard it was to give up dreams that you have held close to your heart since childhood. Yes, she had wanted to travel. Maybe dreams were also stimulated by genetics. She had wanted to touch the walls of castles that had stood for hundreds of years. See paintings that covered the ceilings and walls of Cathedrals, walk through gardens that had been planted centuries ago. There was something majestic about seeing buildings and gardens that had withstood the parade of time. She was in awe of the skills and labour that made such incredible structures. There were old buildings in Australia, and she had visited some of them, but by comparison they were new buildings. The oldest buildings still standing were only around a couple of hundred years old, not three, four or more like the ones overseas.

She thought about all the dreams that she had let go of during her life. She realised that, looking back, many of them really didn't matter that much now. It was funny though, the ones she had grieved for the most were the small dreams. The ones that she didn't think would be that hard to achieve. Probably the hardest one had been her garden. She had wanted a nice formal flower garden, which didn't seem to be that hard to achieve when her and John had got married. After all, the house was fenced in nicely, it wasn't big, making it all seem so doable with the right amount of work. Yet, it didn't matter how hard she worked every time it started to look nice something would happen, either it would stop raining, rain too much, or one of the children would leave the gates open and the stock would destroy months of hard work in a few minutes. The other problem was, of course, that no one, including her, got to enjoy it as no one ever went out into that part of the yard. In the end she had given up on having a flower garden, spending any spare time sewing or knitting for the children. I guess she really hadn't been surprised that Rose had only one flowering plant in her garden, life on the land was tough on women. You couldn't afford to be delicate, you had to be made of steel otherwise the elements would break you and often did in the end. After all, Rose didn't appear to be that old when she had died after having Patrick.

The big dreams, the impossible ones, the ones that you knew were going to take a miracle from God, well they were easier to let go of when they didn't work out. This was because she had truly believed that God had her best interests in mind when He said 'No'. She remembered a time when a trip had fallen through. Yes, she had been disappointed, but at the time when she would have been away on the trip, her daughter had suddenly taken very ill. She was able to be there for her instead. There were other times when, by staying home, they had missed being in the middle of some natural disaster. One time, being a cyclone and another flooding. It amazed her how many times that had happened. Would she have liked to have still been able to do those, yes, of course, but here she was, they hadn't happened, and her life had still been good without them. There were some prayers that had been answered, of course, but the answers had usually surprised her.

No one knows what the future holds for them, only God knows that, and as hard as it had been for her to learn, she had found that it was better to let go of her dreams and trust that God knew more than she did. Mind you, she had shed lots of tears and expressed her anger during the process and while others had called her childish, she didn't see that it was wrong. It had helped her to let go. She thought about her granddaughter, Susan, and realised that she had a much tougher time in life than she had. So much was expected of her. Yes, their generation had been confined, belittled even, by the rules and expectations of society. She knew many women who had hated it. The belittlement of anyone was wrong, she agreed, but what was expected of Susan's generation was incredible. Modern women were expected to be mothers, housekeepers, volunteer workers, make a contribution to the economy by working in some form of paid situation, and then they were also expected to make sure they put time aside to look after themselves. Of course, some were lucky enough to have good partners, like Susan's Greg, who were willing to pitch in and help with the housework. Watching that man swing the vacuum cleaner around the house is hilarious. He creates his own comedy show with it and the kids think it's great. He also looks after the children so Susan can do some things for herself. Mind you, Susan's paid employment was carried out at home, so she is one of the lucky ones, but Mary knows that there are many women who have to carry on by themselves as single parents even though they are married because they are not only looking after children but husbands as well.

The other problem with dreams was, of course, that they don't always live up to their own expectations. A holiday at the beach usually meant kids screaming from blue bottle stings or sunburn or even worse, driving her crazy because the weather wasn't suitable for the beach and they were couped up inside. It was always harder to find them things to do as they were in unfamiliar surroundings. Even trips inland didn't always deliver the scenery that websites and postcards said were available. As for that new lounge that she had dreamed about for so long, well it didn't take long for rodents and children to wreck it. In order, to save it from becoming completely destroyed it had to be covered all the time and she only enjoyed it when she washed the covers.

She made herself a cuppa before she read on.

It's been a couple of days since I was sitting in the train station tearoom. I was sitting at a small table with my head down writing in my diary when I heard someone call, 'Mary!'. Mary is a fairly common name, but I couldn't help but look up. There standing in the doorway was Daniel. He moved really fast to stand in front of me. As I watched him coming towards me, I thought I saw a look of concern on his face, but it disappeared so quickly that I'm not sure if it was real or not. I asked him about it later while we were eating our tea, but He said that he didn't care about me he just wanted to make sure that I didn't run away again. However, I had been too surprised to move. I asked him what he was doing there. He said that he was looking for me. He had enough money for us to spend the night in town before we returned home. It was so nice to be able to sleep in a proper bed when I had been contemplating spending the night on the streets in the cold. Pa and Mr Jackson were minding his farm while he came looking for me. He told me that Pa wanted to come looking for me straight away, but he had convinced them to let him go instead. He had a feeling that I was headed to Dubbo and he had sent a telegram to a friend asking them to find me and keep an eye on me from a distance to make sure no harm came to me. He was hoping that, by waiting a few days I would get the travelling thing out of my system. What he said made me angry. Well, that was an indication that I was just a pest to him. He has just proved that he has no idea or even cares how important my dreams are to me. All he cares about are his dreams for the farm. He is the only male around who is available as a husband and he doesn't give me a second thought. Why is what I want not important to him or anyone else for that matter? I guess it's simple, I'm not important to him at all. I guess this is another dream I have to give up. We travelled home in silence. I was so angry that I couldn't speak. It took us two days to get home and the silence made it a long journey, but Daniel didn't seem to want to talk to me anyway. I keep asking God if my future is really going to be this lonely. I can only hope that God is going to bring a stranger into my life to be my husband.

I talked to God a lot though, not out loud, I wouldn't want Daniel to hear what I was telling God. I even asked Him if my dreams were important to Him, could I really be dreaming about doing the wrong thing all the time? If God made us, why did He give us dreams about things that were wrong. I even asked God if I was important to Him or did, He treat women the same way that men do? Were we really just created to be slaves to men?

When I got home, I expected Pa to give me a real talking to, but all he did was give me a hug. He shook Daniel's hand, who then turned on his heels and went home. Mon made me a cup of tea, Emma gave me the biggest hug, but Joey stood back and looked as if he could kill me. I guess he is angry at me for running away. Pa said later that he was just so relieved that I was ok. It was late, he told me to get some sleep and we would talk later. I'm sure not looking forward to that conversation. I guess it was the strain of sitting next to Daniel without him speaking to me for two days that made me feel suddenly really tired, I must have nearly been asleep before my head hit the pillow.

While I was helping Mon get breakfast the next morning, I asked her about what God expected of us as women. Were we allowed to have our own dreams? Did He give women dreams and then ask us to sacrifice them just as Abraham was asked to sacrifice Isaac only without providing the substitute? Mon suggested that we pray and read our Bibles over the next couple of days because she really didn't have an answer for me.

❧❧❧

One thing was certain, when we read various passages in the Bible, men and women were equal in God's sight. Even though God wanted us to be subject to our husbands we were still equal. Mon suggested that sometimes God might have to say no to our dreams simply because someone that was part of that dream was saying no to God. However, she also said that if that was the case then God would give us something better in its place because He loves us and doesn't want us to miss out on His grace. We might just have to wait a bit longer. It seems to me that not very many men loved their wives in the way the Bible said they should in Ephesians 5:25. They seem more interested in having everything they want.

Today, I met Mr Jackson's younger brother, Anthony. He is about my age and told me that he likes to be called Tony. He had been spending some of his holidays with them. The Jackson's had asked us over to their place for Sunday lunch. He works as a clerk for a solicitor in the city. He talked about his dream to be a solicitor one day. It would mean lots of study. He asked me about what I wanted to do and when I told him that I wanted to write a book and travel he told me that he thought that would be a great thing to do. He seemed to be nice. He told me that women are starting to do all sorts of things in the city. Some were doctors even; he believed that women were capable of a lot more than just running a home. Women like Florence Nightingale, Caroline Chisholm, and Elizabeth Kenny had made the world a much better place. His own mother had set up a school for poor kids in the city. She worked there all day, five days a week and still managed to make sure that the home was run properly. She worked really hard, he said, she got up about five in the morning to make sure that the servants knew what they had to do for the day, and she was often still working at ten o'clock in the evening. I told him that they were my normal hours too. I told him about Ma teaching Mrs Jackson to read before she died. He said there were still a lot of women who were not getting a proper education. There are three boys in the family, the oldest Andrew was working with their father and would one day take on the business, John had always wanted to go farming, so when he had married Martha, their father had helped him to follow his dream and because John loved Martha, their parents had given their blessing on the marriage, even though she had not had the same social privileges. What an extraordinary family. He asked Pa if he could call on me while he is staying with his brother. He will only be here for a couple of weeks, but I like him. I hoped to be able to write to him in the city when he goes back.

Tony managed to talk Pa into letting me go to work in the city. I'm going to train as a nurse. Pa talked to Mr Jackson, Tony's brother and he assured Pa that the family would look after me, they had connections with a small hospital where I would be able to train. I'm so excited. I dream of being able to see Tony every day and carry on our talks. Walking in the park with him on Saturdays and Sundays after attending Church. I can imagine walking into church on his arm and having people around us making very quiet comments on what a nice-looking couple we make. Mon is helping me to make some new clothes and we are adjusting some of her very nice, colourful dresses to fit me. She says that she will no longer need them as they were not really suitable for life on the farm. She didn't seem sad about it though. I would be, because they are beautiful.

11

Life in the city is not all that I thought it would be. The rules and regulations are very strict, the hours are very long, and the work is hard. I only get a few hours off on Sunday. So much for the dreams of walking out with Tony each weekend. I haven't seen him since I arrived here, but I am learning a lot about nursing and I have found that I do actually enjoy it. I wrote to Tony, telling him how much I was enjoying nursing and how I wanted to be a matron someday. I was bold enough to suggest that even if I was to marry, I would be careful to hide the fact so I could keep working, as I really wasn't that keen on having children, since all they do is cause women to die young. I was surprised that I didn't receive a reply and after a couple of months I stopped writing. There was a voice somewhere in my head that told me that he had only told me the things that I wanted to hear. I pushed the thoughts down and still dreamed of being his wife one day. The one thing that I really missed though, is not be able to watch the stars at night.

There was a lot of short entries in this diary, giving credence to the many comments about her exhaustion.

I got called to the Matron's office today. It seems that Pa has written a letter to Matron asking that I be given a whole weekend off. The family wants to visit me, and they needed to ask permission from Matron for me to spend time with them. I get to have some time off in a couple of weeks.

It was a wonderful weekend with Pa, Mon, Joey, Emma, Patrick, and Daniel. I was really surprised to see Daniel with my family. It appears that Mr Jackson offered to look after all the farms for the weekend so everyone could get away. That is a lot of work, so many cows to be milked each day while they are away. Getting to the city means travelling for two days, then they spent two days exploring. We strolled around the city, looking at the new buildings. Daniel seemed to be very impressed by the craftmanship that went into the buildings. We had tea and cakes in a Tea Shop. While we were there, a couple of young ladies were talking about how one of them had travelled overseas as a companion to a spinster aunt. She was telling her friend about all the old buildings that she had seen on her journey. She was speaking so loudly, which attracted some very disapproving looks from other patrons in their vicinity. Daniel was sitting closest to her and as I watched his face, I saw his interest growing. I'm not sure if it was the girl he was interested in or the places that she had visited.

Matron handed me a letter as I was leaving work. I was really surprised to discover that it was from Daniel. It was very general in its tone, talking about how things were going at the farm.

Mary turned the page to discover that the letter had been put in as part of the book. She was able to read exactly what Daniel had written. She could see that he was trying to reach out to her Mary. He mentioned the trip and commented on how impressed he was with the architecture.

As she continued to read, it appeared that Daniel had written to Mary at least once a week for about six months. She noticed that sometimes he did express an interest in seeing the world and being able to see some of the ancient buildings that he had heard about on their visit to the city.

She continued to read the few entries and the letters. She noticed that Daniel gradually started to share his feelings about things that happened on the farm. After six months she noticed that he started to even share his feelings and thoughts about things that happened with his family, particularly his father's health issues and friends. As she continued to read his letters, she was starting to see his feelings grow for Mary.

In amongst all these entries there was one that intrigued Mary.

It was my afternoon off today, Judy Brown and I went for a walk. We ended up in a park and decided to just sit down and rest awhile. We decided that it would be fun to watch those from the social set parade the gardens. We quietly commented on the various dresses and dreamed about being able to afford some of their creations. As we were watching, I noticed a man who seemed to be familiar, even though he was a long way away, I realised that it was Tony Jackson. He was smiling and paying a lot of attention to a young lady, dressed in a very stylish green velvet outfit. She seemed to find what Tony was saying very absorbing. Even from that distance it seemed that these two young people were very much in love. I felt as if someone had slapped me. I sat there transfixed, watching them for what seemed like ages. Suddenly, Judy playfully poked me in the side. She had been talking to me and I hadn't heard a word she had said. She looked at me and asked what was wrong. I quickly looked at her and replied, nothing and suggested that it was time for us to walk back to the hospital. Judy looked around trying to work out what I was upset about and spotted Tony and his girl. The thing was, she had no idea that I knew Tony and had once dreamed about walking out with him.

'Oh, don't those two, look sweet together.'

'Yes, I guess, let's go home' I replied in what I hoped was my most cheerful voice, praying that Judy didn't catch on as to how hurt I was feeling.

❧❧❧❧

It seemed Mary was into her third year of being a nurse when there were several entries that indicated that Mary wasn't feeling very well but continued to work until it was apparent that she wasn't able to work any longer.

Matron allowed me to stay in bed yesterday and when I still wasn't any better this morning, she asked the doctor to visit me.

He told matron that I wouldn't get better living in the city and suggested that I should go home to recover. Matron decided that if that was the case, I would no longer be suitable for nursing. She is sending a telegram to Pa asking him to come and fetch me. I wonder if Pa will come or if he will send Daniel again.

కావ్యావ

I was wrong! Tony Jackson arrived at the hospital this morning. I hadn't seen Tony for almost a year now not even from a distance. When the message arrived, Mr Jackson, our neighbour was visiting Pa, and suggested that Tony bring me home in his horseless carriage. It would mean that the journey home would be much quicker which was important as I am so ill, and the weather is so cold. Tony had me wrapped up in some blankets and a couple of hot water bottles, although I knew they would be cold in a short space of time, they did help to make me feel warm for part of the journey.

కావ్యావ

It was during the journey home that I realised that Tony wasn't really interested in me as a potential wife at all. In fact, I've decided that he was only saying things that he thought would impress me, which they did of course. He went on and on about how his future wife, it appears he is engaged to a Miss Anderson, would be able to mix with those in high society. I felt very embarrassed about the way I had thought that he was really interested in me, but I also realised that I didn't love him either. Maybe it was the way he had pretended to be in favour of women working, just to get my attention, that had hoodwinked me. When I asked about how his betrothed would be able to make her way in the world, he laughed and said that she would never need to do that and that her job was to make him look good to his peers. He even said that he didn't care what she did during the day. He would give her his schedule at the beginning of the week, and he expected her to make sure that they looked like a very happy couple. Oh, my goodness, how could I have been so blind! He didn't want a wife; he wanted a gold-leafed ticket to society's elite. I wondered if Miss Anderson really wanted to be married or just her freedom. His family seemed to so unconventional in their thinking. Like accepting Martha, without the same background. He went on to say that his fiancé's family would be gifting them a large home, so they would occupy a floor each, with staff and all. I was shocked at just how shallow and pretentious he was. I even felt a little sorry for Miss Anderson and when I suggested that it didn't sound like a very loving marriage, he just shrugged and declared that they both would get what they wanted. He was working for her father so money wouldn't be a problem, that meant that she got to live in the style to which she was accustomed, and he got be who he wanted to be with social respectability. Somehow, I got the feeling that he wasn't talking about being a solicitor. I told him that I had seen them in the park about a year ago and that they looked very much in love. He looked at me and asked, you were convinced? I nodded and he just muttered, well if we fooled you, we should be able to carry it off. I asked him what his family thought of this and wouldn't he be expected to produce an heir. He just laughed and said that Jane had an older brother who would carry on the family name and John had already produced the heir for his parents who didn't care what each member of the family did as long as they didn't cause humiliation. That's why they weren't worried about John and Martha, they lived in the bush and very rarely visited the city. Suddenly, I was grateful that he had discarded me. I was thankful that our final encounter made me see the truth and grateful that it allowed me to get home. Right then I felt as if I didn't want to leave the farm ever again, the real world was a crazy place. I didn't even cry.

Mary sighed; well, her Mary had really grown up. Nursing had taught her a few things about the world, it seemed. She continued to read.

I have only been home a couple of weeks and I am beginning to feel a lot better. I spent the first week in bed, but Mon's good care and chicken soup seems to have worked. It was just fortunate that we had a few spare chooks to kill. I still get tired quickly, but I am able to help Mon a lot more. She is still letting me rest more than I am used to. However, it appears that Pa is now suffering from what I have. This means that for the next few weeks Daniel will be coming over to milk the cows. Pa is way too sick to even get out of bed. Mon has insisted that Daniel eat at our place, so he doesn't have to cook for himself when he has finished our milking. John Jackson came over to make sure that I was okay. I got the feeling that he knew that Tony had been leading me on and was concerned that I might still be hurting. I was able to tell him that I wasn't and realised that I really didn't care at all. He said that he knew that the way Tony was living was sinful. He is my brother and the best thing

I can do for him right now is pray. God answered my prayers for Martha, even if it took years, I know that He will answer them for Tony one day'.

৵৽৵৽

The last few weeks have been very strange. Daniel has insisted that he help with the dishes while Mon attends to Pa, Emma, and Patrick who are all sick now. So far, they have been rather silent events. Daniel doesn't say much.

৵৽৵৽

Tonight, while Daniel and I were doing the dishes I asked him how much water he had left at his place. It hasn't rained for weeks. We have plenty of tanks on our house, but I know that Daniel has only a couple. He responded by saying that at least while he was eating at our house the water in the tanks was holding up as he wasn't using any to cook his evening meal. There was still plenty of water in the well, so things were ok. He then proceeded to tell me about all the plans he had for the house. A couple more tanks, another tank above the house so he can gravity feed water down to his vegetable garden, chook yard, and dairy. He wants to have a flower garden. He asked me what flowers I liked. I told him that I liked very bright coloured ones but understood that they would die in the dry times. Ma had given up having flowers many years ago. I had

264

asked her why when I was very little, and she said that it was too hard to keep the Kangaroos and other wild animals away from them, so she settled for having the rose bush at the gate.

ঔৡ৽ঔৡ৽

Daniel is still having meals at our place several times a week, even though Pa is feeling a lot better. Pa isn't protesting about him spending so much time here. I have no idea what they talk about while they are milking the cows, but they share some funny looks around the meal table. I have a feeling that my name turns up in the conversations fairly often. He still helps with the washing up and we talk about all the things that have happened during the day. It makes these jobs so much easier to manage when you are working with someone. I love having Daniel around but I'm not sure how he feels about me. It must be lonely at the farm on his own. He still only talks about the farm, weather, and prices of produce. It has rained and the creeks and dams are filling up again. It's too cold for the grass to grow yet but when spring comes there will be moisture in the soil to help it take off.

ঔৡ৽ঔৡ৽

During our conversation tonight, I told Daniel about how I still wanted to travel. I talked about how I had been asking God to take the desire away so that I could be content where I was but that it didn't seem to be happening. I realised that life is much the same, no matter where you live. People are happy, sad, sick, or healthy because they make the most of what is around them. My heart, however, would still like to see all the places that I dream about but it's no longer the obsession that it has been up till now. What I had finally realised is that it's more important to have a loving family around you because without them it doesn't matter where you live, you will be lonely.

Daniel kissed me tonight. He was leaving to go home; I was walking out behind him to go to my room. Suddenly he turned around and kissed me. It was a very quick kiss on the cheek. He almost ran to get on his horse while I just stood rooted to the spot.

Daniel hasn't stayed for a meal for about a week now. He still helps Pa with the milking but goes home straight after finishing. I don't think I will ever understand men.

Tonight, Daniel stayed for dinner and helped with the dishes afterwards. He didn't say much while we were working but just as we were finishing up, he asked if I would go for a walk with him. The evenings are starting to lengthen but are still pretty cool. Daniel made sure that I had fetched a warm shawl before we ventured outside. The full moon was starting to rise and was sitting on the horizon, throwing enough light for us to see where we were going. I remarked how beautiful it looked but Daniel didn't seem to hear me, he seemed very distracted. We walked to where a big tree had fallen last summer, and the trunk made a wonderful bench to sit on. I often come out here to read or write in my diary when the weather allows. I asked Daniel what was wrong, because he hadn't said a word since we had left the house. He told me to sit down because he needed to talk to me. I tried to look at him, but he lent forward and put his face in his hands. I thought he was going to cry but I knew he hadn't cried since his mother had died years ago. He asked me not to interrupt him because if he didn't say what he wanted to; he would never be able to tell me what was so important to him.

Well, it turned out to be the longest speech that I have ever heard Daniel give. I have trouble remembering exactly what he said because I was so surprised. In essence he told me that he loved me, that he didn't realise how much until I got sick, and it looked like I wasn't going to get better. He explained that he had fought it because he knew that I wanted to move away. He was angry with me for wanting to explore the world and not liking farming life, particularly since it's the only thing that he can see himself doing. He now understands that there are wonderful things out there to be seen and experiencing new things will not kill him, besides, he also realises that no one knows what the future would be like. He continued to talk about all the times he had ignored me, expressed his anger, or said mean things to me because he couldn't bear to think about me not being around and finished by saying "Mary, do you think you could possibly consider loving me enough to go wherever life takes us even if it's no further than the farm?" I responded by saying yes, and in that moment, I knew that it was the truth. I love Daniel, I would be happy with him even if it was at the farm. Daniel looked up at me for the first time since we had sat down, I could see the look of surprise on his face in the moonlight as the night had closed in around us.

"Are you sure?" He must have asked that question three times. When I said "Yes" each time his face broke out into the biggest smile that I have ever seen him wear. He gave me a big hug and kissed me properly for the first time. We continued to talk about our plans until we heard the cows starting to bellow in their paddock.

Suddenly, he realised that it was time to go and milk the cows, we had been talking all night. He turned all stiff and formal on me, saying that we need to take our time and make our plans carefully, after all he wanted to make sure that his plan for his house was completed before we thought about getting married and he still had to talk to Pa. I admit that I giggled a little and said that I didn't think Pa would be the least bit surprised. He stood up and very formally escorted me back to the house. I wish I understood what made him do that and I have a funny feeling that this might be a long courtship, after all, the plans he has for the house are not going to happen in a hurry, considering he is running the farm by himself.

Mary stopped reading. She knew a little about the expectations of society up to about the 1960s when people had indulged in 'free love'. Society, until then, had expected women to behave in a proper manner and they bore the brunt of the blame if things went wrong. What of the men? She was sure that there would have been a number of young men who desired to do the correct thing when it came to being around a woman. Not all men at the time would have subscribed to the attitude that you were allowed to have your way with any woman as long as you were not planning on taking her home to meet the family or marry her. Having a stiff formal approach to women might have been one way they were able to supress their strong natural urgers. After all, birth control was not talked about in polite society and what was available wasn't always very effective.

As Mary continued through the diary, she read about the trials of planning a wedding that seem to keep being pushed into the future in order for Daniel to finish his plans for the house. There was very little mention of what the plans were, but she could feel Mary's frustration at the length of time it was taking for them to be completed. On entry read.

Pa found me today looking at the photo of Ma and himself on their wedding day. It still hangs in the parlour, with a photo of Mon and Pa on their wedding day. I have to admire Mon; she certainly isn't going to upset Joey by moving things around. I asked Pa about Ma's dress, if it was still around but he said that she, being the practical person she was, had used it for many years as a Sunday best and that it was the dress that she had been buried in. They had talked about my wedding day, what she wished for me. Pa said that she wanted me to have a new dress. You haven't had many new things so far and this is the start of a brand-new life. A new dress that could be used as a Sunday best afterwards was what she wished. Queen Victoria had made white wedding dresses popular, but Ma said that they were very impractical in a place where money and dresses were hard to come by. He told me that she had suggested pale pink as it's a colour that I look very pretty in.

❧❧❧❧

We attended Mrs Smith's funeral today. She had diphtheria. I watched both Mr Smith and her son Terry, they were quiet but really didn't look that sad. Terry's wife also seemed to be more relaxed than the last time I saw her. The children didn't cry either. They all actually looked relieved when they didn't think anyone was watching them. How sad is it, that someone could be so nasty that people, if they are honest, they are glad to see you die? I overheard Mr Smith talking to Pa when we were having the 'wake' at his house. He said, "Joe, I know that you think I was mad to stay with her, but I do believe that she made her peace with God just before she died. She opened her eyes, and I could see a real peace in them and then she squeezed my hand. It was a beautiful moment, rare but beautiful. I doubt if that would have happened if I had walked away. I would hate to think that there would be one less soul in Heaven just because I wasn't a faithful servant. He has been faithful to me and has blessed me on two fronts this day, Joe. He has seen to it that I was taught to look after myself and I am grateful to her for that, but I am also blessed because God has seen fit to relieve me of a heavy burden. I thank Him greatly for both".

෴෴

Daniel has spent nearly every day for the last six months working on the house and the garden. All the neighbours had offered their help and the work has finally come together.

Mon has been helping me to make a new dress. It is pale pink with a lace overskirt. Mon said that once we are married, I can use the lace overlay to make food covers or even a mosquito net for my baby's crib, even though I'm still not sure that I want to have children. There was certainly enough material there to be used for a few of those things. She had it sent out from the city just for my dress. By taking the lace off after I'm married, the dress becomes more practical to be worn as my Sunday best. She has sent out the invitations to all our neighbours including Mr Smith, as he is again on his own after the death of Mrs Smith a few weeks ago from Diphtheria. This time I'm sure that he will be alright on his own. His second wife was not easy to live with and made him carry out most of the housework, citing illness. However, we all knew that if she wanted to do something, she managed to get better rather miraculously. Most of the community felt sorry for him and made sure that they did everything they could to help him even when she was alive. It was all done on the quiet, however, Mrs Smith was so self-centred that she probably had no idea how much support her husband received.

Well, thought Mary, his second wife really didn't seem to be very nice anyway. No wonder her son, Terry, wouldn't marry his girl while she was living at home. She knew that the men in her family now would definitely be able to look after themselves and their families, particularly Greg, Susan's husband, if, heaven forbid, anything happened to their wives.

However, she had been surprised recently to learn that even though diphtheria was almost unheard of in Australia today, very few people would survive if they managed to get it. Mary made herself another cuppa and returned to reading.

Pa and Daniel have been killing the 'fatted calf' today as Pa calls it. He seems to be very pleased that Daniel and I are getting married next weekend. The meat will be used all this week and for the wedding on Saturday. What isn't used straight away will be salted and stored to preserve it. Pa is smiling more these days and I've even heard him laughing quite a bit. Mr Smith came over to help Pa and Daniel today as well. I had trouble believing that it was him. He was smiling and laughing, and I think that he has even put on a bit of weight again. I guess that being miserable all the time, like Mrs Smith was, has an effect on the health of those around you. I pray that I will never be like her. If I am miserable, I will try to hide it, so it doesn't make my family sick.

Tomorrow I get married to Daniel. The other night he was helping me to do the dishes, I could tell that he was angry about something. I asked him what I had done to make him so upset, because I couldn't think of anything. It turned out that the kangaroos had jumped the fence and chewed all the flowers in the garden. I told him not to worry about it. I knew that flower gardens were a waste of time in this area and that we would just have to settle for a couple of roses around the gateways the same as Ma had. I hoped that the animals wouldn't eat them on him as well.

I may not be as practical as my mother, but I have a feeling that I'm going to be learning to be from now on. I've decided that since I haven't lost my memory of any other days since that strange Christmas day three years ago that this would be a good time to stop writing. Daniel doesn't know that I completely missed that day which seems to be so long ago now. I also have a feeling that I'm not really going to have time to keep writing anyway. I will keep them in my secret drawer and if something like that happens again, well you never know I might have to take it back up.

12

It was Christmas eve again when Mary got to the last pages of the third diary. The writing had changed, there was more maturity about it. She read the first few lines and realised why.

Today is Christmas Eve, tomorrow I will be going to have lunch with my son, Joseph, at the farm. Two weeks ago, we laid Daniel to rest. It was the first time that I have seen Mon, Joey, Chloe, Emma, Paul, and their families in years. Patrick was killed in a farming accident in his youth. Joey married Chloe Goldsmith. They have only one child, a girl they called Rose, after our mother. Emma and Paul Goldsmith were married a couple of years after Joey and Chloe. They have four children, Paul, Patrick, Martha, and Jane, their youngest is getting married next year. They have four grandchildren. Another farming accident claimed Pa's life about ten years ago. I wonder if farming will always be the most dangerous way of life.

John Jackson, stooped and frail, also made it to the funeral. Martha had died a few years back and he was living with his son who owns a merchant store in town. I asked about the family and he told how proud he was of his children and that his prayers for Tony had been answered a few years back. They both found that Jesus can change their lives and they now have a real marriage.

I was feeling restless and decided to start sorting out the papers on Daniel's desk. Well, it's my desk, actually, Pa made it for my seventeenth birthday. I gave it to Daniel to use after we were married because he needed an office desk, and I didn't have time to write anyway. I needed to clean up the room that Daniel used as an office for Mon anyway. She has been living with Emma and Paul, since Pa died and now that we are both on our own, it was decided at Daniel's funeral that Mon should come and stay with me. I wonder if women will ever be able to be independent people in their own right?

As I was sorting out the papers, I remembered that Pa had put in a secret compartment in the desk. When I opened it, I discovered these diaries! I'd forgotten that I used to keep them in there. I wrapped the books in my favourite tea-towel and kept them in a hessian bag that Emma insisted she had given me for Christmas the year that I still cannot remember. I stopped sorting and skimmed through them. Daniel probably had no idea they were hidden in there all these years. I had stopped writing in them once we got married. I couldn't see the point after that because there had not been any repeats of that Christmas day that went missing. I still don't understand what happened back then and I'm pretty sure that I never will, not in this lifetime anyway.

Somehow though, it seems fitting for me to write a little bit about my life with Daniel before I put them back into the secret compartment. Maybe someone, many years from now, might find them and want to know our story.

We were married for forty years and a few months. Our two children, Sarah-Kate and Joseph were born very soon after we were married. I was terrified from the moment I knew I was going to have a baby right up to actually giving birth to Sarah-Kate. I had nightmares nearly every night. I was convinced that I was going to die. Poor Daniel, he spent many hours with me at night praying that I would have peace about the birth. Even Pa had to be enlisted, reminding me that Ma had given birth to three healthy children with no problems at all before she had Patrick. Once I looked at my baby girl after the midwife placed her in my arms, I couldn't believe the love that I felt for her, and the memories of the pain and fears already started to fade.

She is the eldest and is named after Daniel's mother and Sarah – Mon's first name. Joey, Emma, and I started calling her Mon when she married Pa. Patrick didn't know her by any other name. He was too young to understand that his mother had died shortly after he was born. It is a shortened version of her middle name, Monique. Sarah suggested it because Joey didn't want to call her Ma, since she wasn't our real mother. It would have been improper to call her by her first name. Joseph was born exactly a year after Sarah-Kate and it was a difficult labour. The doctor told Daniel that if I had any more children I would die. He arranged for me to go and stay with Mon and Pa for a couple of weeks to recover. After all, he still had to run the farm and it would be difficult to look after me and two children as well.

I arrived home after three weeks of Mon's wonderful care, only to find that Daniel had sold our marriage bed, purchased two single beds, and rearranged our bedroom. I stood in the doorway and gasped, saying "Daniel what have you done!" He sat me down, held me tight and cried. "Mary, I love you so much. I would not be able to sleep beside you every night and not make love to you. We were both young when we lost our mothers but both of us were a lot older than our children are now. I want them to have their mother around for as long as is possible, so this is the way it's going to be. I cannot risk your life; I will not risk your life. You are too precious to me and our children". So, we slept in separate beds from then on. Daniel was an all or nothing sort of man and for a while he wouldn't even touch me. Our relationship was in danger of becoming so formal that I was worried that our children would find it hard to believe that we loved each other at all. I shed so many tears and prayed so hard for weeks. I made sure that I didn't cry in front of Daniel though, because I didn't want to upset him.

However, one day he came home early and found me on my knees praying with tears because I was finding it just so hard. Daniel fell on his knees beside me and asked me what was wrong. Through tears I told him about what was worrying me. It seemed to me that we had stopped travelling together, something that he had promised me on the night that he asked me to marry him. He looked at me and for a minute he held me tight. I could feel the desire rising in him and so could he, making him pull away from me quickly. I knew he was scared, just like he had been when we had shared our first kiss. He stood up and just said that he had to go and milk the cows. I cried some more. Fear controlled our lives, and I didn't want that. A voice in my head, said, 'it's going to be alright', and I started to feel better. I even felt like singing so I stood up, washed my face, and carried on with the household duties.

That night as we finished our meal, Daniel told me that, while I did the dishes, he would put the children to bed. I gave him a grateful look; I was tired, but I knew that he was exhausted from farm work. He was gone for quite a while and I thought he must have been sitting outside in the cool air. However, he surprised me by coming back to the kitchen and helping me finish my night chores. He said that he was sorry for making

277

me feel unloved and again promised that we would travel our lives together no matter how hard it was.

For the first time in a long time, we talked about all the things that had happened during the day. It was just like the days when he had helped me before we got married. He even managed to kiss me; it was a quick one, but it was a kiss. The next morning at breakfast, Sarah-Kate did something that she hadn't done for a long time. She came up to me, put her arms around my leg, she couldn't reach any higher, hugged it and said, "I love you mummy and Da loves you too". When I asked what made her do that, she told me that when Da (her name for Daniel) had put them to bed he had told them a story about how he had met the most wonderful lady in the world and that he wanted her to be around for the rest of their lives. I had trouble seeing the pancakes I was cooking through the tears. God and Daniel had found a way to let the children know that their father loved their mother and I thanked God by singing the song Jesus loves me. God was right the day before; things were going to be alright.

After that day, things got slowly better, each night Daniel would tell the children a story as he put them to bed and then come back to the kitchen to help with the chores while we talked. I really cherished those times together. There were still times when he went out to the shed to sleep. He had set up a room with a bed for the nights when he really didn't even want to sleep in the same room as me or he needed to sleep in the barn because some animal or other was going to need him to be on hand while they delivered their own young.

Wow, Mary thought. Maybe this explains some of those very formal relationships between Victorian couples that she had heard about. She knew that some marriages were arranged and that set the formal tone right from the beginning but maybe there was another reason for many others. The reduction of the mortality rates for babies and mothers by the sixties meant that people could enjoy the physical side of love without the same fear that previous generations had to endure. The love that Daniel had shown to Mary seemed to be the sacrificial type that the Bible talked about in Ephesians 5. Mary read on.

As the children reached double figure birthdays, we'd had a couple of very good years on the farm, so Daniel decided that it was time to take a trip to England and investigate my family roots. I can still hear Daniel telling the children that visiting the Mother Land would be a great adventure. We had employed a worker to help Daniel, so we promoted him to foreman to look after the farm while we were gone. Mind you, he asked Pa to keep an eye on things as well. Daniel wasn't keen on spending three months on the boat, to start with, as it would take six weeks travelling to England and six weeks home again. However, once he was on the ship, he discovered that there was plenty of things to keep him and the children occupied. He was keeping that promise to travel our life together. We spent a wonderful three months travelling around England, Scotland and Wales showing the children our homeland. However, we spent as little time as possible in London because the air there was thick with smog.

There have been so many exciting things happening in our world. Steam trains take a lot of people at once from one city to another. Bicycles are now being used to travel longer distances instead of walking. That probably won't do our health much good, but it is certainly quicker than walking. Someone said the other day that horseless carriages will be the way to get around in the world in the future. I do vaguely remember having a dream about those. I can't imagine a world without horses to pull carts and drays. What will they do with all the horses when they don't have any work for them? There are printers that enable people to read the latest news on a paper, called newspapers. Things such as typewriters enable businesses to print letters that don't have to be written by hand, which is wonderful for people who don't have good writing skills. So many people have discovered such wonderful things about our world. Science has found ways to help improve our lifestyles in so many different ways. Of course, not all the new things are good, some are just downright scary and some I am sure are completely evil. Many people are having trouble coping with all these changes. All these things I read about being invented when I was a child and now, they are so commonplace that people have forgotten how they got along without them.

The government is now putting in place various rules and regulations that will impact our way of life in the future and I'm not sure that the farming life as we know will survive for very long. I fear that our influence on our society will be killed off by these regulations. I guess that, as long as we can continue to produce our own food, such as eggs, vegetables, milk, wheat, oats, butter, and meat we will be able to ride out most of the storms of life. I'm so glad that we don't live in the city where they are so very dependent on merchants buying food to sell through the stores. The new regulations are only going to *make food more expensive. Farming is still very hard work and going to get harder in the future no doubt.*

I'm looking forward to Mon coming to live with me next week now that we are both on our own. Especially after all the years of caring for all of us, in the good times and bad ones, and she has also given so much of her time to Emma and Paul, helping them with their children, it's time that someone made the effort to look after her. I need to show her the care and love that she has given time and time again. She never had children of her own. She always said that she was just pleased that God gave her a ready-made family in us. She certainly experienced all the same ups and downs. She was the one who found Patrick when the tree fell on him.

Even though Daniel has gone, and my heart is sad, life is good, how long things will stay this prosperous in Australia I cannot be sure.

Mary closed the diary, carefully putting it back in the box with the others, the bag, and tea towel, sealing them up together in the box for Susan. She went out to the kitchen to make some tea. Taking her mug, she sat down in her favourite chair.

Mary felt the sigh that she had let out ripple down through her body, as she relaxed back into the comfortable armchair. It had been a long day and the house felt empty. It was late and the room was dark, except for the flashing lights on the Christmas tree. She quietly watched the lights flashing. She thought about the life that Mary of the diaries had experienced. She realised that both Rose and Mon had preached very powerfully to Mary, her siblings and also to her, not by what they said but by how they lived their lives.

Someone once said that the only Bible some people read is the life that you lead.

Life really was a circle of conflict, resolution, and growth. It really was like a time shift, a recording of lessons that can be put aside in preparation for future reference if we took the time to learn. It seemed that the human race had difficulty learning from the lessons of the past.

She let out another sigh, shifted her head back a little more trying to find some cool air. The night was hot and humid, a common thing in Australia at Christmas time. Summer had returned with a vengeance. It was hard to believe that the weather had been so cold recently.

She checked the clock, it said 2 am, oh well, it doesn't matter! Ascending the stairs, she climbed into bed, relaxed, rolled over onto her side and watched the stars through the window. It was still one of her favourite things to do. As she drifted off to sleep, listening to the birds singing outside, she was thinking that Christmas was about celebrating the beginning of the greatest journey of love. Her final thought was *Times have moved so fast since Mary and Daniel lived; I hope the future is just as good for my grandchildren.*

Susan's Future Hope

For I know the thoughts that I think toward you," says Yahweh, "thoughts of peace, and not of evil, to give you hope and a future.

Jeremiah 29:11

1

Susan laid curled up in her bed. It was early morning, Christmas Eve, and nearly the end of what could only be described as another horror year.

How can your life change so dramatically in one day!

How many times had she thought that in the past eighteen months? That day, in June last year, had started out the same as any other Saturday. Greg had brought her a cup of tea; he had sat on the side of the bed and they had talked about the week to come. She had shared her fears of not being able to finish the three projects that she was working on. They needed to be finished before the week was over. Along with the children being home on school holidays and his work dinner on Wednesday night, Susan couldn't see how she was going to be able to complete them. Despite the fact that she was usually highly organized, these particular projects just didn't seem to gel in the way things normally did for her. Greg, her greatest supporter, had suggested that he take the kids out for the day and give her some extra space to be inspired and do as much as she could to get in front of what was going to be a very busy week.

They had breakfast together as a family and the kids got really excited when their father had surprised them with a day out. She had never seen those kids get their jobs done so fast and she had smiled, it was going to be a very good day!

Mandy had even washed up the breakfast things without complaint, something that was becoming a common rhetoric now that she was ten. The twins, now in the first year at big school, were really excited. They were struggling with the constant routine of having to go to school every day. Six months in and they were starting to get tired, they really needed the holidays to recoup and as they were in different classes, something Susan and Greg had encouraged, they were looking forward to being together all day again for the two weeks.

By 8.30 they were ready. Just on a whim she decided to take a photo of them all before they piled into her small car. She waved as they drove down the road, Greg had a company car which he didn't use at weekends. Little did she realise in that moment that she would never see any of them alive again. She just smiled to herself and headed into her studio to work. The strange thing was that, suddenly, things started to gel. She was surprised when both the covers and the flyer she was working on seemed to be finished and she was even very happy with the results. She hoped that her clients would be just as pleased. She had just finished sending the last email for the day when there was a knock on her door.

She was pleased that she had finished as it would most likely be her mother, her grandmother wasn't up to driving into town anymore. She had aged a lot in the last three years. Sometimes mum would go out and bring her into town, but she was usually just happy to have someone get her provisions and deliver them, taking the opportunity to sit and talk for a while. The stores still didn't provide the internet click and deliver service to properties out of town, even though most of them did for people living in town. The pandemics had ensured a major increase of dependence on the internet shopping portals for almost everything. Gran certainly wasn't as demanding these days; not like she had been before her strange journey on that Christmas five years ago.

It had been weeks since she had last seen her mother, Jennifer. She ran her own Coffee Shop in the next small town. It wasn't far away, only a half hour by car, but it was just far enough to make it difficult for them to catch up in person on a regular basis. They did chat on social media every day, at least once, if not more, depending on how busy each of them was. She had to give it to her mother though, if she needed to come to town unexpectedly, she would always call in for a cup of tea. That was one of the things that Susan loved about working from home. It would be a rare day indeed that she wasn't home to greet any visitors. Maybe if Grandma had been closer to town when her mother was younger, she may not have become so difficult, but then again, you never know what hidden events in people lives make them who they are. Jennifer still didn't know about Grandma's strange Christmas and Susan wasn't going to be the one to say anything, not while grandma was alive anyway. She did, however, have a feeling that grandma was putting pen to paper so everyone could read her story once she died.

The doorbell rang again just as she reached it. She turned the handle, smiling in anticipation of her mother standing on the other side. Instead, there were two Police Officers standing on her doorstep. She glanced up and down the street, were they going to ask her if she knew anything about some crime that had been carried out. It wasn't the first time that they had done a door-to-door canvas, asking if they knew anything about something that one or other of their neighbours had been involved in. It wasn't that they lived in a particularly bad area, but a lot of families living in the street had teenagers and they were known to get into mischief on a regular basis. With busy parents, many of the kids managed to stay home from school way too often and bored teenagers were a recipe for trouble. Most of it was petty stuff in the eyes of the law but petty usually developed into more serious crimes as the adrenaline high wore off, hence the constant Police presence.

'I'm sorry, Officers, I've been working out in my studio. The street has been unusually quiet, so I don't think I'm going to be able to help you much today,' Susan said.

'Mrs Green, is it?' the female Officer asked.

'Yes, I'm Mrs Green', Susan was starting to realise that this wasn't their usual sort of call.

'Your husband's name is Greg?' the other officer asked.

'Yesssss.' Susan could feel panic rising in her stomach.

'May we come in please?' the woman stepped forward as if she wasn't going to take no for an answer.

Susan opened the door wider, stepping back and pointing to the lounge room doorway to let her unexpected visitors enter and at the same time direct them to where they could talk. She closed the door quietly, somehow it seemed like it was necessary to stay calm. When the officers had reached the centre of the room, they turned to face her.

The female officer looked at her with a steady gaze and asked: 'Is there someone you can call to be here with you?'

'My husband will be back later today; he has just taken the kids out to give me some space to get my work done. What is this all about?'

'Please sit down, Mrs Green, we have some bad news for you.' Susan almost collapsed into the chair that was behind her. Was it her mother, her father? Were they hurt, had there been a fire at the shop, was it even her grandmother, after all she lived all alone out there on the farm? Had her brother found that she had died in her sleep. If so, why hadn't he rang her instead of sending the Police. Her mind was racing so much that she didn't really hear what the male Officer was saying until she heard the words accident and Greg's name together.

'Sorry, what did you say?' she asked.

'I'm sorry, Mrs Green, there has been a car accident. A large four-wheel drive vehicle hit your family head-on and there were no survivors. I really think we should call someone to come and stay with you. We are not sure what happened yet, but it looks like the driver of the four-wheel drive was under the influence of alcohol and/or drugs. Can we please phone your mother?'

Susan felt numb, she picked up her mobile phone, logged in and in a daze handed it over to the officer. The woman scrolled through her contacts, found what she was looking for and, as she dialled her mother's number, she walked out of the room. All Susan could hear as she came back into the room was that no they would send a Police Officer to collect her. Susan who had been sitting on the front edge of the chair fell back. Her family were all gone. She was all alone in the world. How? Why? Her family were her life and her future! In an instant it was empty!

The next few hours and weeks were a blur, she barely remembered her mother arriving and hugging her, she cried, her mother cried. She did remember seeing her father holding back tears when he arrived.

Greg was like another son to them. His birth father had died while his mother was pregnant and, as they lived a few doors down the street at the time, he had latched on to her father at a very young age. Her father had found him wondering along the footpath early one morning when he was nearly two years of age. It turned out that he had managed to let himself out of the house and was going on an adventure, so he had told her father. Dad had taken him home to find Greg's mother, Hilda, running around the yard calling his name. After that, Greg had followed her father around like a lost puppy, but he also watched everything her dad did. If dad was fixing the mower, or pruning trees, Greg would be right there asking all sorts of questions.

It wasn't long after he had started school that Greg had turned up at their place on a Saturday morning with his mother's mower. It won't go, Mr Higgins, he'd said. Can you please help me fix it? Her dad had rung Greg's mother to make sure that it really wasn't going and after a short conversation had returned to the backyard and the two of them had got to work and fixed it. It had progressed to push bikes, cars, motor bikes, even his mother's washing machine had been dealt with. He was a part of the family and that was that.

2

Somewhere in amongst all the visitors, Greg's mother and her husband had turned up. His mother was so pale that she looked like she was going to faint. They didn't stay long. It took Susan two days to even remember that this was also really hard on his mother. She had also lost a son and four grandchildren. She rang her to say how sorry she was but really didn't have the strength to do much else. The one thing that was a comfort to all of them was the knowledge that they had all died instantly, there would not have been any pain for any of them. The hope that they clung to was that one day they would all meet again in Heaven. Even the twins had a strong faith, Susan knew that and that provided a crack through which a bright light of hope filtered through into her sadness.

Gran had come into to town and stayed with Susan for the first few weeks. Her mother had a business to run and while she had closed it for the day after the tragedy and the day of the funeral, Susan knew that there was no way she could ask her to do more. She often visited after work though to check on both Susan and her mother. If it hadn't been for Gran's gentle promptings each morning, after she had brought her a cup of tea, to shower and dress, Susan would have most likely have just stayed in bed and shut out the world completely. Susan knew that Gran wasn't going home until she was sure that Susan was willing to make the choice to get up on her own. So, after about week three she determined that she would at least get out of bed and shower by herself, besides, there were still a lot of people ringing her doorbell each day to check on her. Looking back, it seemed as if her friends must have drawn up a roster, taking it in turns to call on her. She was too numb at the time to notice any regular pattern to the visitations and even now she could not be certain, but it was what got her out of bed each day; she must be thankful for that, even if she operated on autopilot. She did most of her chores without really thinking about what she was doing. She assumed that it was one of the benefits of being a creature of habit. They were so ingrained in her life that when there was a crisis her brain forced her body to carry out the everyday tasks with very little actual mental input. Sadly, she was still operating on that level, all these months later, for much of the time, anyway. Would she ever get over this?

The day of the funeral or funerals depending on how you looked at it was just so hard. Greg's boss had spoken about how the workplace was going to miss his tenacity to expand the business. The principals from both the schools the children attended had spoken. Their minister from their church had spoken on behalf of the family. No one felt up to speaking with so many coffins laid out in the front of the church. Greg's mother had cried so much that proceedings had to be paused for a little while. Her husband had managed to calm her, but it had taken a few minutes. Susan realised that in spite of the two families being connected for such a long time, Greg's mother still didn't get it that Heaven and Hell were real places, and our souls would exist forever, in one place or the other, depending on the choices made here on earth.

As the weeks dragged out into months, Susan had started cleaning out her house. It was irrational, and deep down even she knew that, but she rationalised it by telling herself that if the house of void of anything that could trigger a memory she wouldn't keep falling apart. Besides, she wanted something to do, and she couldn't work even if there had been any projects for her. Her brain was still incapable of being creative. Most of her clients had heard of the tragedy, after all it had been big news on the television and social media for weeks, because the boys in the other car had families of influence. Most people were just shocked that what was intended to be a bit of fun had turned into such a tragedy. So, most of her clients had sent their business elsewhere, saying that they would give her some space for a while but promised that, once she felt up to it, they would be only too pleased to send business back her way. So, she cleaned, actually purged might have been a better word. She threw out almost everything that reminded her of her family. She even went through her own clothes. If Greg had liked it, it went. She didn't want anything left to remind her of what she had lost. All the children's clothes were sent to charity shops, except for the ones that her mother had insisted on keeping.

Jennifer had turned up one day just in time to find Susan madly packing all the boxes that held the special baby outfits, made by Mary's mother for her. Susan had used them for her babies and put them aside to hand down to her grandchildren.

'Are you going to put them in storage?' Jennifer had asked.

'No, they're going to charity. I have no use for them anymore. I'll never have grandchildren, so they may as well go.' Susan's voice was angry and determined.

'Look, Susan,' her mother's voice held a note of anger too as she took hold of Susan's shoulders and turned her to face her, 'I know it feels like your life is over right now, but it isn't. Our past, present, and future are always connected. Trying to disconnect from your past like this will only bring you heartache in the future. You are still young enough to meet someone and find love again.'

'Mum, that could take years, I'm nearly thirty years old; I'm getting too old to have children. You know the doctors warned me against having more after I had the twins. Besides, I won't be able to love anyone the way I loved Greg, there is no one else like him for me.'

'It won't be the same as what you and Greg had, but it will still be good. Even if you don't have any more children of your own, there is no reason to believe that there isn't some child out there who needs the love that you could give them. I understand that you don't want these around where you can be reminded of what you have lost right now so I want you to let me take them home and put them away until you are ready. Okay?' Jennifer held Susan's gaze; she didn't move. Finally, Susan nodded, Jennifer let out a sigh of relief, wrapped her arms around her daughter, hugging her tight.

'Oh, mum why couldn't they have been a little bit naughty that day, then they would have been later leaving and wouldn't have been in the path of that car', she cried into her mother's shoulder. Jennifer continued to hug her.

'If they hadn't been good and they still died in another accident, you would be crying to me about being upset with them as you said goodbye. You know what I believe; that it's most likely that no matter what they were doing that day, something would have taken them home to Heaven because it was their time to go.'

'Why did it have to be all of them?' Susan pleaded.

'Darling, I have no idea. I don't understand God's plan in this any more than you do but at least you have good memories to hang onto.'

Eventually they parted and Susan leaned against the wall and detachedly watched as her mother packed those boxes in her car, it seemed that she wasn't going to give Susan a second chance to get rid of them.

How many times in that eighteen months had she read her Bible and thought about the women like Hannah? How strong she must have been to keep her promise to God and give up what would have seemed like her one and only child willingly, but of course Hannah got to see her child at least once a year, she would never see her children ever again on earth.

There were times when she surfaced from her own clouds of despair to remember that Hilda, Greg's mother's pain must be harder than her own. They were both childless now, but she only had one son and as her mother had pointed out, she, Susan, was young enough to have more children, even if they were not going to be her own. Greg's mother would not be able to have more children; the family name and line would die with her now. For some reason, carrying on the family name was important to her mother-in-law. She had been really pleased when Paul had been born. She had gone on and on about how the family name and line was now secure. She had tried very hard to hide her disappointment when the rest of their children had been girls. Susan had no idea why such a thing was so important to her, she never talked about it and Susan felt that there was a barrier put in place by Hilda that made it impossible for her to delve into the subject. She was glad that Greg's mother's husband was there to help her. She realised that without him, she would most likely have committed suicide.

Then came the court case. The Police had said in the beginning that it could take up to two years for the case to be heard. Yet, twelve months later, they were in court.

It turned out that the three teenagers, the eldest was only just sixteen, the others fifteen and fourteen, had not only been drinking the night before but also taken drugs. They had decided it would be fun to take the vehicle, which belonged to the driver's father and go for a drive to get a MacDonald's breakfast. None of them had a licence and the driver had only had a few learner's lessons. The powerful vehicle had been more than the driver could handle, and along with the fooling around that was happening inside, he had lost control just five minutes after Greg had turned onto the same stretch of road. Had they left five minutes later, they would not have even encountered the car and its occupants. The four-wheel drive would have been past that intersection.

Susan had sat in court and watched the backs of the three offenders. She couldn't see their faces, but she got a strong impression from the way they were moving around that they were not remorseful at all. Even the Judge made reference in his closing remarks that they didn't seem to care that they had broken the law and completely destroyed an entire family. These boys, it seems, had come from wealthy families, their world was one of comfort and affluence. Yet, it wasn't enough. They needed the rush that the alcohol and drugs provided. She felt her mother put her arm around her; she must have been watching the boys as well. Even with all their advantages there was still something missing in their lives, while she was surrounded and supported by her family. Susan felt a prompting to actually look around the court room. The only people present were there for her. As the realisation dawned, she had to feel a bit sorry for the boys. Even at seventeen they seemed so boyish, not young men as their ages should have indicated. There seemed to be no parents in court with them, that duty seemed to have been delegated to their solicitors. Susan wasn't sure how she felt about their attitude and was very angry when the Judge saw fit to not send them to jail, that meant that they would be on our roads again putting more families at risk. She prayed that somehow, God would send someone to tell them that they could change their lives with the help of God, but she had a feeling that it was going to take these boys a while to figure out that they even needed to change. It occurred to her that, as the parents were wealthy, they were expecting the solicitors to argue a case for a good behaviour bond. Most likely that is what they were being paid to do. Would this incident awaken them to the realisation that their children needed their presence not presents? That had been the driving motivation for her to work from home. Mind you, she was aware that these rouges had five years on Paul, how would he have behaved in five years' time, tears threatened again. Now she would never know. She looked at the boys once more and prayed, 'Lord, I can't help Paul anymore and I can't help these boys. I know that you want them to come to you for salvation, please send someone to help them'. She didn't even say Amen; she just left it in God's hands. For once in her life, she left something at God's alter and walked away, she could do no more.

❧❧❧❧

Her head knew that God had a plan, but her heart was having a very hard time agreeing with it. Here it was, Christmas Eve, her second since that awful day and she was all alone for the first time in her life. Her parents had taken a very much needed holiday cruise for the whole week between Christmas and New Year. It had been booked in the January before their lives had been turned upside down. They had wanted to cancel or try and get her on the cruise with them as well, but nothing seemed to work. There were no extra bunks available, and the cruise had been fully paid for, so they would lose their money if they didn't go. Besides, Susan wouldn't hear of them cancelling. They both worked really hard, and this was the only time they could take off. She would be fine, she told them over, and over again. Grandma Mary was going down to spend Christmas with her sister-in-law in Tasmania where it was a little cooler, she would be gone for two months. Jeff, her brother, had married towards the end of the previous year and was spending his second Christmas as a married man with his wife's family. He had become an instant father, as Claire already had two children when she met Jeff. The children's father had abandoned her after deciding that he really didn't want to be a father after all. Susan had been surprised at how well fatherhood looked on her brother. It really suited him and with his influence, the children had been transformed from angry monsters into cute, cheeky ones. They were planning on visiting her for Boxing Day. So, it eventuated that Susan, a thirty-year-old widow, would be home alone for Christmas Day.

She placed her glasses on the table. All the computer work that she did had created some damage and glasses were needed in order to avoid the debilitating headaches she suffered. She wiped the tears that had been falling yet again. How many tears can a person cry, she wondered? It felt as if she had cried enough tears to fill the sea. She couldn't remember a single day in the last eighteen months when she hadn't cried at some point in the day. Rolling over onto her back, she looked at the ceiling and for the umpteenth time, asked God, what now? What did her future hold?

The world was such a miserable place these days, not just for her but it seemed for everyone. Every time she turned on the TV there were so many stories about families being destroyed by another car accident, someone going berserk with a knife, gun, their fists, or other weapons. There were days when she wouldn't even turn it on. The days when she was brave enough, she would always hope that she would find some morsel of good news in amongst the bad. There just didn't seem to be any hope for Australia. It seemed that they were returning to the dark ages. Yes, she knew that the world was going to get bad before Jesus returned. Part of her wanted that to happen right now, if it did, she would be reunited with her family and she wanted that so badly. So many preachers were focused on Jesus' return because the world was in such a bad state. The Bible declares that no one knows when He is coming back. If he returned now, there would be so many people who would turn around and say, 'I told you so!' However, what if He wasn't going to return for another thousand years. How would we survive? It feels so hopeless.

Then there were the other problems that she knew her brother was having, going through drought and the numerous farming issues. It seemed that it wouldn't be long before the farming industry in Australia would be completely shut down. When imports were closed down during the pandemics, it had made people realise how important farmers were, for a little while, but everyone was getting comfortable again with the return to normal life. There were those animal activists who were again trying to bully everyone into becoming vegetarians. There were others who decided that animals were more important and needed to be treated better than their fellow human beings. Then there was the drought that seemed to just go on and on and had been pretty much since the year 2000. Yes, there had been times of rain, but they didn't seem to last for more than a year or two. One thing that also frustrated her was the way academics made up stuff, wrote it down in a textbook and so many people decided that it was the absolute truth and would work out in practice. One thing she knew for sure was that theory very rarely actually worked consistently in practice. The other thing was that Australia was such a vast country, and academics expected most theories to work in every situation and that was just not going to happen, there is just too much variety in this country. The world was just a horrible place these days. Tears started to flow again.

She didn't need to get up, so she wouldn't, she decided. The only time she'd move was when she needed to go to the bathroom, or she went to the kitchen for a cup of tea. She had that in common with her Gran. She loved tea; coffee made her sick, so she stayed away from that alternative. Her grief was still so raw after all this time. Why, oh why, couldn't God take away all the sad memories and allow her to move on, or even just take her home to Heaven so she could be with her family again. She had no reason to live anymore, yes, there was her work, but without her family she was struggling to find inspiration and she hadn't done any in the last eighteen months anyway because she couldn't face trying to go back yet. Just as well Greg had made sure he had insurance, and his boss had made sure that they had paid up, their savings had been used up remodelling the house, they had opened up one of the front rooms to provide the wide entry and allowed them to put stairs to the second storey added for extra bedrooms. Otherwise, she would not have been able to survive without depending on her family. Maybe if she'd had to fend for herself, she might have found the creativity deep inside of her sooner. Starvation is a great motivation. Was she being childish, self-indulgent, or worse, selfish? She needed some mission in life, something to inspire her to get up in the morning, some way to create new and happier memories. Either way, she wanted this pain to end. At some point she drifted off to sleep.

3

A feeling of loving warmth wrapped around her, as if she were being cradled like a newborn baby. She snuggled deeper into the pillow as she heard a gentle voice calling her name. She slowly opened her eyes and standing in the room was an angel figurine, which seemed to fill all the space in the room. It was translucent and fluid, unlike the solid concrete varieties that guarded grave sites. As she looked at it, it moved.

'Whoa' Susan yelled, sitting up and pulling the sheet up around her chin.

'It's ok, Susan, I have come to take you on a long journey,' the apparition spoke in a gentle voice.

'Are you the angel of death? Have you come to take me home to Heaven to be with my family?' Susan's words were tumbling over themselves. Finally, God had answered her prayer, she was going home. The relief that she had expected didn't come though.

'No, Susan, it's not time for you to be reunited with your family yet. God has a job He would like you to do. It's a very important mission, one that will save your descendants and many others, getting them through a time of major crisis.'

'I have no family. Surely you know that. God has taken them all from me. I am all alone in this world except for mum and dad. How can I have descendants when I have no children?' Susan responded angrily.

'Your family was only lent to you for a season, Susan. They were not your possessions to hang onto, they were a gift from the almighty to help you and them to grow, learn and be prepared for the time ahead of you all. You and Greg faithfully taught your children about the love of God, that love you now doubt. You did all that you could to see that they understood that the decision made here on earth determines their eternal destination. The Holy Spirit called each and every one of your family, and they await your entry through the gates of Heaven one day, just not yet. God is well pleased with your faithfulness. The only sadness is that Greg's mother is not yet willing to call him Father.' The angel paused and then continued. 'God has a plan, even I don't know the whole story, but God has seen your utter despair and has sent me to help you to understand that He loves you. Your future is held firmly in His hands, just as your loved ones are. Please don't make the same mistake Sarah made and doubt God's capacity to do the impossible.'

'What is your name?' Susan asked, mostly because she really had no response to what the angel had said. Her head knew that what the angel said was true, but her heart still didn't want to let go of the family she had called her own.

'My name is Angelica but just call me Angel,' Angelica smiled.

'That's pretty inane, do all the angels have the same name apart from Michael and Gabriel. They are the only ones mentioned in the Bible.'

'The answer to that can wait until you enter through the Pearly Gates, my dear,' responded Angel. 'Not all questions should be answered this side of Heaven.'

'My biggest question is why!' Susan cried, 'I want to hug my kids so badly that it hurts. I know that I complained about them, particularly with Mandy's attitude, but I miss them so much! I just want Greg to come back and give me a hug and tell me that I can do this!'

'Your parents tell you that all the time', Angel said.

'I know that but it's not the same! Greg was so supportive; I keep remembering the night Greg came home when things had been going wrong all day. I had twelve different drafts of a covers for a book and the client didn't like any one of them, for no particular reason, it seemed. I was so frustrated and the I guess the kids picked up on my frustrations. They were sitting at the dinner table snipping and picking on each other and hadn't heard Greg come home. He stood in the doorway and surveyed the scene. Suddenly he let out a wolf whistle, the kids stopped fighting, looked at him in shock and he said, 'Who let the monsters out? Go to your rooms and lock them back in their boxes and then stay in your rooms until I tell you to come back out.' They had scurried to their rooms, no questions asked. Greg had looked at me, walked over to the counter and said 'Sus, (I loved his pet name for me, even though he had started using it at a time when we were not getting along at all), you look like you need a very strong cup of tea. Go and sit down in the nook and I'll bring it out to you.' We had talked about how I couldn't come up with a cover and how frustrated I felt. I then asked how his day had gone and he said that his day had been much the same as mine. There was some sort of coding problem that he couldn't get a handle on but that he'd had twenty minutes in the car to let it go and hand it over to the Lord. 'Sus, I want you to get your camera and go for a walk just to clear your head, take at least half an hour and I'll deal with the kids.' When I got back the kids had finished their meals, the washing up was done, and Greg was reading to them in the lounge room.

The funny thing was, two nights later, after I had managed to come up with a cover that the client liked and things were going really smoothly, the children were sitting at the table eating quietly when they heard Greg's car pull into the carport. Paul had whispered to the others 'Dad's home' and suddenly all hell broke loose. They started fighting and bickering just like the earlier night. I looked at the children and then at Greg as he stood in the doorway. He must have noticed the shocked look on my face and realised something was very different this time because instead of the wolf whistle he just shouted, "GO TO YOUR ROOMS". They walked slowly to their rooms with slumped shoulders and disappointed looks on their faces. I smiled at Greg as I handed him a coffee and we walked out to the nook, our special place to eat breakfast in the sun during the wintertime.

'What was that all about?' he asked as we sat down.

'Well, they were fine until Paul heard your car pull up, I think they wanted a repeat of the other night. This project that you are on has made you a bit distracted lately. I guess after they managed to get your attention the other night, they decided that they would see if it worked a second time,' Susan had ventured.

'Gosh. Kids, they don't miss a trick, do they!' he stated as he slumped back in his chair.

'You look tired, have you been able sort out that coding problem yet?' I asked him as I leaned up against his shoulder.

'No, and for some reason I haven't been able to let go of it on the way home tonight.'

'Well, now it's your turn to go for a walk and my turn to sort out the children. Maybe you might read them a story when you get back.' By the time Greg had returned home I had sat the children down and explained to them that what they had done wasn't very respectful and if they wanted their father to read a story then the best way to make it happen was to eat their dinner quietly and clean up the kitchen. They had managed to do that before he had got home. Greg had read to them every night after that, as long as the dishes were done, and they had behaved themselves.

'They are two good memories to hang on to Susan, you have them, treasure them.'

'I don't want to; it hurts too much because I know there will never be any new ones.' Susan cried.

Angel let her cry for a few minutes and then handed her a tissue. Susan wiped her face and looked back at Angel.

'So, what happens now?' Susan asked.

'Come with me, I have prepared you a meal that will sustain you for the journey,' Angel instructed.

'Do I need to get dressed?'

'No, you will be fine the way you are, no one is going to see you during the first part and clothes will be provided for the second part.'

Susan climbed out of bed, leaving her glasses and mobile phone on the bedside table, she followed Angel to the kitchen. Angel stood in the doorway, her form now shrinking to just fill the space between the doorjambs. She watched as Susan ate the meal that was ready on the table. Susan had not felt this calm and relaxed for so long that she was certain that it wasn't real, it must just be a dream.

Once she had finished eating, Angel lifted Susan, cradling her as if she was a small child. Reminding Susan of the many times she had picked up her children, in exactly the same way to give them comfort when they had run to her in pain. Rising off the floor, the ceiling started to get awfully close. Susan closed her eyes, snuggled into the Angel's shoulder, which felt strangely solid and real and waited for the impact that she was sure was about to happen. When it didn't eventuate, she slowly opened her eyes to see that they had passed through not only the ceiling but also the roof. They were rising above the earth. Higher and higher they went until they could see the whole of Australia in one glance.

'Oh, how dry it looks again. Will the drought ever finish?' Susan asked, 'So many families are struggling to stay afloat, and it seems that city people do not care where their food comes from. Those ships off the coast out there bring in cheap food from overseas. It gives the impression that food just appears on the supermarket shelves automatically. There are so many people who worship animals, making a mockery of the fact that God gave us dominion over them.'

'Yes,' Angel agreed, 'it certainly is dry, and the treatment of Australian farmers is something that also grieves our Lord.'

'He could fix it, couldn't He?' Susan asked.

'Susan, you know that God won't take away the freewill that He gave to mankind, nor will He do what man can do for himself. God will only do what man cannot do.'

'But He could let it rain? That would solve many of the problems some of these poor people are struggling with.'

'God told humanity way back in the beginning that there would be cycles of heat and cold. Don't you remember what it says in Genesis 8:22, "While the earth remaineth, seedtime and harvest, and cold and heat, and summer and winter, and day and night shall not cease." People think that the cold and heat in that verse, refers to Summer and Winter but if it did then He wouldn't have mentioned those seasons. He told you all this so you could use the God given skills and talents to work out how to make things grow during both the cold times and the hot times. Instead, people have become arrogant and think that they can change the climate to suit them. The answer to the dry is right in front of them. All the politicians have to do is look, instead of just listening to the so-called experts. There are places in Australia that are doing better than others and the difference is that they have stored water nearby. Once those in power actually look, they will see how to solve the problem. As I said before, God doesn't do what man can do for himself. He gave them eyes and brains to use. Things will grow with water.'

'It is so hard to convince them that these things work when so many people tell them they are wrong, Believing the science allows them to absolve themselves of the responsibility of inaction.'

'That's why they need to look.' Angel said, 'They will see it soon, as I said God has a plan.'

Angel and Susan watched as the people moved about underneath them. Angel moved a little higher so the whole expanse of the world spread out underneath them. As she watched, planes whizzed around the sky from country to country. Wow, she thought, how amazing is God. He not only manages to keep track of everything happening down there on earth and its creatures, He knows where each person is, what they are doing, what their future holds, what they are thinking and exactly how many hairs they have. That is only something that He could do. Things started to move faster, as they watched the day and night past before them, getting faster and faster. It reminded her of the time lapse photography used to reduce viewing time for documentaries or instruction videos.

'What is happening?' asked Susan.

'You are seeing the passing of time.'

'Goodness, I'm starting to feel a little dizzy, I don't understand how this could be.'

'God is the creator and controller of time.' replied Angel.

Susan looked around and briefly watched the stars speed across the sky. As she brought her eyes back to the happenings on earth, she noticed that things had slowed down again and off in the distance there were flashes of light.

'There seems to be a storm over there.' She pointed out to Angel.

'That's a manmade storm, my dear,' Angel noted, 'A conflict of interests has developed, and those flashes are firearms not lightning.'

'What year is it?'

'That's of no consequence right now.'

She could see that there were no ships moving into the ports, and the only planes flying were crossing the country. It seemed that Australia had become a true island. Angel moved a little closer to the ground. The strangest thing was that even though she shouldn't be able to see what was going on, she could clearly see as if she was only a hundred feet above the scene. Things seemed to be messy, people were moving around in angry mobs. She could see that there were riots on the ground, and it escalated into civil war. Tears ran down her face, Australia's peaceful record was well and truly shattered. Yes, there had been the Eureka stockade event way back in their early history, but that would have looked like a storm in a teacup compared to what she was watching now.

Oh, my goodness, she thought, how would her children have managed. How would she have managed to watch her children trying to live in such a time. They have been spared. For the first time in the last eighteen months, she saw that God's plan had a gold thread to it. As she watched, she knew that there were so many mother's down there whose hearts were breaking every day as they watched their children deal with circumstances that they didn't see coming. For the first time, she was relieved that her children were safe. They were already in the arms of Jesus.

'Oh, Lord,' she prayed out aloud, 'be merciful on our Land', as tears started to roll down her cheeks.

Angel turned around and Susan could see the scars left by the wars down through the ages. Yes, God's blueprint for creation meant that it had recovered and built over, healing the earth time and time again, but the scars remained, camouflaged perhaps, but still there. Susan found that she could also hear the cries of the mothers who had lost their children too. Right back to Eve, when she heard that Able had been killed by his brother Cain. She had been so pleased when Cain had been born, she believed that he could be the means of salvation for their fall from grace, yet it was this precious child that had committed the thing that broke her heart twice. She had lost a son and any hope of salvation through her first born. Oh, the tears she had cried, Susan could hear them now. It seems that every mother who had lived on earth had shed tears enough to fill all the seas. No wonder the world's oceans are salty, she thought. The sound of their cries continued to reach her, and it was deafening, she covered her ears, but they went on and on. She started to cry herself, not for them but for her own self-absorption. She lived in the safest country, yes, it was still the safest place in the world, and she wasn't the first mother to lose all her children. Yet, all she had done for the last eighteen months was cry out to God and ask Him to take away the pain. What was she thinking? What made her think that she was the only mother with this amount of heartache! There were many who had gone before her and there would be many, many more who would have to wear the shoes that she was using right now.

'Oh, God, forgive me' she cried. 'I have been so selfish, untrusting, overbearing, and unkind to you. I have envied all those mothers who still have their children here. I have not loved you even though I dared to call you, my friend. I don't deserve to be called your daughter.'

'The father loves you and yes, it has broken His heart to see you fight what He knows is the best plan for you, but you have seen the error of your ways, repented, and He has forgiven you.' Angel held her tighter and as she did so, Susan felt her heart heal. She smiled as she remembered each child's face and Greg's loving embrace. She knew that now she would be able to move on, but she still wanted something to do, something to get her out of bed in the mornings. It had to be something more than just her work, something that would make a difference to her world, the world that she was watching fall into chaos.

4

Looking around she could see that the land was still looking very brown and dry. As the stench of rubbish, smoke, and human decay assailed her nostrils she turned her face, looking up at Angel's face she silently asked the question. Angel looked back and sighed, 'Hungry people have very little to lose', was all she said.

Susan noticed that water was being pumped into holes from the ocean. Just then the rains started to fall, and time started to move faster again. Only now as she watched it pass the country started to look green and stayed that way. The farmers seemed to be busy; trucks could be seen moving to and from farms and the cities. What she couldn't tell was if those living in the cities had developed a better respect for those who worked hard every day to feed and clothe them. It seemed that not all signs gave you clear answers just as her grandmother had explained once. She had asked God about some future event. On the way home a few days later she saw a cloud in the sky. It was shaped like a number, leaving her still with the question of whether it meant days, weeks, months or even years.

Eventually the manmade storms ceased, there was an eerie peacefulness and planes started to fly from country to country again. The war must be over thought Susan. As they watched Susan noticed that there were more and more satellites being thrown into the sky. Angel handed Susan a pair of glasses.

'Put these on' she whispered.

Susan looked at her a little surprised but did as she was told. A matrix of green beams appeared between the Satellites and earth, reminding her of the laser beams she had seen in some of the light shows that had been performed as part of some firework displays.

'Wow, that's some show?' Susan said as she removed the glasses and the matrix disappeared only to reappear when she put the glasses back on.

'Those special glasses allow you to see the trails of information being flashed backwards and forwards as part of the internet system. Those beams are only visible through those glasses. It shows you just how much humans are depending on the internet.' Angel informed her.

'It's controlling everything,' Susan muttered to herself, 'It's supposed to be controlled by them not the other way around.' Susan noticed that beams were attaching themselves to virtually every moving thing down there. Some vehicles were being attached to more than one beam. As they watched it grew thicker and thicker until it become almost a solid mass.

'Wow, that's getting heavy.' Looking back at Angel with a frown forming on her face, she asked, 'Why on earth do I need to know this?' Angel smiled.

'In case you hadn't noticed you are not on earth, honey,' she giggled, 'Just keep looking.'

Suddenly, Angel covered Susan with her wing, but Susan could still see through it, it was acting as a protective shield. A sun flair, that looked deceptively like a bright orange finger reached out across the atmosphere. Susan watched and, as if things were moving in slow motion, the tip of the sun flair curled under itself and flicked upwards. It looked like a finger that wanted to flick the satellite into outer space. The satellite didn't move, just like a defiant child, but turned white with the heat of the flair. Angel moved them both higher still. All was still for what seemed like only a few seconds then there was an explosion of activity. Susan watched as satellites were flung off into outer space and the internet system quickly disappeared.

'What happened!?' it wasn't really a question, more of a shriek as she removed the glasses, checked them, and put them back on to see if the matrix had returned. Things got very strange. Lights flickered several times and then went out all over the world. She waited for them to come back on, but they didn't. Aeroplanes started falling out of the sky. Some descended safely but crashed upon landing. It was hard to tell how many people survived the crashes. There were some that managed to get down without incident. Ships on the seas started to drift with the currents.

The world seemed to have stopped in its tracks. The highways were filled with cars and trucks, but the only movement was the masses of humans walking away from their stationary vehicles. Trains were sitting on the lines; she could see that the windows had been broken and they were now abandoned. Most farming vehicles were sitting in the middle of paddocks, doing nothing but Susan noticed there were some that were still working.

Then an explosion of fires in every city appeared. There was hardly a city that didn't have some part of it burning. A thick black cloud started to grow. It started out as a very dark grey and when the storms started, lightning flashes showed that the clouds had turned a deep purple. As she continued to watch she found her view was disappearing under a layer of smoke. It was as thick as tar and so heavy that it hung low over the earth. The smell of chemicals, burning flesh and cries of agony reached her; they were so loud that she needed to cover her ears again. She turned her head into Angel's shoulder again but there was no way she could stop hearing or smelling it. This distress of the human race was too much for her to deal with.

'What's happening?' she cried into Angel's cloak, as her tears flowed faster.

'Man decided that computers made fewer mistakes than humans. They built the internet system so that it would not only create its own programs but was capable of fixing any errors that might occur. That satellite you saw turn white hot tried to fix the program that was damaged from the sun flair. However, it made a mistake and instead of fixing the problem it created a virus which has shut down the world's entire computer system. Some things that used computer systems for cooling systems overheated. When fires broke out, the smoke alarms and sprinklers didn't work as they were controlled by computers and there was no way to communicate to the fire services, which were unable to respond anyway.'

'Are these the fires we are told about in Revelation?'

'There is no point speculating about that. Time must come to an end before Revelation is completely divulged. Many people have tried to work out how it's all going to happen ever since John wrote the book. It was meant to reveal the power and faithfulness of God by showing man that Heaven, Hell, and the day of reckoning are very real places and events. It also makes it very clear that no matter how bad things get, God is the King of Kings and He will win over the evil that creates situations like the one you are witnessing here. People have always wanted to know exactly how the future will unfold, even those who walked with Jesus, but remember what Luke said in Acts 1:7 when he quoted what Jesus said to the disciples: "It is not for you to know the times or the seasons, which the Father hath put in his own power". So many people have been tricked into trying to work out how these things will happen and what they will look like. They've been distracted from doing exactly what God wanted of them. That is why I'm not allowed to give you any specific dates as to what you see happening down there. The great commission has been ignored, which is and always has been the order of business for everyone who follows Jesus. There was a specific reason why it was the last instruction from Jesus in the book of Matthew.'

'Why are you showing me this? This is worse than losing my family, am I going to be the only human being left alive? This isn't fair.' Angel moved slightly so Susan could see that beneath the clouds there were survivors. Many of them were people who lived away from the city centres.

As she watched the people move around, she noticed that not only was the water black with the tar like chemicals in the smoke, but it wasn't moving. Had the tar made the water so thick that it had turned into a solid mass? Angel moved her wing that had been protecting Susan. A blast of cold hit her body. It was the type of cold that seeped deep into your bones and made them ache.

'Oh, it's so cold', it was an involuntary cry that escaped her. 'That water is frozen, isn't it?' She looked at Angel, who nodded, smiled, and placed her wing back again to protect and warm Susan's shivering body. 'So, they have survived this far, but how are they going to continue to manage?'

'These people aren't prepared. When the internet failed, they had no idea what to do. Life is going to be so hard for them from now on.

317

They have to learn how to live without the internet. They have no means of generating their own electricity or ways of living without the assistance of computers.'

Susan watched, it was like a horror movie, you wanted to look away, but you couldn't. It started to rain. The tar layer slowly melted and covered the earth.

The scene below reminded her of the occasion when Paul, aged three, had been really angry with her because she had denied him something that he really wanted. Searching her memory banks, she couldn't for the life of her remember what it was that he had wanted, most likely an Icey Pole or a piece of cake. In a fit of rage, he had taken a black crayon and scribbled all over a printout for a client who had just arrived at the front door. It had been no big deal, they had giggled quietly after Paul had been deposited in the play pen out of earshot, minus his toys as a form of discipline. That had been the hardest part about working at home. Had the client not been present, Paul would have been given a quick smack to show her disapproval. However, society frowned on physical discipline so much that even though she believed that it was better to deal with it swiftly and in a manner that children would understand the pain that they had caused, she was never comfortable dishing it out in front of clients.

As time started to flash forward again, a little more slowly this time, Susan noticed that the crops were withering, waterways also turned black; man had destroyed himself even though the sky had cleared and returned to its usual blue hue. It became apparent that farming was coming to a grinding halt. There were no stockpiles of seeds as a backstop to failed crops. Didn't they learn anything from the droughts that plagued the country in the early twenty-first century?

'They didn't see this coming', Angel said, as if she was reading her mind and heard the unspoken question.

'They should have', Susan stated, swiping away her tears. She could feel anger rising up inside her. 'It's not as if the internet and digital technologies were infallible. How can they believe that humans can make something that is perfect when they are not perfect themselves?'

'Pride goes before a fall; arrogance precedes total collapse. Sometimes God has to allow people to get to the bottom of the pit in order for them to see that they need His help to rescue them.'

'Why would God allow this to take place?' Susan asked Angel with tears running down her face. 'Wasn't there some other way to bring man to his knees without this level of destruction? Surely there is no way back from this, the crops, soil, water; they are all contaminated. It will take years before they are able to get rid of all that black stuff and start again, how will they survive long enough to manage?'

'He tried to get their attention during the early twenty first century, but they hardened their hearts towards Him, just like Pharaoh did when God sent Moses to rescue the Israelites from Egypt. God is patient, for the world, this is another chance to seek Him.'

Angel moved and Susan could see countries in the northern hemisphere, who suffered much longer winters than ever experienced in Australia. Looking around, she noticed that survivors were out and about washing the heavy grime off glass houses. They needed these structures to get plants ready while snow covered their ground. Australia hadn't, until now, known a deep cold winter which meant that glass houses were not a necessity.

Something deep in Susan's memory started to surface. Science had declared that vegetation would take years to return after the nuclear plant had created a major crisis in Russia. What had actually happened was very different, plants had grown, yes, they were radioactive, but the expected moonscape had not eventuated. Plants had an amazing ability to grow in the most difficult of situations. Susan knew that the plants would grow most likely sooner than expected but would they be safe to eat? If only they had stockpiled clean soil and built glass houses before the internet had melted everything in its path.

There were no tractors to plough the ground, no bulldozers to remove the contaminated soil. It appeared that these machines were controlled by computers connected to the internet at the time of the disaster.

Time started to move again, and the country just stayed the same, despite the rains continuing to fall and the ground turning green; the people didn't seem to develop a heathy state. Looking down she was reminded of scenes she had seen on the TV of drought ravaged Africa, third world countries where people struggled to survive, let alone thrive. How could Australia, the country she loved, be reduced to such a state? What she realised was that there would be no help from their allies because they were too busy dealing with the same issues. The whole world had been reduced to famine status. This was a modern 'Tower of Babel' event. With the flick of a sun flair finger, God had again scattered the nations back to their own corners to start again. During the pandemics people had commented that it felt as if God was constantly sending us to our rooms to think about our priorities. Mostly how we related to each other. This, it seemed, would be like God was not only going to send us all back to our rooms but really discipline the world by taking away our privileges as well, in much the same way that she and Greg had with their children when they had misbehaved.

'Well, at least they won't be able to blame God for this disaster, like they do every other one.' Susan muttered to herself, 'they made the computers, not God.'

As she continued to watch the time lapse scenes unfold below her, she found herself mentally making a list of things that would be needed in order to start some sort of recovery programme. They would be able to move forward if they had the types of machinery that her father and grandfather had used but she couldn't see any of those types of vehicles down there. Where would they be able to find those pieces, let alone make sure that they worked efficiently and what about having people that would be able to operate them. So many people, even of her generation, were so used to pushing buttons and sliding things around on a touch screen that being able to operate a piece of machinery that didn't have a computer component attached to it would be so foreign that they more than likely would fall in a heap, the stress would be overwhelming. There was also the need to have sufficient stockpiles of fuel or a fuel refinery that would also work without the use of computers. There is no way there was going to be a recovery programme that would work.

There would also be a need to have a stockpile of clean soil, plant seeds and greenhouses. They would need power stations that worked on fossil fuels just as they did when her great, great, great grandfather was a boy. Back then it had been new and exciting for some people and frightening and wicked to others but in the situation that she was witnessing below her it would be an absolute necessity. The fossil fuels would need to be wood, straw or coal.

Petrol and Diesel would be in very short supply, even if they were able to store some in places that would be protected from those fires burning down there. Susan figured that this was the one element of the future that couldn't be avoided. People and equipment had become so dependent on electricity that it would be the number one propriety. She knew that before electric fridges had been invented, they worked on Kerosene, even if it was possible to find fridges that worked that way before there was electricity in abundance, they were so dangerous that it wasn't something that Susan could even contemplate. She struggled to see how they would be able to stockpile enough Kerosene in order to run a large number of fridges for an unlimited time frame, besides freezers were never made to run on this type of fuel, so electricity was going to be essential.

Suddenly, she stopped and shook her head as if she was trying to shake off a pile of cobwebs and started listing all the roadblocks that would make such an undertaking impossible. For instance, there was no way any of the government authorities would sanction the building of an old-fashioned coal fired power station, let alone a wood burning one. They were so committed to the clean-green renewable energy programme that even thinking about a coal fired power station would be akin to treason. Glancing down again, Susan wondered if there would even be enough wood available to provide consistent power for any length of time. Those fires down there were doing a very good job of turning even living trees to ashes. Would there be a way to get desalination units to work without the assistance of computers. She wasn't aware of any filtering systems that would be able to cope with the amount of water required to maintain the survival of the people, let alone livestock and crops. Besides, it would be necessary to dispose of the chemicals and waste that came out of the water and there was unlikely any satisfactory places or methods for that. She figured there must be some system, however, it was very improbable that the knowledge and equipment still existed and even if it did, finding someone who knew how to work such equipment would be nigh on impossible.

Susan lifted her head and looked into Angel's face.

'You said that God had a job for me that would mean that I would save my family?' Is this what I'm meant to save them from? That's impossible.'

'There you go again, like Sarah, you forget that with God all things are possible. What you are seeing is how things will be if you choose to walk away from the mission that God would like you to take up. He is not going to take away your free will. The choice is still yours to make. You are not meant to save the whole world, Susan. God just wants you to work in your small corner. You are only one of many people who are being inspired and challenged to prepare for such a calamity. As I said before, the answers will be found by looking around you. Believe what you see not what you hear.'

'There would be so much to do.'

'I'm not going to pretend that this undertaking is going to be easy. Like Joseph you have been given the knowledge of what is in front of the community in which you live. You will get to understand how Noah felt, while he was building the ark.'

'Right now, I feel more like Moses, too scared to even take a step forward.' Susan returned.

'Moses wasn't alone, no more than you will be'.

'What year is this all to take place?' Susan asked.

'That is not for me to tell you,' Angel replied.

'But how am I to know how long I have to prepare for such a major disaster, even Joseph knew that he had seven years to get things ready.'

'I'm not saying you won't be told I'm only saying that I'm not the one that imparts that information. What I am telling you is that you need to look. Look at the servants of God that have gone before you. Noah, Joseph, Abraham, David, and Moses have all carried out the commissions that God gave them. Their examples will be the signposts that will show you the way. Just remember to focus on who they were more than what they actually did.' Angel's gentleness never deserted her while Susan's feelings of despair and frustration at the ambiguity of the information that she was being given was mounting.

Angel held Susan firmly, exhaustion was washing over her, and Angel smiled gently. 'It's ok Susan, you can sleep now.' She closed her eyes and only had a vague feeling of being placed carefully in a bed, being tucked in as if she was a small child. Angel's voice seemed to be coming from a great distance away, saying, 'sleep well my child, there are more surprises in store for you tomorrow.' Somewhere in her mind she assumed that she had been placed back in her own bed.

5

When she woke up, her body was aching all over. My goodness I must be coming down with the flu she thought. That was not surprising considering how cold she had felt last night. She opened her eyes, but things seemed to be more out of focus than usual. She reached for her glasses, put them on. She didn't notice that her mobile phone wasn't there.

What was going on! Had she really been visited by an Angel? She thought about what she had seen, was it real or just a nightmare, had she really been shown what was going to happen in the future? The tragedy that she had seen, was it certain or could the outcomes be changed. The Angel had said that God had a job for her to do but hadn't elaborated on exactly what that meant.

She sat up in bed as the bedroom door opened, and someone entered.

'Who are you? How did you get in?' she asked, panic making her voice very high pitched, but Susan also noticed that it sounded a lot like her Gran's voice, weak and feeble.

'Good morning, Gran, it's me, Mary, did you sleep well? Are you alright? You look a little pale.'

Where was she? The room look similar to the one that she had fallen asleep in. Was that yesterday? The walls were a different colour, and the furniture was different, except there in the corner was her desk, the one that Greg and Paul had restored together. Susan felt a lump develop in her throat but there were no tears this time. What was it doing in her bedroom, it should be in the studio?

How did that happen? Her thoughts went around and around like a whirlpool. She had expected to wake up in her own home and yet it seemed that she hadn't; this strange Christmas Eve wasn't over yet! Was it still Christmas Eve?

'What day is it?' She asked the girl standing beside her bed.

'Christmas Day, Gran, it's soon going to be a new century next week. Isn't that exciting Gran" she replied with a smile. The look on her face told Susan that this child was used to being asked a lot of questions.'

'That can't be, my dear?' Susan asked, 'when I went to sleep, we were only just reaching the one third mark of the twenty first century.'

'No way!' the girl replied 'that's ancient history. Grandma, are you playing our secret game with me again? The game, where we pretend you are not really my grandma but someone who comes to visit us by travelling through time.'

'Yes', Susan said taking hold of the lifeline that had been handed to her, deciding that it was probably the best way to find out what was happening.

'We learnt about the twenty first century in school, when the thing called the internet collapsed because the sun flares overheated one of the satellites, causing most of them to fly off into outer space because the computer in the Satellite made a mistake and ultimately destroyed the whole system. Computers all around the world wouldn't work, so everything stopped. The world was a real mess, there were fires, planes fell out of the sky killing millions, cars, trucks, trains all stopped and wouldn't move, even the farmer's tractors wouldn't work, lots of people died in accidents or committed suicide and many companies went broke. Slowly people pulled together, started talking to each other again and learnt to live without computers. The world hasn't had any space programs and only limited computer infrastructure since then, Grandma, do I get 10 points.' Susan nodded, 'I'll go and get your cup of tea now, back soon,' she gave a happy little giggle as she moved swiftly out of the room.

Oh, my goodness, Susan thought, what is going on. Was this the second journey that Angel had spoken about when she had asked if she needed to get dressed, just before she had gone to the kitchen to eat the meal that Angel had prepared. She must have time travelled, just like Grandma Mary, only it appears that she has gone into the future instead of the past! Who was this family? If she had truly been shown the future by the Angel last night, there didn't seem to be very many survivors. Why hadn't Angel put her back in her own bed? Instead, she seemed to have been deposited somewhere even further into the future. Looking around she noticed that the room she was occupying didn't look that different from the one she had left with Angel. So, much for futuristic high-tech living, she thought. It wasn't long before the girl returned holding a mug of tea. Susan looked at it carefully, what did the mugs of the future look like. There had been so many predictions in the 20th and 21st Centuries, about what the future would hold for mankind. Most of it was supposed to be made of steel and the world was going to be run by robots. She decided to test Mary a little more, it was a risky question, but she had to be sure.

'Are you a robot?' Susan asked the girl who was still standing beside the bed waiting for her to take the mug of tea.

'No, Grandma!' her voice was full of indignation. 'Of course, I'm not a robot. Robots were run by computers; they were destroyed in the Meltdown. That's what we call the event when the computer made the mistake. The government decided that they were unnecessary, so no more were built after that. Grandma, are you alright? Your questions are very silly today and we don't usually play the game for this long.'

'I'm a silly person', Susan replied quickly, with a laugh. Susan was thinking fast, her body was aching all over, but her brain was still sharp. If she had in fact travelled down a time tunnel, how could she get this child to tell her all about what had happened without frightening her, after all, the reason her grandmother hadn't said anything about her time travelling experience to her daughter, Jennifer, was to avoid being considered to be suffering from dementia or being delusional and landing her in a nursing home. The last thing she wanted was to be considered mad enough to be admitted into a mental institution. Her family had already broached the subject with her, in view of her seeming inability to surface from the grief of losing her family. She suspected that if she couldn't find a way back to the real world shortly, treatment was going to be forced on her. What she couldn't understand, was why she was the only one that had been left behind. If Angel had been right, and God had a job for her to do, even the massive one that had been presented to her during the night, why, oh why, hadn't He allowed at least some members of her family to stay behind with her to assist in the assignment? Even Moses had his brother to help him.

She looked at the girl, who by now was starting to look worried. She must be about fifteen years old, Susan thought. This child seemed to believe in time tunnels, but there is no way she would believe that she had been dumped here, albeit gently, from so far back in time. Or would she?

'Do you believe in time travel?' she asked with caution.

'Of course, I do', the girl replied, 'Our family is legendary for time travel. One lady went back in time, her name was Mary, and another went forward in time. Her name was Susan, the same as your name and she had a very sad event happen in her life.'

'Which was?' asked Susan.

'Her first family were all killed in a car accident and she was left all alone', the girl replied. 'She travelled forward in time and after she returned, she remarried and had twins, a boy, and a girl. No one in the family knows when or who she is going to visit. Mum and I think that she should probably visit sometime soon but we are not really sure. That was the one thing that she didn't record, the future date that she found herself in. She worked really hard for the rest of her life to make sure that her family, friends, and anyone else that would listen to her had equipment that wasn't dependant on computers to work with, when the computer virus destroyed the world as a result of the "Meltdown".'

The girl looked at Susan, moved her head towards her left shoulder and then over to her right, she seemed to be trying to examine Susan.

'I'm Susan', she said.

'Yes, I know, Gran, your name is Susan.'

'I'm Susan Green, honey, yesterday when I fell asleep, it was still the twenty first century.'

'No way!!,' the girl squealed, 'I'm named after your grandmother the first 'time traveller'. My mum is Jennifer, and she is named after your mother. This is so cool', she jumped up and was about to run out of the room.

'Hey, hang on a minute. Let's not get too excited. We don't want to make too much fuss, maybe the rest of the family will think we have both gone mad.'

'No way, the only one that is likely not to believe us is Dad, his name is David by the way. He's the only one that has trouble with the family legends.'

'Are you two going to chat in there all day or would you like to come out and have breakfast sometime soon?' someone called.

"That's mum, you'd better hurry up, here I'll help you out of bed. It's Christmas morning and we are the only ones here at the moment so no one will mind if you eat breakfast in your dressing gown but usually it's frowned upon. We will be going to church at eight thirty.' Mary said as she helped her into the gown had been draped across the rocking chair in the corner. Again, Susan looked around the room. It was square and looked very much like her own house. Mary took her arm and helped her to stand. Pain shot down her left leg as she put it on the floor making her flinch badly, Mary grabbed her more firmly.

'What happened to my leg?' she asked. 'and there is a lot of pain across my back. Oh, hang on, I've experienced that before.'

'Nothing, Grandma, it's just old age, they haven't found a cue for that yet', she replied as she led her out of the room.

'I think if your grandmother gave up eating Tomatoes, she would find that the pain in her shoulders would disappear. It's worked for me.' Susan said as they walked through the door which swung on hinges, in the same way that the doors she was used to worked. It seemed that the predictions of her time, of houses being like seed pods with doors that slid open when you spoke hadn't eventuated, even yet. They turned right, walked down the last part of a hallway that stretched behind her and out into an open living area. It seemed that her room was closest to the kitchen, the rest could be investigated later.

There was a large wooden table and chairs in the middle of the room, the kitchen was directly on her right and divided from the eating area with a bench, it was what we called a galley kitchen, she thought. It wasn't big but still very similar to those that people used in her time. It seems that the tried and tested systems of the past were still being used. The whole area was bright and airy. Beyond the table and chairs there was a lounge area, with a corner sofa, that sat against the right wall of the room, under the windows and across the room to divide the living area from the rest of the space, very twentieth century in style, Susan thought. The windows were already open to allow a breeze to flow through the room. The window directly in front of her was decorated with a Christmas garland, off which hung a number of envelopes. It was made with Tinsel and a variety of ornaments.

High on one wall, there was a clock, telling her that it was only six o'clock in the morning. The only other thing on the walls was a very strange, large, framed picture. It had a vortex spiral taking up the centre two-thirds of the picture with lots of the modern equipment that she was used to, looking as if it was being sucked down into the tunnel. The bottom sixth of the picture was taken up with old farming scenes. Across the top in very large letters was a date. Wow, exactly 32 years after Greg and her family had been taken from her. I wonder where that came from and what the date means. Is that the date the 'MELTDOWN' started she wondered? Angel's words echoed in her head, 'answers will be found by looking around you'. She looked outside; the grass was green, telling her that it wasn't suffering from the usual drying heat that is part of Australian Christmas weather. The room seemed cool enough and she looked around for an air-conditioning unit. There didn't seem to be one, although she noticed a few vents around the room. There must be a unit outside, she thought, but then why were the windows open, that would be something to look into later. Australian summers were notoriously hot, so how had they solved the cooling of houses in the future?

She was moving a little easier by the time Mary helped her to sit down at the table, Jennifer placed a plate of bacon, eggs, and tomatoes with toast in front of her. 'Good morning mum,' she said, as she kissed her cheek, 'you are looking particularly bright this morning, have a good sleep, did you?' she said with a smile.

'Yes dear, I must have', she replied, looking at Mary with a wink, but I don't think I'll have the tomatoes this morning dear, please.

'Mum, you love tomatoes! What are you two up to?' Jennifer asked, switching her gaze from one to the other.

'Mum, meet Susan Green from the twenty-first century,' Mary said in a very casual voice.

'Really!' Jennifer said, Susan could hear a note of caution in her voice, 'It's really you, finally you get to visit', her excitement was very evident now. 'Oh, wow, I don't believe it. You look just like my mother but if I remember correctly Mary looked like Mary Campbell too when she went back in time. Oh, this is great. We have so much to talk about and Jeff and his family are coming for lunch today. David might think we have all gone mad, but I don't care. It is wonderful to finally meet you, Susan Green'. Jennifer bent down and hugged her tightly and then quietly continued, 'I'm so sorry for your loss, Susan', looking into her face, she asked, 'How long has it been?'

Susan knew that she was asking how long it had been since her family had been killed and for the first time, she answered the question without tears streaming down her face.

'Eighteen months.'

'Well, healing begins today', Jennifer said, 'and it starts with your breakfast'.

Susan looked at her plate of food and smiled. It seemed those 21st century activists who wanted everyone to become vegetarians hadn't got their way completely, or had they? Was this real bacon? Have they done such a good job of creating false food that it looked real? Mary had sat down beside her and accepted a plate of food from her mother with a smile and a thank you.

Susan lent closer to Mary, placing the tomato on her plate, and whispered, 'Is this real bacon from a pig or do they make it in a factory?'

'It's real, Grandma, we get it fresh from Uncle Jeff's farm just out of town. He has the best pigs in the district, and they make the best bacon, ham, and pork sausages too. They'll be here for lunch today. Uncle Jeff is such a fun person. The eggs are from his farm as well, mum grew the tomatoes', Mary said, anticipating Susan's next question.

'Well, I never', Susan said, more to herself, than to Mary.

'Come on you two, eat!' Jennifer instructed as she placed two mugs of hot tea on the table. 'Mary, you say grace this morning please'. Jennifer stood still, while Mary prayed.

'Lord, we thank you for the food that you have delivered for us to enjoy, we thank you for the provision of a good night's sleep and for the gracious way that you have provided for and protected this family in so many ways. Make us truly grateful, until you come again. Amen.'

Oh, my goodness, Susan thought, it's the same grace that Grandma Mary started to use after her trip back in time.

'Where is the rest of the family?' Susan asked.

'Oh, they left early to go and help Uncle Jeff get his jobs done, so he can have some time off today. They left at four thirty and will be having breakfast with them. That's their payment for helping. You got to sleep in grandma. One of the privileges of old age', Mary said smiling. This child seemed to be always smiling. It was nice considering that very few people smiled in her time.

'What, you don't get to have breakfast together on Christmas Day?'

'It happens most Sundays as well. We are family and we help each other. We all get to have breakfast together every other day of the week. Jeff and his family will be here for lunch. It's no big deal. I sometimes go out to help them as well. Dad decided that I should stay here and help mum today, that's all.'

After breakfast was finished, Susan and Mary moved to get ready for Church.

'Where do I find the shower, if you still use such things, Mary?' Susan asked, wondering if they even had showers every day or what the water situation was. Mary led Susan to the room next to her bedroom.

'This is your dressing room, Grandma. Your clothes are in these cupboards there and yes, from what I understand, the showers are much the same as they were in your time', she spread out both her arms towards a cupboard on either side of the doorway. In front of her she could see an en-suite containing a shower, washbasin, and toilet.

'I'll leave you to it', Mary said as she closed the door behind Susan. Susan opened the cupboards to see what clothes she would be expected to wear this morning. There seemed to be a complete set gathered together in readiness for the day. What did the fashions look like these days, she wondered? The predictions were that everyone would wear all-in-one jumpsuits, or trousers and tops. This outfit looked very similar to what her grandmother would wear, stylish, comfortable, and very bright in colour. It didn't take her long to realise that things hadn't changed that much. The underclothes were much the same as what she was used to, and the dress she picked was a loose fit with a nice lace overlay in red. What she noticed was that she only had a choice of two outfits, had society done away with the overfilling of their wardrobes with an abundance of clothes or was it just this family? She found a pair of shoes and a handbag in the cupboard that matched the colour of the dress. The shoes even had a reasonable heel, which pleased her. She loved her heels and while she was used to wearing something a fair bit higher, she realised that with her sudden advancement in age, these heels were a good choice. The tiles in the shower were a non-slip type, which was great considering her confidence was dropping fast with all the aches and pains she was experiencing. She showered and dressed and returned to the living area and sat down at the table as there seemed to be no one else around. The house was very quiet, just as quiet as her house was now that the family was all gone but there wasn't the sadness that hung over her place, this house was full of love, joy, and contentment.

She hadn't been sitting very long when she heard a car pull up outside, doors banged, and various male voices drifted in through the opened windows. A door, that she hadn't noticed right beside the kitchen, opened and three men walked in, placing two baskets on the kitchen counter, one full of vegetables and the other empty. They were dressed in work clothes, very much the same as her brother wore. What really struck her was how much one of them looked like Paul, her son. A lot of people had commented that Paul looked a lot like her. She felt the colour drain from her face.

'Good morning, Mum, you're ready early. Did you sleep well? You look a little pale, are you sure you are ok?' the oldest of the three asked. She knew that this had to be Jennifer's husband, David. She also didn't know if people even got married anymore. It was certainly going out of fashion in her time.

'Yes, thank you, I'm fine, how did you get on this morning?' she replied trying to keep the conversation general and hoping that her reply didn't give too much away.

Mary appeared at this point, saving her from having to say anything more. Mary had a red and green, fifties style dress on, it was narrow at the waist with a full skirt that finished just below her knees.

'Dad, John, and Greg, you're back early today.' She said sounding surprised.

'Things went really well this morning, so where is your mum?' Mary's dad said.

'In your room', Mary replied. The other two men had both moved to her side, kissed her cheek, and said a quiet good morning before disappearing down the hallway. Mary's dad followed them without saying any more to her.

'We'll break the news to them later,' Mary whispered, 'I don't think the time is right yet.'

'I agree, sweetheart, do I look okay?' Susan asked.

'Yes, you look beautiful. You always look good in that dress, it's very Christmassy'. She smiled, and Susan realised that it was going to be a confusing day for Mary.

'Look, honey,' she said, 'it won't matter to me if you mix me up with your grandmother, after all, I'm in her body, so just relax and let's enjoy the day. You look very nice as well, my dear, that dress is also very Christmassy.'

'Thank you, and yes, that's cool with me', Mary replied.

'By the way, if the diaries about the first-time travelling event are correct and I go back to my time tonight, your real grandmother will not remember a thing about today, so please keep that in mind when you see her tomorrow, alright?'

'Sure thing, Grandma', Mary said, smiling broadly.

'At least, she will have someone to explain to her why she cannot remember anything about today. The first Mary didn't have that. She never did find out why she couldn't remember anything about that Christmas Day did she!'

'What is the story behind the baskets on the counter?' Susan asked, looking at the counter, Mary followed her gaze, 'Oh, the vegetables are from Uncle Jeff, they share their excess with us, and we picked our extra stuff yesterday which was in the empty basket. Dad took that out this morning for them. We will fill it for them again later in the week. We grow different things so there is enough variety to go around everyone. The family will take some down to an elderly lady down the street later as well.

6

At eight-fifteen, the family all appeared in the living room. Jennifer was dressed in an elegant shift that looked cool and appeared to be a mix of the twentieth century forties length and sixties style. The men wore suits. Each a slightly different colour but suits were suits and Susan couldn't make up her mind as to what era they reminded her of.

'Won't it be too hot for suits,' she asked.

'It's only supposed to get to twenty-eight degrees today, so we'll be fine,' David responded giving his wife a look that sent a message of concern. Jennifer whispered something to him as she kissed him, and he appeared to relax. What happened to global warming, she wondered but knew that now was not the time to bring up the subject.

'Right, Mum,' he said, 'Do you want to go in the car or are you up to walking today.'

'Walking sounds good to me', she said, hoping that it wasn't too far.

'It'll take us ten minutes at your pace', he smiled, 'So, we'd better leave now'.

'You all walk ahead and save us some seats, I'll walk with Grandma, that way we won't end up having to sit outside', Mary suggested.

'Ok, let's go'. David led the way to the front door. Jennifer picked up a couple of tins waiting on the bench and followed. After everyone was outside, David carefully locked the door, tested to make sure it was definitely locked, and they were off. Susan noticed there were groups of other people moving along the street in the same direction. Many of them also carrying tins, that presumably contained food of some sort.

'All these people are going to church?' She asked Mary in surprise.

'Yes, Gran, when there was nothing else to hang on to, people realised that the only source of strength and power was God, we haven't forgotten that, yet.'

'You don't sound convinced that it's going to last?' Susan asked.

'History goes around in circles', Mary said, 'This country moved away from God back in the Twentieth and twentieth-first century, sadly I believe they will do it again, just as the Israelites did. We are a blessed nation, but we are starting to take those blessings for granted again.' Susan was amazed at the maturity of this child. She was certainly far more mature than the lads that had been driving the four-wheel drive that had taken her family away from her or even the teenagers that lived in her street. It seems that the more people have to struggle the more mature they get.

As they approached the church, Susan noticed that the building wasn't a large one and was very modest in appearance. There were some people sitting around outside, indicating that the seating inside must be taken, unless of course some people just preferred to be outside. There was a small carpark which was now being used for outdoor seating. Susan noticed that there were very few cars around.

'Why are there so few cars?' She asked Mary.

'When the 'MELTDOWN' hit most cars were operated by computers. Some just stopped, others went into the bush on the sides of the roads. The only cars that kept going were the ones that people in the bush owned because the government hadn't put in the infrastructure that was needed for computer cars. They were worth their weight in gold almost. Slowly people realised that walking made us healthier anyway and so the only people who own cars now are those who live a long way from town. Towns people mostly walk and most families only own one car. The town has a large carpark two blocks away. Most of the people who live out of town, park there and walk to church. These cars are only for those who are unable to walk the two blocks. Our town planners worked it out so that there are three very large carparks around the edge of town and are within walking distance of most venues. That way they only had to maintain the three carparks and people get to walk more, which means we stay healthier. There are some limited parking spaces in front of the shops in town, but they are reserved for the disabled'.

Church was surprisingly similar to how they worshipped at home when her mum had been little. There was a piano and an organ for the music. She looked around at the pictures that had been painted on the walls between the windows. They all represented various stories from the Bible. There were paintings about creation, Abraham and Isaac, telling of how God has the answers to our problems. There was the Christmas story, the crucifixion, Paul, and Peter fishing. If someone couldn't hear or read, then they too would be able to learn of the love of God. It was the same thing that stained glass windows achieved in the eighteenth and early nineteen centuries. There was a microphone and there must be speakers outside. What there wasn't, was a screen, not a single PowerPoint display in sight. Susan closed her eyes. She listened to the preacher, yes, even a blind man could get the message of how much God loved them. The dependence on computer technology in church was something that both her and Greg had agreed was not helpful. They had often commented that if a blind man had walked in off the street, he would have no idea what was happening because if you could not see the "PowerPoints" there were a lot of blank spaces in the sermons. It appeared that some things had changed for the better, and Susan let out a quiet deep sigh and relaxed back into the seat. Things had looked so grim yesterday that Susan wouldn't have been surprised if the human race had destroyed itself just as the computer infrastructure had, if Mary was to be believed. Maybe that was the important difference. Mary had indicated that when the computer system had collapsed, destroying itself, people had rallied together after the initial crisis and eventually worked things out and rebuilt their lives. People, unlike computers, had the ability to use their God given imaginations, not just make decisions based on logical patterns and algorithms. It probably took a while, but it appeared that when computers finished telling people what to do, they had managed to start thinking for themselves again. After all, that's how this country moved from the primitive to the more industrial era in the first place. We were known as the most inventive country in the world back in the 19th century.

The service didn't go on for too long, but what impressed Susan the most was the sermon. It was short and to the point. The minister was very clear about why we celebrate Christmas. We gather to celebrate God's entry into our sinful world. His mission was to provide a way to save us from eternity in hell by dying on the cross, something that we will be celebrating at Easter in a few months' time.

Everyone gathered together in a room at the rear of the building for morning tea even though it was Christmas Day. It seemed that no one was in a hurry to go home. Susan sat in a chair that had been provided for her and watched the one hundred and fifty or so people interact with each other. There must have been a dozen or more groups in the room. Someone approached her with a mug of tea and a plate of Christmas goodies.

'How have you been, Mrs Jones', they asked, although Susan had no idea who was speaking to her. 'I've been very well, thank you', Susan replied, hoping that she was actually telling the truth. After all she couldn't say that she had been miserable for the last eighteen months, as that Susan wasn't the Susan who was sitting here being spoken to by this strange person.

'That's good, Susan, I know you like to watch our groups interact, so I'll leave you to it', the lady said as she moved away.

Susan sipped the tea and watched. Some groups were smiling and laughing as they talked. Other groups seemed to be involved in very serious discussions and then in the corner away from the main group, Susan noticed a group of four people sitting in a circle, who appeared to be praying earnestly. What was very clear to Susan was that these people really cared about each other. As she watched, between the short conversations with several people who engaged her, she noticed that the groups moved around. The groups made up of people ranging from the elderly to the very young didn't stay static, new people would join a group and others would leave to join another group, but nobody was in a hurry. There were others sitting by themselves, but they seemed relaxed and comfortable, not lonely or sad.

Somewhere, a clock started to strike, Susan counted the bell-like sounds ten times. Ten O'clock, even that was the same. So much for the predictions of her time. If only her real generation knew how much the future was going to be the same.

'Are you ready to return home now?' Jennifer asked, approaching her.

'Yes, whenever you are ready, but if you have things to do, I'm quite happy,' Susan responded. She didn't feel that tired although she had been glad to sit inside once they had arrived at church.

'Well, give me a minute to collect my tins and we'll be off.'

As they walked along the side of the church, Susan could see a group of people waiting for them. She recognised, David, Mary, and the boys, but there was another family that she didn't know. A man, woman, and two children were also watching them approach.

'They were just packing up the chairs from the carpark', Jennifer explained.

'So, has the future done away with feminism as well?' Susan asked.

'No, not really, I think we have a lot more respect for both sexes now. People are too busy working now to worry about who can do what. If it has to be done, then it doesn't matter if you are female or male, you pitch in and help when it is necessary, and they allow others room to choose when it isn't.' Suddenly, it struck Susan that Jennifer was talking about males and females. Well at least they have done away with that silly nonsense, Susan thought, yesterday she could have been arrested for saying someone was a male or female. Sadly, when she returned to her real world it would still be the same but knowing that, eventually, people would realise that men and women were made as two parts of humanity, gave her hope for the future.

'There are still those who insist on being hurtful', Jennifer was still talking, 'but most people have to work now that there are not as many machines. When the computers stopped working, people finally realised that any job was better than sitting at home doing nothing. There was no television, computers, or social media to be involved with all day. Nothing is more demeaning than not working at all and now there is plenty of work for everyone because the computers stopped doing it all for us. The other people standing with David are Jeff and his wife Monique, by the way, the children are Emma and Daniel.'

When they arrived back home, they all gathered in the living area and sat on the sofa with the children occupying the floor. John carried out the rocking chair that was in her room and she was installed rather regally in it.

Jennifer and David brought drink pitchers and glasses and placed them on the coffee table that she hadn't noticed before. After everyone had a drink in their hand, Jennifer made a noise that clearly told the group gathered that she wanted to speak.

'Before we drink our toast to Jesus today, I want to introduce you to a very special guest. Sitting in my mother's rocking chair today is not my mother, but Susan Green, the Susan Green of time travelling legend.' Susan watched their faces and smiled crookedly at them.

'Oh, come on!' David said, 'There is no way that is a real story.'

'Dad, I can prove it', Mary said, she turned to Susan and said, 'what does the cover of the family history album look like?'

345

'Its cover has a gold tree that takes up most of the space with a pale green background. It's about this big. Susan moved her hand to indicate that the book was in fact about two-foot square in shape rather than the usual A4 size that most people associated with books. The box that I put it in is also pale green.'

Mary left the room and came back carrying a box, Susan recognised it as the box that she had given to her grandmother five years ago, but which was now a little more battered with age, but it was the same box.

'See, Dad.'

'Oh, don't be silly, Mary, your grandmother has looked at that album a million times, of course she would be able to tell me what it looks like.'

There will always be unbelievers thought Susan, people will always be people. Someone will always try to have a plausible explanation for the unexplained. Susan thought, looking at David.

'Mary, can I have the box please.' Susan asked, she wasn't sure why she had done it at the time but now she was glad that she had, maybe. Susan opened the box and checked the back cover. While the album had been well used over the years the cover was in extremely good repair. In fact, there was no damage at all.

'David, if you want proof that I am the person who made this book, I'd like you to lift the top right-hand corner of the back inside cover and underneath you will find my initials in dark green ink, SG inside a circle. If you use some steam the glue should soften enough for you to lift and see if I'm right, after that if you press the paper back down the glue will reset when it dries out.'

David looked dumbfounded but went and did exactly what she had told him to do, the rest of the family silently watched on. They heard David gasp, yes, sure enough there were the initials, precisely as she said they would be.

'Alright, you win', he said, if not a little ungraciously. 'Let's make our toast to Jesus and then we will open the envelopes'. He placed the album on the bench to reset the glue and moved back to the lounge area.

It just proves that humanity is still the same, she thought with a sad smile. Some people, when faced with absolute proof, ignore it in the hope that they will not have to deal with it.

It appeared that it was Daniel's turn this year to give out the envelopes. Gifts had to be small enough to fit in one or a voucher was placed instead. Daniel gave his mother a packet of seeds, David gave Jeff a voucher that said he would help him put up the new fence he was wanting within the next three months. Mary gave Greg a voucher saying that she would wash the family car once a month for a whole year giving him one weekend a month off this job and so on. It was such a lovely time. When it came for her envelope or rather her hostess' envelope, Susan asked that they be put aside and opened the next day. After all, she already had the best Christmas gift ever and that was the knowledge that she still had a strongly bound family that honoured God, with hard work, generosity, and a sensible approach to material goods.

7

Over lunch, the conversation turned to how people had survived after the Meltdown. How the people in the regional areas had a much easier time surviving simply because most politicians had largely ignored the bush. Their infrastructure had not been completely updated and so they were able to use things like landline telephone services, how cars that needed drivers to make them work were suddenly very valuable, as well as those old-time tractors that didn't need a satellite to tell it where to go. If it hadn't been for the neglect of the bush, the country would have had a catastrophe that it may never have been able to recover from. It appeared that the older you were, the more important you were. They had politicians begging them to tell them what options were available now that all this modern technology had destroyed itself and they didn't know how to work without it.

Susan could believe this, she had seen young people who lived in her street who had no idea what some of the things her grandmother still used were, let alone how they worked. Add on another thirty years and yes, technology would be running the world, not humans running the technology, which is how it should be.

At some point Susan realised that what she was being told seemed to be very precise. There didn't seem to be any variations that might occur when stories are handed down from one generation to another.

'How are you all so sure of your facts?' she asked. 'It's been such a long time, surely something might have been mixed up.'

'It's very simple, Susan', Jennifer said, 'We have kept all your diaries. They are locked away in the fireproof cabinet, would you like to see them?'

'I guess so, if it's not too much trouble.'

'Not at all, come with me.'

Susan followed Jennifer out to a back room. When Jennifer turned on the light it was easy to see that it had been built as a saferoom with brick walls and a steel ceiling. It was cool but airless, and Susan was hoping that they didn't need to stay there very long.

Jennifer walked across the room to a steel cabinet standing against the back wall. She opened the door wide to allow Susan to see shelves of books, all A4 in size carefully lined up. Here, these start from when you returned and finish five years before you die. It appears that you were unable to keep writing towards the end of your life. You live until you 89th year. Susan's eyes scanned the cupboard and glancing at the shelf below the books she noticed a box. A box that she had definitely seen before. She reached out, looking at Jennifer as she did so.

'This contains the Mary Campbell Diaries, am I right?'

'Yes, and also a very long letter from your grandmother, telling those she left behind about her trip back in time. I gather that your mother doesn't even know about this yet?' The envelope has written on the front of it "To be opened only after my death".

She opened the box, and checked inside, there was the envelope, the tea towel, hessian bag and the diaries. I'm so glad Gran still has these, Susan thought, otherwise I might have thrown them out a few months back when I was madly getting rid of things. Mum was right, we are all connected to our past and trying to disconnect with it does only bring heartache. I'll be asking mum for those boxes that she took away as soon as they get back from their holiday.

'No,' Susan answered Jennifer as she returned the box to it place in the cabinet, minus the letter. 'I'd like to read this, later, if you don't mind. Can I do that?'

'Sure,' Jennifer said, 'just leave it on the kitchen table when you are finished, and I'll put it back in the morning.'

'You know we don't want to tell mum because Gran is afraid that she will try to make her live with her at the very least, at worst put her in a nursing home. I've had the feeling for a while though that she was writing something. I'm hoping that I will understand what happened a bit more after reading this.'

Her gaze returned to the diaries that she was still to write but were lined up on the shelf in front of her. She lifted out the first one, she recognised it as the one that was already sitting on her desk at home. She had purchased it more out of habit rather than any real suggestion that it would actually be filled it with bookings or information. She turned it over in her hand, just as she had when it had arrived with her office supplies delivery. It was the one that she would use in the upcoming year. It had a full page allocated to each day of the year. Susan opened it on the first page and read, Dear family I have seen what the future holds for all of us. It, like Revelation, gives me hope that even though there are many dark days ahead, both for us as a family and our country, I know that we are going to be able to work our way through the greatest difficulties that this country will experience. However, in order to make that journey a little easier we must make some very definite preparations.

The Bible tells us that Joseph stored up food for the Egyptians when God allowed him to see a future disaster ahead of time. So, we must do the same. Not only do we need to have provisions ready for when the time comes but we must also have equipment ready and able to work without the assistance of computer technology. Yes, my loved ones, computers are not flawless. As improbable as it seems to us today, they will destroy themselves, leaving mankind floundering in nothingness in the same way that mankind floundered in the floods of Noah.

Susan stopped reading, she had gotten the idea of what mission she would be carrying out once she returned to her own time and place.

As she flipped through the rest of the book looking at the entries, she saw that she had handwritten a summary of each day.

'It looks as if I refused to use the computer for these from day one', she mumbled more to herself than Jennifer.

'So, what did I do after the crisis?' she asked Jennifer, after all these diaries wouldn't be available once there were no computer printers.

'Well, you certainly kept writing,' Jennifer said as she moved her hand along the shelf until she came to a book with the year handwritten down its spine.

'I think you must have purchased a stockpile of these books because they are all the same, using them when you could no longer get the dated diaries.' Jennifer pulled out the book and handed it to Susan who flipped through it briefly and handed it back.

'Don't you want to read some of them', Jennifer asked.

'Goodness, no, it's almost too weird seeing them lined up here, knowing that I haven't even started writing them yet. What did David think these were? I take it he has read them too.'

'Yes, he's read them, but he thought that you just had too much time on your hands and wrote them as a work of fiction.'

'Really! That's a massive body of work just for the fun of it, he must have thought I was nuts.'

'That just about sums it up, yes. Shall we go back to the others, this room is so stuffy.'

'Yes, let's.'

As lunch continued, Susan asked many questions, and the family did their best to answer them for her. The first one related to the weather. It's so much cooler now than it was during the 20th century. 'Has the planet cooled down?'

'No', Jeff laughed, 'the climate change debate turned out to be the biggest hoax in history but the drought that you are in at present has a few more years to run yet. Some of the mining companies started pumping their excess water into Lake Aye and any other ground depression they could find. Their theory was that if they increased the humidity of the inland then the rains would come back. If the land continued to dry out, then no one was going to be able to make money out of farming. They contended that while it wasn't raining, it might as well be under water. The government didn't seem to be interested in the possibility of the concept working but they, being foreign companies, did it anyway, surprisingly, with the approval of the farmers. The 'Greens' objected but the rains came in so much quicker than anyone expected and meant they were silenced. Part of their argument was that these people didn't insist on countries, like the Netherlands, returning their land back into swamps that they had drained. These measures were about the survival of the country and pretty much the world, so they carried on. While we still have dry spells, they usually only last a few months now, not for decades like they are for you. More moisture in the air allows the breezes to work as air conditioners and so the temperatures don't climb so high. February can still be hot, but the heat doesn't last for the months like it used to.'

'The farming industry must have been nearly finished by then, though? It's nearly finished now, with the continuation of the current treatment of farmers, the industry must surely have been wrecked. How were they able to hang on for that long?' She asked.

'Well, it didn't really, there were some very tough years until imports of food were unable to get through for a couple of years. The Asian Pacific countries banded together and managed to interrupt the shipping lines. It was retribution for some minor policy that the Australian government had implemented. People in the cities were starting to get very hungry and rioting resulted. With no food on the supermarket shelves, the city populous got very upset.'

'As they would', David injected.

'Suddenly, the government realised that the farming industry was very important. They finally conceded that farmers could look after the land, but they had to let them take matters into their own hands, or the country would starve. It was largely due to the lobbying carried out by a friend of Braxton Withers, who just happened to be the Minister for Agriculture, at the time. He had made the shift from New South Wales state politics into the federal arena only the year before. He was able to get the legislation through parliament.

He was also pretty instrumental in making sure there were laws to protect some of the infrastructure that you want preserved so that the measures you could see would be needed were available at the time of the "Meltdown". They even went back to using coal fired power stations for electricity. They found that the solar panels and wind turbines just didn't work in the post meltdown world, besides, once the rest of the world had their own problems to deal with, the Australian people could get on with looking after itself and do what was best for it without the bullies of the rest of the world telling them what to do.'

'Wow!' Susan exclaimed, 'That's interesting'.

'He also mentored his successor, Claire Withers Stanton, the woman who was to be Prime Minister when the Meltdown occurred. She proved to be a very brilliant leader at a time when the country could have fallen into something like a Mad Max movie. The miraculous thing was that the incumbent Prime Minister died suddenly of a heart attack. He was in the middle of a press conference, ironically about the newest and greatest internet satellites that would be launched in a few weeks, when he suddenly put his hand on his chest, went as white as a sheet and collapsed. Efforts to revive him proved futile. The Agriculture Minister, who was also the Deputy Prime Minister, moved into the position of Prime Minister one month before the meltdown took place. It had very interesting parallels with the story of Ester from the Bible.' Jeff giggled.

'I have a hard time imagining such things, not the destruction of the farming industry of course, you don't have to be Einstein to see that happening. It's the rest of it, but if you are telling me it does then I'll just have to wait.'

'It's a bit like waiting for the return of Jesus, we have been told, but in that case, not when', Mary injected.

'Yes, well it's very easy to have great hindsight after things happen. I guess it would have been the same if someone during World War II had travelled to your time. They must have felt that it was never going to end, particularly when it was still going on after five years. If they had been able to travel forward in time then, they would have found out that it was nearly over.' Jennifer added.

"Oh, well now that there is an end in sight it might be easier for my brother, Jeff, to hang on. I know that he and Clare are feeling very despondent at present. It is so frustrating for them when at every turn they are being forced to do more paperwork and comply with more government regulations. I know that they harbour great fears for what it might mean for Joey and Rose if they want to go into the agriculture industry when they get older. All they can see on the horizon is civil war in order to get back the land sold off to foreign powers.'

'Actually, the best advice you can give Jeff, is for him to start diversifying his farm. He needs to move into the more old-fashioned market gardening, pigs, milk, and butter. Along the lines that Joe and Rose had back in the 1800's. The ways of the good old days are what will save him, his family, and friends. It will be hard work for him. Claire shouldn't give up her job either, not yet anyway, but by doing that they will ensure that their family is provided for when the war starts. His skills will be able to keep all his family fed at a time when many in the country will be starving.' Jeff was thoughtful. 'The survival of our nation doesn't just depend on you alone, it is a collaboration of many people, all playing all their parts and working together.'

'So, it looks like everyone has played their parts well then, if I'm here and things are the way they are?' Susan said.

'Maybe', Jeff was still thoughtful, 'I don't understand how our freewill fits into this, if this is a done deal then all those people are just puppets on strings directed by God.'

'Hmm, yes, I see what you mean.'

After lunch, the family sat in the lounge area and continued to talk. They talked about Susan's role in their family's existence and survival. 'You are the one that insisted that any equipment that doesn't need a computer to make it work should be maintained and kept in top working order. The story goes that she was laughed at a lot, a bit like they think Noah would have been', Jennifer remarked, and the family nodded. 'The family, and other families who had heeded her advice, and there were a few, were extremely thankful once the Meltdown started to unfold. Those who had decided that Susan had gone mad really had to eat humble pie, many of them, not being able to cope, committed suicide, leaving their families with a great deal more unnecessary grief.'

'The best way to get an overall picture of what happened is to read an essay that Mary wrote for school. She did a lot of research and read all your diaries. We are going to visit Mrs Smith, down the street for an hour or so, why don't you sit quietly and read. Then we can answer any questions when we get back', David suggested.

Turning to Mary, 'Go and bring Susan your essay, please and then we'll leave her to read it in peace and quiet'. Mary was already leaving the room as Jennifer finished speaking.

She returned with a small book which she handed to Susan. Flipping through it she could see that there was writing on quite a few pages.

'I thought you said it was an essay?'

'It is, just a very long one', she returned smiling 'I want to add to it and leave it in the cupboard along with all the rest of the family history'.

'Wow!' was all Susan could say.

Jennifer made Susan a mug of tea and they headed out the door.

8

Susan opened the book and started to read.

It started out like any other normal winter's day.
Cold, with a good frost on the ground. The droughts
now only lasted for months rather than the years that
were common during the early twenty-first century.
The good rains had made people comfortable and
optimistic and had allowed farmers to survive during
the Asia Pacific war, if they had been wise enough to
diversify in the years leading up to the conflict.
Farming in Australia was no longer a big business but
largely a cottage industry. Once the conflict had been
resolved, imported food had again become the major
source of substance for the population as a whole.
The politicians still focused their empty promises and
energies on the large settlement areas rather than
those known as the bush or outback.

Small towns and farmers were really starting to feel
the pressure. Government authorities still wanted
farmers to upgrade to high priced computer equipment
which they insisted would not only make things easier,
but also save greenhouse gases, which they asserted
would prevent the return of droughts, and would not

make the mistakes that humans were prone to. The cost of these made it impossible for many farmers as their incomes were still minimal and the infrastructures that these machines needed didn't reach that far out into the bush. What wasn't widely known was that it would also allow a greater amount of tracking of their activities. During the previous month, the Prime Minister had announced that new satellites would be launched in order to make sure that every inch of the country would have internet coverage. Other countries around the world had managed to achieve this years ago and it was high time that Australia caught up with the modern world.

Over the coming days and weeks, they were going to be thankful for being the forgotten members of society.

As the clocks around the country struck the tenth hour, people noticed some strange things starting to happen. Traffic lights started to play up, they flickered in the wrong order causing confusion on the roads. There seemed to be something very different about this failure of the internet system. There had been failures in the system before, but they had been isolated both in the locations and systems affected. Radio stations were next to shut down. They were unable to transmit. Television stations also started to experience intermitted problems until they finally had to shut down.

It soon became very clear that this was a worldwide hacking issue. Communication around the world was becoming very hard, but the little communication that was managed indicated that these issues were not isolated but, for the first time in history, the same thing was happening around the world in real time. Nothing worked the way it was meant to. The world was thrown into an eerie but deafening silence. From that point on no one would know what disaster was befalling those in the next town, state, or country. People soon discovered that the only way to connect was to actually talk to someone. No one even entertained the idea that it was caused by the computer system itself. Why would it do that, it was infallible.

Trains stopped in their tracks, some in the middle of tunnels. Passengers needed to break their way out by smashing the windows and doors in order to save themselves from suffocation as the air conditioning systems failed to operate. Ships stopped in the middle of the oceans and quickly started to drift in the currents as their mighty engines also failed to provide the power needed to keep them in the correct shipping lanes.

The banking system went down, making it impossible for people to buy goods. Over the next two days the computer systems all over the world crashed. The newer planes just fell out of the sky, killing so many people. The older ones, that had more experienced pilots at the controls were able to land but it was chaos as they tried landing at airports using visual cues only. The control tower being out of commission the instant the computer system went down. There were a lot of near misses and even some disasters with some planes landing too close together.

In the small town where my ancestors lived, they gathered together and prayed for the families facing the disaster they knew was happening. There was no need for them to formalise a restoration program. The town had been operating with the minimum use of computers for years so that when this disaster actually happened their town was able to continue operating as usual. Yes, there were some things that had to be done, such as firing up the restored power station, which had been restored under the guise of being a museum piece, allowing the power grid to operate on a local level. Within a few hours, power, water, and telephone communications were restored. The community was finally thankful that they had been able to have the old systems in place alongside the National Broadband Network thanks to a particularly hard-working Agricultural Minister.

It would seem that the country had almost reverted to its colonial levels of operation. Except that now most of those people were situated in the regional areas away from the highly populated areas along the coastal fringe. There wasn't even enough army personal available to help restore sanity to an insane world.

My ancestor, Susan, had visited the future and she knew that this was all going to happen thirty years before it came about. On her return she knew what could be done in order to reduce the amount of chaos that would eventuate. She also knew that if she went around telling people of this, they would consider her to be totally insane and commit her to a hospital. With much prayer, she was able to start her campaign by challenging the young people through an open letter on social media.

The letter went viral, which means that it was seen by people all around the world. Susan was asked to

speak at some schools, where she challenged all the
students to be the leaders of the future by showing
the older generation how it was done. However, not
that many students actually took up the challenge.
They found it too hard. At one school, a student
asked her if she did all the things that she suggested
and her response was, no, not all of them but she
wasn't the one worrying about climate change.

Over the years Susan and her husband used their spare
money and time making, selling, and repairing old
machinery, making sure that they were in top working
order. It wasn't just farm machinery they worked on,
it was also printers, generators, large mixing machinery
used for making bread or baking, sewing machines, quite
a few treadle ones because she knew that electricity
would not be available in some areas for months after
the virus had infected the system. They fixed
anything that would help people get things done when
the computers stopped working. These were not to be
museum pieces, they had to be active working
equipment and they made sure that there were plenty
of people around that were trained to use them,
particularly as some of the equipment required good
concentration to keep the operators safe. There were
many sheds and basements of large buildings that were

being set up as future business ventures, under the guise of a working museums, just waiting for the opportunity to start up and take off.

They set up a network of groups who agreed that life in the computer age was tenuous at best and a disaster in the making. After all the system was already showing signs of being dangerous. A computer operated car had killed its occupant during a test drive and while the manufactures said that the newer models would be better, no one really believed them. The increase in massive hacking of accounts also served as a reminder that these systems could not be trusted with our lives. After all, if humans can make mistakes, how on earth did they expect to make a machine that wouldn't.

Susan and her second family moved to a new home. It had a few acres of land, a very large shed, a large studio for Susan to carry on with her commercial artwork and an established vegetable garden. They made good use of the internet system, while it was working, to spread the word about what they were doing. Some people accused her of being a hypocrite. Why use something that you didn't believe was going to work. However, they kept very quiet about the actual date of the impending crisis. They were being *considered eccentric enough as it was. Many of her friends put it down to a consequence her inability to deal with the loss of Greg and the children and it had driven her back into the past. Most people just ignored her and figured that if she wanted to waste her time and money it was her business and one day, she would die, leaving all this useless equipment behind.*

Susan's second husband was a very good mechanical engineer, and he could make all sort of parts to repair just about any piece of machinery. After their marriage, he spent a lot of time gathering pieces of broken machinery for parts. It was ideal for the work to be carried out on all the machines that would be brought to them to be fixed.

Susan noted that the essay wasn't saying who, where or when exactly these things were going to happen. God was keeping some surprises for when she returned obviously.

They both travelled around the country. Susan would take some of her freelance Artwork to sell, and her husband would go and visit farms always looking for parts to buy and repairing machinery if he was asked. In the early stages there were still enough farmers around who didn't want to be dependent on computers for them to get the message out there and find plenty of work. It got harder as the smaller farms were swallowed up by the big corporations which would insist on using computer guidance systems and working programs.

One month before "Meltdown" the Prime Minster of the country suddenly died of a heart attack. He was speaking at a lunchtime press conference outside Parliament House about some new satellites that would be launched into space the following month. They were to be a new super model that would provide greater coverage and eliminate any blackspots that still existed across the country. He was very excited about their artificial intelligence component that would reduce the cost of maintenance because they were 'self-repairing'. He was going on about how these satellites were going to be a game changer for our country, when suddenly, he placed his hand on his chest, went as white as a ghost, and collapsed. There was pandemonium while security and paramedics tried to revive him and stretchered him off to hospital. At six o'clock that evening, the Deputy Prime Minister stood in the same position, and announced that the Prime Minister had died. He was only the fourth Prime Minister in our history to die while still in office and the first one since Harold Holt in 1967. She also announced that she would be leading the country until the next election that would be held as soon as was constitutionally possible.

What the country didn't know was that she was a believer in what was known as the 'Meltdown Conspiracy' and she had been working very hard to ensure that there was a plan to save the country from complete desolation once it happened. What she didn't expect, was that she would have so much power available at the time of the event. She was prepared to implement the scheme once the internet went down, leaving the Prime Minister standing in her wake, as he was a definite disbeliever. The plan would have been different of course, had the Prime Minister survived his attack, as there would have been no way she could have engineered the disconnection of the internet service to the House of Parliament. The original plan was to have enough old school fire trucks on hand to deal with the fires. They would have appeared to materialise out of thin air to protect their nation's most important building. Thankfully, it was wintertime and so the effects of fire would be dampened considerably due to the cooler weather.

However, once the top job was hers, she worked very quickly and but still quietly behind the scenes to make sure that there were some measures taken to protect

Parliament House. It turns out that she employed some criminals out on Parole to disconnect the internet modems and optic cables on the very morning the 'Meltdown' was to occur. Her theory was that if it wasn't true, she could put it down to vandalism on a major scale and if it was, then Parliament House would be safe when the system overheated and started fires. She also had a special bus parked out of general sight at Parliament House. As soon as the system went down, she got in the bus and drove around Canberra with a loudspeaker, encouraging people not only to stay calm but also gave them instructions as to what they should do immediately. She had managed to get other members of government on side to do the same thing, reading a message that she had ready, to be delivered. In the month that she had been there, she had printed off lists of things people needed to do so that they were able to survive without their computers. There were meetings in every community, which she insisted were held in the local churches, where bottled water was passed out and she assured the public that it would only take 24 hours for the water systems to come back online, thanks to the hard work carried out by her predecessor. Right across the country, even though they were in shock, people started to work together to not only put out fires but help each other get on with life purely because of her foresight. She was hailed as a hero. I am proud to say she was my ancestor.

On the day of the 'Meltdown', the family were ready. They had, over the few weeks prior to the event removed all their money from the banks and stocked up on fuel and food. Susan's studio had suddenly become a bunker. Everyone involved had made good use of the banking system over the years to ensure that they were well provided for during the crisis. In their travels and workshops, Susan indicated that any funds in the banks needed to be removed during the days before the Meltdown and stored safely as many people would be desperate and thieving was still going to be the survival tool for many of those who hadn't heeded the warnings.

Investigations were impossible after the Meltdown. There was a story circulated that a sun flare had cooked a satellite. This sun flair event had been witnessed by a few people who were star watching at the time. It was assumed that the computer on board had decided to repair itself but instead had managed to create a virus that was transmitted to all the other computers in the network, not only forcing them all to shut down but also sending all the satellites flying off into outer space, deactivating all the mobile phone networks. As there was no communication available once the fires started, firefighters were unable to attend, causing large parts of the bigger cities to go up in smoke, literally. The only computers that survived were the ones that, for some strange reason or other, were not "online" at the time.

Within a month of the crisis, Susan, and Braxton, now reaching their sixtieth year, were on the road in a bus that carried tools and printed material to render assistance to those communities that up until now had rejected the whole concept of the 'Meltdown'. She wasn't surprised that people had been sceptics, after all, once before the world had been told that the planes would fall out of the sky when the clocks ticked over at Midnight on the 1st of January 2000. The fear then was that the Y2K bug would render all computers useless. It had turned out to be a great falsehood. Susan knew this and knew that her strategy leading up to this event was going to need a very quiet and long-term approach. She constantly thanked the Lord for the community in which they lived as most people in the area didn't have any trouble coming on board with developing the infrastructure that she envisaged.

The saving grace that allowed the regional communities to take on the projects with a lot more confidence was the fact that the drought had finally finished doing its damage twenty-five years before. Rain patterns had been restored thanks to the audacity of the foreign mining companies who had defied government regulations and pumped excess water into any and every ground depression they could gain access to. Farmers, so desperate for rain, had not objected but had in fact stood beside them and had given them all the assistance necessary. This meant that regional areas now had the water resources available to enable them to contemplate hosting more residents. The necessity to evacuate whole towns when water dried up no longer had to be anticipated.

In the lead up to the Meltdown, Susan and Braxton had encouraged people to make sure that they built glass houses and stored up large quantities of clean soil, knowing that the unattended fires caused by the crisis would contaminate the soil with the chemicals that would be released in the smoke. Seed banks were also established but it was always emphasised that it needed to happen on a local level as travel was going to be limited.

There were many times when they were laughed at and accused of being fear mongers. Computer companies often tried to sue them for damages but that failed as they always encouraged people to use the system while ever it was working as there was no way of preventing it from happening, there was no point in trying to close down the technology ahead of time. It pretty much already existed, so it was important to use it to its full extent until the Meltdown was about to happen. They insisted that what was important, was that those who believed them pull the plug on the system in time to avoid the devastation.

9

As the family headed off to bed at around ten o'clock, Susan was feeling a little overwhelmed and not at all sleepy. She asked if she could take some time to look through the family history album. She opened it and found that a second family tree page had been inserted in the front. She spread it out and was amazed at just how many more family members there were. She thought about how Sarah and Abraham might have doubted the promises that God gave them. How could two people make a great nation. It seems impossible when there were no children and age is advancing at a rate of knots. She understood why it was easy for seeds of doubt to take root.

There was so much information that it just seemed to blur in her brain. However, one piece of information stood out, she noticed that nearly every generation had someone who had been given the name Susan. Mary was still up, and Susan asked her about this.

'The thing is that there was no indication in the diaries as to when you would come to visit. So, each generation named the eldest girl Susan, in the hope that you would return and visit them through her. No one expected that it would take this long to happen.' Mary explained.

'So, why was your mother named Jennifer instead of Susan?'

'Mum had an elder sister, called Susan and she died a few years ago, unexpectedly, no one realised that she was born with a rare heart condition.'

'No one has mentioned her today.'

'No, they miss her very much and she was a lovely person. It's not that we don't talk about her and I must admit that I was surprised that she wasn't mentioned today, it seemed odd to me, but I guess your visit seemed to overshadow everything.'

'What about you, Mary, why isn't your name Susan?'

'Dad was such an unbeliever that he refused to allow mum to call me Susan. He eventually allowed her to name me after another member of the family but flatly refused to have me called Susan.'

'So, what if I hadn't come to visit until you were older?'

'I often wondered about that, but I figured we would get around it some way. There isn't any point worrying about it now.'

'I guess God knew what He was doing when He sent me now instead of later or earlier for that matter. What is it that we have to remember? God's timing is never late or early?'

'Grandma?'

'Yes, Mary,"

'Can I ask you about the desk, please?'

'Yes, what do you want to know?'

'Well, the diaries from the original Mary, say that there is a secret compartment in it somewhere, that is if it's the same desk. Is it? Grandma Susan says that I'm to have it when she dies'.

'It certainly looks like the one I have in my studio'.

'Well, we haven't been able to find the secret compartment, that's all, the diaries don't tell how to find it and I keep wondering if there might be something in there.'

Susan stood up and walked over to the desk. 'Here, let's have a look together, shall we.'

Susan found the catch easily enough and the secret compartment was revealed, but it was empty. Disappointment showed on Mary's face. 'I'll tell you what', Susan said, 'When I get home, I will put something in there, just for you. How about that?'

'Wow, that would be very cool', Mary said her face beaming.

Returning to the bed and the album, she paid special attention to the names of the people who were around in her time. She didn't know very many of these people, however, she did pick up a couple of names that were the same as people she knew. Were they the same people? she couldn't be sure, but it seemed likely. What really struck her was the number of people that God was going to bring into her family from all over the world. They would become part of her future. Some of them were alive already and she knew that they had no idea that their lives would be connected, simply because they didn't even know that she existed yet. She found her page. It was like a shrine to her family. She must have done this, but she knew that up until now she could not bring herself to even think about her lost family without a flood of tears. Now, when she returned home, she knew that she would be able to put this together. There was a photo of her, Greg's favourite wedding photo, a copy of the photo she had taken on that dreadful day, and the funeral order of service for her family. There was also a page for each one of her children and another one for Greg. Each page had her favourite photo and a short exposé outlining what they had accomplished in their short lives. As she read them, obviously written by her, she became aware that they had achieved quite a bit, even the twins and that she could be thankful for the impact that they had on her. It was very confronting but surprisingly she found that, for the first time, she wasn't crying. As she looked through it, she also noticed that she had two pages, the one she had just found and another one. It told her more about what she was already calling her second life. The man's name was Braxton Withers, which she already knew but here she saw his photo for the first time. Wow, she thought, he is really handsome, in a different way to Greg. Where is he? she wondered. She didn't know anyone by that name. It intrigued her as to how she was going to meet him. They'd have two children, Clare Jennifer, and Steven Braxton. Whoa! Claire was the Agriculture Minister that Jeff had been talking about at lunchtime and therefore the Prime Minister during the Meltdown. Goodness, no wonder God didn't want her to go home to Heaven yet! However, it was a bit weird looking at photos of her children who hadn't been born yet.

Overall, there were a lot of pages relating to her and the things that she did, far many more than those before and after her. It seemed that the family's survival had a great deal to do with her ability to motivate people to not let go of the past and yet that was exactly what she had wanted to do so badly the very day before. There was a couple of letters that Susan realised she still had to write. It created a very odd feeling, reading something that in her world just didn't exist yet.

The letters were written to her family. They encouraged them to keep going even under such difficult circumstances because if they didn't there was no hope for the future of the family or Australia. The consistent message was, we improve the world one day at a time and by constant hard work even though it may seem pointless and futile.

It had been a long day, exciting and full of surprises. She opened the letter that her Grandmother had written. Would she better understand the experience that her grandmother had after reading it?

Dear family,

Firstly, I want to thank Susan for not only believing me but also for keeping my secret. Secondly, I want all of you to know that I am very proud of you. I know that I have been telling you all that more often in the last few years, but I want to say one last time. I want you to remember that, even though I am not with you anymore, you have all been the greatest gift that God ever entrusted me with. Yes, sadly I didn't always treat you in the manner that He would have wanted me to. I have asked Him to forgive me. I have had conversations with each of you, but I am aware that there may still be things that we have not yet covered. If that is the case, I ask that you forgive me too. You may think that it is strange that I ask you to forgive me now that I am no longer here. The truth is, forgiving me is not about giving me peace or for me to find out even, it is about freeing yourselves and allowing yourselves to move on with your lives. Jesus has forgiven me, and I am grateful that you treated me with kindness when I was less than generous in my treatment of you all after John died. I could plead it was a result of grief, but I have to be honest and say that it wasn't the entire truth. My anger at John's departure caused me to question my faith and to drift away from his guiding hand. I am grateful that God was always as close to me as a breath. It was the Christmas you gave me the family album as a gift when God reached out and brought me back into the fold. The way He did that was in a most unusual way.

It happened that during the night I travelled back in time and met the parents of Mary Campbell and experienced a day in their life at what appears to have been the early days in Australian settlement by Europeans. That Christmas Eve I had been thinking a lot, more than usual, about my life as a child. It was very late when I finally went to sleep in my own bed. I woke up to hear my name being called but when I got out of bed and looked in the mirror (one that hadn't been in my room the night before) I was looking at the body of a sixteen-year-old girl not an eighty-six-year-old woman. I wasn't sure if the experience was real or just a very realistic dream. I found that I was on a mixed farm owned and worked by Rose and Joe Campbell. Mary, whose body I seemed to be occupying, had two siblings, Joey, and Emma, aged 10 and 5. Yes, I was possessing the body of sixteen-year-old Mary Campbell. Her clothes were uncomfortable and consisted of many layers of petticoats and pinafores or an apron. Her socks were made of real wool and shoes were solid and heavy. Life was hard for them. There was no electricity, refrigeration, or air conditioning and the hot water was heated on the open fire, that had to burn in the kitchen, all day, every day. There was no escaping the heat. The best place to get any comfort was on the verandah, where a grapevine provided extra shade and cooled the air a little as it passed through the leaves. To make matters harder for Rose, their aboriginal help, both farmhands and housemaids, had gone walkabout that morning without giving notice. The kitchen was separate from the rest of the house so that if there was a fire the rest of the house stood a chance of being saved.

It was hard to tell that it was Christmas Day to start with because work had to be carried out in the same way as any other day. The cows had to be milked and the pigs fed before breakfast was eaten. The heat, like now, was unrelenting and instead of taking it easy there were in fact there were extra duties to be done. Joey was required to give the horses an extra rub down because it was Christmas Day.

Gifts were handmade but, all the more precious because of the thought and care that was taken in the making of them. There were no supermarkets to buy food or shopping centres to purchase mass produced goods. Preparations would have taken months of thought and work. Joe gave Rose a wonderful sewing box that would have been planned and worked on for much of the year. Emma gave Mary a hessian bag with her name sewn in wool on it, the pleasure on her achievement was something to behold. When the Jackson family turned up unexpectedly with nothing to give and nothing left after the fire destroyed their home the family rallied to collect what they could to make sure that they had a roof over their head and clothes on their backs.

Rose had invited neighbours and friends for lunch, which consisted of a full baked dinner. Lunch was interrupted by a rider announcing that there was a bushfire, started by lightening from a morning storm, on another neighbour's property. Everyone downed tools and went to help put out the fire. Rose didn't question Joe going to help and quickly prepared extra food for Joe to take with him and inviting the men to make sure that the lady of the house and her twins be sent back to their place so they could be safe. This lady wasn't the nicest person in the district but still Rose extended the hand of friendship to her. Rose's kindness allowed Martha Jackson to see that God had a loving nature and allowed her shared the gospel of salvation with her. She shared her fears about having another child. I learnt later, through the diaries that were sent to Susan, that the child would be a boy, whom they named Patrick and that Rose would not recover from the delivery. What we don't understand is how unsafe it was for women to have children back then. The medical services were not what they are now. What Rose did on that day, changed my life forever. She made me see that I had allowed my relationship with God and my family to become something less than what God wanted. I asked God to forgive me for my sins.

Mary's diaries continued to fill me in on the lives that I had a glimpse of that day. Mary struggled to look after her family after the death of her mother. Her responsibilities overwhelmed her at times, and she found the confines of the society stifling. She ran away and for a time her family let her try the freedom that she thought she had but when the time was right, they went in search of her and found her, just as God our father looks after us when we stray.

Rose's faith in the future of our country has become a reality. Somehow, she knew that God had great plans for our land, and she was glad that her future family would be part of it. However, I see those blessings being taken very much for granted and in fact being scoffed at. I pray that those who have been the recipients of those blessings will respect the hard work and care taken by their ancestors and return to the ideals that they held so dear.

The diaries are there for all of you to read and I encourage you to read them. I even suggest that Susan might like to have them published as they are a great way to discover that love has many different aspects to it. There is the generous love that Rose showed her neighbours. There is the humble love that Joe showed to both his wives. Sarah's compassion for Rose's children and the care that she took to make sure that their lives were not disrupted too much tells us much of God's strength given to each of us who ask. There is the resolute love that Mr Smith showed his second wife which he was hopeful allowed her to find peace with her creator albeit as her last breathes were being expired. The sacrificial love that Daniel had for Mary. We might only experience a couple of those but remember that God is love and that He loves us with every aspect of love there is.

While many of you may think my experience to be a fanciful delusion of an old women – the reason that Susan is the only one that knows about that journey – it felt very real. My explanation is that while God, for the most part, works within the rules that He set in place for this world, He can, and sometimes does, break those rules simply because He is the creator of all things and the sovereign God and that allows Him to do whatever He pleases with his handiwork.

Remember this, my loved ones, He loves everything about you, and He has a plan for your life that He will bring about when He is ready. He is never early and never late.

Love Mum

10

In Susan's mind, there were still a lot of questions and some pretty large doubts. There was also the question that Jeff had raised at lunchtime. Was this plan set in concrete, so to speak? What would happen if she or others made mistakes or worse, exercised their free will, and decided that they would not carry out their part of the plan. As far as she could see, for everything to work out so that the world reached this point in time, in the state that it apparently existed right now, everything that had happened, had to take place exactly the way it was, yet she was the only one who was aware of what had happened. Besides, wouldn't she have to visit again when the world reached that point in time again. Wouldn't it create some sort of constant time loop. Then she asked herself, if this was the outcome, why did she witness the devastation with Angel last night. Angel had said that she had a choice, she could step up and carry out the work God had for her or she could walk away. She knew that God didn't treat people as puppets on strings, so was He so sure that everyone would do as He had planned. There was so much to take in. Where was Angel when she had so many new questions?

"I'm here, what would you like to ask me?" Susan looked up at where the voice had come from. Angel was sitting in the rocking chair that David had put back in the room after lunch.

'Well...'

'Come on, ask away', Angel encouraged.

'Ok, my question is this. Last night you said that God wouldn't take away our free will, so if I chose not to do what He has asked me to do, or make a mistake along the way, what would be the consequences for me and for the country?'

'You know that God will still love you regardless of your choices, don't you?'

'Yes, but…'

'Ok, so last night when I arrived, you wanted to go to Heaven and be with your family, am I right?'

'Yes.'

'My instructions were to show you what might happen if you went to Heaven now, so what I understand is that if you decided to just carry on the way you were when I collected you, life would be what it was last night. Today is what could be if everyone who is part of the plan makes the best choices that God has for them and completely does His will. What actually happens will, therefore, be something in between depending on how many people make their choices in accordance with God's plan', Angel said.

'I don't understand', Susan said puzzled.

'What I am saying is this, when the world gets to this point in time again, there will be some things that will be different. If some people, make different choices then the final picture will be different. Think of it as being like one of your poster projects. Someone wants you to produce a poster similar to that picture hanging out there in the living room. Using the internet, how many photos of spirals would you have to choose from?'

'Millions.'

'That's right, so you pick one that you like or maybe two but then you need to add in some farm equipment pictures and how many of them would you have to choose from?'

'Millions again.'

'Correct, maybe the first one that you pick, doesn't really work, so you have to make a second choice or maybe you need to use more than two photos to get the desired effect. Then you need to select the background colour of the poster. There would be dozens of colours that are part of the photos that you could use for that, right?'

Susan nodded,

'So, how many versions of the same cover could you potentially come up with in the end?' Angel looked at her questioningly.

'At least a couple of dozen maybe more but some of them would look really, dreadful,' Susan stated a bit defensively.

'Yes, granted there would be some that would be absolutely dreadful and there would be some that would be absolutely perfect and in between there would be a whole lot that could be used by your client if they wanted to, but they would still be the end result of the same plan, wouldn't they?'

'Yes.'

'So, what you have seen this Christmas, is the worst, if no one makes a choice to serve God, the very best, if everyone makes the right choices. What will actually happen is somewhere in between. For instance, if the Prime Minister at the time of "Meltdown" has made good choices leading up to the event and doesn't die, then the Deputy Minister's plan may have to be carried out covertly but in the end the effects will be the same, it just gets there in a different way. When the world gets to this point in time again, things will be different, but they won't know and nor will you. What will be, will be. That is what has been hidden from you, but it will still be the same end result of the plan that God has for Australia. You are only responsible for doing your best with what you have been given to do. God created time and while ever it exists, He can manipulate it for whatever purposes He chooses.'

'Wow', it was all Susan could say and when she looked at the chair again, Angel was gone.

Ok, so what she was starting to realise was that this journey was only a small part of God's plan. Was it even a real journey or just a couple of visions? That question was pretty rhetorical. He had shown her His "project brief" if you like. Her choices, and those of the many other people who would be involved at different times would affect the outcome. She couldn't, and God wouldn't, control this plan like a computer program. It would be the result of His people's choices but in the end it would still work. What that meant though, was that they still had to live by faith. They still had to trust Him and do the best they could because they couldn't know exactly how things were going to work out. He would still be there to guide her and show her how to do her small part in this great colossal plan of His.

When she returned to her own time tomorrow, if she did and she was pretty sure that she would, she had a lot of new reasons to get on with her life. God had blessed her with a glimpse at the future and with it He had given her a mission to carry out and, with it, a sense of hope. She must remember though, that the most important thing to do is to continually remind people that God loves them and that He is allowing them to be prepared for this disaster.

Just as Joseph had been able to help Pharaoh, in Egypt, prepare for the upcoming famine, so she was in a position to assist her family to be ready for the disaster that would be theirs to navigate. She was under no illusions that it would be plain sailing. Her future family had already warned her that things would be difficult. That people would consider her to be paranoid and dismiss her concerns but that didn't matter to her tonight, she had sure knowledge that there was a better future in front of them. She wondered if that is how St John felt after his revelation. He had seen into Heaven and he knew beyond a doubt that it was real. It's the rest of us that have trouble with the interpretation of his vision, just as people in her time would have trouble with hers.

She turned the events over and over, thinking about how the family had expected her to turn up, and the fact that they didn't know when it would happen. That's just like the return of Jesus, Susan thought, the Bible tells us that it's going to take place but no-one, not even Jesus, knows when that event will be. She even remembered that she had been told, in her other life, that at the time of Jesus' arrival as a baby on that first Christmas, Jesus was actually a very common name. This was because everyone was hoping that their child would be the one to rescue the Israelites from the nasty Romans. It looked as if this family had a very similar hope, that each Susan would be the one whom she would visit. They just kept the name going until she arrived. While her mission, when she returned home, would be to save as many people as she could, she knew that she would only be able to help a few and that she wouldn't be able to help everyone. Most people wouldn't believe in her assignment. She also realised that Jesus would know what that felt like. There are still a lot of people who don't believe that He even existed, let alone came down to earth as a baby, grew up living and learning just the same as we do without even committing one single sin. They cannot comprehend that He would choose to die on a cross. By doing so, he made available a way of salvation to each, and every person on earth provided they are willing to accept the gift that His love offered.

She checked the clock, noting that it was 2 am. If things happened the same way that they had worked for Grandma Mary, she would wake up on Christmas day in her time. She would have the whole day to herself to start making lists of things that could be done to help when the "Meltdown" happened. It would be very sensible of her to write most of what she could remember down somewhere where she could pull it out and check it over again from time to time. Yes, her first Christmas without any members of her family around her wasn't going to be so bad after all, she had good reasons to be hopeful now. She whispered, 'Thank you, Lord,' as she pulled the blanket and sheet up around her head, curled up and dropped off to sleep with a smile on her face.

11

Her mobile phone was ringing, but every time she tried to answer it, it wouldn't let her. As she drifted into wakefulness, she realised that she had been dreaming and the ringing mobile had been part of that dream. She opened her eyes, looked around, things were clearer than they were yesterday. Yes! Her body didn't feel like she was getting the flu anymore. She was home again!

She sat up in bed, reaching for her phone and glasses as she did so. Her mobile rang again. It was Jeff. Once she had put on her glasses, she quickly registered that there were three missed calls from him and two from her grandmother.

I wonder what's wrong now she thought as she swiped the screen.

'Hi Jeff, what's wrong?' She asked.

'Nothing this end, but are you okay? Grandma tried to ring you twice yesterday to see how you were getting through Christmas day on your own and you didn't answer. She's worried about you.'

'What do you mean yesterday?' Susan asked.

'Grandma tried to ring you yesterday, Christmas Day, to make sure that you were okay and see how you were getting through your first Christmas on your own.'

'What day is it?' Susan asked.

'Boxing Day, are you sure you're ok?' Jeff responded.

'Are you sure?' She asked surprised.

'Yes, I'm sure, its Boxing Day and Grandma wanted to check on you yesterday.'

'Ok, I was away and didn't take my phone with me, I've only just woken up. I'll give her a ring in a little while.'

'It's eight-thirty! Are you sure you are okay? I've never known you to sleep in that late before.'

'Yeah, I'm fine. That's the best night's sleep I've had since the accident.'

'You certainly sound better this morning. So, why am I ringing?'

'What? Nothing to do with grandma being in a panic'. She giggled.

'No, actually it isn't. You know how we are coming around for lunch today.'

'Yes, Boxing Day lunch' she added more to convince herself than Jeff.

'Yes, well, we met someone at church yesterday who has just moved into the area. I was wondering if you would mind if they came to lunch with us as they're at a bit of a loose end. Is there anything extra that you need us to bring?'

It seems like Jeff wasn't really going to take no for an answer, Susan thought.

'Um, I don't think so, just give me a minute to check the fridge.' She replied walking to the kitchen while she was talking. She opened the fridge and noticed that there was still plenty of salad makings that had been delivered last week. Nothing extra was needed.

'You're still bringing the ham, aren't you?'

'Yes.'

'Good, then everything is okay, and yes, it's fine if you bring an extra guest', she said. Probably another counsellor or shrink that he hopes will help me get over my grief, she thought as she told him that she would see him at twelve-thirty and pushed the disconnect button.

So much for having Christmas Day all to herself if this was Boxing Day, she thought, Oh, well plan B it is. She started compiling a mental list of the things that she wanted to do before lunch. First, she needed to shower and get dressed. Next, she had better ring her grandmother or she really would be in a panic and she had so much to tell her. Then she wanted to spend some time in her studio. It was time to get back to work. So, a list of things that she needed to do, such as send out emails telling her clients that she was ready to go back to work, tidy up her desk, and so on, needed to be written on her white board, now. Yes, the new year was still almost a week away, but the rest of her life was starting now.

She realised that she was walking into her future with a lot more sight than most people would ever have. What was it that Jesus said to Thomas? "Jesus saith unto him, Thomas, because thou hast seen me, thou hast believed: blessed *are* they that have not seen, and *yet* have believed". Susan repeated the verse in her head, paraphrasing it to relate precisely to her situation: *Susan, because thou hast seen your future you have hope, blessed are they that have not seen, and yet still have hope.* Yet, this morning she felt very blessed. Realising that there is still hope in the future after someone goes through any form of grief takes time, she knew that. Had God withheld her realisation of that hope for so long, in order to bless her in this special way or would she have been taken on that journey regardless.

She remembered what Angel had said during that first night, 'The answer to that can wait until you enter through the Pearly Gates, my dear,' Well Angel was right, she wasn't going to worry about the answer to that question now or in the future. One day she would face her Heavenly Father and He would give her the answer. Susan stopped, shook her head, and smiled. Suddenly, she knew that when she got to Heaven, the answer to that, particular question wouldn't matter. The only thing that would matter would be whether she had carried out the work that God had given her to do faithfully. Having Him say to her, 'Well done, Susan, you can now rest with us for eternity', that was her greatest desire.

Susan finished her shower and got dressed, then found her grandmother's contact on her mobile and rang her, turning her computer on to warm up while she made the call. Mary answered almost straight away.

'Susan are you okay, I tried to ring you yesterday, but you didn't pick up', her grandmother's voice sounded full of concern.

'Gran, I'm fine, guess what, I couldn't answer my phone because I wasn't here, I've time travelled too!'

'You what?'

'Yes, I time travelled, this time into the future. It was different to your experience. Gran, I'm not sure if you are going to believe me but I was visited by an angel. I thought it was the angel of death to take me home to my family. Instead, she took me through time, showing the things that are going to happen in the future. It was like that time lapse photography, where images just flash by. She carried me all the way. Then after I went to sleep in her arms, she tucked me up in bed. I expected to wake up in my own bed, but I didn't, I was in the home of our future family. Yes, Gran, I'm going to have a second family. And guess what, Gran, they were expecting me. They told me about what I can do to help the family and many others get through a time when the internet crashes leaving the world without computers.'

'Wow, sounds interesting?'

Susan continued to talk about what she had seen and what she knew. How they had kept all her Gran's diaries, the letter she was writing and the ones that weren't even written yet.

'I didn't read mine, Grandma', she said, 'that just felt too weird, but at least I now know what I am meant to do with the rest of my life', she exclaimed enthusiastically.

'You know, dear, one of the problems I'm having is that my memory of my experience is fading. Whether it's to do with my advancing age or the passage of time, I'm not sure, but from what you are telling there were a lot of things where our experiences had common ground. There also seems to be a lot of differences, such as precise dates that need to be remembered. It might be worth writing something down in the next couple of days to make sure that the real important things that you want to recall are there in front of you all the time.'

'That's such a good idea, Grandma, I was going to do that yesterday because I thought that it would be the same as your experience, that it would still be Christmas Day when I returned, but it wasn't. You know what! I have another idea about how I can make sure that I see it every day. I have to go now, as Jeff's family and someone he met yesterday at church will be here for lunch soon and I want to do a quick draft before they get here. Bye, Grandma, I'll catch up with you properly when you get back home. Love you!'

'Love you too', Mary replied, and they disconnected the call.

When Susan checked the time, she realised that she had been talking to Mary for nearly an hour. She also realised that she hadn't even asked how her Grandmother was or whether she was enjoying her holiday. Oh, I am going to have to be careful that I don't neglect my family, she thought, cringing at her thoughtlessness. It was nearly ten o'clock. A cup of tea and a slice of toast in hand she headed to her studio. She knew what she wanted to do. It was the picture that she had seen hanging on the wall the day before. She now knew what it was all about. It was the perfect way to remind her of the date that the world would fall apart. If it hung in her studio, she could see it every day for the next thirty years and it would be a constant reminder of what her mission in life was.

As she started to look for the images to put together, she found, just like Angel had said, that there were so many to choose from. Even now she couldn't really remember exactly which pictures had been on that poster. Well, it wasn't going to matter, she told herself, she would pick the ones she wanted to use. Yes, it might be different to the one she saw yesterday but so what? The one she came up with would still do the job it needed to. It didn't take that long to come together. The picture of a vortex that appeared to be sucking up all the stuff that cluttered their lives in the centre worked really well and the date, the day, on which the disaster was to start happening across the top in very large letters was a reminder to her of the deadline that she needed to meet.

After all, if they were going to survive as a family, she needed to remember the exact date. Then she could ensure that all their funds had been removed from the banks in time. Cash was going to be very important in the weeks after the crisis, as nobody would be able to sell or buy anything using the internet. Cash was going to be their saving grace. Just for good measure, to ensure that she remembered how they were going to be survivors she inserted a string of photos along the bottom of the page, depicting life using old fashion equipment, this too was to serve as a reminder of her mission from now on. It also served as the start of that very long list of things that needed to be done, that list that she had been making while she watched the catastrophe unfold below her. Susan stopped working and looked at the screen for a while. Why would God select her for such an undertaking? It was such a large project. No wonder Moses felt incapable of the task in front of him, if what he was feeling was anything like how she felt right now. There were going to be a lot of tough times ahead for her and her family, but she was certain that God had a plan, and her family had a part to play in it. Wow, that was a very sobering thought, she wondered if Mary, the mother of Jesus, felt a little bit like this when she was told of her part in God's plan for man's ultimate salvation. Yes, it was a large task, a bit like building the ark, but God wasn't going to leave her or her family without His strength, courage, imagination, or power. Her visit from Angel had proved that beyond any doubt.

First, she found a card which had a lovely photo of her house on it and wrote a note to the future Mary just as she had promised to. She then took off her wedding rings and included them in the envelope. If she was going to start a new life, she must put behind her the ties to her past. She had a feeling that the future Mary would be impressed with her gift. She opened the secret compartment and placed the envelope safely inside, locking them away for safe keeping for the next hundred or more years. As she closed the compartment, she knew that she had made a connection with a different Mary from a different time, and it felt good. She then turned to her computer and started working on the other project that she wanted to get done before Jeff and Clare arrived.

She was just printing off an A4 copy of what she had worked out, planning to enlarge it later, when the front doorbell rang. Checking the time, she realised that it was now twelve-thirty. She hadn't even started putting lunch together and that would be Jeff, his wife Clare, kids Joey and Rose and whoever they had decided to drag along with them. Poor thing, she thought as she headed towards the front door.

Never mind, Jeff was her brother and for all his faults, she knew that he really did care for her. She had given him a lot to be concerned about, particularly in the last twelve months when she just didn't seem to be able to surface from her grief. The first six months, most people expected her to be grief stricken, particularly given the enormity of the tragedy but she also knew that they were really starting to worry that she would never be able to move on. It wasn't that they were putting a time limit on her grieving process, but she knew that they were concerned about the depth of her depression. She was thankful that they hadn't insisted that she go on medication. Of course, it had been offered and there were times when she had thought about allowing the doctor to prescribe something. The thing was though, she had such a sensitivity to medications that she really didn't want to go down that road unless it was absolutely essential. Her family understood that and had made sure that other measures were in place if at any time she had got to the point where she wanted to do something really stupid. How good was her Heavenly Father, He had given her a family that really understood her and loved her the way she was? She knew that there were many people out there who didn't have half of what she had been given.

Some people might accuse her of being ungrateful and selfish, but grief affects everyone differently. No one asks to be depressed or to have their loved ones snatched from them. Looking back now, she could see that God had been there watching over her during the darkest time of her life. Yes, most of her family had been taken home early but, as Angel had reminded her, families are gifts, but they are not permanent gifts, they are borrowed for a short time. In some cases, like hers, that time is shorter than others. Mind you, she had to remember that there were a lot of people out there who have and would in the future experience grief far greater than hers. She would need to be careful and remember her trials so that when God brought such people across her path, she would be able to have some sympathy for their situation.

Things were different now and she was about to make sure that Jeff knew that she had turned the corner. She opened the door, stepping back quickly as the children rushed in, wrapping their arms around one leg each and looking up at her with cheeky grins.

'Hello, you two,' she said looking down at them, smiling 'did you have a good Christmas day.'

'Yes, thank you', they sang in unison. 'We had a great time. Santa bought us…'

'Alright you two, give Aunty Susan some space.' Clare instructed as she moved into the house, deftly disengaging her children and kissing Susan on the cheek on her way past.

Susan looked back at the doorway, standing there was Jeff, and Braxton Withers! She knew exactly who he was because she had seen his photo the day before. To be honest, his photo didn't quite do him justice. He seemed way more handsome in real life. Talk about love at second sight. Well, she couldn't exactly call it first sight, could she, because this was the second time that she had seen him.

'This is..' Jeff started to introduce them.

'Braxton Withers', Susan cut in extending her hand for a handshake, 'I'm Susan Green, Jeff's sister. How do you do?'

'Have we met before?' he asked, puzzled?

'No, not in this lifetime but don't worry about it, I'll explain it to you sometime. Right now, we should put lunch together, I've been working in my studio this morning, so lunch hasn't been started yet and I have a feeling that those two kids are going to want to eat pretty soon, unless something really strange has happened to them over Christmas', she said, smiling as she led her guests through into the kitchen. She felt as if she was walking on air.

Yes, the rest of her life was starting now, and God had brought her future husband into her life, even if he didn't know it yet, just in time to start it with her. Yes, there was hope for the future after all.

Other Books by Helen Brown

All these books, with the exception of Whispers from on High, are available as eBooks.

Turning Water into Wine
100 Stories of God's Hand in Life

More Water into Wine
100 Stories of God's Hand in Life

Still More Water into Wine
100 Stories of God's Hand in Life

Reflections
Australian Stories from my Father's Past

365 Glasses of Wine
Short Devotionals for each day of the year

Conversations with Myself – Volume 1
100 Stories of Hope, Faith and Determination

Whispers from on High
Poems and short stories

Fireside Stories:
Australian Family Tales

Follow Helen Brown on:
Facebook: https://www.facebook.com/HelenBrownCollection/

Instagram: https://www.instagram.com/helen_brown_books/

Pinterest: https://www.pinterest.com.au/helenbrown58726/

Connect with Reading Stones for other great reads:
https://www.facebook.com/Reading-Stones-Publishing-and-Editing-Services-252366958298920

www.ingramcontent.com/pod-product-compliance
Lightning Source LLC
Chambersburg PA
CBHW070200120726
47909CB00001B/189